The Best American
Mystery Stories 2017

GUEST EDITORS OF
THE BEST AMERICAN MYSTERY STORIES

1997 ROBERT B. PARKER
1998 SUE GRAFTON
1999 ED MCBAIN
2000 DONALD E. WESTLAKE
2001 LAWRENCE BLOCK
2002 JAMES ELLROY
2003 MICHAEL CONNELLY
2004 NELSON DEMILLE
2005 JOYCE CAROL OATES
2006 SCOTT TUROW
2007 CARL HIAASEN
2008 GEORGE PELECANOS
2009 JEFFERY DEAVER
2010 LEE CHILD
2011 HARLAN COBEN
2012 ROBERT CRAIS
2013 LISA SCOTTOLINE
2014 LAURA LIPPMAN
2015 JAMES PATTERSON
2016 ELIZABETH GEORGE
2017 JOHN SANDFORD

The Best American Mystery Stories™ 2017

Edited and with an Introduction
by **John Sandford**

Otto Penzler, *Series Editor*

A Mariner Original

HOUGHTON MIFFLIN HARCOURT

BOSTON • NEW YORK   2017

ISSN 1094-8384 (print)   ISSN 2573-3907 (ebook)
ISBN 978-0-544-94908-9 (print)   ISBN 978-0-544-94920-1 (ebook)

Printed in the United States of America
DOC 10 9 8 7 6 5 4 3 2 1

These stories are works of fiction. Names, characters, places, and incidents are products of the authors' imagination or are used fictitiously. Any resemblance to actual events, locales, or persons, living or dead, is entirely coincidental.

Contents

Foreword

The Best American Mystery Stories can now drink legally, turning twenty-one with this edition, and has been fortunate to have led a happy life through its early years. It was conceived at a lunch with my agent, Nat Sobel, a festive dining experience that we have shared every month for more than three decades. The series was fed by hundreds of the best writers in North America, and given a wonderful, caring home by Houghton Mifflin (now Houghton Mifflin Harcourt).

BAMS has had a blessed life from birth, eschewing the expectable growing pains of a newborn into a mature adult. The guest editor of the 1997 edition was the distinguished Robert B. Parker, and it made several bestseller lists. The next guest editor was America's sweetheart, Sue Grafton, and that volume outsold the first. Sales, reviews, and, most important, the stories in each edition continued the excellence and success of the first books. Perhaps not surprisingly, the series hit a bump in the road when it hit its teenage years, the hardcover edition being dropped after 2008 because of reduced sales, leaving it exclusively a paperback. It quickly rebounded as it grew a little older, however, filling out and coming closer to realizing its potential by adding e-book editions.

It would be reasonable to expect a lot of changes over the years, and there have been some, but mostly behind the scenes so that readers would be unlikely to sense them. When stories were being read for the first book, my invaluable colleague, Michele Slung, without whom it would take me three years to produce this annual volume, examined about five hundred stories to determine whether they were mysteries and whether they were worth consideration.

When the Internet became a greater part of our lives, we learned of more literary magazines, more little regional publishers, and electronic magazines (e-zines) that published mystery fiction. She now reads all or parts of three to four thousand stories every year. She then sends me those she thinks I should read, a stack that I whittle down to the fifty best, which are sent to the guest editor, who selects the twenty that go into the book; the other thirty make the honor roll. I can think of no other substantive changes, which I regard as a good thing. As Tony Hillerman said to me about thirty years ago (yes, yes, I know it's a cliché, but that was the first time I heard it, and I can still hear it with his little bit of a twang), *If it ain't broke, don't fix it.*

One thing that changes every year is the guest editor, and everyone who has agreed to perform this task has done it as an act of generosity and self-sacrifice. Once an author has achieved the fame and success that comes with being a national bestseller (as all the guest editors have been), the drain on his or her time and energy is almost unfathomable. To put aside their books, to risk losing the battle with their own deadlines, should earn them immeasurable thanks (which I am happy to send).

John Sandford (the pseudonym of John Camp) had a long career as a journalist, resulting in a Pulitzer Prize in 1986. He decided to write fiction full-time three years later, when his first novel, *Rules of Prey,* became a huge success. He has produced approximately forty novels, every one of which has been on a national bestseller list in one format or another, but he is best known for the Prey series, starring Lucas Davenport, the handsome, well-tailored cop who drives a Porsche.

It would be inappropriate not to thank the previous guest editors, who, like Mr. Camp, gave so much time and effort to make the books in this series as good as they could be. I've offered kudos to Robert B. Parker and Sue Grafton, who were followed by Ed McBain, Donald E. Westlake, Lawrence Block, James Ellroy, Michael Connelly, Nelson DeMille, Joyce Carol Oates, Scott Turow, Carl Hiaasen, George Pelecanos, Jeffery Deaver, Lee Child, Harlan Coben, Robert Crais, Lisa Scottoline, Laura Lippman, James Patterson, and Elizabeth George, and I am in debt to them all.

Presuming that you are familiar with these giants of the mystery world, you will quickly perceive that despite their literary excellence, they produce very different kinds of fiction, ranging from hard-boiled to traditional detective stories to international thrillers to crime stories and more. The literary genre described as "mystery" is large and embraces multitudes. I define it liberally to mean any work of fiction in which a crime, or the threat of a crime, is integral to the theme or plot, and you will find a great range of styles and subgenres in the present volume. Please don't call or write to complain that many of these stories are crime or psychological suspense rather than detective fiction. I know. Tales of observation and deduction, the staple of the so-called Golden Age (between the two world wars), have become more difficult to write (Agatha Christie used up too many plot ideas!), and we have seen the "whodunit" and the "howdunit" pushed more to the side of the road that has become dominated by the "whydunit." This change has often resulted in superior literature, with character development and exploration unheard of in the 1920s and 1930s.

The hunt for stories for next year's edition has already begun. While Michele Slung and I engage in a relentless quest to locate and read every mystery/crime/suspense story published during the course of the year, I live in terror that I will miss a worthy story, so if you are an author, editor, or publisher, or care about one, please feel free to send a book, magazine, or tearsheet to me c/o The Mysterious Bookshop, 58 Warren Street, New York, NY 10007. If a story first appeared electronically, you must submit a hard copy. It is vital to include the author's contact information. No unpublished material will be considered, for what should be obvious reasons. No material will be returned. If you distrust the postal service, enclose a self-addressed stamped postcard, on which I will happily acknowledge receipt of your story.

To be eligible, a story must have been written by an American or Canadian and first published in an American or Canadian publication in the calendar year 2017. The earlier in the year I receive the story, the more it is likely to warm my heart. For reasons known only to the blockheads who wait until Christmas week to submit a story published the previous spring, this happens every year, causing much severe irritability as I read a stack of stories while everyone else I know is busy celebrating the holiday season. It had better be a damned good story if you do this, because I already hate you. Due to the very tight production schedule for this book, the absolute firm deadline is December 31. If the story arrives two days later, it will not be read. Sorry.

O. P.

Introduction

I've read a stack of stories—fifty of them, to be exact—sent to me after a preliminary selection by Otto Penzler, with instructions to pick twenty. I've done that. Some decisions were close, some were not; of the top twenty, I would rank most of the stories to be close, and the close calls probably extended to the top thirty. Dropping a third of those was tough.

Some of the previous editors pooh-poohed the idea of an intellectual tour of the history or theory of short story writing. I wouldn't pooh-pooh doing a history, but I don't know enough of the history of short stories to write about it with authority. Sure, I've read Poe and Hemingway and O. Henry and Mark Twain, Ray Bradbury, Guy de Maupassant and Stephen King and Faulkner and O'Conner and Philip Dick and Kafka and Proulx and many more than I can remember—I majored in American history and literature in college, so I'm heavy on Americans and a little light on others—but there are more terrific short story writers than you can shake a stick at. That's my take on the history.

Ah, but theory. As an occasional teacher of writing, I do have a taste for it.

Of fictionoid© literature, there are several varieties that most people wouldn't usually consider as relevant to the short story . . . but I do.

The newspaper column, for example. A newspaper column is often about 750 to 800 words and is an unusual hybrid of fact and opinion, the opinion leaning hard on fiction. A good newspaper column generally has the structural aspect of a short story: a fast, mood-setting opener, the rapid development of an interesting character, a few hundred words of exposition, frequently for the purpose of jerking a tear or two, and a snappy ending.

They're almost short stories, except for the problem of the facts, which can really clutter up a good piece of fiction. There's an old newspaper line about taking care to stop reporting before you ruin a perfectly good story.

As a newspaper columnist for a few years, I wrote several hundred columns, some good, some bad, some okay. I wrote on demand, four of them a week. No writer's block allowed — the space was always waiting for me. (My friend and fellow novelist Chuck Logan and I were once on a book-writing panel at a St. Paul–area college, and Logan was asked by an audience member what he did about writer's block. Logan asked the woman what she did for a living, and the woman answered, "I'm the president of this college." Logan asked, "What do you do when you get college-president block?" The answer, of course, is "Work harder.")

The biographic profile of the kind you frequently see in the *New York Times,* the *Wall Street Journal, The New Yorker,* or *The Atlantic* may also be similar to the short story. They begin with a catchy opener and the careful construction of character. Since the reporting often involves interviews with the character himself/herself, it usually produces a raft of fiction, intentional or unintentional. Then we get a few unexpected twists of fate and a snappy ending. A profile of Donald Trump, for example, even if carefully documented from the Donald's personal speeches and tweets, would arguably comprise mostly fiction, and certainly the twists of fate. Whether the ending will be snappy, of course, we don't yet know. My personal opinion is that it might tend more toward sloppy; we'll have to wait to see.

Haiku, carefully
groomed, may be the tightest
form of short story.

And has much to teach the short story writer, in my opinion. Especially about an opening. Read haiku: it's like taking your vitamin pills in the morning.

*

Then there's the novel. The novel is not a long short story but uses all the techniques of the short story, except length. It may be—I think it is—an ultimately more important form of literature, because of some of the inherent difficulties of the short form, but novels are not "better" in the purely literary sense.

They are usually a bit lazier, because they have the space to be; they can allow the reader to breathe, and to contemplate between sittings. They can present more author-nuanced character. Most important, they create a world of their own, which is comprehensible even hundreds of years later. How many people have gained a greater knowledge of the Napoleonic Wars through Tolstoy's *War and Peace* than they have through any number of histories? Tolstoy created a world that survives today.

Novels, then, are an object of their own.

The short story, I believe, is not usually an object that stands on its own. Unlike a novel, a good short story is an intense collaboration between reader and writer. A novel may create an entire new world; a short story usually depends on the intelligence and understanding of the reader, because the elements of the story—the characters, the scene-setting (the total environment of the story) and the plot, whatever it may be—are usually so condensed that the short story is almost like an extended haiku.

The story is dependent on author implications and reader inferences. To take Poe as an example, his creepy dungeons are painted in few words; the shiver they send up the reader's spine depends on the reader's imagination as much as Poe's, and Poe knew that. He was a master at tripping off the guilty hidden thoughts and imaginings of his readers.

So what would be the essential working parts of an ideal short story?

The story must be tight and well written; a novel can take a few fumbles without much damage, but a short story really suffers from them.

The opening must be catchy and quick and set a mood—the story should be rolling with the first line. No space here for the dark and stormy night.

From C. J. Box's "Power Wagon": "A single headlight strobed through a copse of ten-foot willows on the other side of the overgrown horse pasture. Marissa unconsciously laced her fingers over her pregnant belly and said, 'Brandon, there's somebody out there.'"

Single headlight strobed/ten-foot willows/overgrown horse pasture/laced her fingers/pregnant belly/somebody out there.

All that bound in two sentences, thirty-six words.

What, you're going to stop reading right there?

Scene-setting should be integral to the story, part of the fabric rather than long blocks of exposition. The scene-setting ideally should contribute to the mood and texture of the story. If you set a dark, morose story on a sunny summer's day, you're fighting yourself. Not to say that it can't be done.

From Charles John Harper's "Lovers and Thieves": "It was the kind of rain favored by lovers and thieves. A misty November rain. The kind that hangs low, veil-like, obscuring the dark, desperate world beneath it. The kind that sends lovers into their bedrooms and thieves into the night . . . I was more like the thief, waiting outside the Bon Vivant on La Brea, a tired, three-story, stucco apartment building with a name more festive than its architecture. Waiting inside my gunmetal-gray 1934 DeSoto Airflow Coupe . . . It wasn't where I wanted to be. It wasn't where a PI makes any real money in this town."

Now we get to character. The physical description of the characters is critical, and what the reader sees in this physical description should tell us much about the character's personality. There's a reason for that: it creates an immediate image in the reader's mind, so that laborious explication isn't necessary. If a guy has a twice-broken nose, a fedora, a double-breasted suit, and is smoking a Lucky Strike Green, we've got a pretty good idea of when and where the story is coming from, without even knowing much more.

From Dan Bevacqua's "The Human Variable": "Standing out front near the bug light was an incredibly tall, incredibly thin man with an orange beard. He had the word SELF tattooed above his right eyebrow. MADE was above the left. Ted asked him [where he was.] . . . 'Liberty' . . . 'Thanks . . .' 'Yut,' SELF MADE said, as if he were offended by language, as if it had done something horrible to him as a child."

*

Of course, a major factor in short story writing is that the story itself has to be good. One of the biggest problems of too many short stories is that they're boring and occasionally stupid, and you feel that the editor who chose it for publication has some unstated motive for choosing it.

By "good," I mean the reader has to want to continue it, the story should have something interesting to say about the characters (and about character in general), and it should have something surprising about it.

Not surprising in a jack-in-the-box way, where something weird pops up in the last paragraph, but something logical, something that develops directly from the story line, but something that the reader didn't see coming. And preferably something that contributes to the resolution of the story. Something like the dog that didn't bark in the night.

Almost all the stories in this collection work that way: I can't quote them because I'd be giving too much away. I can say that one story that I *didn't* like, and didn't select, was doing fine until the last moment, when all the questions were answered by a jack-in-the-box.

And finally there has to be some resolution. You can't just end a short story; you have to wind it up.

As Doug Allyn does in "Puncher's Chance" (not a spoiler): "And because it's the flat-ass truth."

Some people might tell you that crime short stories, unlike the more precious kind, are a kind of fictional ghetto, full of cardboard characters and clichéd situations.

Not true. These stories are remarkably free of bullshit—although there's always a little, just to grease the wheels. And as a guy who writes a lot of crime, I love the language, the kind of language you don't generally find in *The New Yorker.*

I personally have used the phrase "douche-nozzle" to characterize a low-life character in an upcoming novel, and have to say that I'm nothing if not proud of myself; you'll find more of that kind of fine stuff in this collection.

And so . . .

Here they are.

JOHN SANDFORD

The Best American
Mystery Stories 2017

DOUG ALLYN

Puncher's Chance

FROM *Ellery Queen Mystery Magazine*

MY SISTER FINISHED me in the third round. It wasn't a big punch. It stung, but didn't do serious damage.

But it definitely got the job done.

We were sparring in the ring of our family gym, tuning each other up, getting prepped for fights only a few days away.

Jilly's bout would open the show at Motor City Stadium, Detroit's version of Madison Square Garden. Home of the Red Wings, Big Time Wrestling, and the Friday Night Fights. Chick boxers are mostly a diversion, eye candy tacked onto a program to pump up the crowd. No one takes them seriously. Yet.

Jilly's trying to change that, one round at a time. Cute, blond, and blocky, she could pass for a junior-college cheerleader.

Who punches like a pile driver.

I was hoping my opponent wouldn't be much tougher than hers. I'd be facing Kid Juba, a middleweight from Chicago. He's been away from the game for a few years with drug problems, looking for a big comeback.

So am I. Juba will be my first bout since I ripped a rotator cuff last fall.

The docs say my shoulder's healed now, good to go. I can curl my own weight again and spar all damn day with only an occasional ache. But boxing careers can crash and burn in a few tough years, and the six-month layoff to rehab my shoulder has been driving me bonkers.

I was desperate to get back in the ring, desperate to get my life back on track.

I come from a Detroit family of fighters, the Irish Maguires. Boxing isn't a sport to us, it's been the family business for three generations. We own our own gym, train ourselves. My grandfather Daryl was a welterweight contender back in the eighties. Fought Ray Leonard and Tommy Hearns in their primes. My Pops, Gus Maguire, won silver in the Olympics and coached U.S. boxing teams three times.

I'm next in line, with little brothers Sean and Liam only a few years behind me.

Jilly is the first female Maguire to step through the ropes. And if the game doesn't take women seriously, nobody told Jilly. She fights every round like a freakin' headhunter. No mercy, no quarter asked or given.

Pops didn't want her in the ring, said it was no fit place for a woman. When she pushed it, he matched her with Liam, who's only fifteen but a strapping lad with fifty-plus Golden Gloves bouts under his belt. He promptly put her on the deck.

No big surprise. Every green fighter gets clocked, especially if she's fighting a Maguire. But Jilly shook it off, and the next round she threw an elbow in a clinch and busted Liam's lower lip open. The dirty foul ended the bout. It took sixteen stitches to close the wound. But it got my Pops's attention.

After she sent Liam to the emergency room, Pops quit blowing Jilly off. Noted that she could take a punch, refused a hand up when she got dropped, and came back fiercer than before.

And most of all, noted how *hungry* she was. It takes more than guts and skill to prevail in the ring. It takes smarts and tenacity and, above all, the will to win. Jilly's got the whole package. She can take a punch and she's even better at dishing them out.

Usually.

But not today.

As we boxed, I realized Jilly was holding herself in check, pulling her punches. My freakin' baby sister was actually taking it easy on me in the ring.

Screw this! I slipped her next hook, then clinched, pinning her arms tight against her sides.

"C'mon, little twit! Put some steam on it, if you got any!" I gave her a rabbit punch as we broke, and she swung an elbow, barely missing my nose.

"Time!" Pops yelled, before we could do each other serious harm.

I didn't bother with the stool, stayed on my feet, dancing in my corner, steaming.

"Keep your guard up, Mick," Pops chortled. "Your sister's gettin' miffed."

"Good! Hey, Jilly! I won't be fighting a girl come Friday night," I yelled across the ring. "This Kid Juba will be lookin' to drop a Maguire, make a name for himself. Crank it up, goddamn it! Show me something!"

And she did. She showed me I was finished.

At the bell, Jilly came out of her corner like Smokin' Joe Frazier, punching like a machine, a steady drumbeat of serious blows, every one dead-eye accurate.

Which was exactly what I needed. It woke me up. On full defensive alert now, I was picking off her punches with my gloves and forearms, fighting on autopilot, more interested in her skills than my own.

I threw a right-hand lead to slow her roll; she countered it with a stiff left hook to the base of my rib cage. I dropped my elbow to block the punch . . .

But I missed it.

Her hook grazed my arm, then struck home, digging under my ribs. It wasn't full strength, but it definitely stung. And I winced. And read the shock in her eyes.

As we both realized I'd just missed a basic block.

Because I couldn't make it.

My surgically repaired shoulder had a glitch. My range of motion had been reduced by an inch. One critical inch. The healing was done, and so was I.

I couldn't drop my elbow far enough to defend my gut. It was a fatal flaw. One that any schooled fighter would spot in a round or two. And when he did, he'd start firing body shots that would snap me in half.

The same way my little sister had nearly dropped me by sheer accident.

"Time!" Pops called, though we were only forty seconds into the round. "Time, goddamn it!"

Jilly followed me to my corner.

"What the hell was that?" they demanded together.

"I missed a block," I growled, though I was as shaken as they were. "No big deal."

"It looked big to me," Pops growled. "Lower your elbow."

I did.

"All the way down!"

"That *is* all the way," I said, swallowing bile. "That's as far as it freakin' goes."

"Ah, sweet Jaysus," he said, turning away. Pops looked like he wanted to throw up, and Jilly was nearly as green.

I knew exactly how they felt. Because we all knew what it meant.

As long as I could throw leather I'd have a puncher's chance. The hope of landing one big punch that'll turn a fight around. Or end it.

But the permanent gap in my guard meant I'd never have the prime-time career I'd trained and sweated for all my life. In a single round, with a single punch, I'd gone from being a contender to a burnout.

I could still earn for a while. Guys could pad their records by beating hell out of me, and even losers' purses add up. But every bout would send me further down the road to Palookaville.

Stick a fork in me. I was done.

I dropped down on the stool in my corner, staring down at my shoelaces, seeing the wreckage of my life swirling in the spit bucket. Don't know how long I sat there. Eventually I came out of the fog. Realized Jilly had hit the showers. Probably to hide her tears.

But Pops hadn't gone. He was parked on a wooden bench against the gym wall, looking even worse than I felt. Which was saying something.

I climbed through the ropes and eased down beside him.

"C'mon, Pops, it ain't the end of the world. Liam's almost of age, and his punch is bigger than mine—"

"Liam will never train here," Pops said flatly. "We're going to lose the gym, Mick."

"What are you talking about?"

"Your last fight," he said. "Against Clubber Daniels? He was made for you, Mick. Looked scary as hell, had all them iron-pumper muscles. He'd won eight straight, but most of 'em were tomato cans. Watchin' the film on him, he was just a brawler, with no real skills. I figured he'd punch himself out in the first couple rounds. By the third, you'd own his ass. Put him away in the fifth or sixth."

"But I tore my shoulder in the third," I said, shaking my head at the memory.

"And then tried to fight him one-handed." He nodded grimly. "Got decked twice before the ref stopped it."

"That was stupid, Pops, I know, but—"

"No. That was Irish heart, Mick. Not smart, maybe, but amazin' brave. The stupid part is, I bet on you. Bet heavy."

"What?"

"You heard me, Mick. I bet the freakin' farm."

"But . . . managers can't bet. It's illegal—"

"The gym's been bleeding red for months, son. We needed a payday to tide us over. I knew you'd be earning big soon, and with Jilly coming up, and Liam only a few years behind, we'd be back in clover in no time. But instead of a fat payday . . ." He shook his head.

"That's why they call it gambling, Pops," I said. "How much are we down?"

"Almost ten."

"Thousand? Sweet Jesus, Pops!"

"I got greedy," he admitted. "It was my first time crossin' over to the dark side, and since I knew it was a sure thing—"

"You went big." I groaned. "Where'd you get the money?"

"I borrowed half from the bank against the gym. The rest I spread around on IOUs. Still owe most of that. But that's not the worst of it."

"Seriously? It gets worse?"

"I doubled down, Mick."

"You . . . doubled?"

"I bet big on you again, for Friday against Kid Juba. After losing your last fight, then the long layoff? You're the underdog, Mick, with odds against you three and four to one. We ain't had a payday since you got hurt, and I knew you could take him—"

"Only I can't, Pops. Christ, I probably can't take Jilly."

He didn't argue the point. We both knew I was right. He walked away, silver-haired, pudgy, looking every damn minute of his fifty-plus. I stayed on the bench. Where I belonged. I wasn't going anywhere.

"Mr. Maguire?"

A woman was standing in front of me. Hadn't seen her come in.

Tall, slim. Black slacks, black turtleneck. Boots. Raven-black hair
cropped short as a boy's.

"I'm Bobbie Barlow," she said, tapping my glove with her small
fist. "*Ring Scene Fanzine*? Our interview was set for eleven, but I
came early. And I'm glad I did."

Sweet Jesus!

"How long have you been here?" I managed.

"Long enough to catch the drama. What was all that about?"

"Just a sparring session, lady. Boxing practice."

"I know what sparring is, Mr. Maguire. I also know what a liver
shot is. And it looked like your little sister hooked you with one."

"I wasn't hurt."

"That's because she didn't have much on it. But it's a deadly
punch. Joe Louis won half his fights with it."

I stared at her.

"Joe Louis Barrow?" she prompted. "The Brown Bomber? His
fist is on display over at Hart Plaza. Twenty-four feet long, eight
thousand pounds, cast in bronze? Maybe you've seen it."

I still didn't say anything. Still trying to shake off the darkness of
Jilly's punch. And the end of my world.

She eyed me a moment, then shrugged. "It was nice meeting
you, Mr. Maguire. We probably won't talk again, since you won't
like my story. Irish Mick Maguire almost clocked by his little sister.
Would you care to comment?"

I couldn't think of one. She turned to walk away.

"Wait," I said. "If you write that, you'll get me killed."

She faced me. "I beg your pardon?"

"If you write that my sister caught me with a liver shot and Juba's
people see it? You might as well tattoo a target on me, lady. He'll
break me in half."

"He'll probably kill you whether I write it or not. He's a seasoned
fighter, Mick. He'll pick up on it."

"He's been out of the game. Drug problems."

"Is that what the promoter told you? Juba's been serving a three-
year drug sentence in Joliet, fighting for the prison team. He's been
training hard every damn day, desperate for a comeback. Dropping
an Irish Maguire will get him ink and face time on TV. Especially if
he's standing over your dead body."

I didn't say anything. This day kept getting better and better.

Barlow was watching me, reading my reaction. Our eyes met and held. She had a strong gaze. Honest. And attractive. I couldn't help smiling and shaking my head. At her. At the whole damned crazy business.

"You didn't know about Juba's prison time, did you?" she said. "You were expecting a tune-up fight?"

"It won't matter when the bell goes off. Maybe Juba will be in top shape. Maybe he'll be rusty from fighting second-raters."

"Second-raters?"

"If they're in prison, how smart can they be? Either way, I'd appreciate it if you didn't tip him off about . . . what you think you saw."

"I *know* what I saw, Mick. And if there's a weak point in your defense, Juba will pick up on it."

"Maybe. If he has enough time."

"A puncher's chance? That's what you're counting on? You're hoping to clock him *before* he can spot the problem?"

"A puncher's always got a chance, lady. If you stand in there and keep throwing leather, one punch can change the fight, change your luck. Change everything."

"My dad used to say that. A lot," she scoffed.

"He was a boxer?"

"A club fighter. Loved the game more than it loved him. He's in a hospice now, Mr. Maguire. Dementia. From taking your puncher's chance one time too many."

"I'm sorry it went that way."

"It always does. It's a savage, bloody sport."

"If you hate it, why write about it?"

"I'm my father's daughter, I suppose. And there's an endless fascination to the fight game. With all the corruption, the mismatches, the wheeling and dealing, in the end it comes down to two guys in the ring. Facing off, one-on-one, with the crowd screaming for blood. The last gladiators."

"But they always have the same chance," I said. "It's tough about your dad, but don't fault a guy for loving the game. And as long as he kept on swinging, he did have a puncher's chance. The next punch can change your whole life."

"Wow, you actually believe that, don't you?"

"Belief's got nothing to do with it, lady. It's the flat-ass truth. Hell, you just saw it happen."

*

I was back in the gym at first light the next day. Desperate. The flaw Jilly revealed would definitely finish my career, *unless* I could find a fix for it.

Preferably before I faced Juba in the ring.

I spent hours in front of a full-length mirror, shadowboxing, turning this way and that, studying my form, looking for a solution to my problem.

Not finding one.

Pops came in early too. He circled me slowly as I worked out, watching for the better part of an hour. Neither of us saying a thing. But finally he shook his head.

"There's no way to compensate, Mick. You can't drop your elbow low enough. Beyond that point, you start to hunch down—"

"Which leaves me open for an overhand right," I agreed, "which will drop me even faster than the liver shot. I might as well close my eyes and hope Juba knocks himself out."

"I'm pulling you, canceling the fight."

"The hell you are! We need the damn money, Pops, even if it's only the loser's share. And it's not a done deal. We know the problem, but Juba doesn't. If I can get to him before he spots it, I've still got a chance."

"A puncher's chance?" Pops snorted. "Guys who count on that get carried out."

"It's the only shot we've got, Pops. Now quit bugging me, I need to work on this."

He disappeared into his office, taking my last hope with him. My Pops was an Olympic coach, a brilliant ring general. If there was a solution to my problem, he would have seen it. Since he didn't . . . ?

I was on my own. With a puncher's chance.

Assuming Bobbie Barlow didn't take that small hope away. If she mentioned my problem in her daily blog—

But she didn't. Her column was totally focused on Jilly, the rising star of the Irish Maguires. She only mentioned my name to plug my bout with Juba. Didn't mention the sparring match at all.

Which must have been a tough call. It would have been a big scoop to pinpoint the exact moment Irish Mick Maguire's career ended. And Jilly's began.

Or so I thought.

*

The first bout of the Friday Night Fights opened with a bang. Jilly had drawn a UFC cage fighter who was making her big debut in the boxing ring. The cage fighter had a fierce rep, years of fighting experience, a cauliflower ear, and fists the size of country hams.

It didn't save her.

Jilly exploded out of her corner like she'd been shot from a cannon, taking her rage and frustration out on her opponent, firing off punches in bunches, accurate as sniper fire. The cage fighter covered up, trying to weather the storm. But the barrage just kept coming, numbing her arms, until she could barely defend herself.

Hurricane Carter in his heyday would have had his hands full against Jilly that night.

She had the UFC fighter so clearly outclassed that midway through the second round, after a murderous flurry, Jilly actually dropped her hands and stepped back, glaring daggers at the ref.

"Are you going to stop this slaughter or what?"

The cage fighter used the break to take a wild swing at Jilly's head, a huge mistake. Jilly answered with a salvo of savage body shots, jamming her opponent into a corner, beating her senseless. The referee finally leapt between them, waving Jilly off, earning a chorus of boos from the crowd.

They were hoping to see a clean knockout, a rare event with female fighters. And they would have gotten one. A few more punches would have sent the cage fighter to dreamland. Or the ER.

Jilly was so deep in the zone she popped the ref three times before she realized he'd stopped the bout. He was an old-time heavyweight, Bozo Grimes. He'd once gone the distance with Foreman, but he winced at the power of Jilly's punches. I felt sorry for him.

But not for long. I was too busy feeling sorry for myself.

Bobbie the reporter was right. My tomato-can opponent was anything but. Joliet Prison is one of the toughest gladiator schools in the country. Kid Juba had been training all day, every damn day, fighting for his cherry.

Following Jilly's example, he came charging across the ring at the bell like Dempsey jumping Willard, firing off blows in a blur, so fast it took every bit of ring craft I owned to fend him off. A few struck home, getting my attention. But the others came on in a steady drumbeat, jab, jab, hook, cross. Jab, jab . . .

In a set pattern. Predictable.

Juba wasn't a smart fighter, more like a schoolyard bully who'd picked up some skills. He was throwing too many punches too soon, desperate for an early knockout. It took me less than a minute to pick up on his rhythm. After that we were trading leather for leather in the middle of the ring. The crowd cheered the action, but it was all flash and dazzle, no serious harm done. We were fencing, probing for weaknesses. Seeing what worked, what didn't.

Juba was short on technique but he had *power.* I got that message when I slipped a right cross. The punch flashed by like lightning, missing my jaw by an eyelash.

And it definitely widened my eyes.

The sheer force of it sent me a message. Big-time. This stud was dangerous.

Put-your-young-Irish-ass-in-traction-type dangerous.

Fully focused now, I picked up my rhythm in the second round, taking Juba seriously now, taking him to school. Pugilism 101.

I went in low, hammering the ex-con's rib cage with stiff body shots, sharp punches with serious snap to 'em, dealing out some pain. The barrage forced Juba to drop his guard a few inches, then quickly raise his hands as I finished every flurry with a hard right to the head.

The attacks didn't do much damage. Juba was blocking most of my shots, probably thought he had me figured. Anticipating that final right, he started lifting his left a little sooner every time. A rookie mistake.

As the round wound down, I suddenly reversed the pattern, firing off a flurry of body shots, then dropped the last punch four inches lower, digging a hook under Juba's elbow as he raised his guard. The punch drove home like a battering ram, halfway to his spine!

Juba gasped, then quickly backed away, grinning, shaking his head like the punch was nothing. Nothing at all.

But that punch was something.

I charged in, working the same combination again before he could figure it out, delivering a second body shot to the same spot, flatfooted this time, a sledgehammer blow with serious steam on it.

Juba couldn't clown this one off. Wincing in pain, he backpedaled, dancing away as fast as he could. He stayed up on his toes the last fifteen seconds of the round, then walked stiff-legged back to his corner at the bell. His knees wobbled when he collapsed on his stool.

I nodded in satisfaction. Gotcha! Juba was definitely in the House of Hurt.

"You hooked him good there, Mick." Pops grinned as I dropped onto my stool, breathing deep with my nostrils flared, sucking down all the air I could hold, inhaling the stink of the ring, the crowd. "How do you feel?"

"I'm good, Pops." Then I tuned him out, focusing on the ex-con across the ring.

Tall and rangy for a middleweight, Juba had long arms, like Tommy Hearns. Had a honey of a scar on one cheek, gleaming through the Vaseline, giving him a fierce, predatory look.

But beneath the savage mask, I could *feel* his pain. Juba was keeping his teeth bared in a fierce grin to camouflage it, but his brow was furrowed and he couldn't quite straighten up on his stool, even when his trainer tugged on his waistband to relax his abdominals.

I knew that agony. I'd drilled him with the same punch Jilly had caught me with earlier in the week. I'd stopped one like it once before, early in my career. The pain was so bad I thought the guy had ruptured my spleen. Somehow I answered the bell, stayed on my feet, but I could barely defend myself. My opponent toyed with me for a round, setting me up. Then dropped me flat in the sixth.

But I couldn't wait for the sixth. Juba was tough, with real power, and his flashy punches were piling up points. I had to put him away now, before he could shake off his misery. And find the chink in my guard.

Normally Pops would be yelling instructions in my ear. Not on this night. No need. We both knew what had to be done.

"Seconds out!" the timekeeper called, slapping the ring apron with his palm for emphasis.

"You did some damage," Pops said, rinsing off my mouthpiece, sliding it in as I rose. "He thought he was getting a tune-up fight. So tune his ass up!" Grabbing the stool, the old man hoisted himself through the ropes.

Across the ring, Juba was already dancing in place, angry, hurting, and hungry for payback. And if we started trading body shots?

He'd kill me.

It had to be now. I had to put him on the goddamn deck.

Slamming my gloves together, I sucked in extra air, ready for Freddie.

At the bell Juba came charging out of his corner, firing away like a machine gunner. Pumped up on pain and rage, he was desperately trying to smother my punches, keeping me too busy to land another body shot.

No problem. I let him flail away. I was headhunting now, picking off Juba's blows, waiting for a puncher's chance. One clean shot for a knockout. Waiting . . . waiting . . . Bobbing, ducking . . . Knowing it could come any second now—

Suddenly there it was! Juba threw a left hook so hard it carried him around when it missed, out of position, leaving his jaw wide open for a counter!

Perfect!

I threw a hard right, swiveling my hips into the punch, giving it everything I had—but Juba's desperation-flailing roundhouse landed first, grazing my temple.

Totally focused, I barely felt Juba's punch. But it had just enough zip on it to make me miss mine. Big-time.

The force of my blow spun me off balance, and as I straightened up, I stumbled over Juba's left foot, dropping to one knee.

Jesus! What the hell just happened?

I jumped up immediately, more embarrassed than hurt. But the ref was already counting, giving me a standing eight.

"Hey!" I shouted around my mouthpiece. "No knockdown! I freakin' tripped!"

Across the ring, Juba was dancing in his corner, arms raised in victory, showboating for the crowd. And the fans were eating it up. Screw the fine points of pugilism. Your freakin' grandma can understand a knockdown. *Goddamn it!*

"You okay, Maguire?" The ref was peering into my eyes intently.

"Dammit, Bozo, I tripped!" I mumbled around my mouthpiece.

"Answer up, Maguire! Can you continue or not?"

"Hell yes!" I roared, desperate to get back into the fight. "Get out of the way!"

Grabbing my gloves, Bozo wiped them off on his white shirt, then stepped back and waved us on.

I charged into Juba's corner, but he danced out of reach, grinning, hot-dogging around the ring for the last half minute of the round.

"You're blowin' it, Mick," Pops yelled as I sagged on his stool. "Dammit, I told you—"

I leaned back, closing my eyes, tuning him out. Knowing he was right.

Crap! Decked by a dumb-ass lucky punch. Juba hadn't laid a glove on me all night. And he wouldn't have to, now. The knock-down would decide this bout. Pops was ranting at me, practically frothing at the mouth, more frantic than I'd ever seen him—

The ref was leaning over me, checking me out. "You good to go, Maguire?"

"Terrific," I snapped.

"Glad to hear it," he said dryly, then trotted back to the center of the ring to wait on the bell. I noticed he didn't bother asking Juba if he was okay. This fight was over unless I could nail Juba and put him down—

But I couldn't. The traditional glove touch before the final round was the closest I came to landing a punch.

Juba danced the last rounds away, running for his freakin' life but looking good doing it. Every time I tried to close with him, he got on his bicycle, firing flurries of flashy, pitty-pat punches with nothing on them, confident he had the fight in the bag.

Which he damn well did.

Bozo cautioned Juba twice about the running, but that didn't mean squat to the fans. Juba was still showboating at the final bell. Five seconds to confer with the judges and the ref was raising Juba's hand in victory while the ring announcer bellowed the unanimous decision. There was a smattering of applause, but the crowd was already thinning, headed for the johns and beer booths before the next bout.

"Lucky goddamn punch," Pops said glumly, cutting the laces off my gloves in the dressing room. "You rocked him good in the second. What the heck happened?"

"I had him hurt, I went for the knockout. I was so paranoid about catching a liver shot—"

"This is all on me," the old man said. "I should have pulled you."

"You didn't make me trip over his damn foot, Pops."

"I know, but . . ." He swallowed. "We've got more trouble, Mick. Them IOUs I spread around? They've been bought up. All of 'em."

"By who?"

"Tony Dukarski. Used to fight some himself—he's a promoter now. Do you know him?"

"Tony Duke? He's not just a promoter, Pops, he's mobbed up. How much are we down to him? Exactly?"

"The better part of fifteen grand. It might as well be a million. I don't have it."

"The loser's purse is a thousand, but—hold on. Fifteen grand? Dukarski's in the business. He must know we don't have that kind of money lying around. Why would he buy up your paper?"

"He's backing a new fighter, a stud from L.A., Toro Esteban. Bad-lookin' dude, prison-yard muscles, tattoos, dreadlocks. Big puncher. Killed a Mexican fighter down in Tijuana. They call him Toro the Terminator now."

"What's that got to do with us?"

"Toro's wins are nobodies, Mexicans from Dago or Tijuana. Everybody's fifty and one down there, no way to confirm their records. I hear Tony Duke's lookin' for some . . . local bouts."

He looked away, unable to meet my eyes.

"My God," I groaned. "You mean Dukarski's lining up mopes his boy can knock down to pump up his win record? Mopes like me, for instance?"

"It don't matter what he's doin'," Pops said. "Bein' down fifteen to Tony Duke ain't like owin' the Bank of Detroit, Mick. We're in deep shit here. We gotta talk to the man."

We found Tony "Duke" Dukarski holding court at a third-tier table overlooking the main floor. A dozen people around him, all as drunk as he was, except for his bodyguard, Cheech Gamez, a hawk-faced Latin in a gray silk suit, narrow tie. Cheech was strapped, nickel-silver automatic in a shoulder holster winking from beneath his sport coat. Tony Duke was carrying too, a piece tucked in his waistband. Not really concealed; he clearly wanted folks to see it.

His new fighter wasn't armed, but didn't need to be. He was at the end of the table and Pops was right. Even in a slick new sharkskin suit and tie, Toro the Terminator looked bad to the bone, prison-yard muscles straining the seams of his tailored jacket.

Dukarski looked bad too, in the original sense of the word. Big and fleshy, with thinning blond hair, he was clearly on a downhill slide. His cheeks were splotchy from booze, seamed with smile lines from his fixed salesman's grin. His brows were shiny with scar tissue from his time in the ring, but his fighting days were a while back. Looked like he was carousing himself into an early coronary now, laughing all the way.

"Mr. Dukarski? I got word you wanted to talk to us?"

"Irish Pops Maguire and his star fighter," Tony Duke said, not bothering to offer his hand. "Hey, everybody, say hello to Irish Mick and his Pops."

A couple of drunk chicks at the table glanced up. Cleaned up, in a clean white shirt and jeans, I'm saloon-society passable, if you ignore the scars around my eyes and a deep nick in my upper lip, souvenir of a head butt. The girls weren't interested. They'd just seen me lose.

"Siddown, have a drink," Tony Duke slurred. "You'll probably want a shot to go with the one put you on your ass, Mick. Nurse!" he bellowed at a passing waitress, stuffing a ten down her bra. "Scotch all around."

"I'll have a beer," I said, swallowing my anger. I sat opposite Dukarski with Pops beside me. Pops went with the Scotch. A double.

"Have you met the Terminator, Mick?"

Toro offered a sizable paw, but it wasn't a contest of strength. He shook gently, Spanish style.

"Tough break, trippin' like that, Irish," he said. "Your last fight was bad luck too. Your shoulder was screwed in the third. Why didn't your papa throw the towel?"

"I was ahead on points, tried to go the distance, squeeze out a win."

"Gutsy, but stupid. I would have busted you up like a wrecking ball. Hit you so hard whole damn family would've spit blood for a month."

I eyed him, but let it pass.

"Want some advice, Irish?" Toro said, leaning forward, his massive mahogany face only inches from mine. "You looked different in the ring tonight. Fought different too. Like you were scared. I think you were. You should back away from the game now, before your brains get scrambled or you get kilt. Maybe I kill you."

"Maybe you'll talk me to death," I said.

"You got a smart mouth, white boy." Toro grinned, not backing off an inch. "Gonna be some fun bustin' you up."

"Hey, hey, let's not have any fightin' at the fights," Tony Duke interrupted, with a bleary grin at his own wit. "Your Pops tells me we got a problem, Maguire—"

"We owe you," I said, turning to Dukarski. "We understand that. If you want me to fight this gorilla, I'll do it for free. But I won't dive, Mr. Dukarski, not for you or anybody else."

"You ain't callin' the shots here, sonny." Dukarski snorted. "And you ain't the one I want to talk about anyway. It's your sister."

"Then there's nothing to talk about," I said, standing up, flushing with fury. "I'm the fighter, Mr. Dukarski—"

"Not from what I seen," Toro said.

"If you want to try me, bring it!" I flared, whirling on him.

"Dammit, Irish, cool your jets!" Tony Duke snapped, waving me back to my seat. "You Maguires are into me for fifteen, which your old man lost bettin' on you, Mick. Have you got my money?"

"Not tonight, but—"

"Then it's a done deal." Duke leaned back, confident now. "You're in the toilet, swirlin' around. I can flush the lot of you down, or we can all get well. A sweet deal, one time. One and done."

I turned away a moment, fighting down the urge to punch Tony Duke's lights out. But I knew what would happen to the family if I did.

Out on the arena floor, acres of boozy spectators were cheering or cursing two gladiators in the ring. Fight night, Motown style. Shirtsleeves and summer dresses, not a tuxedo in sight.

Half an hour ago I'd fought an ex-con to entertain these stiffs and got my head handed to me. And now we were deeper in the hole than before.

"What's on your mind, Mr. Dukarski?" Pops asked.

"Your girl, Jilly? Hasn't lost a bout since she turned pro. Your family name alone makes her a heavy favorite every fight now, and after seeing her tonight, she'll be five or six to one to win her next bout. Crazy odds, and that's the beauty of it. Nobody takes female fighters seriously, they're strictly for glitz. So losing one bout won't mean squat to your girl's career. But at five to one, we could all make a pile. Enough dough to get you off the hook, Pops."

"Jilly won't tank," I said.

"Then you can give her a lesson." Toro smirked. "Show her how to trip."

"I hear she's got a temper," Dukarski said coldly, his sham friendliness gone. "That's why I'm talkin' to you two first. You're gonna explain the facts of life to her, guys. She drops one lousy fight, we're all even again."

"Unless somebody figures it out," Pops said. "Then we're all in jail or on the street."

"I can put you on the street tonight, old man. It ain't like you got a choice. Which brings us to Irish Mick here."

"What about me?"

"You got a temper too, Maguire, and I don't trust hotheads. So you're gonna fall too. You want Toro, you got him. In six weeks. Same card as your sister. I'm betting you fall in the fourth. Understand?"

"I won't—"

"Deal," Pops said.

"What?" I said, whirling on him. "Are you out of your freakin' mind?"

"The man's right, Mick," Pops said, "neither loss will mean much in the long run. With your shoulder, you're all but done, son. Liam, Sean, and Jilly are the future now. So we'll do this one thing, one time, to make sure they get their chance."

"Pops—"

"Mick will fall in the fourth, Mr. Dukarski," Pops said, turning back to Tony Duke. "But he don't get hurt. Nobody bleeds, you understand me? Or I'll feed you that damn gun myself!"

"Relax, Pops, no need for drama." Dukarski grinned, offering his hand. "We all understand the stakes. Don't we, Mick?"

I didn't say anything. Couldn't.

Then the man I've worshipped my entire life reached out and shook the gangster's hand.

Done deal.

"Don't look at me like that," Pops said. We were in the dressing room collecting my gear.

"How should I look? You sold us out, Pops."

"I saved the family," he countered. "Pull on your big-boy pants, Mick. Grow up."

"To be like you? That's what I always wanted."

"I wanted to be heavyweight champ." He sighed, slapping his belly. "All I ever made was the weight. Maybe Liam will be a champion one day, but first we gotta get ourselves out of this jam."

"I thought we just did. By selling Jilly out."

"Get over your snit and start thinkin', boy. The only true thing Dukarski said back there was about us circlin' the drain. The rest was a crock. Something's wrong about the deal."

"Hell, every damn thing's wrong with it, Pops! Dukarski's a hood—"

"Gee, a thug in the fight game? Do tell. He ain't the first we've met. They're like lice on the biz, and always have been."

I opened my mouth to argue, then closed it again. He was right.

"So what are you saying? What's wrong with the deal?"

"You tell me, dammit! *Think*, boy. I know we're missing something, I just don't know what!"

I mulled that for a moment.

"For openers, it *won't* be one and done. We do this once, Dukarski will freakin' *own* us."

"He can't burn us without burning himself," Pops pointed out.

"Sure he can. If we get busted for illegal gambling, Dukarski will pay a fine, maybe spend time on the county, and be right back in business. But the Maguires will be done, Pops, barred from the sport forever. It'd be the end of us. You'll be the Pete Rose of boxing."

"Maybe I should be, if I've brought us to this."

"Maybe we both should," I conceded. "But we can't let our mistakes wreck Liam's future, or Sean's. And Jilly's most of all. We gotta make this right, Pops."

"We still ain't seein' it clear. One thing, though? When Toro talked about killin' you, he was dead serious. He ain't a fighter, Mick, he's a murderin' son of a bitch. You need to be ready when you fight him."

"I'm not afraid of him, Pops—" I broke off, considering what I'd just said.

"What is it?"

"Dukarski was sweating," I said. "Did you notice?"

"He seemed jumpy," Pops acknowledged. "So?"

"So the man was strapped, so was Cheech, and the Terminator kills people with his fists."

"I don't—?"

"We were in a public place—he had a gun and two bodyguards. Why the hell would he be nervous? What was he afraid of?"

We both mulled that one over but came up empty.

Pops left to collect our purses, a winner's share for Jilly, loser's for me.

I was zipping up my gym bag when Bobbie Barlow rapped once and stepped in. Dressed casually in jeans and a Detroit Tigers baseball jacket, she still managed to look classy.

"Hey, Maguire. Tough luck tonight."

"Puncher's luck." I shrugged. "Didn't go my way tonight. I'm glad you came by, though. I wanted to thank you for not writing about that sparring business."

"I wrote the important part. Jilly's going to be a star."

"You know what I mean."

"I'm a sportswriter, Mick; obituaries are a different department. It would have been a false alarm anyway. You owned that mope until he tripped you."

"It was my fault, actually. I stumbled over his foot. But anyway, I owe you one. Buy you dinner?"

"I never date my stories, Mick."

"I'm not a story anymore, lady. I'm yesterday's news."

"Not to me. I came by right after the fight, but you were already gone. So I went looking for you and there you were, making nice with Tony Duke. And the Terminator."

"We were doing a deal," I said simply. "I signed to fight Toro in six weeks."

"With your shoulder messed up? Are you out of your mind?"

"It's what I do, Barlow."

"But cutting a deal with a sleaze like Dukarski—"

"The family needs the money. Simple as that."

"No, it's not. Toro killed another fighter—"

"In Mexico. I know. But—"

"My point is, that's *all* he's done. Toro's a nobody, Mick, and you're coming to the end of your career. Even if you beat him, it won't fatten your purses or build your image—" She broke off, staring at me.

"But it'll build *his* image," she went on. "When he beats you."

"You mean *if* he beats me."

"I don't think so. When promoters cut a deal, both sides look for an edge, but in the end, no matter how they finagle it, it comes down to the fighters. Two guys squaring off in the ring. But it only takes one to fix a fight. Is that what I saw, Mick?"

I didn't say anything to that. Which was an answer, of sorts.

"You owe me, Maguire. You just said so."

"I don't want to lie to you, Bobbie."

"Well, that's *something*, at least. Forget dinner, but I'll toss you a bone for free. If Dukarski promised you a payoff? You won't see it. He doesn't have it."

"What are you talking about?"

"Duke bet the wrong way on the last Mayweather fight, and borrowed big to do it. He's down fifty Gs to Fat Jack Cassidy, a loan shark out of Warsaw Heights. And people who can't pay Fat Jack tend to disappear. One way or the other."

"Where'd you hear this?"

"Sorry, Maguire, one freebie's all you get," she said, shaking her head. "And you still owe me a story."

"I'd rather buy you dinner."

"I'll settle for the truth," she said from the doorway. "If you ever remember what it is."

"Duke's in the hole to Fat Jack Cassidy?" Pops mused when I told him. "No wonder he's worried. He damn well should be. He's in deeper trouble than we are. How much did she say?"

"Fifty thousand. Which is a huge problem. For us."

We were in the gym office, Pops behind his desk, watching something on his computer, me in a chair facing him. The walls around us were lined with dozens of photos and trophies, the bloody plunder won over three generations of war in the ring. Barely worth a few hundred bucks to a collector.

Worth everything to a Maguire.

"Which part is the problem?" Pops asked, still frowning at his computer screen, his face blue in the reflected light.

"The fifty Gs," I said. "Duke can't lay a bet anywhere near that against Jilly. A wager that big on a girl fighter would raise too many red flags."

"You're right." Pops nodded without looking up. "Even if he spreads it around, winning more than ten, fifteen grand on an upset would draw the gaming commission like crows to roadkill. But the fifteen might be enough to keep Fat Jack Cassidy from capping him while he waited for the real payoff."

"What payoff?"

"Take a look at this," he said. "Tell me what you see."

"What is it?"

"Fight film, from Mexico. Toro Esteban versus Momo Benitez. It wasn't easy to come by. There are laws against snuff films."

"Benitez is the fighter Toro killed?"

"Take a look," Pops repeated. "What do you see?"

There was no sound, and the film was grainy, an overhead-view shot from a cheap-ass videocam suspended above the ring.

I wasn't sure what I was looking for. Toro came out of his corner cautiously, feeling out Benitez. His opponent looked sloppy to me. I spotted a half-dozen openings that Toro missed.

They wasted the first round feeling each other out, but halfway through the second, Toro suddenly picked it up, firing off a dozen hard body shots that clearly hurt Benitez . . .

"Watch this," Pops said, leaning in.

In his corner, between rounds, Benitez and his manager were arguing. But in Spanish and without sound? I had no idea what the beef was.

Third round, Toro jacked up the action again, a full-body attack. Benitez had no counter for it; he kept taking the punches, clearly hurt, until Toro caught him with a low blow, then laid him out with a hammer strike to the temple. Benitez hit the deck, didn't move. The screen went dark.

I stared at the blankness.

Staring at death, I suppose.

"What did you see?" Pops pressed, his eyes intense.

I considered that a moment.

"The body attack," I said. "Benitez wasn't expecting it. Is that what he was arguing with his manager about?"

"I think so. The question is, why didn't he expect it? Toro's a body-puncher, they must have known that. So why were they surprised?"

It took a moment for the answer to register. And when it did, I went utterly still. Realizing what I'd just seen.

"It wasn't a fight," I said slowly. "It was murder."

"Benitez was set up," Pops agreed. "I think he was fixed to fall in the fourth. So when Toro came at him full on in the second, it caught him by surprise. He wasn't ready to fight, or defend himself properly. He thought he was going to dance a few rounds, then drop."

"Instead, Toro used him for a punching bag, knowing he

wouldn't fight back," I finished. "The poor bastard had no chance at all."

"Still, they couldn't have known they'd kill him," Pops mused.

"Probably not. They double-crossed him, figuring to end his career, put him in traction. His death was a bonus."

"Toro's whole reputation, the 'Terminator' business, began with that fight," Pops said. "Before Benitez, Toro was just another pug. And even the killing didn't make him a headliner, because Benitez was a nobody, and it happened in Mexico."

"But if he kills a second fighter? Say an Irish Maguire, in Detroit? Dukarski will be minting money off this guy."

"Jilly diving is only a smokescreen," Pops agreed. "To get you into the ring with your guard down. So Toro can make his name by stomping you into dog meat."

"Or killing me. If he can."

"We've got to go to the law, Mick."

"To say what? Toro killed Benitez? Hell, everybody knows that. He's proud of it. And if we admit we're mixed up in a fix with Dukarski, we'll be flat broke, barred from boxing forever, while he waltzes away without a scratch. The law can't help us here, Pops. We have to settle this on our own."

"How?"

"We do what we've always done. We're Irish Maguires. We come up with a plan, then step in the ring and swing away."

There's a famous quote from former heavyweight champ Joe Frazier. My Pops has it painted on a banner that hangs over our training ring:

"You can map out a fight plan or a life plan, but when the action starts, it may not go the way you planned . . . That's where your roadwork shows. If you cheated on that in the dark of the morning, well, you're going to get found out now. Under the bright lights."

We took Smokin' Joe's advice, kept our fight plan as simple as possible. First we brought Jilly up to speed on the fix. Pops told her she was supposed to lose, and why.

"Duke needs to make two things happen," Pops explained. "He bets heavy that you lose and makes enough to hold off the loan sharks. Then Toro beats Mick real bad, maybe to death? And Duke gets himself a big earner for the long run."

"That's his plan." Jilly nodded grimly. "What's ours, Pops?"

"The exact opposite," Pops said flatly. "You win your bout and bankrupt that son of a bitch. Then Mick calls in the ring doctor, admits his shoulder's injured, and cancels out. And Toro stays a nobody who can't make Duke a nickel."

"Sounds like a plan." Jilly nodded, frowning, mulling it over.

"And?" Pops asked.

She glanced up with the feral flare of combat in her eyes. "I like my part of it just fine." She grinned. "Who do I have to beat?"

"A Russian called Olga the Borg," Pops said warily. "A cage fighter out of Duke's stable. She's tough and tall, a lot taller than you, with a longer reach. And she'll definitely be in it to win it. Duke won't tell her nothing about the fix."

"What fix is that?" Jilly asked, all innocence.

"Exactly right." Pops nodded. "Ain't no fix, girl, not anymore. Just make damn sure you win!"

That was our fight plan. And we trained hard for it, Jilly to win, me to look like I was serious about a fight Pops would cancel at the last minute.

It was a good plan. Until the night of the fight. When it all went south.

I was alone in my dressing room, sitting on the massage table. Jilly's fight was being announced and I was waiting for the ring doctor so I could cancel mine.

The door burst open and Pops charged in, his eyes wild.

"What the hell?" I demanded, jumping to my feet. "Why aren't you in the ring with Jilly?"

"Dukarski," he said. "He sent a limo for Liam and Sean. They're sitting at ringside between him and Gamez. Gamez is strapped and Duke is too."

"Jesus! Did he threaten them?"

"He don't have to! The message is plain. The boys don't know nothing. Hell, they're happy as clams to have front-row seats."

"What about Jilly?"

"She ain't said nothing either, but she can see what Duke expects her to do. Them boys are there as insurance to keep her in line."

"Then it's gotta be on Jilly," I said flatly. "She's the one in the bright lights tonight, Pops. Whatever she decides, we back her up. Now get back out there, look after her."

"What are you going to do?"

"Wait, for now. If I go after them like this, they'll see me coming a mile away. Get out there and follow Jilly's lead, whatever it is."

Pops hurried back through the crowd to the ring. Standing in that doorway, watching him go, was harder than any fight I've ever been in. All we had going was Smokin' Joe's advice.

The action had started, it wasn't going the way we planned, and our only hope was to trust Jilly. She was the one in the ring under the lights. It was her call to make.

And I had no idea what it would be.

But subtlety ain't Jilly's style. She didn't keep me waitin'.

She was dancing in place, glaring up at the Russian all the way through the ring announcements. Ready for Freddie. Her opponent was big and battle-scarred from the cages, looked like she ate lions for lunch. Experienced and sure of herself, she glared back at Jilly with open contempt.

An expression she didn't wear for long.

At the bell, Jilly came rocketing across the ring like a cruise missile, trapping the Russian coming out of her corner. Facing a much shorter fighter, Olga thought she could fend Jilly off, keep her at bay, out of reach.

It was like trying to hold back a hurricane with a parasol. Jilly's punches just kept raining in furiously from all directions, nonstop. And I felt my heart drop.

Jilly was going all-in in the first minute, gambling everything on this round. It was an impossible pace to maintain. If her strategy failed, Jilly'd be totally burned out by the second—but it didn't fail.

Trying to duck away from the rain of punches, the Russian caught a right cross flush on the jaw. Rocked by the blow, she lunged desperately at Jilly, trying to wrap her up into a clinch.

But she didn't make it.

Her arms closed on air as Jilly danced back a step, just out of reach. Then charged back in firing off a half-dozen straight shots that caught the Borg off-balance and out of position, driving the Russian to her knees.

Waving Jilly to a neutral corner, the ref began his count: one . . . two . . .

Before he could say three, Olga's eyes rolled up and she toppled. Wrapping a protective arm around her, the ref took a quick look into the Borg's vacant stare, then waved Jilly off, stopping the bout!

The crowd exploded with cheers and applause, galvanized by the explosive action that ended with a first-round knockout. By a girl? Freaking amazing!

Jilly was even more excited than the spectators, bouncing around the ring like a dervish, pumping her fists in the air, celebrating . . .

Which was totally out of character. Irish Maguires don't celebrate. We're all business, all the time.

But not this time.

Jilly was over the moon!

And then she was over the ropes.

Scrambling up the ring post, she pumped her fists, saluting the fans, bringing the audience to its feet with a deafening roar. Then she leapt into the crowd!

Dropping onto the ring apron, she launched herself into the ringside seats, catching Dukarski totally by surprise as he lurched to his feet.

Slamming into Big Duke chest high, Jilly's tackle carried him backward into the next tier, though I doubt Dukarski had any idea where he was at that point. She was hammering him the whole time, with the same furious barrage of punches that had demolished the Borg. Dukarski was lights-out before he hit the floor.

Gamez was apparently smarter than he looked. Seeing his boss laid out on the deck, the gunsel immediately backed away from Jilly and the boys with his hands raised, then turned and fled up the aisle, running like a scalded dog.

The place dissolved into pandemonium as security guards charged into the crush, trying to wrestle Jilly off Tony Duke. It took them a while. The fans fought for her, pushing them back, defending their new princess.

But chaos at a fight isn't unusual. Order was quickly being restored. And I was on next.

Stepping back into my dressing room, I did a few quick pushups to get my heart pumping, then faced the mirror.

It was definitely time to call for the ring doctor.

But I didn't.

I started to dance instead. Tuning up, getting my mind right.

Getting ready for Toro.

Pops found me there a few minutes later, shadowboxing.

"What the hell are you doing? Where's the doc?"

I just shook my head and kept on punching.

"Dammit, Mick, you don't have to do this! We're off the hook now."

"It's got nothing to do with the fix, Pops. However it goes, this is probably my last night. We both know that. Dukarski and Toro are poster boys for everything that's wrong with this sport. Jilly took care of the one, now I'm going to settle with the other. I owe it to the game, and to that poor bastard they killed in Mexico."

"But—"

"I owe it to myself, Pops! If it's my last shot, I want to take it. There's no time to argue about it. I'm going on. Get me ready."

And he did. When a gofer came to call us to the ring, he found the Irish Maguires throwing leather as hard and fast as we could, both of us grinning like feral dogs.

I was halfway down the arena aisle when the ring announcer roared out my name. I got a huge ovation that had more to do with the show Jilly'd just put on than my own record.

It didn't matter. I wasn't fighting for the crowd.

I was here for the guy across the ring, dancing in his corner, his face hidden by his black silk cowl. My emerald-green trunks seemed boyish as the ref called us to the center.

Neither of us heard a word he said. We both stood like stone statues, staring each other down. When the ref told us to touch 'em up, neither of us even offered. He asked again, then shook his head and sent us to our corners.

Across the ring, Toro was snarling as he slammed his fists together. Pumping himself up, his eyes locked on mine. He knew the fix was off. Knew it the moment Jilly won her prelim. Knew I'd fight him now. Straight up.

He didn't care.

Neither did I.

Because Bobbie was right. In the end, it comes down to the fighters in the ring, matched fairly or mishandled, with the crowd screaming for blood.

With my shoulder lamed up, I knew I had no real chance against Toro.

Except the one.

A puncher's chance. The same chance Bobbie's father took one time too many.

The same chance we all get, every single day.

We choose to keep punching or not. To speak up or keep silent, stand our ground or step off. To tell someone we care for them. Or not.

And as long as you keep punching, one split second can change a fight. Change your luck.

Change your life.

Every fighter believes that.

Because we have to.

And because it's the flat-ass truth.

JIM ALLYN

The Master of Negwegon

FROM *Ellery Queen Mystery Magazine*

"It is not a garment I cast off this day, but a skin that I tear with
my own hands."
　　—Kahlil Gibran

ON THIS WARM August morning Josh Zuckerman thought he
was alone on the beach. He didn't know he was being watched. He
didn't know he was being regarded by a set of eyes that considered
him just another enemy in a country that contained nothing but, a
country that Josh had never seen and never would see because he
had less than ten minutes to live. He was going to live that last ten
minutes on a pristine stretch of Lake Huron shoreline named after
a long-dead Chippewa chief: Negwegon.

Josh was thrilled to be away from his invalid mother. During the
school year, a home-care nurse helped her in and out of her wheelchair, helped her with personal things, and did routine chores.
In the summer, though, to save money, they dispensed with the
nurse and Josh did the work. None of the summer jobs he could
get would earn as much as the nurse cost. So Josh didn't get the
summer break most kids got. But right now he had a break and was
scary happy. Scary because he knew the huge, lightly used wilderness park and its seven miles of undeveloped beach was protected,
off-limits to four-wheelers. He'd snuck his Yamaha Raptor into the
forests and fields of the park before and there he stayed well concealed, never daring the beach. That much was easy, because the
park boundary was long and roadless and only two miles from the
family farm on Black River Road. But tearing around on the open

beach—that was risky: just what he needed to shake the boredom of weeks of caring for a beloved cripple. He had successfully negotiated the broken trails without being spotted. Now the broad empty beach was all his, a perfect place to release the muscle of his Raptor, a gift on his fourteenth birthday.

If he had been standing, he would have been taller than the cluster of young six-foot Scots pines in front of him. But he was crouching, peering through the green needles at the roaring four-wheeler doing figure eights in the desert sand. He wasn't sure where he was. His best guess was about two miles from where the Euphrates emptied into Lake Huron. He watched as the giant beetle straightened, accelerated and soared over the top of a small dune, and splashed into the shallow waves. He couldn't understand why nobody was shooting. The son of a bitch was running wild inside the perimeter. Frigging thing might be loaded with explosives. Why wasn't anyone shooting? Skidding, spraying sand into the water, the fat treads of the Mud Wolf tires were ripping up a beach that had been unmolested for centuries.

He couldn't see who was driving. It didn't matter. He was going to kill him. Carve a deep red smile into his throat and let the blood spray out over the hot sand. The desert sand of the Holy Land has an unquenchable thirst for human blood. Yes, he would kill him and throw his body in the alley with the rest of the corpses that had welcomed his unit this morning in Fallujah. The religious and ethnic factions were engaged in fratricidal butchering of biblical proportions. Bombings. Kidnappings. Murder, because it's the only thing you know and the only job you can find. Home invasions. Drive-bys. Sunni against Shiite against Kurd against Christian, tribe against tribe, clan against clan, family against family. The only good thing about that was that when they were busy killing each other they weren't busy trying to kill the infidel invaders. And now come the Internet-savvy, joyfully murderous thugs of the self-proclaimed Islamic state—ISIS. He'd seen their black uniforms and black flags in the *Alpena News* and on the tube. It was only a matter of time until the butchers showed up here.

Josh Zuckerman didn't see the lean, bearded, half-naked figure break from the pines like a jungle cat and sprint across the sand. He didn't realize someone had jumped on his back until a strong hand grabbed his chin from behind and jerked his head back. The searing pain, the profound and final gagging, lasted ninety seconds. Like vanishing music, his strength and vision faded, his last image a lone magnificent cloud moving unhurriedly across an open blue sky.

He shut off the engine. Now the sounds were as they should be. The gentle lapping of the waves, the screech of a gull, the wind trailing through the towering white pines. He dropped from the Raptor and jogged back into the forest. The beach was quiet again . . . and all his.

A warm, breezy August night in northern Indiana. Joy Gunther and Hank Sawyer had opened all the bedroom windows of the old farmhouse that sat isolated about twenty miles south of South Bend. Hank was wrapped in Joy's arms and legs with the wind dancing across his back. He had reached that wonderful state when the mind finally shuts down and all that's left is warm, damp, exciting rhythm. That's why Joy had to make a fist and pound him on the temple to get his attention, not exactly one of her usual playful moves. It hurt.

"Hey, take it easy."

"I heard something. I think there's someone at the door."

"If you knock me out I won't be able to check on it."

She giggled. Together they became still, like someone had pulled the plug on a washing machine. Quiet, just the curtains rustling. Then Hank heard it too. A gentle rapping at the front door. He grabbed his snub-nosed Colt off the nightstand. Trouble usually doesn't knock, but it was one a.m. and he was definitely a little dazed and confused, not to mention naked and aroused. With domestic violence a routine part of his work, he had noted the menacing glances the husband Joy was dumping had sent his way. Without turning on a light he tied Joy's blouse around his waist and went out into the living room. He looked sideways out the bay window at the front door and saw a stocky white shape. He let his head clear for a moment. His heart was still beating fast. He called out through the screen.

"Who is it?"

"Hank, it's Frenchie. Open up."

It's funny how people you were close to in your youth remain familiar always. You bump into them after years have gone by and start talking to them like you'd seen them only yesterday. Hank hadn't seen Frenchie Skiba in five years, but somehow it seemed perfectly natural that he was at his door in the middle of the night. He flicked on the porch light and opened the door. Frenchie Skiba stood there in a rumpled white baseball uniform with navy pin-stripes. ALCONA WILDCATS was emblazoned on a patch on his left shoulder. A black Alcona County Sheriff's Department prowler sat in the driveway. Hank smiled. Even with all the windows open wide, they hadn't heard the prowler pull up. They wouldn't have heard the space shuttle land either.

"You here for the tryouts?"

"You gonna shoot me or invite me in?"

Hank glanced down at the Colt. "I'm on the fence."

Frenchie pushed by Hank. "You never could hit shit anyway." From behind Hank got the smaller man in a friendly horse collar and gave him a big hug.

"Jesus, if you're gonna do that put some pants on."

Hank laughed and led him to the kitchen that Joy was restoring and sat him down in the breakfast nook. He put the gun on the counter. "My girl is separated, getting a divorce," he said. "Thought you might be her husband dropping by to cast his vote."

"Husbands that knock you don't have to worry about."

Hank went back into the bedroom. "It's Frenchie Skiba," he said as he put on baggy khaki cargo shorts and a white T-shirt. Joy had never met Frenchie but she knew him as the stocky, somber, heavy-bearded black man omnipresent in photos from Hank's youth. In the pictures he looked short, but most people looked short standing next to Hank.

"Why is he here at this ungodly hour?" she asked, rummaging around for something to throw on. "Some kind of emergency?"

"Don't know, but I expect so. He's driving a prowler and wearing a Little League uniform. I'd say he hit the road in a hurry."

"He didn't tell you anything?"

"Not yet. Frenchie tells you things when he's ready. Come out to the kitchen and we'll talk."

She leaned into him. "This is just halftime, you know."

"Not a good analogy," he said.

"Why not?"

"Because there's no sport where both sides win. How about 'intermission'?"

"Mmmmm . . . I like your logic." Together they went out to the kitchen. Like the rest of the sprawling old farmhouse, the kitchen was in the middle of a transformation. About half the cabinetry was still covered by original blistering and peeling white paint. The other half was lovingly if sloppily painted light yellow with light green trim right over the old paint, no sanding or scraping done at all. Joy's choice of colors was odd, but like everything else she did it exuded casual charm. It was that touch that made her the youngest vice president in South Bend's biggest marketing firm. Clients loved her, were wowed by the pretty blonde with the purring engine and creative mind.

"Frenchie, this is Joy Gunther."

Frenchie sprang awkwardly from his chair, banging the table as he did so, eyes fixed on Joy. What she had thrown on wasn't much.

"It's great to finally meet you," she said, taking his rough, outstretched hand in both of hers. "Hank doesn't have many pictures, but you're in all of them, and that makes me feel like I already know you. He talks about you all the time." She excused herself and padded barefoot down the hall to the bathroom. Frenchie watched her all the way. "Holy shit," he said. Hank grinned and set about making coffee.

"Make detective yet?" Frenchie asked.

"Few months ago," Hank said.

"That's fast. Congratulations . . . This is quite a spread."

"Yeah, it's a handful, but it's fun. Ten acres. Monster of an old barn. Joy's making it all into something special. That's a gift she has. Takes beat-up, discarded things and makes them special." Hank was letting Frenchie move at his own pace. He owed Frenchie a lot. They say it takes a village to raise a child. When Hank was growing up in northeastern Michigan, there wasn't a village to be found. What he had was Frenchie Skiba. Frenchie pushed aside the whiskey bottles Hank had for parents and gave him a hand to hold on to and a hand up.

Earl, Joy's big orange tomcat, jumped up on the counter and sat down next to the coffeepot.

"You let the cat up on the counter?"

"His ass is cleaner than yours."

"That's not saying much. Besides, I'm wearing pants and I'm not the one sitting on the counter."

Hank nudged Earl off the counter. "All excellent observations. They didn't make you sheriff for nothing."

"Speaking of asses, how's the sand in yours?" It was a reference to Iraq.

"Less and less," Hank said. "Less and less. You never wash it all out, do you?"

"Never met a combat vet who ever forgot he was in combat," Frenchie said.

Hank sat down at the table, waiting for the coffee. They waited in silence, perfectly comfortable, like a pair of worn hunting boots in a corner. They waited for Joy, for the coffee, for Frenchie to get down to it.

"You serious about this girl?"

"Pretty serious. I like the hell out of her."

"You love her?"

"Every chance I get."

"You love her?"

"We get closer every day. Pooled our money to buy this place. We haven't talked marriage but we're already joined at the hip."

"I'm glad to hear it."

Joy returned as the coffee finished up. "I'll get it," she said. "What did I miss?"

"An analysis of Earl's behavior," Hank said.

"We spoil our animals," Joy told Frenchie as she served the coffee. She sensed the natural silence and left it alone. Hank was waiting for Frenchie, so she did too. Frenchie sipped his coffee, set his cup down, and folded his hands on the table.

"Lee murdered a fifteen-year-old boy."

Hank let the statement sink in, instantly wrestling with memories and emotions he hadn't tasted for a long while and didn't miss. They weren't repressed exactly, but close to it.

"That's a hell of a stretch. I don't believe it."

Frenchie sat in glum silence. He knew it would take Hank a while to get his arms around this.

"Killed or murdered?" Hank asked.

"You think I don't know the difference?"

"When?"

"Yesterday around noon."

Silence descended once more. This time it was anything but comfortable. Joy's face was moving, full of questions. She looked at Hank. "Lee, Lee Weir, right, your Marine friend, the one in all the pictures? The one you never talk about?"

Hank didn't say anything. His lips were moving slightly: a conversation with himself. Joy looked at Frenchie. "There's always three guys in Hank's pictures. You, Hank, and the one who looks like his brother."

Frenchie nodded. "That would be Lee."

"So what happened?" Hank asked.

"Some kid from Black River was rodding around on a four-wheeler. Lee jumped him. Slit his throat from behind. Left him dead at the wheel and took off."

"Jesus. Was it a fight? I mean, did the kid provoke him somehow? Or did Lee just finally flip out?"

"Don't know for sure. Lee's not in custody, so all we've got is the crime scene and a dead kid."

"Witnesses?"

"No."

"Well, there you go. You don't really know for sure, then, do you?"

"We've had some incidents with him at that location leading up to this. Fits a pattern. And I know in my gut. Think about it, Hank. Think about the Lee that came back from Iraq. Not so much of a stretch when you think about it that way."

"PTSD is one thing. Murdering a kid is another. Vets mostly just murder themselves. And your gut won't get you far in court. You think he's headed here for some reason. That why you're here?"

"No. We know where he is." He paused. "He's holed up in Negwegon. Killed the kid on the big beach there."

"Negwegon, huh. That's like saying he's holed up in Pennsylvania."

Frenchie nodded, looking intensely at Hank. Hank went cold. The purpose of Frenchie's emergency visit was now perfectly clear. Hank could tell by the concerned look on Joy's face that she understood as well. Hank was being recruited.

"Correct me if I'm wrong, but Negwegon is in Alcona and Alpena Counties in northeastern Michigan. I'm not an Alpena or Alcona County sheriff. I'm not a Michigan state cop. I'm an Indiana state cop. This has nothing to do with me."

Frenchie scowled. "Come on, Hank. You know better than that."

"Come on, Hank, my ass," Hank said.

"He's the nearest thing to a brother you'll ever have."

"We went our separate ways, Frenchie."

"You had a political disagreement. Lee was never political. He was just a soldier."

"Horseshit!" Hank barked, slamming the kitchen table with his fist. Fat Earl scrambled across the linoleum to get out of the room. Joy pushed her chair away from the table. "Soldiers don't break into homes at night and muster families out on the street," Hank hissed. "And they don't carry drop weapons."

"It's a volunteer army," Frenchie said.

Hank's face sagged, as if someone had knocked the wind out of him. He knew it was as close as Frenchie would ever come to saying, "I told you so." Frenchie had simply told them both, "I wouldn't go to war for that crowd."

Hank stood up, walked over to the window, and stared out into the warm darkness. Shame was the worst of it, shame for giving his life over to "that crowd." Green as grass, galvanized by 9/11, and perfectly positioned between high school and college, Hank and Lee had joined up. In retrospect, Hank saw himself as good old reliable unquestioning rural cannon fodder: smart, tough, fierce, and stupid. The more the mission creeped, the more betrayed he felt.

"It's a volunteer army before you join, not after," Hank said. "Point is, I got the hell out when I got the chance. Lee saw the same things I saw, but stayed in. Shipped over, for Christ's sake. In the end, it's your trigger finger. Nobody else's. And you don't get kicked out with a general discharge because you're a good Marine. Maybe he developed a taste for it."

"Hank," Frenchie said, drawing his name out, as if admonishing him for suggesting something ludicrous. "I saw him a couple times after he got out. He was screwed up, pounding down the beers, but I never sensed anything like that."

"But he was violent, wasn't he?"

"If you call garden-variety bar fights violent."

"I call them precursors," Hank said. "He never did that kind of shit before. And you don't know why he got a general discharge, do you?"

"No."

"No. They keep that stuff confidential for a reason. That kind of discharge is usually for guys too shaky to keep around. I'll lay odds it involved a bad kill. And a bad kill by military standards would get you the chair stateside."

"Gets kind of tricky when you start talking about good kills and bad kills in a wrong war," Frenchie said. He sipped his coffee thoughtfully. "Okay. Fair enough. You're probably right and I should have seen it coming. But I mean, we're talking about Lee, Hank. Lee. I took him in one night after a bar fight and he gave me the creeps. Wasn't the kid I remembered, but I never figured him for a walking time bomb. He was jabbering. Said the world was coming for him."

Hank snorted. "Well, if it wasn't before, it sure as hell is now. You look ridiculous in that uniform, by the way."

"I was holding a practice at Harrisville when I got the call. Went to the scene and then drove straight here."

"You still haven't told us why you're here."

"You haven't figured that out yet? I thought you made detective."

"I want to hear it."

Frenchie was irritated that he had to ask. He was hoping for a volunteer. "Okay. You're the only one who's got a chance to bring Lee in solo with no more violence. No one knows the man like you. No one knows Negwegon like you."

"Lee knows Negwegon better than anyone."

"Maybe, but you're a close second and no one else is even in the same ballpark. Plus you've got a shared past you can use to talk him out. Hell, you've even got experience counseling vets through your Wounded Warrior work."

"It should be called 'Wounded Warrior for What?'" Joy interjected heatedly, "and he doesn't do that anymore. It was making him sick." She went over and stood by Hank. "He's done enough. And let me ask you something, Frenchie. Would Lee Weir have killed this boy before he went to Iraq?"

"No way."

"Then what makes you think he won't kill Hank?"

Frenchie hesitated. "I didn't say it wasn't dangerous."

Drawing herself up in her best boardroom persona, Joy stepped toward Frenchie and said sharply, "I think you should get out of our house." Standing there barefoot, all of five foot two and wearing a pink robe with a white fluffy shawl collar, her order did not have the desired effect: Frenchie grinned broadly and Hank laughed.

"Whoa, tiger," Hank said, putting his arms around her. "Frenchie's talking business. He's just talking business. We should hear him out."

"We'll hear him out and then you can say no," she said. Hank could feel the tension in her body.

Frenchie rubbed his tired face with both hands. "Look, I've only got two options. You're one. The other is to let loose the pack, and that scares the hell out of me."

"The pack?" Joy asked.

"The northern Lower Peninsula is nothing but state parks, national forests, state forests, big private hunting clubs . . . it's really a single forest about a hundred miles wide and two hundred miles long, with Lake Michigan on the west and Lake Huron on the east.

"Lee grew up in Negwegon, in the north woods. Guy with his skills, if he decides to hide or fight, hell, it'll take a ton of manpower to flush him out. I'll have to round up city cops, state cops, sheriff's deputies, National Guard to comb the woods section by section. Plus everybody up there owns a gun and knows how to use it. Lee will be just another blood sport to a lot of them, and they'll be out in force trying to get their picture in the paper. If I go with that pack, we might be seeing body bags until there's enough snow to track 'im. And today is August thirteenth."

Joy leaned her head back to look at Hank. He nodded in agreement.

"Hank," Frenchie said, a look of defeat clouding his face, "I could go to your boss, but you know I won't do that. But if you do this, whatever decisions you have to make, it'll be okay with me. I'll back you, no questions asked. No one expects you to subdue him. Just get him." That meant no rules—Frenchie was giving Hank an open license to kill.

"You know, Frenchie, for the first time in a long time I feel pretty good about life. Stopped the tailspin." He squeezed Joy tight. "Why should I take a chance on starting that whole thing again?"

"Because Lee hasn't been so lucky."

"Luck has nothing to do with it. It's about choices. I'm living with mine. He can live with his."

"You guys walked into a shit storm. What happens in a shit storm is all about luck. You tellin' me you don't think it's possible Lee could be sittin' here with this pretty lady while you're half nuts and hidin' out in Negwegon? Why, because you're so pure of heart?"

Hank said nothing, smiling slightly. That's why Frenchie was a damn good coach. He knew the buttons to push.

"Nobody knows his favorite spots like you. He won't be expecting anybody to know that."

Hank gazed at Frenchie. His de facto father was older now; his black wiry hair had gone salt-and-pepper and his face had earned more wrinkles, particularly around his eyes. So many wonderful days Hank had spent with Frenchie and Lee on the sunrise side of the Big Lake.

"I'll do it," Hank said abruptly. "Take me about an hour to gear up."

Frenchie nodded his head once, emphatically, acknowledging and thanking Hank in that one motion.

"Got the park locked down?" Hank asked.

"Best we can with the manpower. Blocked off both ends of Sand Hill Trail and put a car at the dead end on Lake Shore Road. Got a prowler driving back and forth on Twenty-three between the mountain and Nicholson Hill Road so no one parks and hikes in. Got two deputies at the crime scene. Yamaha is still there. Didn't want to stir things up, do any searching, until I heard from you. So it's been quiet at the park."

"Good. That's good," Hank said.

Stunned by the suddenness of Hank's decision, Joy said nothing and simply followed Hank as he moved toward the bedroom. He stopped halfway down the hall and turned back to Frenchie. "Why didn't you just call me? Could have saved you a trip."

"Red said a call wouldn't be enough," Frenchie responded. "Said I'd have to talk to you face-to-face. I figured she ought to know."

Hank winced but said nothing. Red was a struggle he kept to himself.

"Is Red that big girl that's in some of the pictures?"

"Probably," Frenchie said. "Coached her just like I coached Hank and Lee. She was the Queen of Title Nine in our area. Real jock."

"Her hair doesn't look red."

"It's dark red, almost black."

"Dark auburn," Joy said.

"She's one of my deputies now," Frenchie said. "She was always Lee's girl, since about the seventh grade."

Joy sat on the edge of the rumpled bed. She was angry that Hank had reached a decision without involving her. She knew Hank's relationships with Frenchie, Lee, and probably Red were at the core of the boy he used to be and the man he had become. What did she matter compared to them? She wasn't sure. She now knew Frenchie for all of twenty minutes and Lee and Red not at all. She had tried to get Hank to open up about them, even tried to get him to take her camping at Negwegon. "Maybe someday," was all he said.

She sat quietly, clearly at a loss. This was the first time she knew ahead of time that Hank was headed for certain danger. Not an abstract understanding of his job or a talk with him after the fact, but going one-on-one after a crazy ex-Marine who had killed a kid.

Hank stopped stuffing a duffel bag and sat down next to her. "Talk about going from heaven to hell in a matter of minutes."

"It doesn't have to be hell. You sounded like you weren't going to do it, then all of a sudden you said you would. Why? Frenchie said he wouldn't go over your head. And whatever Lee Weir was to you before, he's not that anymore. You said so yourself."

Hank took her hand, kneading it thoughtfully. "At first I figured, easy call . . . no way. But as he talked I saw something in his face I've never seen before—dread. Pure dread. Everybody has a breaking point. I got a bad feeling that Lee's blood on Frenchie's hands might be more than he could handle. I mean, the guy practically raised us. And Lee . . . hell, we both did things . . . things that couldn't be helped, things beyond our control. But kill a kid on a beach at Negwegon? Can't see it."

"Frenchie sees it."

"Yes. Frenchie sees it. And everything he says points to it. But I can't see it. And if I don't go, the pack will gun him for sure. He's gonna run. He'll run at 'em or he'll run away from them. They'll kill him either way. Frenchie and Lee . . . I can't leave it hangin' like this."

"What if you have to . . . do something to Lee? How's that different from anything else that might happen?"

"It's different because Frenchie trusts me completely. He'll know he did everything he could to save Lee. He thinks I'll bend over backward to bring Lee in alive. He's wrong, but that's what he thinks. Anybody else drags Lee out in a body bag and it could send Frenchie into a guilt trip he'll never get over. That pack he was talking about, that's no joke. He won't have any real control over those guys. He'll feel responsible for anything they do."

Joy nodded. She understood. Hank believed this was the most important thing he could ever do for Frenchie and he had to do it. She squeezed his hand and put her arm around him. "Maybe you won't find him and you'll just be back in five days like nothing happened. Just a longer intermission than we thought."

Hank smiled. "Maybe," he said.

Resigned, Joy returned to the kitchen, where Frenchie was nursing his coffee.

"Sorry to meet you with a mess like this," he said.

"You ought to be," Joy snapped.

"You're a hard woman."

"You could get him killed."

"Hank can handle himself . . . Mind if I borrow your couch while he gets ready?"

"Go ahead. Take your shoes off, if it's not too much trouble."

"That kind of trouble I can handle," Frenchie said. He rose slowly from the table, stiff from hours of driving. Joy watched him move creakily over to the couch, take off his sneaks, and sink into it. He didn't look at her. He wasn't eager to talk.

Joy followed him over. "I'm being a bitch," she said.

"That's okay," Frenchie said. "You've got cause. And anyway, you're a saint compared to the mother of my second baseman."

"Frenchie, how dangerous is this?"

"Not dangerous at all," Frenchie said, turning to face the back of the couch. "Unless he finds Lee."

Joy managed a small good-luck smile as Hank pulled out in his dark green Jeep Cherokee, his battered sea kayak strapped on the roof like a turquoise torpedo. He was geared up, already thinking strategy for the hunt. He was nervous. Lee was trouble. They had always competed in a friendly way, all kinds of contests, from bench presses to swimming to running. Truth was, on his best day, Lee was damn near unbeatable.

With Hank trailing Frenchie's prowler they crossed the northern Indiana border into southern Michigan and tacked steadily northeast across the state. Then they veered as far east as they could go onto U.S. 23 North, the traffic immediately dwindling to almost nothing. The two-lane highway hugged Lake Huron so closely that the big lake was now visible through the trees and the yards. The lake bathed the early afternoon in coolness.

Hank slipped the Jeep into four-wheel drive as he turned from Black River Road onto Sand Hill Trail, the entrance to Negwegon. It was Sand Hill Trail that practically eliminated tourism at the big wilderness park. The poorly marked, narrow, twisting dirt road discouraged most vehicles. If people can't drive to it, most won't go. Negwegon was a huge park that was hugely unknown. Locals called it "the hidden beach."

Frenchie spoke briefly to a deputy stationed near the turnoff and they continued some three miles through a mature mixed conifer and hardwood forest until they reached the main gravel parking lot at the heart of the park. They pulled up next to the lone prowler parked by the band of forest that lay between the lot and the lake.

Hank stepped out into a familiar deep-woods quiet and the soft, soothing murmur of water rushing to shore. It was his old haunt, his escape, his and Lee's. Lee didn't have a poisonous home life to escape. It was his love of the natural world and all things physical that made him a perfect match for the big park and Hank. Frenchie forged them together. The two had camped, hunted, swum, fished, worked out, partied, kayaked, grown tall and strong here, and loved every minute of it.

Frenchie and Hank took the short trail to the beach. The shiny blue Yamaha was perched on a small dune like a prehistoric bird of prey. Standing next to it in a uniform of dark brown pants, khaki shirt with brown epaulettes, and black belt and holster—tall and Norselike—was Red. Hank stopped.

He frowned. "Do you think it's a good idea to have Red involved with this? I got enough on my mind without worrying about Red." Hank's eyes had been hungry for Red for as far back as he could remember.

"She's here because she's a cop with a special relationship with Lee, just like you. She could come in handy, help talk him out maybe. She's steady. You know that." He eyed Hank. "Make sense?" Hank nodded grudgingly.

The puddles of blood on the Yamaha were baked black like tar.

Frenchie laid a big hand on a Mud Wolf tire. "How's it work that the mess in Iraq kills the Zuckerman kid here on the beach? Man, that's the long way around." But they all knew how it worked. You trip and fall in Iraq and hit the ground in Michigan. Or anywhere.

"Thanks for coming, Hank," Red said.

"Hey, Red," Hank said. He grinned and in a herky-jerky dance shed his cargo shorts. "Damned if I won't get something good out of this trip. Be right back."

In his navy boxers he charged into the gently rolling surf. Home was not people to Hank. Home was a place. This place. Woven into the fabric of his childhood. He was home.

He high-stepped a few yards, then dived into the shockingly cold water. Breaking the surface with a gasp and a whoop, he lay still, floating like mercury in space with his face toward the icy bottom, his back absorbing the friendly warmth of the sun.

Hank was a superb athlete. He had reached his height of six foot three while still in high school. At 190 pounds he was fast, rangy, and strong. He and Lee, under Frenchie's tutelage, had honed their considerable genetic gifts to become small-town sports phenoms, as close as you can get to canonization. Everybody knew the guy who caught forty-yard passes that beat the bigger schools from down south. Passes that came from Lee Weir.

The athletic prowess of the two boys brought them to the attention of Frenchie Skiba. He brought them stability, affection, and discipline. They brought him championships.

Hank kept swimming straight out until his veins opened up. On the job, over time, his veins collapsed. Oh, he stayed gym-rat fit. But his standards were higher: boot-camp hard, survival-training hard. What the world throws at you doesn't get thrown at you in a gym.

Chest heaving, tiring a little, he stopped his machinelike strokes about a quarter mile out. He was completely relaxed, a natural part of the spectacular panorama around him. Returning to shore was a frolic. Diving here and there, holding his breath as long as he could. Close to shore, where the water was shallow and warm, he flopped on his belly, crawling with his fingertips and letting the little waves nudge him along.

He staggered up the beach, fatigue from the long drive and hard swim coursing through him. He dropped on his back, making an angel in the hot sugar sand.

Red and Frenchie were smiling. It was quintessentially the Hank they used to know.

"Feel better?" Frenchie asked.

"Much."

"Your secret playground is now a crime scene."

Hank sighed and rose to his elbows, surveying the quiet blue bay. "Yeah. Can't believe it. So what are you thinking, Coach? What's the plan?"

"That you search alone, but keep Red close. Whether you use her or not is your call, but communicate through her. She'll communicate with the rest of us. She knows all the contacts we might need. We'll try to keep the place locked down for however long you say."

Hank recognized that it was a good approach, using Red to handle the problem of his being an outsider. "If I don't catch him or cut a hot trail in three days then I don't have an edge and I'm gone," Hank said. "I won't hang around for the tally-ho enterprise, thank you very much."

"Can't keep the lid on this much longer than three days anyway," Frenchie said.

"I thought I'd take Potawatomi Trail and camp tonight at South Point. Start out first light. Red can drop off at Pewabic on the way there." Negwegon had four pocket parks along its shoreline, all consisting of a small open beach, picnic table, privy, and firepit: Pewabic, Blue Bell, Twin Pines, and South Point.

"I got a two-seventy with a big Zeiss in the prowler if you want it."

Hank considered. The moment was like so many that had occurred in the last decade. Utterly incredible. Four-ton Humvees tossed in the air like toys. Half-conscious terrified souls getting their heads sawed off in front of cameras. Endless streams of impoverished refugees. Now, here, take this rifle son and go shoot the guy who used to be your best friend and by the way since you've been gone your house is only worth half of what it used to be.

"I'm not here to be a sniper. I'm here to try up close and personal. Putting one into him at three hundred yards is a job for someone else."

"Lee is not a job," Red said.

Frenchie looked hard at her. "Take a knee," he said. Without hesitation Red dropped to a knee. Hank pulled himself up from

the sand and took a knee beside her. It was a familiar position for
them and they couldn't help exchanging a smothered smile at
Frenchie's unique mixture of coaching style and law-enforcement
leadership. He didn't look particularly impressive standing there in
his Little League outfit.

"Feel kind of awkward," Hank said. "I'm the only one not in
uniform."

Frenchie ignored him. "You said Lee's not a job. You're wrong.
That's exactly what he is. You're not here because you're friends of
his. You're here because you're cops, cops who have an advantage
that just happens to be friendship.

"A good argument could be made that you're exactly the wrong
people to do this job — too close to the perp. Judgment will be
for shit. But I figure my job is to minimize bloodshed and you two
have the best chance of doing that. I won't have this command for
long. Crime's too big. If I have to bring in the pack, my jurisdiction
will be the smallest and they'll take command away from me in a
heartbeat. This is my only chance to do the job my way . . . and
you're the best tools I've got. The goal here is to avoid a manhunt
that could become a shootout. The goal here is to protect your-
selves. The goal here is not, I repeat, *not*, to *protect* Lee. The goal is
to *get* Lee.

"Time to imagine," he said. "Time to imagine." He let the words
hang in the air.

Red and Hank recognized the introduction. It was the visualiza-
tion exercise. See yourself launch the three-pointer from the cheap
seats and hear the swish as the buzzer sounds. See the pigskin drop
from the sky into your hands as you outjump the defensive back
and cross the goal line as time expires. See success in your mind
and then go make it happen. It won't be a surprise. It will be an
expectation.

"See yourself killing Lee," Frenchie said softly. He waited a moment. "See yourself killing Lee. If you can't, go home, because for
all we know he'll kill us all if he gets the chance." Hank and Red
remained where they were. Frenchie left in his prowler.

They unloaded Hank's Jeep, lashing the kayak, a few supplies,
and Red's backpack to a two-wheel cart. They didn't talk. They
were thinking about what Frenchie had said. They headed out on
the northern branch of Potawatomi Trail, which started at the end
of the parking lot. There could be no awkwardness between them.

They had grown up together, been through too much, most of it filled with extraordinarily fine moments.

"Life used to be simple," Red finally said. "Used to be Lee's biggest concern was whether he'd work in the lab or in the field and my biggest concern was how many kids we'd have."

"Life was never simple," Hank said. "We were. Young, simple, and having a hell of a good time."

"We're not young anymore?"

Hank patted her shoulder. "Haven't been young for a while now." Hank had never touched Red, never made a move. Would have blown their wonderful triangular friendship sky-high. Fortunately, he'd always had girlfriends around to take the edge off.

They continued walking down the sun-splashed trail, the cart an easy pull. It dawned on Hank that Lee could be around anywhere. Maybe even near this trail. He began looking around more warily, watching for signs of movement in the woods or unusual shapes. He did that for a while and stopped in his tracks.

"There's something screwy about the woods," he said. "Looks different somehow. What am I missing?"

"Look at the ash," Red said.

Hank picked out a tall ash among the oak and maple and birch and pine and spruce. Its normally dark bark was mottled with tan streaks and large tan areas that looked like rub marks. He looked at other ash. Their dark bark was also mottled in various degrees, and he noticed that some branches were entirely without leaves.

"What is that?"

"Emerald ash borer. Invasive species from Asia. It's killing all the ash in the park. If we were in one of the ash swamps, you'd have noticed right away. All those trees are dead already."

"Jesus, if Lee's been wandering around through all these dying trees, maybe we can lure him out with Prozac. Red, did Frenchie give you any tips about how to handle this thing?"

"Yes. He said not to take any chances with Lee and not to take any chances with you." She cast him a sideways smile.

Hank laughed. Shit, he'd probably always been an open book to Frenchie and Red. "So what's your take on this? Frenchie's sure Lee did it. Are you?"

They walked a bit. Red said, "I would have killed that kid myself if I saw him tearing up our beach with that rig."

"Amen," Hank said, glancing at her. The black-red hair against her fair skin always got to him, as did the memory of watching those smooth slabs of muscle at work in basketball and volleyball games. What a specimen she was. Some women are the flame and you rail against being the moth but you never quite make it.

"I made a big mistake," Red said. "You know how pissed I was at you guys for enlisting. Both of you. You acted like it was a lark, just another sport to go be heroes at. But I had watched my dad walking home from Vietnam all his life. He never made it, so my mom and I didn't make it either. I didn't want Lee to bring that kind of life home to us."

Which is exactly what happened to a lot of vets, Hank thought. Christ, how many times do we have to see this movie?

"When he got back I wanted to punish him. I always intended to go back to him. Just couldn't bring myself to act like nothing happened. So I froze him out for about six months. By the time I tried to make up, he was way weird. Dancin' with himself. No room for a partner."

"As a general rule, vets don't need any more punishment than they already got."

"I know that now. I shouldn't have done it. Lee and a family was all I ever wanted."

"So what'd you do finally?"

"Tried seeing him for a few months. Mostly couldn't find him or we'd go out and he would immediately get drunk. Couldn't get a fix on him. Last time I talked with him he was nowhere to be found. Started dating a little."

"What was that like?"

"Like meeting strangers with problems they wanted to make mine." She shook her head. "Why on earth did he reenlist? Why didn't he get out when you did?"

"Don't know. Never figured it out. Might have got hooked on war-think—it's like a drug. Or might have believed in it. They're not the same things. Some guys couldn't care less about the mission, they just crave the action."

"What are you going to do if you find him?"

"Try talking sense to him. Of course, he might be short on sense. Way I see it, he doesn't have any real options. Can't play Master of Negwegon forever. He must know that. If that doesn't work, I'll just have to wing it." He thought about some of the vets he had counseled. Good days, bad days. Catch them on a good day, everything's cool. Catch them on a bad day—way, way past common sense.

Red looked like she was tearing up. A small sob slipped out, but she kept striding straight ahead. No Jody had warmed her bed while Lee was away or since he came home. She loved Lee, always had. She gripped Hank's arm hard. "You know he'd never hurt you."

"Right," Hank said. "I wonder if that's what the kid on the Yamaha thought."

When they reached Pewabic, Hank gave Red a hug and said he'd call a couple of times a day. He lugged the kayak the remaining mile to South Point, crossing a little bog with planks for steps and his favorite cedar-lined meadow. Alone on Potawatomi Trail a feeling was creeping up that was not much different from the ice in his gut when he was driving a Humvee down a dirty street in Fallujah.

Hank was tired and didn't bother organizing his little camp. He tossed his mummylike sleeping bag on top of the picnic table, curled up in it, and was out.

He awakened in the cool predawn mist and put his hunch into action. He carried his weathered Necky across the marshy fringe of South Point, a rocky finger that jutted out into Thunder Bay. When the marsh gave way to calf-deep water and tall green reeds, he slipped into the boat, using the light, double-bladed graphite paddle to push himself along. He positioned himself at the end of the point but remained a few yards back in the marsh to conceal the boat. From this vantage point he could use his binoculars to scan the entire sandy beach of the horseshoe bay, almost two miles point-to-point.

The sixteen-foot sea kayak was essentially a light, hollow fiberglass and Kevlar tube with a centered cockpit. Hank's weight was spread out over such a long, light surface that water displacement was minimal, allowing the craft to float and maneuver in extremely shallow water.

Hank knew Lee could be sitting in an open, breezy birch grove or hiding out in the low, huddling cedar swamps. He could be lying on his back in a meadow. But it was August. He wasn't hiding out in Negwegon for the muggy forest. He was hiding out in Negwegon for the open water.

If Hank was right, Lee would show up on this beach. Seeing that it was deserted, he'd come out of the woods for a swim. He'd come out to bask in the sun. He'd come out to walk along the fresh, bracing shoreline. He wouldn't linger—too exposed—but he'd have to get his big-lake fix. And when he did and after he left, Hank would paddle quickly across the bay and pick up his trail. At that point Hank would be minutes away from catching up to him and Lee would be ignorant of his pursuit. Surprise would be on his side.

The antithesis of the desert is not the ocean. You can die of thirst in either place. The antithesis of a vast, arid desert is the magnificence of a great sweet-water lake. Hank and Lee had both swallowed the gritty sand of the high desert and the rocky dust of the low desert. Their skin had been dried out by desert winds, like dried plants in a florist's window. Immediately after his discharge, Hank had camped on the beach at Negwegon for several weeks. He couldn't get enough of the big lake. The craving was deep and abiding. You didn't shake it. He was betting Lee felt the same way. Hank's impulsive swim upon arrival had not been entirely within his control.

Hank took a quick look at tiny Scarecrow Island to the east. His glasses went by a couple of black ducks as he returned to study the beach. He scoped the beach carefully, then let the binoculars hang from his neck as he folded his arms and leaned back. His lower body was stretched out comfortably inside the boat. He sat perfectly still. He was "still hunting," just as if he were waiting for a nice eight-point to walk into his line of sight. The dawn had broken clear and calm. It would be straight, fast, flat-water kayaking this morning—if he did any paddling at all.

He smiled to himself. If Lee didn't show, this might turn out to be the best stakeout he'd ever had. Damn near a vacation. Kayak as prowler, marsh as darkened street, the tree line a doorway from which Lee could emerge at any moment. He should have brought a fishing pole, try to pull a big tasty smallmouth out of the reeds. He dozed a little, rousing himself just enough to scan the beach with the binos.

For a change of scenery he occasionally looked at Scarecrow Island and was doing that when he realized he'd been suffering from what the shrinks call "inattentional blindness," where you see what you expect to see rather than what's really there. The black ducks he'd been passing over weren't black ducks. Now, brought into better focus because they were closer, he saw a swimmer with a partially submerged stowfloat bag behind him on a dragline.

Hank's binos froze on the swimmer. There was no doubt. He

couldn't believe his luck. Instinctively he reached down to the waterproof bag nestled by his seat and took out his little "get off me" .38 Smith backup and stuck it in the waistband of his cargo shorts. Then he called Red.

"Cecil."

"Red, the best thing that could have happened has happened. He's swimming toward the beach from Scarecrow Island. Must have been holed up there. I'm hidden in my kayak at the tip of South Point watching him. Come to the edge of the woods about one hundred yards south of the point. If I'm not in yet, stay out of sight. Don't come out on the beach until I bring him in. Seeing you might set him off. I don't want any distractions until he's cuffed."

"Roger that . . . Try not to hurt him, Hank."

"Christ, he's in the water, Red. Never had a better drop on anybody. It's going to be all right."

Hank sat for a few minutes waiting for Lee to swim deeper into the bay and past his hideout at the point. He wanted to paddle up behind him, remaining unnoticed as long as possible.

He watched Lee swim through the dark blue water with strong, rhythmic strokes and it was as if he were swimming back through time. Hank was struck by a powerful sense of déjà vu. The moment itself was singular and beautiful and like so many shared before. Lee's bronze face bearded and hard but still somehow boyish. Sky and lake and beach from years ago, but this time no scholarship waiting, no bright future. What was waiting was a cage somewhere, a cage that was going to be his home for a long, long time. His pulse quickened as he slid the paddle into the water and pushed the boat out of the reeds.

The turquoise craft moved swiftly across the calm bay. In silence Hank came up about thirty yards behind Lee and shipped his paddle, just drifting along. He could hear Lee's heavy breathing; the distance Lee had covered would be almost two miles. Then Lee rolled over to move into a backstroke, saw the kayak, and his motion stopped. He began slowly treading water.

Hank eased the kayak a little closer.

Hank said, "Had breakfast?"

"Thought you were bringing me some."

"Got some MREs in my kit."

"You call that breakfast? Why should we eat that shit now that we're out?"

"Because it's all I got," Hank said.

"You been gone a while," Lee said. "I thought you were finished with this place."

"I don't think that's possible, Lee. Not for me. Not for you."

"Frenchie called you, huh?"

"Frenchie and Red." Hank wanted Lee to know they were both involved and nearby.

Hank studied the man in the water. Didn't look threatening. Looked calm. Didn't look like a throat-slashing kid killer. But he knew Frenchie had contacted him; must have had a reason to think that. Still, Frenchie might be wrong. After all, no witnesses.

It shouldn't have been a languid moment, but it turned into one. They were just floating there on the glassy, sparkling bay, Hank rocking gently in the kayak, Lee on his back, moving his arms and legs like a willow in a breeze. The sunlight spread over them like a fine warm oil. A lazy warmth, the kind that tempts turtles and snakes out onto the rocks and puts them right to sleep. A slight offshore breeze wafted over them, carrying the scent of white pine, red cedar, and other essences of the north. Swept away were the alien experiences that had shattered their friendship.

"I remember we were out here two days after you hit that walk-off against Bay City," Hank said. "Just floatin' on inner tubes, mindin' our own business. Red grillin' hot dogs on the beach."

They began to chat about old things, about pre-9/11, prewar things. It went on for a while, just a reunion of two old friends gabbing away and laughing at events recalled.

"Doesn't seem possible that it was just fifteen years ago," Hank said.

"It wasn't fifteen years ago," Lee said. "It was a million years ago."

"Amen, brother, amen." A million years ago. A million years ago and a war ago and maybe a murder ago, Hank thought. But there was no point in pressing Lee. Hank thought of it as similar to a hostage negotiation. If they're talking, you're winning. And he had the drop.

"So you were hanging out at Scarecrow, huh?" Hank asked.

"Yeah. Had a camp at the mouth of the Euphrates on the south side of Squaw Bay but it got overrun."

Hank almost laughed and said that the Euphrates was six thousand miles away, then saw it for what it was: the first signal of delusion. He became cautious with his words.

"Overrun by who?"

"Can't be sure, there's so many splinter groups around here." Lee's face darkened. His movements in the water became jerky, agitated. "They get inside the perimeter. Them and the ash borer. Killing everything. You seen the ash?"

"Yeah, damn shame. They're a huge chunk of the park."

"Not just the park. Of the whole country," Lee said, his voice rising. "Fifty million trees so far."

It looked to Hank like a paranoid episode was on the way. They were hard to deal with under the best of circumstances. How you deal with one from a kayak he had no clue. He tried to take control.

"Lee, why don't we talk this over on the beach. Why don't you start swimming for the beach."

"And if I don't, you gonna blow me in half right here in the bay?"

"Now why would you say that?"

"Because I figure you've got a nine-millimeter or a forty-five handy in the cockpit there."

"Believe me, Lee, I'm here to help you . . . Come on, why don't you keep going like you were — straight to the beach."

"Hell, Hank, you're not taking me to the beach. You're taking me somewhere a hell of a lot farther away than that."

Hank straightened up in the boat. "Lee, stop jawing and start swimming."

Lee kept treading water. He turned his face into the water and turned back spitting out a narrow stream. "You can taste the Euphrates," he said. "Everything's changing." He slipped out of the loose dragline attached to the stowfloat bag. "Hey, Hank?"

"Yeah?"

"Is it a nine or a forty-five?"

"Does it matter?"

"Not really, 'cause holdin' a gun on somebody only works if they give a shit."

Lee exploded straight up out of the water almost to his thighs. He came down with a tremendous splash and from the white spray launched a thrashing, powerful butterfly straight toward the kayak, closing the distance like a killer whale speeding toward its prey. Hank froze for just an instant. He grabbed for his Smith but hesitated, saw Lee dead, saw Red crying, and in those few short seconds Lee reached the kayak, latching onto the stern and easily flipping the slim arrow of a boat.

Hank saw the sky spin and found himself hanging upside down, choking in cold water, his lower body jammed into the boat. As he tried to slide out, he saw Lee swimming toward him like a ghost, a combat Bowie in his hand. His face was flat and unemotional, a death mask. Then a strong arm had Hank in a steel-like hammerlock, pulling him down where it was deeper and darker. His life didn't flash before his eyes. What flashed was the simple understanding that he'd never used a kayak to land a man before and had done the whole thing all wrong. His lungs gave out in a white bubbly cloud.

Hank rose through a cylinder of blackness until all was light, coming to in a coughing, gagging cloud of confusion. Completely disoriented, he turned on his side and kept coughing up water. His throat was raw. He was freezing. The August sun was a godsend. He was on the beach, barely out of the water.

Red was leaning over him. Her shirt was off and Hank realized it was draped over him. He remembered Lee coming for him, felt his arm around his neck.

"Lee?" he rasped.

Red straightened up, tugging at a strap of her black sports bra. She nodded toward the lake. Close to shore in shallow water the kayak was floating unevenly, its bow forced skyward by the weight of the body draped over the stern. Bronzed shoulders gleamed in the sun.

"I came out of the woods," Red said. "Lee had you laid over the boat. I called to him to move away from you but he pulled a knife. I had no choice."

Hank nodded. He was hazy but he knew the water where Lee had attacked him was much farther out, well over their heads. For the boat and Lee to be this close to shore Lee would have had to be bringing him in. But Red wouldn't have known that.

Hank looked at the boat and the body. It wasn't really suicide by cop. It was something a hell of a lot more personal than that.

His throat was burning. He looked at Red. Her face was distraught but she was dry-eyed. Her father had been walking home from Vietnam until the day he died. Would she be walking away from this until the day she died? He didn't think so. Red was tough, knew how to stay within herself. Frenchie had taught her that.

Red fumbled in her pocket for her phone. "I haven't called Frenchie," she said, her hands shaking. "There wasn't time. We have to get you to the ER. Bad things can happen the first few hours after near drowning."

Hank looked out at Lee, the gentle waves washing away the dust from someone else's desert. That's where Lee would want to stay, as far away from the desert as he could get. Not a part of Negwegon exactly, but close enough. Hank put his hand on Red's and squeezed gently, stopping the call.

"Let's not call Frenchie just yet," he said.

DAN BEVACQUA

The Human Variable

FROM *The Literary Review*

THIS PART OF Northern California was too dark, Ted felt. It freaked him out. Without a moon, the lack of streetlights gave everything a creepy redneck vibe. Driving with his high beams on reminded him of certain back roads in Vermont—little pit-stop towns he used to speed through when he was a teenager and first had his license. He couldn't remember the last time he'd ventured this far out of San Francisco. Palo Alto for work at the startup, yes. Oakland to visit friends. But those places weren't like wherever he was now. The overwhelming, almost chemical smell of the pines blew in through the open car window. At a stoplight, he heard a coyote howl. The old, dense forest was otherwise silent, and Ted flinched when the console in the Prius beeped and the Bluetooth said, "Incoming."

"Boo!" Kathy said.

"Hey."

"Where are you?" she asked.

"I don't know." Ted stared at the GPS. "I'm just a red dot on a blank screen."

"Well, find out," his wife said.

He pulled over at a gas station. Standing out front near the bug light was an incredibly tall, incredibly thin man with an orange beard. He had the word SELF tattooed above his right eyebrow. MADE was above the left. Ted asked him.

"Liberty."

"Thanks."

"Yut," SELF MADE said, as if he were offended by language, as if it had done something horrible to him as a child.

Ted got back in the car and locked the door.

"Liberty," he told Kathy.

"Keep going north," she said. "Another twenty miles. You'll see a condemned Mexican restaurant called Señor Mister. Pull into the lot and then text me." Ted drove on through the darkness of Liberty, SELF MADE shrinking in his rearview, and considered once again the fact that he needed $350,000 by tomorrow. Without it, MicroWeather.com, his baby, was finished. He'd lose his house too. His wife probably. But what should he say when he got to the weed farmer's? How should he act? As if it were a regular business meeting? More casual? He had no prior experience interacting with marijuana kingpins. He bought an eighth sometimes. That was it. It would last him a month. It was a Friday-night, smoke-a-joint-out-on-the-patio kind of thing. He wasn't the guy for this.

"Be your normal self," Kathy had said that afternoon. "He's from New Hampshire. He's New England. Like you. Be New England together."

"What the hell does that mean?" Ted asked his wife.

They were in the offices of MicroWeather.com, which took up half a floor in a once-industrial building on the outskirts of Palo Alto. To the south, out the floor-to-ceiling windows, was the promised land: Google, Facebook, various other big ideas that had turned people into billionaires. MicroWeather.com was five geeks Ted knew from Caltech and his wife. The company was seven desks, seven chairs, and a very large room, basically. The geeks were out to lunch.

"How do you even know him?" Ted asked.

His wife was thirty-five and beautiful. She had long, straight blond hair, an MBA from Stanford, and ran four miles every other day. But there was a tattoo of a unicorn on her inner thigh that told a story of forgotten dreams. Only the month before, she'd disappeared to Chicago for the weekend in order to catch the final three Grateful Dead shows. Her first ever email address had been indigochild79@hotmail.com. She knew how to roll a blunt.

"I know him from the old days," Kathy said. "The rave scene. He was around."

"And you just called him?"

"I just called him," Kathy said. "I explained the situation."

"The whole situation?"

"The whole situation. I told him about the bank. How this was all very time-sensitive," Kathy said. "But Ted, he's a businessman. He's not going to give us the money out of the kindness of his heart. He's willing to hear the pitch. But please, sweetie, do me one favor."

"What's that?" Ted asked.

"Make it sound cool," Kathy said.

Like its founder, "cool" had always been a problem for the company. While at Caltech, Ted, and every other grad student who cared about these sorts of things, noticed how localized weather websites and apps were becoming all the rage. He also noticed that they were all terrible. They relied on National Weather Service info combined with wonky algorithms. For months Ted thought about the problem, the inefficiency, and the ways in which, as an engineer, science had taken over his life, but then one day he looked at his iPhone. Radio waves streamed in and out of it 24/7. He could map the waves and chart the way they flowed inside the pressure systems. With enough subscribers, with enough data pinging back and forth, the information would domino. Essentially, the future—whether it would rain, sleet, or snow—would always be known, and down to the square inch. No more surprise storms. No more *Whoops, here comes a tsunami!* How many cell phones were in the world? Seven billion? More? *That's* an accurate forecast, Ted thought. *That's* the new weather.

"But it is cool," he said to Kathy. "It's totally cool."

"I know it is, honey. I believe that, really," Kathy said. "Just don't, you know, overdo it on the algorithms."

Kathy was the cool one, Ted knew. Everybody thought so. Friends said it to his face all the time, like it didn't hurt, like he didn't know what that made him—the uncool one. There wasn't room for two cools in a marriage. He understood that. There could be only one, like in *Highlander*. The same was true for business. But that meant his wife should be the spouse/business partner pulling into Señor Mister's empty parking lot. *She* should be the one texting her. But instead Kathy was out to dinner with the loan officer, trying to flirt out a few extra days on the repayment, and Ted was texting to his cool wife: *I'm here, Kath!! Now what? Now what do I do?!?*

*

She sent the reply and then smiled back at the red, drunk face of Mr. White.

"Oh, I know," Kathy said. "Believe me, I know. It's a bubble. Only a matter of time."

She was glad he was old. Old and a little fat. Had he been young, it might have been a different story, one she didn't want to think about.

"I mean, theoretically, a bubble should never burst," Mr. White said. "It should swell, sure. It should contract, yes. But it should never burst, not really."

She'd heard all this before. At Stanford. Regurgitated Friedman. The market will prevail. Live long and prosper. Have faith. At the time she'd believed it enough to have had two Republican boyfriends. Like that was okay. Like that was something people like her did. But it was her choice, Kathy reminded herself. She was the one who'd student-loaned her way into the club. She was the one who'd grown tired of being poor. Tired of having nothing. Tired of being tired.

"But then people," Kathy said.

"But then people, yes," Mr. White said. "The human variable."

"They're unpredictable."

"That's one way of putting it," he said.

"What's another?" she asked.

"Foolish," he said. "Delusional. Unrealistic."

Like an old pro, Mr. White quarter-turned the last of the Barbera into her glass. They were seated by the front window. To Kathy's right, the dining room was awash in men and women eating alone. Everyone had a cell phone in one hand and a fork in the other.

"Which of those am I?" Kathy asked. "Foolish, delusional, or unrealistic?"

"If you're one of them, you're always all three," Mr. White said.

Kathy looked at the people in the restaurant—they were talking, texting, masticating—and thought of a diner in Fresno called the Chat 'n' Chew. For years her mother had waitressed there.

"We need two days," Kathy said. "Two more days."

"What's changed?" he asked.

"We have an investor. Ted's meeting with him now. But we need time for everything to clear."

"You've had eight months."

"I know that, Mr. White," Kathy said. "So what's two more days?"

"Who is it?" he asked. "One of the hedge funds?"

"No. It's a small company. Privately owned."

"An angel investor then."

"Of a type," she said.

Kathy had left Rome (the weed farmer Ted was driving up a dark mountain road toward) because she'd had a revelation. She wasn't going to be one of those women—one of those women like her mother—who didn't live the life they wanted to. She refused to be among the legion of kept, kept down, or kept from. She'd loved Rome—and had loved the money that came along with him—but she couldn't plan one more trip to Burning Man for their anniversary. Couldn't host another end-of-the-season barbecue for the gutter punks who trimmed. Couldn't be the weed king's common-law. She'd begun storing up her *fuck yous*, hiding them away like Rome did duffel bags of cash, and she didn't like the feel of it.

"They believe in MicroWeather?" Mr. White asked. "And they know about the FCC, the FAA, the privacy lawsuits you're sure to get?"

"All of that's hypothetical," Kathy said. "None of that's happened."

"It will," Mr. White said. "Trust me."

"Maybe," Kathy said. "Warning letters are only warning letters. MicroWeather doesn't need to know if you're cheating on your wife. It only needs to know if it's raining where you are. Is it wrong to ask a stranger's phone if the wind is blowing? If the temperature's dropped? If it senses an earthquake two miles underground?"

When in doubt, it was best to hit them with tragedy and disaster. You had to give their wives cancer, Kathy thought. Shoot their children in the street. Blow the world apart.

"This is likely?" Mr. White asked. He was very, very serious now. "The investment?"

Kathy didn't know. But for the call she'd made to him that morning, she hadn't spoken to Rome in five years. She'd caught him early, at six, before he'd had time to head out to the fields.

"I know you're married, Kath," Rome had said over the phone. "I'm on Facebook. I know a lot of things about you."

Kathy knew a lot of things about him too. He was dating some woman named Monarch. She was young, and looked like a tramp. Her Twitter feed loved life. She Instagrammed horses.

"How bad is it?" Rome asked. "The money?"

"Bad," she said.

"And the idea? This Internet thing?"

"Very good," Kathy said. She explained it to him. "Does that make sense?"

"Yeah," he said. "It's the weather."

"But perfect," she said. "Perfect weather."

"All this technology," Rome said, "and all anybody wants to talk about is the weather."

"It's the end of the world, Rome," Kathy said. "Don't you know that? Flash floods, heat waves, tornadoes."

"It's the end of people," he said. "Not the world. Once we're gone, the world will be fine."

"Put it however you want," she said. The man was infuriating. He knew what she'd meant. "Either way, it's an opportunity."

Even as she considered the position she was in—and Kathy was begging him for money; they both knew that—she found it difficult to be fake with Rome. With anyone else, Ted even, she would have immediately agreed, sacrificed her own opinion, and done whatever was required of her to get what she wanted. But it was different with Rome. Her instinct was to attack. With him, her love had always come out wrong. She would want to be gentle, but would end up pushing him away instead. She would pick a fight, or find herself in one despite not wanting to be. Something about Rome, his closeness, the way he'd lived in her, and she in him, had been unsettling. It had felt claustrophobic. It had driven her mad.

"Will you meet him?" Kathy asked. "Will you please do that for me? I've never asked you for anything."

She waited in silence. The tension between them—old and comfortable—was like a worn T-shirt that needed to be thrown out. Kathy felt herself disappear. She experienced the folding nature of space and time.

"Fine," Rome said. "Send him up. But later tonight. I've got work to do. Some of us do actual work."

He clicked end and noticed Monarch standing in the kitchen doorway. She wore a towel, but her hair was dry.

"Who was that?" she asked, and yawned.

She was beautiful, sexy, and kind, and Rome loved her, he thought, but for an instant he couldn't remember who the hell she was or what she was doing there.

"No one," he said. And then, "An old friend."

Monarch was half Mexican, with dark eyes and even darker hair. A pleasant sleepiness clung to her in the mornings.

"Kind of early," she said. "Who?"

Rome understood that if he lied to her, it would only end up being more of a thing.

"Kathy," he said.

The sleep burned out of Monarch's eyes. She'd heard too many stories around the farm. *One time she did this. One time she did that.* Over time, Rome had come to understand that Monarch's obsession with Kathy had very little to do with him. Maybe nothing.

"What did she want?"

"Oh," Rome said. "Business."

"Business?" Monarch asked. "Your business?"

"Her husband and her. They're having some . . . some money stuff."

"And she called *you?*"

"Isn't that what I—" He stopped himself. "Yes," he said.

"What do you say?"

"I said I'd hear him out."

"Who?"

"Her husband," Rome said. "He's got a pitch. Some company. A weather thing."

"When?"

"Tonight."

"Jesus fucking Christ," Monarch said. She readjusted her towel, made it tight, and then walked out of the kitchen. She went down the hall toward the bathroom.

"Monarch!" Rome shouted. He tried to be gentle about it. "Mon!"

He heard the bathroom door close. A moment later the shower came on. He did not hear the curtain, which meant she was either peeing or standing there in front of the mirror, being angry. Monarch was an emotional person. She cried a lot. Something would bother her, and then she would start. He had learned to let her cry, like that Hootie and the Blowfish song. What was that guy doing now? Rome wondered, his mind suddenly gone left. Singing country music? What was that about? How did that work? America did the strangest things to people.

He filled his thermos with coffee and went out to the truck. On a morning like this, when he felt behind, having to drive slow on the gravel driveway was annoying. But it was a good thing, the gravel. The rocks were a cheap security measure—he'd never *not* heard an approaching car—but more than a few were sharp. Sometimes, if a guy came up from San Francisco or flew in from wherever, New York, Boston, there would be a puncture.

Sitting in his living room, Rome would hear the tire blow. After the first few, he learned to keep spares around. The buyers he sold to spent a lot of money to get out his way. Plane tickets. Rental cars. Once they reached him, they spent a whole lot more. He tried to be accommodating. The tires. Plenty to eat and drink. It was in his nature, but it was also good business practice. Everything was reputation. It wasn't like he sold coke or heroin. He wasn't cooking meth. Those trips were for maniacs, paranoiacs. The people he transacted with were decent. The idea was to make a nice living. In ten years, Rome had harmed very few. On occasion he would have to scare someone. He would have to put the fear of God in them. But that was the nature of any business.

After the gravel came the dirt road. The kids who trimmed camped in the pines. On his right he saw last night's campfire. It still smoked. A thin gray line like something drawn with a pencil rose up into the branches near the sun. The kids' pup tents were scattered here and there, and one of their pit bulls lapped up water from a tin pan on the ground.

Rome saw Brian standing on the side of the road. He pulled the car over and rolled the passenger-side window down.

"Mornin'," Rome said.

"Mornin'."

Brian had to hunch over to get his head in the cab. Rome hardly noticed the tattoos anymore. SELF MADE, my ass, he thought. ROME'S GUY was more like it.

"How's it goin' with them?" He nodded at the campsite.

"Pretty good," Brian said. "Should be done with the first grow house end of the week."

"Good, good."

"Little problem last night, though."

"What's that?"

"The new kid. Botherin' one of the girls. Well, not girl."

"Right," Rome said. "Which one?"

"Okie."

Rome liked Okie.

"Real problem?" he asked.

"That's what she—that's what Okie said."

"Okay, okay," Rome said. "I'll stop in."

Brian didn't emote. Not really. He stared. He stood there. New Hampshire or California—Rome knew it didn't matter. The country was the country.

"What?"

"The fence. We got a serious issue up there," Brian said. "Near the southeast corner."

"Show me," Rome said. "Get in."

They drove up toward the hidden fields. On the left side of the rise, staked tight across the ground, was half an acre of black plastic sheeting. Kathy had mentioned flash floods, and Rome knew about those. After six months of drought, a monsoon off the coast. The loss of that plot had cost him $60,000. He didn't need Kathy to tell him about anything, let alone the end of the world. The apocalypse wasn't sexy anymore, someone should have told her. It was boring. It was here, and it was going to cost a lot of money. Lots and lots. More than the world could ever know.

One of the things Rome paid Brian for was to check the perimeter fence a few times a week, but during the harvest this proved more difficult than usual. In the grow room for most of the day, Brian inspected for quality and made sure the kids weren't pinching more than they should. The gutter punks, like Okie, took only small amounts—a fat bud here, another there—but the hippies were greedy. You had to watch them all day and for part of the night. It was annoying, but necessary. Pounds were known to disappear between their fingers.

Rome parked the truck outside the south gate, and he and Brian walked east beside the scrub brush and vines that grew across the fence; it was chain link, and rusted in places. They stopped at the corner where the path took a sudden left. Brian squatted and pushed aside a pile of branches and Rome saw the bolt cutters. They were brand-new, two feet long, with red rubber grips.

"And over here," Brian said. He slid over on his haunches like an ape to where the fence met the ground and pulled apart the cut links. "Half a foot, maybe. You think it's—"

"I don't think," Rome said. "I know. They hit Bill. They hit Julie. We're up from Julie. We're next." He went down on his knees and examined the cut. "Those assholes worked for me for three years."

"Could be the other thing."

"It's not the other thing," Rome said. "The other thing is they come here with machine guns, offer me money, and I say, '*Muchas gracias, señors. No problemo.*' Then I retire. This isn't that. It's them."

"I saw the one yesterday," Brian said. "The young one."

"I thought we were straight?" Rome asked. "I bought the land. I paid a fair price."

"They've been here a long time," Brian said. "They're an old family."

OLD FAMILY, Rome thought. That would have made a better face tat. OLD FAMILY or WHISKEY BOTTLE or PILL HEAD. TRUST FUND would have been hysterical, but Brian didn't do irony.

"I know that, Brian," Rome said. "I know they're an old family."

"They used to be all right."

"Not anymore," Rome said. "Now they're trash. They're gonna rob me here."

Rome stood up, then Brian. On the other side of the high fence were five hundred plants. Afghani indica. It was early in the season —they were still in the stretch—but Rome could smell them: their oils, their resilience, their profit. He could do three fifty.

He could make that happen for her, if he wanted to.

"Whaddya think?" Brian asked.

"Put everything back exactly where you found it," Rome said. "I'm gonna get the Bobcat up. I'm gonna dig a hole."

He went at it all day and the better part of the evening. The vibrating interior of the Bobcat cleared his mind, and it was that, the work, the repetitive nature of it—even more than the money —that he was addicted to. He dug the hole eight feet wide and eight feet deep. He put beams in the corners to keep the walls from collapsing. He made twenty or thirty trips in the Bobcat so as to hide the dirt a quarter mile away. All of this he did in a kind of trance. When he was finished, after he covered the hole with tree limbs and branches and looked up to see the last of the shadows on the mountain, he began to think in a more regular fashion, his past forming, becoming, like the dark. It was an experience Rome found he didn't care for. Instead of dealing with it, he went down to see about Okie.

It had taken Rome years to think of Okie as only Okie, and never as "she" or "her." Kathy had always said "they" was fine, "they" was *preferred*, and Rome used it, sure, but the plural threw him off, not least of which because Okie was one person. He knew it was unfair, but the word "they" brought to mind multiple personalities. Also, after a lifetime of gendered pronoun usage, it was hard to break the habit. Rome was sympathetic to the cause, but the language flummoxed him. Still, he tried. He made the effort. He hadn't left New Hampshire for nothing. The last thing he wanted to do was to become the kind of asshole he'd hoped to get away from.

The Coleman lanterns were on at the camp. The kids hung them from the lowest tree branches and left them on inside their tents. Red and yellow, green and blue: bubbles of color were scattered around. The kids moved from the fire to the woods, from the woods to the fire. They cooked their pinto beans, and the half-rotten meat they'd scavenged from town.

Rome saw Okie. They were sitting on the ground outside their tent. They were cleaning their knife. He went over.

"Mind?" He nodded at the ground beside them.

"It's your land," they said.

Rome sat. He watched them as they cleaned their knife with a green rag. It was a Bowie, with a brass-knuckle handle. The blade caught the firelight. Okie's neck and arms were covered in a dense mosaic of black ink. Their hair was cut short, and their septum was pierced with a silver ring. They were self-conscious about their lips—the full, pink beauty of them—and they tried to keep them chapped by biting them all the time. In eight years, Rome had never seen Okie in anything other than fatigues and a black T-shirt. Rome could smell their body odor, their not-unpleasant sweat. They kept their breasts bound tight against their chest. They said it was their last season, but they'd said that every season. Who didn't need forty grand? It didn't matter who you were. A lot of the kids had run away from lives of privilege even, away from the inbred dysfunction of too much old money. Okie was one of those, Rome thought, but he couldn't remember for sure. They'd mentioned a father once, a sailboat accident. He knew they hopped trains.

"Where were you this winter?" he asked.

"Tennessee for a while, in Nashville, and then down to this jamboree thing," they said. "It's on an island. It's crazy. Everybody's queer or trans. Then I was in New Mexico for a few months."

"Doin' what?"

"Hangin' out. I went on a spirit quest."

"In the desert?" Rome asked.

"Yeah. I took peyote. I saw an angel with a black face. I thought it was a sign."

"But it wasn't?"

"No," Okie said. "I asked it."

"What did it say?"

"It said, 'Fuck you. I'm just a black angel. There's black angels too, you know.'"

Okie went into their tent. Rome could hear them moving around. In their absence, he looked at the campsite, at the kids. At one time he'd known them all. He'd known their names, and stories, and where they were from, and how it was they'd come to him. But that was years ago, with Kathy, who took the time to get to know people. She was cool like that, or had used to be. Now when Rome looked at the kids, he saw compensated strangers. Except for Okie and a few others, he didn't know their names. He kept them straight in other ways. There was the kid with the one-eyed dog; the boy who never wore shoes; the girl with earlobes that hung down to her shoulders like loops of taffy. The new kid sat Indian-style near the fire. He wore a fedora with the feather of a hawk in the band. He gnawed an ear of corn. He was either choosing to sit alone or was being shunned. Aside from the kid's hat—which was stupid, plain stupid—Rome didn't see the problem.

Okie crawled out of the tent with papers and a small bud in their hand. They sat down next to Rome. They broke the bud apart and rolled.

"Is that the Silverlight?" he asked. It was his design. The strain was mellow, for the body. Monarch said it hit her in the third eye.

"Yep," Okie said. "Brian said it was cool. He put it down in the book."

Okie lit the joint. They took a small hit to check the draw. They waited a second, then took another, bigger hit. Okie passed the joint to Rome. As he exhaled, they asked him how his day was.

"Kinda fucked up," Rome said. "Kathy called."

"That explains it," Okie said.

"Explains what?"

"Why you look so sad," Okie said. "A ghost called. *The* ghost called."

"I did feel sick," Rome said. "Like in my stomach."

"Yeah, man," Okie said. "That's exes. They're like the dead, except they can call you on the phone. My mom can't do that. My dad can't. You know why? Because they're dead. They can't call me up just to see how I am."

Hitting the joint again, Rome remembered: it had been the both of them; Nantucket; a freak storm; the maid and the harbormaster crouched in the playroom, consoling; the fortune had been left to a blue-blooded grandmother who wouldn't acknowledge them.

"What did she want? Can I ask you?"

"Money."

"Ouch," Okie said. "You still love her?"

Rome shrugged his shoulders.

"Jesus, man. *Really*?" Okie said. "That woman is a force of nature."

"She really is," Rome said.

"But I always liked her."

Rome passed the joint to Okie.

"Me too," he said. "When we were together, Kathy never asked me for money. I'd give it to her, but she never asked me. She said it made her feel kept. She had a chip on her shoulder. It was the size of a planet."

"I get that," Okie said. "That makes all sorts of sense to me."

"Now she calls."

"She must be desperate," Okie said. They passed the joint back to him and picked up their knife again. "You remember desperate? It's a terrible place."

"I remember."

"But not really," Okie said. "No offense, but not really. That's not how money works. It doesn't help you remember. Not the desperation. Not the fear. Not in this world."

"I've been desperate," Rome said.

"I'm sure you have been," Okie said. "But you don't remember."

"Sure I do," he said.

"No you don't," Okie said. "Once you've got the money, you know? It's not your fault. Once you have it, certain receptors, they get clicked off. It's just the way it goes. It's just how it is."

Rome hadn't come by to argue, and he didn't need a lesson in sympathy, or whatever it was Okie thought they were talking about. If he wanted to, he could tell them his own little sob story. A description of his own father would make them happy theirs was dead. He could say, "I remember desperation, you little asshole. I remember crackers for dinner, and hiding in a closet whenever he came home." But Rome wouldn't do that. He couldn't. The gentleness people required so much of depended entirely on his not being cruel. He tried to live this way, but would forget from time to time. It was a battle.

"What's the issue over here?" He nodded at the kid with the feather in his hat.

"He gets drunk and weird," Okie said.

Rome got that. That made all sorts of sense to him. "Does he need to go?"

Okie looked up from their knife. They eyed the kid.

"No," they said. "I don't think so. I told him if he looks at me again I'm gonna cut his balls off."

An hour later Rome sat in his living room. Across from him, on the other, lumpier couch, was this guy, this husband of hers, this Ted. Rome looked at his phone. *Following Duhursts*, Brian had texted earlier, and then, right that second, *On mountain road*. Rome finished repacking the bong. He sent the letter *K*.

"What makes you any different?" he asked. "Your company?"

"A fair question," Ted said. He was so, so, *so-so* high, and it was pretty clear this Rome person didn't care for him. But who knew, really? Maybe he did. Maybe he didn't. Ted was so paranoid he couldn't trust himself. One thing was certain: there was zero chance they were going to "be New England together," as Kathy had suggested. This was actually impossible—because they weren't from the same New England. Ted's parents lived in Woodstock, Vermont, on the same road where Michael J. Fox kept a house. He'd attended Phillips Exeter, and *not* on scholarship. He'd skied! He'd skied all the time! That was the New England Ted belonged to. This Rome guy was from another one. It was written all over his sexily creased face. Enormous pickup trucks splattered with mud had rumbled through his childhood. Drunk uncles had thrown horseshoes at the pig roast. He clearly knew how to change his own oil. All that frightening reticence! Ted thought. How would he get his money?

"We're *way* better," Ted said. "I think that's the main thing." As soon as he'd said it—he'd said nothing! he couldn't think! why was he yelling?!? was he?!?—he wanted to crawl under the couch and hide there until morning.

At that moment, as if to rescue him, the most beautiful woman in the entire world walked into the living room. She held a glass of water in each hand and had long dark hair, like Pocahontas. She was Pocahontas. She set the waters down on the coffee table, smiled at Ted, and then disappeared.

"Who was that?"

"Monarch," Rome said.

"Oh, yeah," Ted said. "Monarch. Right."

Shit, Rome thought. Ted was stoned out of his mind. The poor idiot didn't know what was going on. Rome wanted to help—he'd made up his mind to help—but they had to talk terms at some point. No matter how you looked at it, it was a lot of money. What would come back to him? How would percentages work? When would he get to see her again? Beyond logistics, Rome couldn't launch Ted back into the world like this. He'd crash his car maybe, or get pulled over. Rome asked himself (he was high too—the Silverlight was headier than expected), did he like Ted? And the answer was no. He did not like Ted. He hated Ted's guts. He wanted to smash Ted's well-bred face in. But Rome got it. The guy was sort of sweet. He was nice. Good for her and all that shit. In any case, nice guy or not, Rome had to get this thing over with. The Duhursts were coming.

"Why don't we step out onto the porch?" Rome said. "Get some air?"

"That sounds amazing," Ted said.

"Bring that water," Rome told him.

After a few minutes Ted was able to communicate more effectively.

"It's precision, basically," he said. "That plot you mentioned, all those plants you lost—you could have saved them."

"Really?"

"Really," Ted said. "You would have known."

The air was nice up here. It cleared his head. While he was looking at the stars, he heard Rome's phone go off.

"Yeah?" Rome said. "How many?"

Ted stepped down the porch steps to give him some privacy.

"I don't care who ran away," Rome said. "Who's in the hole?"

Ted thought maybe he had him. He'd seen a look in Rome's eye, one he'd witnessed before. It was the look of a man who believed in MicroWeather. Standing there among the jagged driveway rocks,

Ted allowed himself a grin. After all, wasn't this how it worked? Didn't you come close to ruin? Didn't success, like fame, reject you first? One day, years from now, he would look back upon all this hopelessness. He would look back upon a moment in time when the dream appeared to be lost . . .

"Ted."

Rome took in the man's face. What was this preppy asshole smiling about? God, he hated him. Did he not know anything? Did he only know the weather?

"I wanna show you something," he said. "Get in the truck."

He rode in Rome's truck up the mountain. They passed a camp of homeless twentysomethings. He saw a pretty, short-haired girl throw a knife into a tree and then walk the ten feet to pull it out. Laid across the ground, a big sheet of black plastic caught the starlight. They drove up another, smaller road and parked outside a fence. The fence was twelve feet high and topped with razor wire. It was in the middle of the forest. The sky was down upon them. The stars were low. The angry voices of men came through the trees.

He followed Rome down a path that went along the edge of the fence. Suddenly they turned. Were they going north? After a few more seconds, Rome's flashlight app illuminated a man. Ted couldn't believe it. It seemed impossible.

"Over here," Brian said.

"For fuck's sake. I know where I dug it," Rome said. "Help me get the branches off."

The little Duhurst down in the hole had stopped talking shit. Rome had heard him shouting the whole way down from the truck.

"The rest of 'em?" Rome asked Brian. Together they moved what was an entire felled tree to the side.

"They took off," Brian said. "I heard their truck. They're gone."

"You hear that, you little fuck!?!" Rome shouted. "They left you! You came up here to rob me, and they left you alone!"

"Fuck you, Rome!" the kid shouted. "My fuckin' leg's broke!"

"That's the least of your problems," Rome said. "A broken leg won't matter after I cut your head off!"

"You won't!" the kid shouted.

"Watch me!" Rome screamed down into the hole. "Watch me kill you!" He could just make out Donny's face. It was covered in dirt. What was he now? Sixteen? Seventeen?

"This land was *ours*," Donny moaned.

"It was yours," Rome said. "I bought it. Now it's mine. That's how property works. First one thing is one person's, and then it's another's. Things change hands like that all the time. Something belongs to you for a while, and then it doesn't. Isn't that right, Ted? Isn't that how it works?"

Ted was over near the fence. He realized he was hanging on to it. He could hear the child crying down in the hole. Kathy and Rome: he got it. He didn't want to live in California anymore.

"I guess," he said.

Rome walked over to where Ted stood. He kneeled down in the grass in search of something.

"You're not really going to kill him, are you?" Ted said into the air.

Rome stood up and looked into Ted's face. They were close enough to feel one another's breath.

"No," he said. "Of course not. Whaddya think, I'm some kind of lunatic?"

Ted looked down at the bolt cutters in Rome's right hand.

"I'm gonna cut off one of his fingers," Rome said. "Two maybe. Three at the most."

Power Wagon

FROM *The Highway Kind*

A SINGLE HEADLIGHT strobed through a copse of ten-foot willows on the other side of the overgrown horse pasture. Marissa unconsciously laced her fingers over her pregnant belly and said, "Brandon, there's somebody out there."

"What?" Brandon said. He was at the head of an old kitchen table that had once fed a half-dozen ranch hands breakfast and dinner. A thick ledger book was open in front of him, and Brandon had moved a lamp from the family room next to the table so he could read.

"I said, somebody is out there. A car or something. I saw a headlight."

"Just one?"

"Just one."

Brandon placed his index finger on an entry in the ledger book so he wouldn't lose his place. He looked up.

"Don't get freaked out. It's probably a hunter or somebody who's lost."

"What if they come to the house?"

"I don't know," he said. "I guess we help them out."

"Maybe I should shut off the lights," she said.

"I wouldn't worry about it," he said. "They probably won't even come here. They're probably just passing through."

"But to where?" she asked.

She had a point, he conceded. The old two-track beyond the willows was a private road, part of the ranch, and it led to a series of four vast mountain meadows and the foothills of the Wyoming Range. Then it trailed off in the sagebrush.

"I saw it again," she said.

He could tell she was scared even though there really wasn't any reason to be, he thought. But saying "Calm down" or "Don't worry" wouldn't help the situation, he knew. If she was scared, she was scared. She wasn't used to being so isolated—she'd grown up in Chicago and Seattle—and he couldn't blame her.

Brandon found a pencil on the table and starred the entry he was on to mark where he'd stopped and pushed back his chair. The feet of it scraped the old linoleum with a discordant note.

He joined her at the window and put his hand on her shoulder. When he looked out, though, all he could see was utter darkness. He'd forgotten how dark it could be outside when the only ambient light was from stars and the moon. Unfortunately, storm clouds masked both.

"Maybe he's gone," she said, "whoever it was."

A log snapped in the fireplace and in the silent house it sounded like a gunshot. Brandon felt Marissa jump at the sound.

"You're tense," he said.

"Of course I am," she responded. There was anger in her voice. "We're out here in the middle of nowhere without phone or Internet and somebody's out there *driving around*. Trespassing. They probably don't even know we're here, so what are they doing?"

He leaned forward until his nose was a few inches from the glass. He could see snowflakes on the other side. There was enough of a breeze that it was snowing horizontally. The uncut grass in the yard was spotted white, and the horse meadow had turned from dull yellow to gray in the starlight.

Then a willow was illuminated and a lone headlight curled around it. The light lit up the horizontal snow as it ghosted through the brush and the bare cottonwood trees. Snowflakes looked like errant sparks in the beam. The light snow appeared as low-hanging smoke against the stand of willows.

"He's coming this way," she said. She pressed into him.

"I'll take care of it," Brandon said. "I'll see what he wants and send him packing."

She looked up at him with scared eyes and rubbed her belly. He knew she did that when she was nervous. The baby was their first, and she was unsure and overprotective about the pregnancy.

During the day, while he'd pored over the records inside, she'd wandered through the house, the corrals, and the outbuildings and had come back and declared the place "officially creepy, like a mausoleum." The only bright spot in her day, she said, was discovering a nest of day-old naked baby mice that she'd brought back to the house in a rusty metal box. She said she wanted to save them if she could figure out how.

Brandon knew baby mice in the house was a bad idea, but he welcomed the distraction. Marissa was feeling maternal, even about mice.

"Don't forget," he said, "I grew up in this house."

The old man hadn't died at the ranch but at a senior center in Big Piney, population 552, which was eighteen miles away. He'd gone into town for lunch at the center because he never missed it when they served fish and chips, and he died after returning to his table from the buffet. He'd slumped forward into his meal. The attendants had to wipe tartar sauce from his cheek before wheeling him into the room where they kept the defibrillator. But it was too late.

Two days later Brandon's sister, Sally, called him in Denver at the accounting firm where he worked.

"That's impossible," Brandon said when he heard the news. "He was too mean to die."

Sally told Brandon it wasn't a nice thing to say even if it was true.

"He left the ranch to us kids," she said. "I've talked to Will and Trent and of course nobody wants it. But because you're the accountant, we decided you should go up there and inventory everything in the house and outbuildings so we can do a big farm auction. Then we can talk about selling the ranch. Trent thinks McMiller might buy it."

Jake McMiller was the owner of the neighboring ranch and he'd always made it clear he wanted to expand his holdings. The old man had said, "Over my dead body will that son of a bitch get my place."

So . . .

"Do I get a say in this or is it already decided?" Brandon had asked Sally.

"It's already decided."

"Nothing ever changes, does it?" Brandon asked.

"I guess not," she said, not without sympathy.

Will and Trent were Brandon's older brothers. They were fraternal twins. Both had left home the day they turned eighteen. Will was now a state employee for Wyoming in Cheyenne, and Trent owned a bar in Jackson Hole. Both were divorced and neither had been back to the ranch in over twenty-five years. Sally, the third oldest, had left as well, although she did come in from South Florida to visit the place every few years. After she'd been there, she'd send out a group letter to her brothers confirming the same basic points:

> The old man was as mean and bitter as ever.
>
> He was still feuding with his neighbor Jake McMiller in court over water rights and road access.
>
> He was spending way too much time drinking and carousing in town with his hired man Dwayne Pingston, who was a well-known petty criminal.
>
> As far as the old man was concerned, he *had* no sons, and he still planned to will them the ranch in revenge for their leaving it.

The brothers had been so traumatized by their childhood they rarely spoke to each other about it. Sally was the intermediary in all family business, because when the brothers talked on the phone or were in the presence of each other, strong, dark feelings came back.

Like the time the old man had left Will and Trent on top of a mountain in the snow because they weren't cutting firewood into the right-size lengths. Or when the old man "slipped" and branded Trent on his left thigh with a red-hot iron.

Or the nightmare night when Will, Trent, Sally, Brandon, and their mother huddled in the front yard in a blinding snowstorm while the old man berated them from the front porch with his rifle out, accusing one or all of them of drinking his Ancient Age bourbon. He knew it, he said, because he'd marked the level in the bottle the night before. He railed at them most of the night while sucking down three-quarters of a quart of Jim Beam he'd hidden in the garage. When he finally passed out, the family had to step over his body on the way back into the house. Brandon still remembered how terrified he was stepping over the old man's legs. He was afraid the man would regain his wits at that moment and pull him down.

The next day, Will and Trent turned eighteen and left before breakfast.

When their mother started complaining of sharp abdominal pains, the old man refused to take her into town to see the doctor he considered a quack. She died two days later of what turned out to be a burst appendix.

When the Department of Family Services people arrived on the ranch after that, the old man pointed at Sally and Brandon and said, "Take 'em. Get 'em out of my hair."

Brandon had not been back to the ranch since that day.

"It's a car with one headlight out," Brandon said to Marissa. "You stay in here and I'll go and deal with it."

"Take a gun," she said.

He started to argue with her but thought better of it. Everyone in Sublette County was armed, so he had to presume the driver of the approaching car was too.

"I wish the phone worked," she said as he strode through the living room to the old man's den.

"Me too," he said.

Apparently, as they'd discovered when they arrived that morning, the old man hadn't paid his phone bill and had never installed a wireless Internet router. The electricity was still on, although Brandon found three months of unpaid bills from the local power co-op. There was no cell service this far out.

Brandon fought back long-buried emotions as he entered the den and flipped on the light. It was exactly as he remembered it: mounted elk and deer heads, black-and-white photos of the old man when he was a young man, shelves of unread books, a lariat and a pair of ancient spurs on the wall. The calendar behind the desk was three years old.

He could see half a dozen rifles and shotguns behind the glass of the gun cabinet. Pistols inside were hung upside down by pegs through their trigger guards. He recognized a 1911 Colt .45. It was the old man's favorite handgun and he always kept it loaded.

But the cabinet was locked. Brandon was surprised. Since when did the old man lock his gun cabinet? He quickly searched the top of the desk. No keys. He threw open the desk drawers. There was a huge amount of junk crammed into them and he didn't have time to root through it all.

He could break the glass, he thought.

That's when Marissa said, "They're getting out of the car, Brandon. There's a bunch of them." Her tone was panicked.

Brandon took a deep breath to remain calm. He told himself, *Probably hunters or somebody lost.* Certainly it couldn't be locals, because everyone in the county knew the old man was gone. He'd cut a wide swath through the psyche of the valley where everyone knew everybody else, and the old-line ranching families—who controlled the politicians, the sheriff, and the land-use decisions —were still royalty.

As he walked to the front door, he smiled at Marissa, but he knew it was false bravado. She looked scared and she'd moved behind the couch, as if it would protect her.

He pulled on one of the old man's barn coats that hung from a bent horseshoe near the front door. It smelled like him: stale cigarette smoke, gasoline fumes, cows. The presence of the old man in that coat nearly caused Brandon to tear it off. He shoved aside the impulse and opened the door.

Three—no, *four* people were piling out of a dented white Jeep Cherokee with County 23 plates. So they were local after all, he thought.

The driver, who was standing outside his door waiting for the others, was tall, wiry, and bent over. He looked to be in his seventies and he wore a wide-brimmed cowboy hat and pointed black boots. He saw Brandon and grinned as if they were old friends.

An obese woman grunted from the back seat as she used both hands on the door frame to pull herself out. For a moment her feet stuck straight out of the Cherokee while she rocked back and threw her bulk forward to get out of the car. She had tight orange-yellow curls and wore a massive print dress that looked to be the size of a tent.

Two younger men about Brandon's age joined the wiry older one while they waited for the fat woman. One of the younger men had a shaved head, a full beard, and tattoos that crawled out of his collar up his neck. The second man looked like a local ranch hand: jeans, boots, Carhartt coat, battered and greasy KING ROPES cap.

Brandon stepped out on the porch and closed the door behind him. He could feel Marissa's eyes on his back through the curtains.

He said, "What can I help you folks with? There's no need for all of you to get out."

The wiry man continued to grin. He said, "You might not re-member me, Brandon, but I sure as hell remember you. How you doing, boy?"

Brandon frowned. There was something familiar about the man, but whatever it was was inaccessible to him at the moment. So many of his memories had been locked away years before.

"Do I know you?"

"Dwayne Pingston. I remember you when you were yay high," he said, holding his hand palm down just below his belt buckle. "I don't blame you for not remembering me from those days, but I was close to your old man."

Brandon nodded. Dwayne Pingston.

The Dwayne Pingston who Brandon had discovered butchering a deer out of season in the garage. The Dwayne Pingston who'd lifted Brandon off his feet and hung him by his belt from a nail while he finished deboning the animal.

"This is my lovely wife, Peggy," Pingston said, nodding the brim of his hat to her as she struggled to her feet next to the car and smoothed out her dress.

"My son, Tater," he said, and the man in the jeans and ball cap looked up.

"And my buddy Wade," he said, not looking over at the bald man.

"Nice to meet you all," Brandon said. "Now, what can I do for you?"

"I guess you could say I'm here to collect a debt," Pingston said.

Brandon tilted his head. "A debt? You know the old man passed a couple of weeks ago, right?"

"Oh, I heard," Pingston said. "They wouldn't let me out to at-tend the service, though."

"What kind of debt?" Brandon asked. "I'm officially going through his books now, and he didn't leave much of anything."

"Tell you what," Pingston said, moving over to Peggy and slid-ing his arm around her. "Why don't you invite us inside so we can discuss it? If you haven't noticed, it's snowing right now and it's getting colder by the minute. I nearly forgot how much I didn't miss Big Piney until I stepped outside this morning and the hairs in my nose froze up."

Pingston started to lead Peggy toward the front steps and the two other men fell in behind them.

"Hold it," Brandon said. "My wife's inside, and we really weren't planning on any company. She's expecting our first baby, and now isn't a good time. How about we discuss whatever it is you want to talk about tomorrow in town?"

"I wanted to talk about it with you today," Pingston said, still smiling, still guiding Peggy toward the porch, "but when I called they said the phone was disconnected. So we had to come out in person. I didn't realize Peggy's Jeep had a headlight out. Those are the kinds of maintenance things I used to take care of before they sent me away."

Sent me away, Brandon repeated to himself in his head. *They wouldn't let me out to attend the service.*

"Really," he said. "You folks need to get back in your car and we'll meet tomorrow. How about breakfast or something?"

"Won't work," Pingston said, withdrawing his smile. "I got to hit the road first thing in the morning. I'm only here for the night."

"That's not my problem," Brandon said. "Look, there's going to be a legal process in regard to everything my dad left behind. You need to contact his lawyer about your debt—not me."

Pingston shook his head. "Brandon, you're the one I want to see. We don't need no lawyers in this."

Wade with the shaved head stepped out from in back of Pingston. "Open the door," he said. "Let's get this over with."

His glare sent a chill through Brandon that had nothing to do with the temperature outside. Wade was tall and solid and the bulk of his coat couldn't hide his massive shoulders.

"Give me a minute," Brandon said. "Let me talk to my wife."

"Don't take all day," Pingston said. "It ain't getting any warmer."

Brandon entered the house and shut the door. Marissa was still behind the couch, rubbing her belly almost manically.

"They want—"

"I heard," she said.

"I'm not sure what to do," he said, keeping his voice low. "Pingston used to work for the old man. My guess is he wants back pay or something like that. Knowing the way my dad was, they probably had some kind of dispute."

"What did he mean, they wouldn't let him out to attend the funeral?"

Brandon shrugged, because he didn't want to answer.

"What are you going to do?" she asked, incredulous. "Invite them in?"

"What choice do I have?"

Before she could answer, the front door opened and Tater poked his head in.

"Look, folks, my mom is standing out there in the freezing snow. She's gonna get pneumonia and die if she don't come in here and warm up."

Brandon looked from Marissa to Tater to Marissa. She was saying *No* with her eyes.

"Come on, Mama," Tater said over his shoulder. Then he walked in and stepped aside so Peggy and Pingston could enter, one after the other. They couldn't do it shoulder to shoulder because Peggy was too wide.

"Thank you kindly," she wheezed. Her cheeks were flushed and she labored the four steps it took to reach a recliner, where she settled in with a loud sigh.

Pingston came in behind her and looked around the house. Wade slipped in behind him and shut the door.

"Hasn't changed much," Pingston said, removing his hat and holding it by the brim with both hands in front of him.

"Please," Brandon said, moving from Marissa closer to Pingston. "There's nothing I can do for you. All I can do is make a recommendation to the lawyers on selling the assets and either splitting up the estate or selling it. I couldn't write a check from his account if I wanted to."

Pingston smiled as he nodded his head. "That's just blah-blah-blah to me, Brandon. We don't need lawyers to settle up accounts. We can do this man-to-man."

Brandon didn't know what to say.

Wade had positioned himself in front of the door with his arms crossed over his chest. Tater stood behind Peggy and had opened his coat. Brandon wondered if Tater had a weapon tucked into the back of his Wranglers and had opened his coat to get at it more quickly.

Suddenly Marissa said to Pingston, "You were in prison, weren't you?" It was an accusation. "You just got out."

Pingston shook his head sadly and looked down at the hat in his hands. "I'm afraid so, ma'am. It isn't something I'm proud of, but I paid my debt to society and now I'm back on the straight and narrow. Peggy here," he said, nodding toward his wife, "waited for me for the past five years. She struggled, and it wasn't fair to her. Now I've got to make things right with her and my boy."

"Make things right?" Brandon asked cautiously.

"Now you're gettin' it," Pingston said.

"So how do we make things right?"

"You were in prison with him?" Marissa said to Wade.

"We shared a cell," Wade said. "We got released within a couple of days of each other last week. I'm just here to support my buddy Dwayne."

"*Support him,*" Marissa echoed.

Brandon looked over at his wife and implored her with his eyes to please let him handle things. But she was glaring at Wade.

"You people need to leave this house," she said. "You have no right to be here."

Wade raised his eyebrows and shook his head. Nobody moved.

Peggy asked Marissa, "How far are you along, honey?"

It broke the tension slightly. Brandon looked on.

"Seven and a half months," Marissa said.

"Boy or girl?" Peggy asked Marissa.

"A little boy. Our first."

"Well, God bless you," Peggy said. Her face was strangely blank, and it didn't match her words, Brandon thought. "The last thing you need right now is a bunch of stress in your life, I'd bet."

Marissa agreed with a pained smile.

"That's what I thought," Peggy said. "So what I'd suggest to you is to talk to your husband here to get this thing over with. Then we'll all be out of your hair and you can get on with your life. How's that sound?"

As Marissa thought it over, Pingston said to Brandon, "It ain't gonna be as bad as you think. It's going to be downright painless."

Brandon and Marissa exchanged a glance, and Brandon said, "So what is it you want with us?"

"First of all," Pingston said, "I need to tell you a little story. It'll explain why I'm here."

"Go ahead," Marissa said.

"Six years ago this area was booming with oil-field workers. That's before the bottom dropped out of the market. I'm sure you know about that," he said. "Them boys had more money than they knew what to do with, and for a short time there were four banks in town. Now we're back to one, as you probably noticed.

"The old man resented the hell out of the oil boom, because none of it was on his land. Plus he didn't like it that a bunch of out-of-staters had moved into the valley and they were acting like big shots. As far as your old man was concerned, they didn't deserve to run the county.

"Well, somebody got clever and hit one of the Brink's trucks after it picked up a bunch of cash at one of those fly-by-night banks they had then. Nobody got killed, but the driver and the guard were pistol-whipped and tied up and the thieves stole all the cash out of the back of the truck. Something like a hundred and seventy-five thousand dollars, if I recall. It was quite the big story in Sublette County: an armed robbery at gunpoint."

"I remember reading something about that," Brandon said. Maybe in one of Sally's letters?

"At the time it happened I'd just told the old man I was quitting the ranch to seek employment in the oil patch," Pingston said. "I thought to myself, why should I bust my ass for that mean old bastard when I could get a job driving a truck or delivering tools for twice what I'm making out here? Peggy deserved a better life, and Tater was in junior high at the time. So why should I put up with that old bastard?"

Brandon shrugged.

Pingston continued, "The old man didn't like that. He knew the word was out up and down this valley that he was a bastard to work for and he didn't pay much. So he said he needed help around here and he wouldn't let me quit. He said I had to pay off all this damage he claimed I'd caused when I worked for him—wrecked trucks, cattle that died during the winter, anything he could think up at the time and pin on me. You know how he was," Pingston said.

"I do," Brandon said.

"I told him to shove all that up his ass," Pingston said. "I didn't owe him a damned thing. You can imagine how well he took it. The last I seen of him, he was limping toward this house to get his gun so he could kill me. He was so mad smoke was coming out of his ears. So I jumped in a ranch truck and beat it toward town. It was that old '48 Dodge Power Wagon that had been here forever. I figured I'd leave it in town for the old man to pick up later."

Pingston paused and looked around the room. Brandon guessed that Wade, Peggy, and Tater were about to hear a story they'd heard many times before even if Brandon and Marissa hadn't.

"The sheriff's department intercepted me before I could even get to Big Piney," Pingston said. "Lights flashing, sirens going, the whole damn deal. The old man must've reported a stolen Power Wagon, and they had me on that. But before I could explain I was fleeing for my life they had me face-down in the dirt and I was being arrested for that armed robbery and for hurting them two Brink's guys."

Pingston lowered his voice now for effect. He said, "The old man said it was me who did that Brink's job. He told the sheriff some bullshit about me being gone the day it happened and that he'd suspected it all along. If you remember the sheriff and the judge here at the time, you know that ranchers like your old man pretty much told them what to do and they did it.

"Supposedly the sheriff found a pistol in my duffel bag in the truck that matched what was used in the armed robbery, but I always suspected he planted it there after the fact. I was in prison in Rawlins at the Wyoming State Pen before I knew what hit me, just because I quit my job here. Your old man put it to me, and hard.

"To make matters worse," Pingston said, "Peggy had to get a job to survive, and the only one she could find was at the senior center."

Peggy spoke up. "So two or three times a week I had to ladle the gravy on your old man's lunch and pretend I didn't know what he'd done to my Dwayne," she said. "There he was with that big roll of cash he always kept in his pocket for buying drinks for politicians, but he never missed a free lunch at the senior center with old folks who didn't have two nickels to rub together. I'd look out from behind the counter at your old man holding court with his cronies and think of my Dwayne down in Rawlins surrounded by murderers and rapists."

She turned to Marissa. "Honey, you may think having a child is hard. But what's really hard is putting a fake smile on your face and serving the man who put your husband away."

Wade shifted his weight and sighed. It was obvious he was bored by the story he'd no doubt heard a thousand times before.

Brandon said, "If you're asking me to make you whole out of the proceeds of the ranch, I don't know how I can do it. There are liens on the equipment and the cattle, and the old man hadn't paid any bills in months. He might have always had a roll of cash on him, but he didn't use it to pay off his debts. All those people are filing claims, and they get their money first when everything gets sold. I sympathize, but I just don't know what I can do."

Pingston stared at Brandon for a long time. Finally he said, "I kind of figured that."

"So why are you here?" Marissa asked, exasperated.

"I want that '48 Power Wagon," Pingston said.

"What?" Brandon asked. A wave of relief flooded through him, but he tried hard to conceal it.

"It's a goddamn classic," Wade said.

Pingston nodded and said, "People don't realize what a work-horse that truck was. The greatest ranch vehicle ever made. Three-quarter-ton four-by-four perfected in WW Two. After the war, all the rural ex-GIs wanted one here like they'd used over there. That original ninety-four-horse, two-hundred-and-thirty-cubic-inch flat-head six wouldn't win no races, but it could grind through the snow and mud, over logs, through the brush and willows. It was tough as a damn rock. Big tires, high clearance, a winch on the front. We could load a ton of cargo on that son of a bitch and still drive around other pickups stuck in a bog."

Brandon shook his head, puzzled. "That's what you want?"

Pingston nodded. "Look, I suppose you're thinking that if I restored that beast to its former glory, I could make a lot of money on it, and you're right. I've seen where some of 'em sell for seventy thousand or more in cherry condition. But I don't give a crap about that. I want to fix it up and get it running. This one is too damned beat up to ever amount to much."

"Then why do you want it?"

"It means something to me," Pingston said. "That was the truck I drove every damned day I worked on this ranch. Twelve years, Brandon. I know that truck as intimately as I do Peggy."

Peggy smirked at that. Brandon thought that odd.

Pingston said, "I know when to downshift going up a vertical hill, how to power through six-foot drifts, how to use that winch to pull myself up the side of a damned cliff. If I ever go elk hunting again, that's the vehicle I want to take.

"Plus," Pingston said with a wink, "it's the truck I borrowed to go to town when your old man sent me up the river. I like the idea of that old bastard rolling in his grave knowing I'm riding around in high style in the Power Wagon he owned all his life. It gives me a small measure of satisfaction, if you know what I mean."

Marissa said, "If we give you the truck, will you all go away?"

"That was rude," Peggy said. She folded her thick arms over her bosom.

Brandon said, "I should discuss this with my brothers and sister, you know. We all have a say in how the assets are divided up."

That's when Wade stepped forward and said, "We don't have the time."

Out of the corner of his eye, Brandon saw Marissa tense up and move back.

Brandon said, "If I give it to you, how are you going to get it out of here? I doubt it'll start after all these years. I don't even know if it still has a motor in it—or tires. And I don't even know if it's in the shed out there."

"Oh, we brung a tow rope in the Jeep," Pingston assured him.

Brandon hoped that the Power Wagon was not only in the shed but also in good enough shape for them to take it away that night. He was still basking in the relief he'd felt at the words *I want that '48 Power Wagon.*

Even if it didn't make any sense. Four people to retrieve a truck? In the snow? At night?

"If it's there, it's yours," he said to Pingston.

Wade grinned and said, "Let's go check it out."

"I'm going too," Tater said.

"No," Pingston said sharply. "You stay here with your mother and Marissa."

And Brandon felt the fear creep back inside.

"Why don't you all come with me?" Brandon asked.

"No," Pingston said sharply. "Peggy don't need to stand around outside in this weather while we mess around with an old truck."

But Brandon heard, *I want my son to stay in here and keep an eye on Marissa so she doesn't try anything.*

When he looked over at his wife, Marissa nodded to him and mouthed, *Go.*

It took a while for Brandon to locate a set of keys in the old man's desk that might open the old shed. While he searched, Wade kept a close eye on him from the door. More than once, Brandon caught Wade glancing toward the gun cabinet.

"Okay," Brandon said when he found a ring of ancient keys. "I can't guarantee anything, but one of these might work." None of them were marked or labeled.

"We'll follow you," Wade said, closing in behind Brandon as he left the room.

Brandon pulled on the ranch coat and looked over his shoulder at Marissa. "Back in a minute," he said.

She nodded, but her mouth was set tight as if holding in a sob.

Pingston and Wade followed Brandon outside into the snow. It was coming down harder now and the flakes had grown in size and volume.

He led them away from the house toward a massive corrugated-metal shed where the old man kept his working ranch equipment as well as the hulks of old tractors and pickups that no longer ran. The pole light that had once illuminated the ranch yard had long ago burned out, so Brandon had to peer through the snowfall to find the outline of the shed against the snow.

"I told Wade I wasn't sure if I have the right key," Brandon said in Pingston's direction.

Pingston didn't reply.

The shed had a side door but it was clogged with years of weeds that were waist-high, so he figured it hadn't been used in a while. Brandon walked through the snow to the big double garage doors that were closed tight. A rusty chain had been looped through the handles and secured with a padlock.

Brandon bent over and tried one key after another in the lock.

"I need some light," he said. "Did either of you bring a flashlight?"

Instead of answering, Wade extended a lighter in his hand and flicked it on. The flame lit up the old padlock in orange.

The next-to-last key on the ring slid in, and Brandon turned it. Nothing.

"Jerk on it," Pingston said.

Brandon did and it opened. Tiny flakes of rust fell away from the lock into the snow below it. He closed his eyes with relief. Wade reached over his shoulder and pulled the chain free.

"Okay, step aside," Pingston said, reaching forward with both of his hands and grasping the door handles. He groaned as he parted them. The old door mechanism groaned as well.

"Give me a hand here," Pingston said to Wade. The two men wedged themselves into the two-foot opening and each put a shoulder to opposite doors. With a sound like rolling thunder, the doors opened wide.

Brandon watched Pingston walk into the shed and disappear in the dark. A wall of icy air pushed out from the open doors. It was colder inside the shed than outside, Brandon thought. Then a single match fired up in the corner and he saw Pingston's finger toggle a light switch. Above them, two of four bare bulbs came on.

"See, I remembered where the lights were after all this time," Pingston said.

"Good for you," Wade said without enthusiasm. "You figured out how to operate a light switch."

The shed layout was familiar to Brandon, and much of it was the same as it had been. Some of the equipment was so old it looked almost medieval in the gloom. Thrashers, tractors, one-ton flatbed trucks without wheels, a square-nosed bulldozer, a faded wooden sheep wagon as old as Wyoming itself, a lifetime of battered pickups. And there, backed against the far sheet-metal wall, was the toothy front grille and split-window windshield of the '48 Power Wagon. It sat high and still on knobby tires, its glass clouded with age, the two headlamps mounted on the high wide fenders looking in the low light like dead eyes.

"Son of a bitch," Pingston said. "There it is."

Wade blew out a sigh of relief.

"How you doin', old girl?" Pingston said to the truck. He approached it and stroked the dust-covered hood. "It looks like the old man backed it in after they arrested me and it hasn't been moved since," he said.

Brandon put his hands on his hips and took a deep breath. He said, "Then I guess my work is done here."

"Not so fast," Wade said, stepping over and placing his hand on Brandon's shoulder. Then to Pingston: "Check it out."

Check out what?

Pingston nodded and opened the front door of the Power Wagon and leaned inside. Brandon was surprised how obedient Pingston had been to the command. Then he realized Wade was actually the one in charge, not Pingston.

"What's he looking for? The keys?" Brandon asked.

"Shut up."

Brandon pursed his lips and waited. He could see Pingston crawl further into the cab and could hear the clinks of metal on metal.

After a long few moments, Pingston pushed himself out and looked to Wade. Pingston's face was drained of color.

"It's not there," he said in a weak voice. "The tools are on the floorboard, but the toolbox is gone. The old man must have found it."

Wade closed his eyes and worked his jaw. Brandon felt Wade's hand clamp harder on his shoulder. Then Wade stepped back quickly and kicked Brandon's legs out from under him. He fell hard, half in and half out of the shed.

When Brandon looked up, Wade was crouching over him with a large-caliber snub-nosed pistol in his hand. The muzzle pressed into his forehead.

"Where is it?" Wade asked.

"Where is what?" Brandon said. "I don't have a clue what you're looking for."

"*Where. Is. It?*" Wade's eyes were bulging and his teeth were clenched.

"Honest to God," Brandon said, "I don't know what you're talking about. I haven't been in this shed for years. I wasn't even sure the Power Wagon was here. I have no idea where the keys are."

He tried to rise up on his elbows, but the pressure of the muzzle held him down.

"Fuck the *keys*," Wade said. He barked at Pingston, *"Look again."*

Pingston practically hurled himself into the cab of the truck. His cowboy boots stuck out and flutter-kicked like he was swimming.

"Don't lie to me or I'll kill you and your wife," Wade said, and Brandon didn't doubt it. "Where is it?"

Brandon took a trembling breath. He said, "This is my first day back on this place. I have no idea what you're asking me. I've not been in this shed. You saw how rusty that lock was, Wade. It hasn't been opened in a long time."

Something registered behind Wade's eyes. The pressure of the muzzle eased, but he didn't move the gun.

"My old man was in this shed since I was here last. Hell, Dwayne Pingston was in this shed after I left. I don't know what you're looking for. I'm an *accountant,* for God's sake."

Wade appeared to be making his mind up about something. Then his features contorted into a snarl and he withdrew the revolver and hit Brandon in the face with the butt of it. Brandon heard his nose break and felt the hot rush of blood down his cheeks and into his mouth. Wade struck again and Brandon stopped trying to get up.

Wade got off him and Brandon tried to roll to his side, but he couldn't move his arms or legs. He was blacking out, but he fought it. For some reason he thought about the fact that the only violence he had ever encountered in his life was here on this ranch. And Marissa was back in the house . . .

His head flopped so he was facing into the shed. Through a red gauzy curtain, he watched Wade stride toward the Power Wagon with the gun at his side.

And he heard Wade say to Pingston, "You stupid, miserable old son of a bitch. I knew I should have never believed you about anything. You kept me on the hook for years so I'd watch your back inside."

Pingston said, "Wade! Put that down."

Pop. Pop.

Brandon didn't want to wake up, and each time he got close, he faded back. He dreamed of freezing to death because he was.

He groaned and rolled to his side and his head swooned. He threw up on the sleeve of the old man's ranch coat and it steamed in the early-morning light. His limbs were stiff with cold and it hurt to move them. His face throbbed and he didn't know why. When he touched the area above his right ear he could feel a crusty wound that he couldn't recall receiving.

But he was alive.

He gathered his knees under him and pushed himself clumsily to his feet. When a wave of dizziness hit him, he reached out and grabbed the end of the open shed door so he wouldn't fall again.

It took a minute for him to realize where he was and recall what had happened. He staggered toward the Power Wagon, toward the pair of boots that hung out of the open truck door.

Dwayne Pingston was dead and stiff, with a bullet hole in his cheek and another in the palm of his hand. No doubt he'd raised it at the last second before Wade pulled the trigger.

Brandon turned and lurched toward the open shed door.

The morning sun was streaming through the east wall of willows, creating gold jail bars across the snow.

The Jeep was gone, but Tater's body lay face-down near the tracks. Peggy was splayed out on her back on the front porch, her floral dress hiked up over blue-white thighs. Both had been shot to death.

"Marissa!"

He stepped over Peggy's body like he'd once stepped over the old man. The front door was unlocked, and his eyes were wide open and he was breathing fast when he went inside.

His movement and the warmth of the house made his nose bleed again, and it felt like someone was applying a blowtorch to his temple. He could hear his blood pattering on the linoleum.

"Marissa!"

"Oh my God, Brandon, you're alive!" she cried. "I'm in here."

She was in the old man's den.

When he filled the door frame and leaned on it to stay up, she looked up from behind the desk and her face contorted.

"You're hurt," she said. "You look awful."

He didn't want to nod.

Five tiny hairless mice, so new their eyes were still shut, wriggled in a pile of paper scraps on the desk in front of her.

"What are you doing?" he asked.

"Checking on my babies."

It was incomprehensible to him. "What happened?"

She shook her head slowly and said, "When I heard the shots outside I ran upstairs and locked myself in the bathroom. All I could think of was that you were gone and that I'd be raising this boy by myself.

"I heard Tater yell and run out, then Peggy followed him. There were more shots and then I heard a car drive away. I didn't unlock my door and come out until an hour ago. I went outside and saw you lying in the snow and I thought you were gone like the others."

Brandon said, "And the first thing you did after you saw me was check on the mice?"

"They're helpless," she explained. Then he noticed her eyes were unfocused and he determined she was likely in shock. She'd succumbed to her maternal instincts because she didn't know what else to do. His other questions would have to wait. He hoped their baby had no repercussions from her terror and tension throughout the night.

"I'll get the car," he said.

"Can I bring the babies?"

He started to object but thought better of it.

"Sure."

As he turned he heard her say, "There's a towel in the bathroom for your face."

Brandon was shocked at the appearance of the person who looked back at him in the mirror. He had two black eyes, an enormous nose, and his face was crusted with black dried blood. A long tear cut through the skin above his right ear and continued through his scalp.

Wade, he thought. Wade had stood over him after he'd shot Pingston and fired what he'd thought was a kill shot to his head. He'd missed, though, and the bullet had creased his skull.

He *looked* like he should be dead.

When Brandon went outside he saw that Wade had left them a present: all four tires on their minivan were slashed and flat, and there was a bullet hole in the grille and a large pool of radiator fluid in the snow.

When he shook his head, it ached.

Then he turned toward the shed.

When he went inside, long-forgotten memories rushed back of observing the old man, Pingston, and various other ranch hands working on equipment, repairing vehicles, and changing out filters, hoses, belts, and oil and other fluids. The old man thought it was a waste of time and money to take his equipment into town for repair, so he did it all himself. Those were the days when a man *could* actually fix his own car. And as the men worked, Brandon would hand them the tools they requested.

It had been another world, but one Brandon eased back into. A world where a man was expected to know how a motor worked and how to fix it if necessary.

The battery in the Power Wagon was long dead, so he borrowed the battery from his minivan and installed it. The air compressor in the shed sounded like an unmuffled jet engine, but it sufficed to inflate the tires. He filled the Dodge's gas tank from a five-gallon can he found in the corner. Then, recalling a technique the ranch hands had used on especially cold mornings, he took the air filter off the motor and primed the carburetor with a splash of fuel.

Like they were for all ranch vehicles, the keys had been left in the ignition. He opened the choke to full and turned the key and was astonished that the truck roared to life.

The Power Wagon reminded Brandon of a grizzly bear that had emerged from its den. It shook and moaned and seemed to stretch. The shed filled with acrid blue smoke. Pingston had been right when he'd inferred that the old truck was indestructible.

When Brandon eased it out through the doors, he saw Marissa standing open-mouthed on the front porch.

It was a rough ride, and Brandon couldn't goose it past thirty-five miles an hour. Blooms of black smoke emerged from the tailpipe. The heater blew dust on their legs when he turned it on. The cab was so high that the ground outside seemed too far down. He felt like a child behind the massive steering wheel.

He'd forgotten what it was like to drive a vehicle without power steering or power brakes. He didn't so much drive it as point it down the road and hold on tight to the steering wheel so the vibration wouldn't shake his teeth loose.

On the way into Big Piney, he glanced over at Marissa, who was holding the box of mice in her lap.

"When did you go into the shed?" he asked. He had to raise his voice over the sound of the motor to be heard.

"Yesterday, after I found the nest of mice."

"How did you get in? The doors were locked."

"The side door wasn't locked. The one with all the weeds? That was open and I went right in."

He nodded and thought about it.

She said, "Are you accusing me of something, Brandon? Your tone is mean."

"I'm sorry," he said, reaching over and patting her thigh. "I'm just confused. There are three dead people back there and my head hurts."

"It was Wade," Marissa said. "Peggy told me after the three of you left. Wade was behind it all."

"I get that. But what were they after?"

Then, before she could answer, he reached into the box of mice and grasped a fistful of the shredded paper. He downshifted because the brakes were shot, and he eventually pulled over to the side of the dirt road and stopped the Dodge. The motor banged away but didn't quit running. He could smell hot oil burning somewhere under the hood.

"What is it, Brandon?" she asked.

The strips of paper in his hands were blue and old. But when he pieced them together he could see the words "Trust," "Security," and "Stockman's" printed on them.

He said, "Stockman's Security Trust. That's the bank that got hit years ago. These are bands that held the piles of cash together. Where did you find them, Marissa?"

"I told you," she said. "They were in the nest. I didn't even look at them."

He tried not to raise his voice when he asked, "Where was the nest?"

"It was in the back of this truck. When I found it and realized their mom wasn't around, I looked for something to put them in so I could save them. There was a toolbox under the seat of the truck, so I poured all the tools out and put the babies in the box. Brandon, why are you asking me this?"

He sat back. The water tower for Big Piney shimmered in the distance.

"Pingston did that armed robbery and hid the cash somewhere inside the Power Wagon. Probably beneath a fender or taped to the underside. He got pulled over and arrested before he could spend it or hide it somewhere else. And all these years he thought about that money and worried that the old man would find it—which he did."

Marissa seemed to be coming out of shock, and she registered surprise.

"Either that," Brandon said, "or my old man was in on the robbery all along and fingered his partner. That way, he could always have a big roll of cash in his pocket even though the ranch was going broke. We may never know how it all went down.

"Pingston told his cellmate Wade about the cash and promised him a cut of it when they got out. I heard Wade say something about protecting Pingston inside, and that makes sense. Wade kept Pingston safe so they could both cash out. Only the money wasn't there, and Wade thought his old pal had deceived him all along. He went berserk and killed Pingston, then Pingston's family."

Brandon put the truck in gear and turned back onto the road. "We've got to let the sheriff know to look for Peggy's Jeep so they can arrest Wade and send him back to Rawlins."

"Why didn't he kill us and eliminate all the witnesses?" she asked.

"He thought I was dead," Brandon said. "I think maybe he panicked after Peggy and Tater were down and just got the hell out of there. Maybe chasing down a pregnant woman was too much even for Wade."

"Or maybe," she said, "he thought he was stranding me out there to freeze to death without a car, that bastard."

As they entered the town limits of Big Piney, Brandon had to slow down for a dirty pickup that pulled out in front of them. The legs of a massive elk stuck straight up from the bed, and sunlight glinted off the tines of the antlers.

Marissa said, "I can't believe you grew up here."

Brandon patted the steering wheel and said, "We're keeping the Power Wagon. I don't care what my brothers or sister say about it."

"Why?"

"I don't know," he confessed. Then: "Maybe because I got it to run again with my own two hands."

GERRI BRIGHTWELL

Williamsville

FROM *Alaska Quarterly Review*

BY THE TIME Matthis crests the last hill and catches sight of what must be Williamsville, his old bones ache from three days of riding ·and his tongue's dry and rough behind his teeth. Each time he licks his lips he tastes dirt, and when he touches his jacket puffs of dust rise off it. But there spread before him is the valley at last, and there hazed by distance the town, smaller than he'd imagined and untidy as a heap of crates dumped on the far bank of the great Pine River. As for that river, it's nothing but a shallow surge frothing between boulders, a river a man could easily ford, this time of year at least.

Williamsville — the sort of town Matthis knows so well he's wearied by this glimpse of it. There'll be a bank and hotel and general store with men in starched collars and oiled hair, and smaller, shabbier businesses straggling out along the main street: a blacksmith, a livery, a bathhouse and laundry, a carpenter who'll knock together a few planks just good enough to carry a dead man the short walk to the cemetery. Staked out on the raw ground just beyond, shacks and tents where the town will grow, if it lasts long enough. And everywhere filthy gaunt men, the very men Matthis took care to steer clear of out in the hills, because miners are a distrustful breed. In towns like this they skulk along the streets, ghostly with dust and morose from cheap liquor, while the lucky few who've dug up some kind of riches sit down freshly bathed to a hotel dinner and halfway decent whiskey, or take a whore to bed.

Matthis clucks at his horse, dry tongue against dry mouth, then sits back as the horse leans away down the slope, its head low, its hooves scraping as it finds its way around boulders and oily-leafed thornbushes. When the horse stumbles Matthis lays one hand on its neck, says gently, "Hey, old boy, steady now," and together they wait as rocks knocked loose shiver off down the hillside and leave a gasp of dust on the air, no breeze to push it away, no breeze at all. Matthis tips back his hat. With his cuff he wipes sweat from his forehead, feels the rasp of grit across his skin. How hot it is. He never used to mind, but now in these hills—it's enough to sap a man's spirit, to make one day melt into the next.

Away to the north clouds are bunching up above the hills. Across the narrow plain nothing moves. Even the pale track of road from the south is empty, as though the press of the afternoon sun is too much for any creature, and when Matthis touches his heels to the horse's belly and the horse shifts one foot then another down the slope once more, suddenly his chest tightens and in all this heat he shivers. For a moment he holds still, that clutching around his heart almost painful, an old unease stirring, then he breathes deep and hard and he fixes his attention on the route ahead because just below lies a jumble of rock from an old slide. He nudges the horse to the right of it, a long way around perhaps, but when at last they reach the cracked earth of the valley bottom they're headed north to where the river widens and slows just above the town's cemetery.

Here on the flat Matthis kicks the horse into a canter. One hand grips the gritty leather of the reins but the other rests just above his thigh, fingers cupped, muscles ready to swing that hand down to his holster then fast up again bearing the weight of his gun, and to fit that gun precisely into a spot a few inches from his chest. But not yet. The valley's empty, after all, and the town still some way off, puckered by the heat. This is his way—to make himself ready, to guard against what he himself is, the bringer of death to men that other men want dead. It occurs to him that maybe today this wariness is more than just habit. The ache in his bones. That clutch of unease around his heart, as though there's something he's overlooked. The way the buildings of the town swim a little, even now that he's closer, and his eyes can't quite settle on them.

Soon over the beat of his horse's hooves comes the dull tock of an ax chopping wood, and the hollow barks of a bored dog. If he's learned anything, it's that a man can tell a thing or two about a town by looping around its ugly backside where outhouses stand like sentries, past warped back steps and unpainted walls, past smoldering heaps of trash with smoke twitching from them and dogs sniffing stains on the earth. Here now across the river is a stout woman splitting wood, the slick crack of her ax coming a moment after she raises it because Matthis is just far enough away, an unsettling sensation like time's come loose. Here's a white dog lifting its leg, and its piss feathering out through the sunlight onto a clump of weeds. And here is a man in a stained apron upending a pan of scraps into a pigpen, and his head turns just enough for Matthis to know he has seen him, but a moment later the man's shaking the pan and slouching off to the dark mouth of a doorway.

Now Matthis is close enough to hear the muttering of the river, to catch the green fuzz of grass along its edge, then his horse is slowing. At the bank the horse dances back until Matthis urges him into the sudden shock of the water, and he lays a hand on the horse's neck and leans down to murmur, "Once it's up to your balls it don't get no worse, so you get going now, fella," and he keeps muttering as he digs his heels into the horse's belly, and the horse feels its way into the water, plunging into it and soaking Matthis right up past his knees, and god it's cold.

The man that Matthis has come to kill is called Flyte. He is a card-sharp, a man who has cheated other men out of hundreds of dollars, thousands maybe, a man who is traveling with another man's wife and whose existence is an affront to mankind, especially to Henry Pearsall, that wife's husband, who is paying half up front and half upon completion to have Flyte wiped from the face of the earth.

There is always a reason for wiping such men from the face of the earth. Such men are a blight. Or a plague. Or a canker. Such men are slanderous or larcenous, or have corrupted other men's wives or sisters, daughters or sons. Such men are beyond the attention of the law in places where the sheriff is a lone man with his own idea of what the law should be. Not that it matters to Matthis what the sheriff's ideas are, except when that sheriff is an overly righteous man who aims to apply the letter of the law rather than the general spirit in which it is meant. But sheriffs of that kind don't last long out here. It's become Matthis's habit not to notice lawmen, and in turn they look right through him—to a dog scratching its ear in the middle of the street, or a whore on the boardwalk scraping muck from her boot. In this way a certain moral code is applied:

men who are a blight on a town are removed, and if a man like Matthis should make his living by it, what does it matter?

With a great splashing Matthis's horse heaves itself out of the river and stands splay-legged, shedding water onto the dirt. Just a few yards away a fence is staked around a handful of wooden crosses driven into lumpy ground baked hard by the sun.

Not a town where there's much dying, then, likely because much of the dying is out in the hills, where miners are buried in rock falls and cave-ins, and Matthis settles his hat more firmly on his head. From the shade of its brim he takes in the ragged edge of town. A bathhouse. A livery. A few cabins, their wood already cracked by the sun, and around them a scatter of chickens pecking at the dirt. From the doorway of one cabin an old guy stares out. Matthis touches his hat to him as he passes, and he makes a show of it so that his eyes can linger, just in case, watching that old man's expression, and his hands, until he rounds the corner into the main street.

From here he can see clear through to where the street becomes the road south. There isn't much to this town after all, and yet it's a town like so many he's seen. Matthis's horse shakes his head, then comes the raw crunch of his teeth on the bit. He can smell the feed in the livery across the street and he shakes his head again, harder. Not much forage in the hills, and now that they're in town he expects to be fed. It might be hours until Matthis finds Flyte, and hours more until he can corner him somewhere private enough to shoot him without a whole bunch of ballyhoo, so Matthis lets the reins go slack and the horse turns toward the broad doorway of the livery.

Just inside the entrance the horse halts. It's late afternoon and Matthis has been in the saddle since sunup, except to relieve himself midmorning. In the sudden gloom he lifts one leg, stiff as an old dog, and lets himself slide to the ground. Except the floor's uneven, or he didn't bend his legs enough because his wet pants are clinging to them, and he lands hard and staggers against his own goddamn horse. The horse spooks and rears up so that Matthis, yanking on the reins, is pulled up on his toes and has to use his whole weight to haul the horse's head down to his chest and hold it there. Its breath comes hot through his shirt while behind his ribs his heart crashes about.

If the stable boy noticed he doesn't say a thing. He drifts out of the shadows, a hollow-chested kid with orange hair who nods when Matthis says to feed his horse good and rub him down, and deftly snatches the coin Matthis tosses him out of the air. A moment later the boy's turning away and taking the horse with him, then Matthis is back in the sunlight. From out of nowhere a breeze has started up. It swirls dirt along the street, sending it hissing against Matthis's wet pants, slamming a door hard against its hinges not far away, and that push of wind, that sudden sense of movement when the few men Matthis can see are leaning against walls or propped against posts—it doesn't feel right. Nor does being on foot after days high up on his horse, and he wipes a hand across his face just for the feel of it, then sets off down the street.

From the shadow of the buildings watch grim-faced men, but as he passes not one of them moves, nothing moves except for that wind licking up dust. Matthis cocks his head to one side then the other so these men know he's watching them back. A flash of black from a doorway—Matthis's arm stiffens, his fingers curl to the shape of his gun just an inch from his holster. A man hurrying into the street. A prim little man in a stiff collar, the sleeves of his coat worn to a sheen, his pants slack and creased around his boots as though they once belonged to a taller man, and he hasn't even noticed Matthis just a few yards away. The man's squinting against the dust and the sun, and across the street he goes, arms pumping, eyes on the gleaming windows of the bank.

Matthis watches him, stretching his hand, fiddling his fingers like he's letting go of something. That man is not Flyte. Flyte dresses fancy but wears a dark low-crown hat, a thick black mustache, and has a squint in his left eye. Matthis wasn't given a description of Henry Pearsall's missing wife, but then, it's not her he's been sent after. He's sure to see her, all right. After he's shot Flyte she'll come hurrying down the stairs or rushing out through a doorway. She'll wail and grieve, she might even chase after him—some women do—and beg him to kill her too, because now she's so on her own, and he'll pull himself away and walk off slow and steady to his horse, then swing himself into the saddle like a man who can't concern himself with such matters.

Still, it's a rotten business, leaving a woman with a man to bury and no resource. Sometimes he's wondered what they do—do they go back to their homes? Would a man like Henry Pearsall take back the wife who shamed him? Surely this whole business is about revenge and nothing more, about a man like Henry Pearsall having the money to pay for that revenge to be exacted on his behalf, revenge on a man for stealing his wife, and revenge on his wife for allowing herself to be stolen.

Sooner or later a man like Flyte would abandon Pearsall's wife anyway. Matthis knows this to be true, and he lets himself glance over to where that prim man in his worn coat is slipping away into the bank. It is not as though Matthis expected to see Flyte in the street within minutes of arriving in town, though such things have happened. No, up ahead there's the unmistakable frontage of a hotel, and just beyond it a saloon. A man like Flyte might still be asleep, even at this time of day. He might be busy with a plate of steak and potatoes, or already set up in the saloon with whiskey and cards. Henry Pearsall couldn't tell him what kind of man Flyte is, though the fact that Flyte is here in a sprung-up town like Williamsville says a lot: he's not a top-of-his-game cardsharp, and his fancy clothes might be the only fancy thing about him.

It could be that Flyte is expecting Henry Pearsall to come after him, or one of the many other men he's cheated, but not a man like Matthis—a man bearing him no grudge, a man he does not even recognize. In the sliver of a second between Flyte seeing Matthis raising his gun and the bullet hitting him in the chest he'll understand that this stranger has come to shoot him dead, and his face will register shock at the world for having caught him out.

The wind's blowing harder now and sending up ghostly waves of dust that spin and spin. Matthis ducks his head and clamps one hand to his hat. He turns his back too, so when the wind settles a little he's looking past his own shadow laid out before him, out beyond the north end of town where great dirty clouds have piled up above the hills. If Flyte can't be found, or he can't get Flyte on his own by evening, he might be trapped here by the river swelling with storm water, and he walks a little faster now, right past the hotel to the saloon.

As soon as he's through the doors, the used-up reek of the place is all around him. Cheap tobacco, spilled liquor, old grease, the smell of men who haven't washed in a month. The rumble of voices tells him, even before his eyes have got used to the dimness, that the place is at least half full. A few faces glance toward him and he looks back, not at them exactly but through them so that no man feels the weight of his gaze as he takes in the whole room, never mind that he's already spotted the man who must be Flyte at a table over by the stairs. The dark low-crown hat, the mustache like a smudge of soot, the squint that looks like he's closed his left eye against the smoke from his cigar. Then Matthis is heading to the bar as though the only thing on his mind is a drink.

He sets his elbows on the counter and one boot on the foot rail. He orders a whiskey, and only as the man pours does he let his eyes drift up to the mirror behind the bar. From under the brim of a filthy hat a man's watching him, his hair lank and gray and his face so old it looks rendered down to the bones. His heart squeezes tight like a fist and his hand drops for his gun, and only when the old man mirrors him—his face hard, his hand dropping out of sight—does Matthis understand he's looking at himself. The surprise of it burns through him, a scorching of nerves that feels familiar, as though he has been taken unawares by himself before, and he looks away to the corner of the glass to find Flyte.

Flyte's with three other men, glasses in front of them. One man's skimming cards to the others from the deck in his hand with surprising speed and grace. The men are miners, foreheads and noses burned brown by the sun, chins smooth and pale where they've just had their beards shaved off. Two of them are hunched forward with their arms on the table and their hands close to their money, but Flyte's sitting back, that cigar jammed into the corner of his mouth and one arm over the back of his chair as though he's settling in to tell a story.

Already Matthis has looked away. There's the barman lifting the bottle from his glass and a little whiskey slopping onto the counter, there's the glass being pushed toward him and the whiskey trembling and spilling some more, and Matthis searches his pocket for a couple of coins and drops them into the barman's hand. He picks up the glass. The spilled liquor is a slippery coolness under his fingers, and as he lifts his head to empty the whiskey into his mouth, he finds Flyte in the mirror once more.

Flyte is on his feet. He's stepping away from the table, and he stumbles a little and has to steady himself against his chair. Between the miners flickers a self-satisfied look, and Matthis catches the sharp scent of trouble rolling in, of a setup, because a man like Flyte doesn't let himself get that drunk in the afternoon, not during a card game with a bunch of miners, not unless he's an utter fool, and it was no fool who cheated Henry Pearsall out of a substantial sum and took off with his wife.

From the depths of the saloon comes a wink of light as a door opens. Flyte's letting himself out a back way. Matthis stiffens: Was Flyte expecting him? Is he slipping away? But a man like Flyte would know better than to take off out back by himself. No, Matthis realizes, by an incredible stroke of luck, Flyte's gone to relieve himself, right now, out behind the saloon, and moving nice and slow he tilts up his glass a second time and waits for the last drops to slide onto his tongue before he follows.

Out behind the saloon the wind's fierce now. Matthis has to grab his hat as it tips away, and the world's bleary with dust. A few yards off is an outhouse, a lopsided thing with a door flapping against its frame, but Flyte's relieving himself nearby on a pile of broken crates, legs wide, his back to Matthis. The air snaps. On a clothesline sheets are flapping in the wind, lifting and billowing and folding back on themselves, and from beneath them an overturned pail comes spinning and clanging across the dirt. Flyte doesn't turn around. Why would he? So Matthis waits, ready, and though Flyte has a gun in his holster—a cheap thing that probably hasn't seen much use—he doesn't take aim, not while the man's back is turned.

The wind spits dust into Matthis's eyes and he blinks it away. A woman's thin voice calls out, "The wind's gonna bring 'em down," and maybe she's nearby, or maybe her words have been carried on the wind, but there's Flyte buttoning himself up and turning back to the saloon, and when he catches sight of Matthis his face goes flat. He's not dressed so fancy after all. His pants look worn, and on his shirtfront, half hidden by his jacket, is a yellow mark where someone's been careless with an iron. Out here in the glare of afternoon he looks younger too, his eyes blurred with drink, and that's the thought arcing across Matthis's mind as his hand dips for his gun and brings it up so fast that Flyte hasn't moved when the bullet hits him right where his shirt's been scorched.

Flyte stands there with his mouth open, then all in one go he topples to the ground as though the wind's blown him over, and his hat goes rolling out toward those crates still wet with his piss. A few tremors shake him, then his body goes slack and Matthis, gun holstered, head down against the wind, walks over to him. All he needs is something small—a cigar case, a ring, something personal of Flyte's to take back to Pearsall. He crouches and tugs at a watch chain, then he cradles the watch in his palm. It's still warm. A raindrop shatters against it, and another. He springs the cover open: *Paul H. Dewar.* What man is this, Matthis wonders, who carries another man's watch in his pocket, a watch he must have won in a game and wears as though it's his?

But what does it matter? Flyte is dead.

The rain's pocking the dirt and the mineral smell of it's suddenly everywhere. Matthis heaves himself to his feet and slips the watch into his pocket. Just beyond where Flyte lies the sheets are still lifting and flapping, only now there's a gap like a tooth knocked loose where one's missing. In its place stands the stout woman who'd been chopping wood, the sheet bundled over her arm. Her face has gone stark. Her mouth opens and she wails, "Paulie! Paulie!" then she's running toward Matthis crying, "What you have to go and do that for?" and Matthis raises his gun slowly so she'll see it, and when she keeps coming he fires a single shot that stops her dead.

A thrashing rain is falling now, blurring everything. Matthis slips around the side of the saloon, but the street is not how he remembers it. It is longer, and wider, and though he slogs through mud and puddles, the livery's nowhere to be found, and he wonders if this is still Williamsville or if this is some other town and Williamsville was where he shot Flyte a month ago, for he remembers a man in a dark low-crown hat who seemed to have a squint, and a woman raging after him as he walked away and how he had to stop her. He slows and looks over his shoulder. Through the downpour the street's filling with the dim shapes of men, and he pulls out his gun and hurries on, but where the livery should be is the cemetery, and the men are closing in.

There's nothing for it but to take off through the graves. Mud sucks at his boots and he loses his footing and falls, nearly drops his gun, then he hauls himself up and lurches away between the crosses, slipping and stumbling through the blinding rain, then there, suddenly, is the river right before him, only now it's a torrent raging past.

From the way Matthis pushes his hat hard down onto his head, it's like he means to swim it. Instead he turns to the men coming after him, dozens of them swarming across the cemetery, and he wipes the rain from his face to see more clearly. Among them there's a man in a dark low-crown hat, and Matthis fires at him and fires again, though he's certain he's already killed him, that in fact he killed him only a few minutes ago behind the saloon.

He is still puzzling over this when he's shoved hard in the chest. He stares down in wonder at the blood blooming on his shirt, and what a curious sensation it is to hear the air cracking apart all around him while he floats, weightless, away from it all. The men are gone, and the rain is gone, and as he's swallowed up by a drenching cold he thinks he should have stayed and fought. There was a man he was supposed to kill, but when he tries to catch hold of the gossamer memory of who that man was, it's dissolved to nothing. What does it matter? His hands are empty, and his thoughts so thrown apart by a furious roaring that he stops trying to remember, and what a relief it is to stop at last and let himself be borne away.

Abandoned Places

FROM *St. Louis Noir*

"YOUR DAD'S A bastard, kid. You should be mad. Hell, you should be madder than me. The fucker ran off and left you with someone you hardly know. You know what I think?"

He knew what Vickie thought. He'd heard it over and over the past couple of days. Tuning her out, he pressed his forehead into the window, the dust along the edge tickling his nose as he watched the cars pass through, hoping to catch a glimpse of curly blond hair and his dad's wide, wide smile, the one he called his "fuck me" smile. He'd never seen it fail to bring a girl to her knees. Sometimes he locked himself in the bathroom and practiced that smile, trying to make it reach his eyes so they crinkled at the corners and blue shined.

She slammed the door on the washer, the vibration tugging at him through his hip. He turned, studying her short black hair spiked like porcupine quills, her eyes squinted against the cigarette smoke as she flapped one of her shirts. He didn't understand why she bothered to wash them. They stank like smoke before they even made it to the closet.

Vickie was only seven years older than Ian and had been married to his dad for two. She hadn't been thrilled with him before his dad left; now he kept waiting for her to call social services and have him taken to a home.

"Everybody needs a vice. Val could've had the decency to leave me some damn money." Dropping her cigarette to the concrete floor, she ground it under her heel, hand digging her pack out of her pocket. "Are you listening to me?"

"Yes." He didn't call her ma'am because that usually pissed her off.

She paused long enough to light her new cigarette, cheeks hollowing as she sucked against the filter. "I saw that look you gave me."

He turned back to the window, staring through the grime to the world outside, wondering how it could keep functioning when everything in his life had turned upside down.

Vickie stopped hiding her smoking the day Valentine left, moving from behind the shed to lighting up inside the house, and every day since then she kept accusing Ian of giving her looks. Maybe she just felt guilty for ruining her lungs, but every time he saw her light up, the pit in his stomach opened just a little wider. Either she'd stopped caring if his dad found out or she knew he wasn't coming back.

"I take good care of you. I feed you, make sure you're clean. Fuck, I'm damn good to you, considering you're not my kid."

Ian supposed she was right; she did feed him, and so far she hadn't called anyone about him, but he wished she'd stop making him feel like he owed her something for being there.

"I need a vice, and mine left, walked right out the door while you were at school. Didn't even tell me where he was going."

Ian bunched his hands in the sleeves of his shirt, the back of his head tight. He knew this part of the story too. She kept repeating the same things over and over, until the more she said, the less he believed her. Vickie reminded him of Sandy Robinson, the girl at school who kept saying Justin Bieber was her brother. She kept repeating it as if it would make it true, as if they'd start believing if she said it enough. Even he was a better liar than Vickie was, and she had seven years on him. It was a little shameful.

"It's such fucking bullshit. At first I was sort of relieved. No offense, kid, but do you know how much foundation I was using to cover the bruises from your daddy's fists? There's vice and then there's vice. Shit, it's sick. I know it's sick." She paused to take a draw off her cigarette, the tip of her tongue poking out between her lips as she picked off a stray piece of tobacco. "It's odd what you can get used to. When I look in the mirror, my face seems empty without the occasional black eye."

He wondered if she stood in front of that mirror and rehearsed the things she said. It was like seeing the same play over and over again. That was one thing about lying: you never wanted it to sound rehearsed.

She stood, pulling an armful of clothes from the dryer and dropping them in the basket. He couldn't tell if she was using any less makeup. It still looked like a painted mask, the edge of it not quite meeting her hairline. Sometimes he thought about seeing if he could peel it back to reveal what lay underneath.

"Mean fists or not, the bed gets lonely without someone in it. Shit, I haven't been alone in bed since your daddy came and I crawled out my window." She dumped ash on the floor before sticking the cigarette back into her mouth, one side clenched down around the filter, making her face uneven, like old Mrs. Ashworth after she'd had her stroke. "I didn't know I was trading one bad man for another, but at least your daddy was better in bed than mine."

He didn't want to hear this. Rolling his eyes, he pushed off the washer and started up the stairs, palm skimming the handrail.

"Hey, runt, you're supposed to be helping me. Get your ass back down here."

Ignoring her, he yanked his dad's old union jacket from the chifforobe in the entryway and pulled it over his shoulders, the sleeves hanging to his fingertips, shoulders still too wide. He closed the door on her—"Ungrateful bastard"—and loped off the porch, body all right angles, his joints loose as if he wasn't securely put together yet. The wind blew up the street, ruffling his hair as he stared at the red-brick duplexes across Tamm Avenue, satellite dishes sticking out like malignancies. He kept his eyes trained on Cindy McClellan's upstairs window, hoping to catch sight of her moving behind the glass. At night he sat in the dark, watching as she changed without pulling the blinds. He liked it best when she raised her arms, her breasts jutting out in small peaks, her nipples perfect exclamation points. One of these days he was going to try out his "fuck me" smile on her.

The sun was just starting to go down, highlighting the tower on the old Forest Park Hospital along the east side of the neighborhood. Soon they would gut it, tearing it down to build another parking lot. It was what happened to abandoned places.

He walked past green, white, and orange, the Irish flag painted on the curb and flying high, down past the faded shamrocks on Tamm Avenue. Concentrating on taking deep, burning breaths, he walked through the fog of each exhale, pretending it made everything new.

There were still kids climbing on the giant stone turtles poised midcrawl over Turtle Playground, arms out as they walked along the back of the long stone snake, moms and dads watching, laughing. The constant hum of traffic on 64 edging Dogtown followed him as he turned from their laughter and made his way up to the swings at the end of the park. At this time of day it was mostly grownups in this part of the park. It was his favorite time to swing. With them here he didn't feel too old to be playing. Maybe growing up wouldn't be so bad if he could still swing.

He closed his eyes, pumping his legs and thinking about his dad as he listened to the squeak of the chain. It wasn't unusual for Val to leave on business, but he always said goodbye, and he always let Ian know when he was coming back. Ian knew better than to think his dad was a saint. He'd overheard Mrs. Donovan say Valentine had a quick smile and an even quicker zipper. He'd never knocked Ian around, but he knew his dad had quick fists as well. He was loud and boisterous, and life seemed to bend itself to his will.

The thought of going back to a house filled with Vickie's practiced monologue and the choking haze of cigarette smoke twisted his stomach up. Pulling his dad's coat closer around himself, he watched as the sun set, the children's laughter disappearing as they made their way home.

That night he could hear Vickie laughing through the wall, her high, fragile cackle scattered by a deeper rumble. For all she talked about her bed being lonely, she hadn't spent much time alone since his dad disappeared. Ian couldn't figure out if she thought he was deaf or just stupid.

He curled up on his side, listening to the squeak of the bed and her grunting moans, his stomach tight, face hot. Tension coiled in his belly, cock hard whether he wanted it or not. Reaching down into his pajamas, he touched himself, the warnings of Sister Theresa running through his head. He didn't want to think of Vickie, of her makeup mask and ashtray stench, so he turned his thoughts to Cindy. Cindy McClellan's tits, Vickie's moans, and his hand, and he was coming over his fingers, eyes closed against the tears, the heat in his stomach burning to ash as he pressed his face against the pillow to soothe the sharp sting in his eyes.

*

Benny had violin practice on Tuesdays so Ian was walking home alone. He tucked his hands into the pockets of his dad's jacket as he walked, the smell of fried food following him down Tamm. It was a straight shot from St. James the Greater once he crested the small hill. He could see Vickie sitting out on the stoop, her long legs stretched out until the tops of her shoes lit up in the sun. The cafeteria macaroni and cheese turned to a hard lump in his stomach. Staring at her was like looking at a black hole.

Letting his pack slip to the ground, he sat down on the bench outside the Happy Medium Barbershop and focused on the people walking back and forth. He closed his eyes, listening to the sounds of the neighborhood as he tried to find the familiarity in its daily routine. The traffic hummed along 64 and the radio droned from the patio behind Seamus McDaniel's farther up the avenue. It was the same as every other day, except it felt empty, a vital piece of Dogtown missing.

"Your daddy is still gone, huh?"

Mr. Allen settled on the bench next to him, cane propped between his legs, wrinkled face hidden under the brim of his hat. Ian glanced at the squashed slope of his driving cap and away, staring up the street toward the gazebo. "Yes sir."

"It was bound to happen." He tapped his cane on the sidewalk, snorting and then spitting into the flowerpot by the bench. "You can't run with the types of people he did and not get into trouble." Mr. Allen glanced at him and then down the road toward the house. Ian wondered if he was staring at Vickie's long legs. "She taking good care of you? You're looking a little peaked."

"Yes sir." He'd found it was best to stick to yes and no when you weren't sure what to say. Glancing at the rheumy paleness of his eyes, Ian wondered what Mr. Allen would say if he told him how he woke up in the middle of the night, sure the world had ended because the house felt so empty. What if he told him he sometimes thought Vickie had killed his dad? He opened his mouth, unsure of what was about to pour out, and then caught Vickie with her head turned, watching him.

Swallowing the grit in his mouth, he dropped his gaze. "She feeds me, does the laundry, sometimes she cleans."

"She feeds you, huh?"

"Yes sir."

"Guess you can't ask for much more than that." He patted Ian across the back and stood, pulling himself up by his cane and walking back into the barbershop.

Someone drove by in a golf cart and Ian settled into the seat to wait Vickie out. Closing his eyes, he listened to Mr. Allen's voice through the open door of the shop.

"Poor kid. You know Valentine started running with the Miller boys. They knew he was part of the hit on the Pulaski Bank last year, they just couldn't prove it. Now it's come back to bite him on the ass."

"Richard, shut your mouth. Door's open. You keep that up and you'll be neighboring with Valentine at the bottom of the Mississippi."

There was a rustle and then Mr. Beech, low and urgent: "The kid's still out there, you big oaf."

The door closed and he was left with a crushing hollowness in his chest, his arms and legs numb as reality receded, taking the air with it and leaving him alone in the still, discarded world. He sat there, blind and unfeeling, until a passing car blew its horn, shattering the bubble he was caught in. Pulling in a deep, shuddering breath, he folded over his knees, the flood of sight and sound making his stomach cramp until he gagged, nose running and eyes burning.

When he was five his Grandma Shone had died, leaving his world a little more gray, a little more empty. It'd been one of the few times Valentine allowed him to cling, and Ian anchored his world to his dad. It wasn't always a steady anchor, but it'd always been there, whether it was in the raised echo of his voice or the rumble of his engine as he pulled out of the drive. Now that anchor had been ripped from him.

What am I supposed to do?

The question was present in every beat of his heart. Each time it ripped through him, pulling dry heaves from the depth of his guts. The vague feeling of wrongness solidified until it was too heavy to breathe around. He sat there, bent over his knees, waiting for the profound weakness to pass.

The question wouldn't leave. The constant knowledge of his father gone and his own uncertain future darkened his world. Cars passed on the street and Vickie watched, and nothing changed except for the dropping temperature, the cold solidifying his legs.

Wiping his mouth with the back of his hand, he stood and hefted his pack over his shoulder and continued down Tamm. Ian stopped on the street, staring at Vickie squatting on the stoop of the house he'd lived in his whole life. She stared back, eyes hard and sullen as she flicked her butt into the yard. Dropping his gaze, he crossed to the house, cheeks and head hot, eyes burning.

"What's wrong with you?"

He tried to step around her, but she reached out and snagged the sleeve of his jacket.

"Hey, kid, I was talking to you."

The last week had grown too big for him. All he could think about was her heavy moans and the banging on the wall every night. The shadow of his missing father was a vise, squeezing his chest until he couldn't breathe. Dropping his bag, he jerked out of her grasp, and using the momentum of his turn, he smacked her across the face, a fingernail raising a welt under her eye.

She stared at him, mouth opening and closing in a perfect purple *O*, and then she stood, catching him across the cheek with her knuckles. The punch sat him down on his ass, the shock reverberating up his spine to ring against his head like he'd stuck it inside the church bells.

"You little shit. I may have taken that from your daddy, but I'll be damned if I let a little runt like you hit me." She ran a hand through her hair, spikes popping right back into place, and glanced around as she tugged at the hem of her shirt. Bending, she hauled him up by the lapels of his daddy's coat and leaned close, her hot breath stinking of cigarettes and mint. "Keep that up and maybe I'll look real hard, make sure you end up with your daddy, you understand?"

He still couldn't think, the world gone plastic and shiny around him. Shoving her off, he left his bag on the porch and stumbled up to his room. He wiped at the warm trickle from his nose and stared at the red smear across his fingers. It looked like they'd both learned something from his dad.

That night he couldn't sleep, his chest tight and aching as he thought about his dad tangled in the murky current of the Mississippi. The swollen side of his face throbbed with every beat of his heart, a constant echo of Vickie's knuckles across his face.

He'd climbed into bed in his school uniform and now his pants were twisted around his legs, his shoes dirtying the sheet. Across the room his Iron Man action figure threw its shadow at the wall, the outside light catching the childhood guilty pleasure. The house was silent in a way it never was when Vickie was there. Even at night she left the TV or radio on, as if she was afraid of what she'd hear in the quiet.

Maybe I'll look real hard, make sure you end up with your daddy, you understand?

Sitting up in bed, he shoved the covers off and pulled on his dad's jacket, the nylon slick in his hands. The house was cold against his belly, the brick scraping his shirt up as he lowered himself from the window. The world was lit by scattered streetlights, their jaundiced light spreading along the sidewalk like watercolor. The low hum of conversation floated down the street from Seamus McDaniel's, sprinkled with the rise and fall of laughter that colored his idea of adulthood.

Ian started down Tamm, away from the noise and laughter, past the empty lot with its foundation rising from the ground, lost and haunted. Wind blew down the street, trapped from spreading by the buildings along either side, rattling the broken fence with its overgrown lot and crooked BEWARE OF DOG sign. Pausing, he turned and looked back, expecting to see Vickie standing in the door, laughing as she locked him out, but the small brick house was still and dark, empty.

The barking of the big red mutt down the street pulled him forward toward the swings, the miserable squeak of the chain floating over the neighborhood. Cutting across the street, he stopped in the shadows by the house on the corner of Graham and watched the woman as she arced out over the highway. The light caught her hair at the apogee, shining blue-black and unmoved as she hung suspended above the river of lights along the freeway. Vickie crested again, legs out as if she would fly off the swing right into the traffic along 64.

Up the street, people spilled out of Pat's Bar and Grill onto the sidewalk, heading toward their cars. A man broke off from the crowd and started down Oakland toward Vickie, passing the silent stone turtles, their shapes rising from the playground like burial mounds.

Shifting closer, Ian tried to catch a glimpse of his face, wondering if it was the man in his dad's bed. Vickie started across the avenue, away from the light. She was so close Ian could hear the click of her mint against her teeth. The man looked both ways and crossed, the light catching him full in the face. He had long stringy hair, the brown shot through with silver, his tall, lanky frame stretched too thin.

Tucked in the shadows, Ian held his breath as they passed, studying the man's doughy face. When they were a good ten feet past, he turned and followed, staying along the edges of the light.

He didn't remember his mother much, just the fuzzy picture his dad kept in his wallet. Her name had been Barbara, and Valentine used to say she was an angel. Ian wondered if his mom had made his dad happy, though. She'd been blond and fair, and in that faded picture she'd laughed with her mouth open and eyes crinkled. Sometimes he liked to pretend he could hear that laugh. He bet it was a good one, high and wild, and not at all like Vickie. Vickie was lucky if she could wash the stink of brimstone off in the morning.

When Vickie and the man reached the corner they turned away from the house, toward Hampton and the abandoned Forest Park Hospital. Ian stopped in the last of the shadows and watched as they paused between the hospital and the empty parking garage. The man swung his doughy face about, looking around before he pulled the fence back, letting Vickie climb through and following after.

He could feel his heartbeat through his teeth. They'd come here sometimes after school, smoke cigarettes and dare each other to go inside while they remained safely on the opposite side of the street. They'd tell each other stories about the horrible disfigurements and deaths, about the ghosts that wandered the halls and the gray lady who Stevie swore he'd seen in the tower.

No one ever took the dare. They would tease and taunt, but nobody was stupid enough to go inside.

Ian sank to the concrete and watched as they walked along the other side of the fence. His bed was calling, safe and warm, even if his life had turned upside down. It would smell like him, and the blanket would scratch just as it did every night. He wanted to turn back, bandage the crack in his world, but he had to know what Vickie was up to, if she really knew where his dad was.

He slipped in after them, something catching him by his jacket, biting into his skin. He froze, a terrible pressure squeezing his heart and filling his head until he couldn't hear past the trembling rush of his blood. Jerking forward, he ripped the collar of his dad's jacket, sharp pain filling his mouth as he bit his tongue. Gravel gouged into his hands as he sprawled across the pavement, head turned back to stare at the jagged edge of the metal fence. The emptiness of the night behind him left him shaking and he collapsed forward, taking deep, aching breaths.

Remembering Vickie, he craned his head up, staring at the hospital rising in front of him, jutting out in odd, painful angles, the tower pointing to a black sky. A shiver gripped him, cold settling into his insides like ice had frozen over his bones, locking him in place. He stared at that building with its brick the color of skin and waited to hear it breathe, the lumbering beast to move, to pulse, creaking on its misshapen joints.

Vickie and the man had disappeared into an alcove on the south side, fading into the dark. Making himself move, Ian followed, head down so he didn't have to see the building. He reached the corner just as they climbed through a broken window into the black behind the brick. Waiting until the flare from their flashlight faded, he boosted himself through the window, stopping just inside. The room reeked of rotting blood and old disinfectant, fetid and sour.

Little light trickled through the window behind him, the dark in front deep and alive. Somewhere ahead he caught the ineffectual sweep of a flashlight and pushed forward. He tried to breathe through his mouth, but the taste of stale sickness settled on his tongue. Starting through the debris, his foot caught, hand bracing against something warm and soft. He jerked back and stumbled forward into the hall. Outside light spilled through the windows and into the empty rooms, creating islands of safety in the hungry dark. Ian knelt behind an old bed, watching as something blacker than the rest moved at the end of the hall.

"Damn it, Vickie."

There was a meaty smack and then silence.

He licked the dust off his lips and watched as they disappeared through a door, the metal clang reverberating through the hall. He hadn't realized how noisy they'd been until they were gone. Now it was quiet, and the light spilling into the hall didn't seem so bright, the silence thickening the shadows. Starting down the hall, he passed room after room, not wanting to look but unable to turn away. He catalogued the oddities: the dark rusty stains pooled in one room, tiles from the ceiling missing and broken, a giant light hanging like something from a space movie, a pile of phones, cords twisted and grimy, and in one what looked like the hips of a man. Ian froze, staring as he tried to make sense of it. It was chopped off at the knees and just above the stomach. There was no blood, no bone, just rubber and plastic, and the taste of his pulse on his tongue.

Turning from the sight, he ran, ears straining for the quiet whisper of pursuit.

The door at the end of the hall was heavy, his breath loud in his ears as he leaned against it, easing it shut. Stairs stretched before him, light flickering through the metal grating like hellfire below. Their voices rose, cadences sharp and brutal. Everything he'd learned in chapel escaped him, leaving him stuck with the beginning of an Our Father and the end of a Hail Mary.

Our Father who art in heaven, hallowed be thy name. Blessed art Thou amongst women and blessed is the fruit of Thy womb, Jesus. Pray for us sinners.

Pray for us.

Their voices bounced off the metal pipes and tanks, spreading and overlapping until it was like listening to the crazy people at his Aunt Marsh's church as they knelt at the pulpit. The bottom of the stairs spread out before him, filled with tile and plastic ghosts, the showers ragged with their curtains partially ripped from their rings. Squatting next to a bank of metal lockers, he stared at the poster fixed to one of the doors, the woman's legs spread, her fingers opening her pussy as he listened to the voices around the corner.

"Tell me where you hid the money, brother."

The man's voice was deeper than he thought it'd be, bouncing off the tile. It was followed by another one of those meaty thuds. The rapid beating of Ian's heart stilled as he stared at the blonde on the poster and listened to his dad grunt through the half light.

"Val, don't be a fool. Tell us where you hid the money and we'll leave you alone. We'll even call the cops when we get out of the city, tell them you're here. You can go back to Ian." Vickie's voice wavered like the dying battery in their flashlight.

Ian closed his eyes, listening to his dad's thin laugh. "Vickie, sweetheart"—he paused for air—"I tell you and Brady Miller'll be after me. Between the two of ya, I'll take my chances with you and Spastic Shortcake over here."

His dad screamed. He screamed until his voice broke, freezing Ian's insides as it repeated over and over, caught against the tile.

The cold locker pressed against his cheek as he watched the man cut off his father's pinkie with a pair of shears. Vickie kept her back turned, like she couldn't bear to watch.

The man leaned close, his mongrel face pressed against his dad's. "You'll tell me, or I'll bring your little runt down here and gut him in front of you. Shit, brother, I'll hoist him up right over-head and let his insides rest against the top of your head while he screams your name."

There was blood on his dad's chin, painting it red like he'd been eating strawberry pie. His dad closed his eyes and let his head fall forward, a thin line of drool stretching from chin to chest. "It's in the basement coal chute," Valentine said.

Ian huddled in his corner, watching as the flashlight trembled in Vickie's hand, throwing shadows around the walls with their grungy caulking and bloody tile. His father's skin was gray, hair matted dark. He didn't look like Valentine anymore. His father was big and strong, and when he walked into a room you knew it, felt it, because he brought life with him. The man in the chair was hollow, broken. Ian shoved his fingers into his mouth, biting as the world went soft and watery.

He couldn't hear; everything echoed in his head like he'd been stuffed into a drum. He sat there, watching the man beat his father while Vickie trembled on the sidelines. He sat there, tucked safe in his corner, his insides shaking and trembling, the world far away as he watched the man put away his shears and pull out his knife. He sat there, piss warming the crotch of his pants, the world roaring around him as the man slid that knife over his father's throat, un-zipping his neck.

The skin gaped on either side of that opening, giving his dad a second smile.

He tried to make himself crawl forward, to press his hands against that hot grin, but he couldn't. He tried, but he'd lost his sense of direction, crawling the other way and tucking himself into one of the showers, face pressed against the tile, cooling his heated cheek. The iron-rich scent of blood and the darker scent of mold touched his nose: death and hunger. The world devoured them.

After a while the tile was no longer cold under his cheek, the world gone dark, as if it had started with its tail and just kept swallowing, a giant ouroboros. The seat of his pants was cold and wet, the denim rough against his legs. His body ached as he crawled forward, head loose on his shoulders. The metal of the stairs felt distant under his numb fingers while he crawled out of the hospital.

Outside it had grown cooler, as quiet and dark as that basement. It was as empty as he was, an abandoned place. Nothing worked right. He wasn't sure he was feeling the ground under his feet, the asphalt giving with every step. He walked up the middle of Graham, passing in and out of the pooled streetlight until he overshot Berthold and had to turn back down Clayton toward his house. He could still hear his father scream.

It sounded like the swings down at the park. (It sounded like the squeak of his dad's bed.)

Slipping into his open window, he stood in the middle of the room, listening to the squeak of the bed next door. Ian pulled off his jacket and folded it on the bed, running his hand along the too-long sleeves. Moving down the hall, down the stairs, down to the basement, he found his dad's ball-peen hammer and hefted it a couple times, the wooden handle cold in his hand. He dragged his feet back up the stairs until he stood on the other side of his dad's door, listening to that monotonous squeak, a machine that needed oiling. He pushed open the door, the light streaming through the window highlighting the man's back as he rutted into Vickie. Ian stood there, watching the grunting flesh, the man's shaggy head lowered so he couldn't see his face.

He didn't time it, but each step he took coincided with a squeak from the bedsprings, adding to the rubbery feeling in his knees.

The man's head gave with a dry crack, like breaking Easter eggs.

He was thrusting into Vickie when the rounded side of the hammer sank into his skull, causing him to collapse. At first everything was still, and then he moved, shoulders rising and falling, a marionette with tangled strings. Ian pulled the hammer loose and brought it down again, the crack a little wetter this time, as if that egg hadn't been completely boiled.

The man stopped moving, and a thin, pale arm snuck out from under him to grope up his back. "Bruce?" Vickie's hand continued up his neck to the back of his head. "Bruce, what's—" Ian watched as her finger sank into the hole in his head like a thumb into a pie.

She shoved, her voice cracking like his dad's had. Squirming, she wriggled out from under him enough to meet his eyes and stilled, the mascara trailing down her face like clown makeup. Ian raised the hammer, ready to bring it down against her forehead, and Vickie closed her eyes, hunching in on herself.

He paused, watching as she waited for the hammer to fall. She was as evil as the man on top of her, but more than that, she was pathetic. He could see it in her eyes, the same nightmares in his. She would continue to see the smile in his dad's neck and taste the copper on the air. They'd never be rid of that.

She reached for him, nails ragged and spiked hair tangled against the top of her head. "Ian . . ." Whatever she was about to say died on her lips, eyes closing as more mascara ran down her cheeks. "Kill me." He didn't answer, and she opened her eyes, shoving at the dead weight on top of her.

He dropped the hammer and walked away, abandoning that place.

Flight

FROM *Ellery Queen Mystery Magazine*

BIRDS. THEY COME in like birds through a door left ajar, a window opened.

Stand for a moment, head tilted to one side, beads for eyes. Peck, peck, peck at us. Then leave.

Some flutter and coo. Flap around the room. I know they feel trapped. *But they have no idea.* Because they get out.

We stay. We stay until we die.

Thursday

"Wake up, my dear."

His fingers slide across my hand. Cold and dry as snakes.

"It's time for one of our little chats."

My right hand is cramped shut. He pries my fingers open. It hurts.

"I know you're awake."

He reaches over the railing of my bed, turns my head so that I face him, not that I can see anything in this darkness. *Useless, useless, can't even pull away.*

"I have something new to tell you."

Clattering. I can close my eyes, but I can't block out the sounds. Breakfast on six-foot-tall steel carts banging along the hall, wheels rattling, plates and trays bouncing on the shelves. Jim Landeman two doors down howling at the morning. I tell myself, *Really it's no different than when the alarm clock shrilled before you leaned over to slap it quiet.* I tell myself a lot of lies to get through each day.

"And how are we all doing?"

Ida lets me blink and yawn before she cranks up the bed, pushes her hands in my armpits to slide me half upright. Her dyed black hair smells of coconut and her breath smells of coffee.

Sam's hand on my shoulder, me turning to him, wrapping my legs around him.

Paper bib crinkling, tied around my neck.

"Jenny's helping you with breakfast today. Helping you and Noni both. You girls be nice to her, all right?"

She's standing in the doorway, watching, caramel-brown hair hanging in a braid over one shoulder. She'll learn to tie it back.

"Jenny, after I get Noni set up you don't worry about her. She feeds herself fine. Just keep an eye out for when she's near done, and take her tray before she throws it." Ida chuckles deep in her chest. "Make sure you get out of the way if she lets fly. She's got a pretty good arm."

"Ten minutes?" he'd say after I shut off the alarm. Now I wish I could have turned off the clock. All the clocks.

"You want a little more sleep?" I'd ask.

"Hell, no." Words from his lips moving down my neck, felt more than heard.

"Can't be more than ten minutes."

He'd laugh, and always oblige.

Jenny comes over, sits by me, picks up the plastic fork. Her hand shaking a little. There's nothing I can do to help. She's young enough to be my daughter. I haven't seen my daughter in two months.

"How do I know what she wants to eat?" Jenny asks Ida.

"Just look at her face, honey. She'll smile or blink. But if you can't tell, just go ahead. Rachel won't fight you, not like some."

Scrambled eggs. Two pancakes. Bacon dry as paper. Coffee. Orange juice that tastes like the inside of an old freezer. Jenny is slow, careful, and I am grateful. She gives me time to chew and swallow.

So many important things are small, so small I never noticed them before. Bits of life that just happened now have to be intentional, and always under someone else's control. How long a cup is held to my mouth. How big a piece of food is on the fork. If every wrinkle is smoothed out of the sheet beneath me. Life and death in those little things. So I don't choke. So I get enough fluids. So my skin doesn't break open in pressure sores down to the bone. So I can hold on to the pieces of life I have left.

"This is my first day." Jenny's eyes are green and intent, watching me eat.

I smile and nod. She lifts the fork with the next clump of syrup-soaked pancake and I open my mouth like a nestling.

"I hope I'm doing this right. Will you let me know if I'm not?" she asks.

I smile, nod again. She has to look closely to see that I'm nodding. It's all I can do for an answer today. Some days there's more. I used to be such a talker. Loved to argue, loved to debate. I'd interrupt people—didn't mean to, it was a bad habit, but I'd so want to get my point across.

"Rachel, would you just let other people get a word in?" my mother said time and again.

"Sorry, sorry," I'd tell her, and I'd try to listen, but then somebody would say something that made me think of another idea, and off I'd go, explaining, excited, my hands waving, drawing pictures in the air, even when I was old enough to know better, to control myself.

Not a problem anymore, is it? Wouldn't my mother be proud? I'm such a good listener now. Even in my dreams. In the ones that I tell myself are just nightmares. Couldn't be real, couldn't be someone really coming into my room night after night, whispering, whispering.

"What's wrong?" Jenny's voice has gone tense. "Are you okay?"

I must have let the fear show on my face. I force a smile back. I've learned that happy patients get treated better.

Time for a distraction. I cut my eyes over toward Noni, back to Jenny, over to Noni again.

"Oh, is she done?"

Noni definitely is. She's staring at her tray, bushy eyebrows drawn together. Her gnarled hands roll the aluminum spoon and fork carefully back in the paper napkin, turn the coffee cup and juice glass upside down, leftover brown and orange liquids sloshing around on the plate. She's reaching under the tray, but Jenny lifts it away just before Noni can get a good grip and send it flying like a rectangular Frisbee. Noni always aims for the door. I think she's trying to help clean up; the aides only get hit if they're in the way.

By the time Jenny's taken the tray out to the cart in the hallway and come back, Noni is off the bed, feet pushed into her worn pink slippers, bathrobe slung over one arm. She's heading out. Jenny looks in the hallway and clearly finds no one to tell her what to do, because she turns to me and asks, wide-eyed, "Do I let her go?"

Just try to stop her, I think, but settle for nodding and rolling my eyes. Jenny seems to get the message, because she contents herself with arranging the flowered chenille more neatly on Noni's bony shoulders as she pushes by.

Ida comes in, looks us over. "Everybody fed, you got the tray in time? Good. I passed Noni making her rounds out in the hallway."

"I hope that's okay, to let her go?" Jenny asks. "Rachel said that it . . ." and then she stops, realizing that of course I hadn't said anything.

"She did, huh?" Ida shakes her head. "Come on, something I want you to help me with. We don't deal with it every day, thank God. It's a good chance for you to practice."

Jenny smiles at me as she leaves, and I tell myself not to like her too much. Getting attached to friendly aides is pointless. They come and they go. And why should they get attached to us? We go too.

Ida doesn't look at me when she says, "I'm afraid it'll be longer than normal before we're back to get you dressed and in your chair, Rachel."

I can't ask her why, but there's no need. She closes the door behind her. Not usual here. Privacy is just one item on the long list of what we've lost. Half an hour later I hear the gurney rattle in the hall. I can't see the parking lot from my window, but I know there's a hearse in it.

And I know what he told me during the night was the truth.

Friday

"We haven't discussed my criteria, have we? The selection process?"

His hand rests flat on my forehead. Palm heavy. Sweating this time. *Is he sick?*

"No. I didn't think so. But regardless, it bears repeating. Especially as I'll be starting again soon, once a prudent amount of time has passed."

He sighs, gently, like my teachers used to, years ago, giving me time to think of the implications of a new piece of information. Noni stirs in her bed, her feet kicking at the steel side rails. His fingers tighten on my face until my bones ache.

"Well, I see I must explain it to you tomorrow, my dear. I wouldn't want my presence to disturb your roommate enough to earn us a visit from the night staff."

He pats my cheek. I can hear his slow careful footsteps as he leaves in the darkness. Noni is deaf as a post, she has never heard him, never will. All that disturbs her are her dreams.

But hers aren't real.

Today is shower day. It's quite a production. Poor Jenny, having to hold my slippery, floppy self on the shower chair. Even with the straps tightened it's hard. I know it is safe enough. I've never fallen, and I'm not so scared anymore. But it's never easy.

I can feel the water. I haven't lost any sensory capacity. Once I'm settled in and she's washing my hair (still dark, but cut so short now), the water running over me, I close my eyes. Try to escape.

Every August at Twain Harte. Gold-leafed aspens lined the rocks between water and tall mountains all around. We swam in shore water warmed by the high summer sun, water clear enough to see the minnows, light moving in ripples around them. The brown and green pebbles smooth under our feet until we were deep enough to stretch out. It felt like flying, arms become wings. Splashing, chasing each other, swimming into the colder water. We turned on our backs and floated, buoyed, weightless, Sam twining his fingers in my long hair that streamed and coiled between us like black ribbons.

After I'm dried and dressed and in my wheelchair, Jenny pushes me out to the common room. I'll be here for the rest of the day, except for lunch and dinner. It's a pretty enough place, windows on three walls, a fireplace that's only used on Christmas. Dried flowers in oranges and yellows fill it now. *Cheerful colors abound for the benefit of our residents!*—I remember that from the brochure Sam showed me when we were deciding.

"Is here okay?" she asks me. She's looking a little bedraggled, strands of fine hair escaping from her long braid, her name tag askew.

I smile my answer. Any place is fine as long as I can see the trees and birds. I sit with my back to the room, watching for the floating gulls, the bright blue flash of a Steller's jay. Listening to the voices of the people slowly coming in around me. They keep our rooms so dark, I've never seen him clearly, and couldn't, even if I could talk, tell anyone what he looks like. He's part of the darkness.

I don't hear his voice. Almost everyone's here, and there aren't that many men in the whole place. Besides the patients, there are a few orderlies, custodians, the occasional repairman, visiting doctors, patients' relatives. Female patients outnumber the male patients ten to one, and flutter around the coherent ones like faded butter-flies. When the tables are set out for late-afternoon bridge, there is a fuss to make sure the men are shared equally, but some groups still end up with four women, and angry looks are exchanged.

"Rachel, come on now," Mina calls to me, "we need our third partner." It's kind of her to pretend that I can travel the twelve feet across the carpet on my own.

Liz bustles over and wheels me to the corner of the table by Mi-na's chair, then sits down with a theatrical sigh.

"Finally ready, ladies?" she asks, looking pointedly at or-ange-haired Geri and blond Bea. She picks up the cards and deals. When she comes to Mina, Liz reaches across the table and slots each card into the plastic tray that holds them upright. Mina hasn't been able to hold cards for years now.

Geri and Bea aren't happy about missing out on having a man at their table. Their faces mirror sulky images of each other—pursed wrinkled lips, and eyelashes drooping under the weight of layered mascara. They're constantly glancing around the room. I can see from the smiles on my partners' faces that they've noticed and intend to use our opponents' distraction to our advantage.

"One spade," Liz bids quickly.

"Wait a minute," Bea whines, "I'm not ready."

"Snooze and loose," Liz says.

Bea counts points to herself in a whisper. She's rattled. Mina tilts her head to listen, and Liz never takes her eyes off Bea. Geri doesn't notice. She's too busy scowling at the flirting going on at the table next to ours.

"Pass." Bea glares at Liz.

Mina looks at me, softly taps her bent fingers twice on the jack. I nod. "Two spades," she says.

No response from Geri.

The table shifts and the ashtray jumps a little, dislodging a puff of smoke from the ashes already accumulated there.

"What!" Geri snaps, and Liz does her best to look innocent and aggrieved, even though she was the one doing the kicking under the table.

"Time to bid, dear," Liz tells her.

Geri sucks on her cigarette. Everyone around the table looks at the ceiling and waits.

"Three. Diamonds."

No one is surprised. The rest of the bidding also goes as expected. They resolve at four spades.

Mina's the dummy, and the other three pitch in to set her cards out flat. She'll let them do that much for her. But when Liz calls which card to play, Mina sets the backs of her fingers against the card and pushes it to the center of the table herself. Fingers like bent twigs that used to handle dozens of glass test tubes a day. That used to hold the smallest of camel's hair brushes and transfer grains of pollen from one flower to the next, and write in perfect tiny script the results of each hybridization. She's shown me her lab books. The covers worn and cracking now, but everything inside still neat, precise—observations, numbers, and the curving black-line illustrations, colors washed in afterward. I look down at my own hands, smooth skin, straight fingers. *Aren't I lucky?* I try to move just one finger. Just an inch.

Wednesday

"It's not as easy as when I was young, of course. But here, it takes so little, that I can still . . . even being as frail as I find myself. One must adapt, after all. When I hold the pillow over them, that is just the beginning. They finish the work themselves. The fear, you see. It's never been determined to be anything other than heart failure. Only to be expected. Nothing to raise any alarm. I just need to not be greedy, since I am practicing in such a limited field now. It is good, isn't it? That I have learned to be patient? I find the anticipation almost as good as the act. Almost.

"It will be next month, I think. Yes."

Tuesday

Mina's roommate has moved out. Helen had been waiting for one of the private rooms at the ends of the halls to become available. Mina never speaks ill of anyone, but I could tell she was glad.

Saturday

No one sleeps deeply. We keep at least one hand twisted into the sheet, or on the bed rail, the thin pillow, anything to help us find our way back in the morning. The only bright pool of light is over the nurses' station, where the four hallways converge. I saw it once at night, when I ran a 105-degree fever and they had to take me to the acute-care hospital over the hill. *Noise pounding in my head with every heartbeat and people's steps on the carpet loud loud never so loud before and thin towels wrapped around ice shoved in my armpits and between my legs and around my neck like a necklace of cold but my skin melted everything it touched and the light glowed around Mel her red hair fraying around her face and her white cap reflecting the light so hard and bright even when I closed my eyes everything was on fire the edges of walls and people and*

But now it is full dark, even shadows lost within it, and he is here again, has reached in, pushed the door almost shut behind him, and I cannot see him, can only feel the cold as he turns my face so I look at him, and see nothing.

He is whispering. "I don't choose them for themselves, you know, I never have. What matters is who loves them. What it will do to the ones left behind. That is what I want to accomplish, something that lasts. The effect I have upon my nominal victims, well, that is transitory, isn't it?"

He stops. I hear him swallow. "We all have thought about it, I expect. What we do in our lives. If anyone will remember? Everyone who comes here must have, at one time or another, mulled over what kind of mark they will leave on the greater world, don't you agree? Even the now mindless ones like her."

His fingers brush across me in Noni's direction. *No, not her,* I shout at him, and no one but me hears anything, *she's so strong and alive and I think sometimes she's even happy.*

He laughs a little. "No, not her. Weren't you listening to me? Who comes to visit her? Who would mourn? You? That's not enough, not at present anyway. No, I am still considering which other choice would be best." He is humming, the wordless tune high and buzzing, and he taps the rhythm.

1,2,3, 1,2,3, it's a waltz, over my face, cheeks, forehead, *1,2,3, 1,2,3,* my mouth, *1,2,3, 1,2,3*

"This stage is very enjoyable, a bit unfocused perhaps, but so alive with possibilities." His fingers quiet, then push, his hands are strong, and my face is half buried in the pillow. "Oh, my dear," he says, when he realizes what he's done, "I am so very sorry. I was musing." He adjusts my head, smoothing the rumpled pillowcase away from my mouth and nose, leans down: "I don't want anything to happen to you."

Today the sun is shining, the air outside looks clear and cold. We're gathering in the common room for a concert by the a cappella quartet from the community college over the hill. I know I have to be one of the last brought in. My chair is so tall in back, solid all the way up past my head, straps and pads to keep me straight, I block anyone's view sitting behind me, but it's hard to wait. No, that's a lie, isn't it? It's the easiest thing in the world now, waiting. Really. Waiting to be fed. Waiting to get the food brushed off my teeth and the cowlicks brushed out of my hair. Waiting to be dressed in one of the hospital's thin gowns and one of my two robes. ("Green or blue today? Oh, the green one's in the wash, so it's the blue. You like the blue, don't you?") Waiting to be moved or turned so I can see what someone else wants me to see.

Jenny sets me by the window. "Is this all right here, Rachel?" And bless her, she did wait for as much of an answer as I could give her. A look.

Their voices are beautiful, and so young. I don't understand the words. The lyrics might be Italian, or French, or Latin. It doesn't matter. All I care about today is the music. Glowing threads of sound weaving over and around each other. Music like sunlight.

I could never sing. I even failed my audition for the school choir in fifth grade. I'd been diligently practicing at home. "This Land Is Your Land" over and over. In the car. In my bedroom. In the bathroom. My mother finally knocked, loud enough for me to hear, told me through the closed door, "Rachel, some of us just can't sing." I still tried out. Later, when I was a mother, I could sing to my daughter when there was no one else around to hear.

There is pink lemonade and three kinds of cookies. The four singers separate and circulate among us. Families have been invited and the grandchildren have started zigzagging around the grownups, faster and faster, all that pent-up energy. The young curly-haired boy right in front of me during the concert had sat still for the first song, then started fidgeting, I could see his legs swinging back and forth, his hand reaching up to pull on his mother's shoulder, then he turned around in his seat and stared at me, silently. I didn't mind.

One of the singers sits down beside me. She's tall and thin, and has to lean over as she introduces herself—"I'm Sheila"—and tries to make conversation. It's difficult. The weather—"So glad it's sunny today . . . usually so foggy here." The music—"We all love singing. I so hope you enjoyed it." I wish I could tell her how happy it made me. She sets down her napkin and cookies on the windowsill and gestures toward my food that someone who didn't know me had brought over and set on my lap. I try to shake my head; it's enough to get the point across. We'd both be embarrassed if she tried to feed me. *Drink me?* Too late now to ask anybody why we never say that.

I start to laugh, and she says how glad she is to have met me, how "inspiring and wonderful" my attitude is. I wish I could tell her I'm just laughing about grammar, and Alice in Wonderland, and the particular rabbit hole I've fallen into. Which for the last hour hasn't been so bad. Then I hear him.

He's behind me, talking. "So many visitors," he says. "How wonderful it is to see the families gathered around." Sheila is already turning away. If I could only just reach out. Sometimes I can, sometimes a bit of control comes back to force an arm, a hand to function, to do something. Grab at her arm and pull her back and somehow make her understand she has to turn me around so I can see who he is. See if I can tell who he's looking at, who he is choosing.

Liz talking as usual, cigarette in hand, smoke circling around her. Politics, probably. The war. One of her grandsons fled to

Canada, and judging by the long hair on the young man sitting by her, the peace sign sewn on his ragged army-surplus jacket, this one might be next. She's told me she'd go too, if she could.

Mina smiling, so happy. Her family is around her, so many of them. *Oh Mina,* I think, *don't be happy, don't let him see how much they love you, kisses, little presents piled on your lap, the orchid on your shoulder, please don't let him see.*

Sunday

A month. He has not come in the night. I have not heard him during the day. *Is he gone? Is he dead?* All I can do is wait.

There is a glassed-over inner courtyard. They call it the greenhouse. Shiny leaves, bright flowers. The hospital cat loves it in there. Lies on the tiles, stares at the hummingbirds that fly in through the opened skylights. Ruby and emerald feathers, glinting, just out of reach. I'll go in there for Mina's sake, to keep her company, but I have to fight to stay awake in the damp, hot air. A heavily pruned lemon, more bush than tree, fills a corner. Mina leans toward the yellow-centered flowers, her nostrils flaring, faded eyes closed. Jenny moves me close enough to catch the scent on the air, sharp and sweet at the same time. Mina lifts her hands, points her curled knuckles toward a smaller plant.

She turns to me. "Do you remember this one, Rachel? Of course you do. You never forget anything I tell you."

Of course I'm the best student she ever had. Never a wrong answer, after all.

Softer, pure white flowers, their scent a perfume that makes me think of stars and lost nights.

Back in Mina's room, she has Jenny take one of the old lab books off the shelf. "Page forty-three," she says. "*Jasminum sambac,* you both knew that, didn't you? You too, Jenny?" Mina wants to think that what she knows, what she learned, what she did with her hands, will last longer than her, will ripple out into the world like the scent of those flowers.

I watch as Jenny lifts Mina onto her bed for her nap. Slim arms, young strong back, lifting the old woman curled back into herself like the petals in a bud. Jenny's movements are easy, she's sure of herself, comfortable now in what she does. She pulls the green covers over Mina's shoulders. The other bed is empty.

"Would you like to go outside?" she asks me. I close my eyes for the length of a breath. It's become our signal for *yes*.

The outer courtyard is different. But not different enough. Enclosed on three sides, it opens out toward the east, toward planted cypress trees dark against the yellow-gray hills. I blink twice, three times, quickly. *No.*

"All right," she says, and wheels me around the building to a narrow walkway on the other side. "Here?"

I close my eyes, open them slowly. Then open my mouth and breathe. We are at a place between pine trees that opens to the west, to the wide gray ocean and the cold wind. There is salt on the air. I'll taste it on my lips when I'm taken back inside.

There is a rough stump. Jenny sits down on it. We're the same height now.

The worn edge of the letter sticks out of her tunic pocket. She pulls the envelope out now, I see the FREE written in the corner where a stamp would go if the sender wasn't a soldier on the other side of the Pacific.

"He doesn't tell me much." She chews on her lip. "Trying not to worry me." Her hands clench shut, crushing the letter. I try so hard to reach out, to pat her arm. Two fingers move.

"When Brian comes back, he'll go on his dad's fishing boat full time. He does write about that. Plans. Where we'll live. He says he's glad he's in the infantry, not on one of the river gunboats, even though that'd be safer. Says he doesn't want to be on a boat hunting people." Her head is bent, not looking down the hill to the harbor. Not looking at me. I try again and my right hand moves, slow, so slow.

Sunday

Eight days. I can't call it getting better, but it's something. We think it is the cold. That it helps, a little, even if unreliably. She brings in ice packs. Only my right hand ever moves, but oh God, to see that. To choose.

Blue with cold, lifting my hand away from the plastic bag beaded with water. Drops hang from my palm.

I wanted to surprise Sam and Maggie this morning, imagined the look on their faces, but they didn't come. It was a different Sunday, the last time they came.

Sometimes they don't come, for weeks, or months. Then they do. Then they're gone again. And if I could wish myself dead I would.

Monday

The charge nurse (not Mel, who is on vacation; Mel would have listened) stands on one side of my bed, speaks over me to Jenny, saying the degree of movement is insignificant, an expected transient effect in secondary progressive MS. No reason to call the family. Orders her to stop the cold packs, cites the possibility of spasms and tissue damage. Jenny looks at me and I blink *No*.

Tuesday

The darkness changes, thickens. He is here.

He says how he's missed these talks, says so ill, says incompetence, says frustration, says plans in place now, still weak, needs someone won't struggle, says choice made.

Says Mina.

He does not need to touch me to make me stop breathing.

When Jenny comes in to wake us, leans close to slide me up, my hand becomes a claw catching on her breast pocket, where her pen is.

"Rachel?" she asks.

The pen is in my hand.

I don't let go.

"You can't write, Rachel."

No.

She looks at me, both of us thinking.

One of us screaming, *I don't know how long how much time.*

She gently loosens my fingers. It doesn't hurt.

*

She makes a grid on the back of her notepad. Shows me.

Six letters across: *a b c d e f*

Four rows. Two letters left over for the fifth row. Her pen moves across them. I blink. Her pen stops.

mina in

She thinks I'm repeating, stuttering. She shakes her head.

danger

Talking now: "What?"

I close my eyes *Yes,* again *Yes.*

not crazy

Her pen stops. "I don't understand."

man patient comes at night tells me

"Tells you what?"

that he is killing us

"Who?"

It takes too long. She has to leave, to care for her other patients. She doesn't believe me.

But when her shift is over, she comes back.

"I can't tell them what you said. You haven't seen anything. You don't know who he is. They'll think you're crazy, we're both crazy. They'll fire me. They'll sedate you. Mel won't want to, but they'll make her."

No no.

"How soon?"

I start to cry. I can no longer form even the shadows of words.

"If he can't hurt"—she can't say what he really does—"Mina, will he go right to someone else?"

I don't think so.

An hour later they're moving me into Mina's room. Jenny convinced them by pointing out how I wasn't sleeping at all. She said it was Noni thrashing around, yelling in her sleep, cursing when she was awake. The effects true (dark circles under my eyes, tremors), the cause true enough, even though it's not the reason.

"I'm so glad you're here, Rachel," Mina tells me. "I've been afraid they'd move in someone noisy." She winks at me. "Promise me you'll be nice and quiet."

I grin at her, forgetting for a moment.

She carefully pushes one of her flower vases closer to my side of the little table between our beds. "Jasmine. You remember. Don't let on that Liz is picking it from the garden for me."

Jenny goes out to the nurses' station to tell them she'll wait until I fall asleep. They won't object, glad of the extra help. She comes back, curls up in the armchair, pulls a blanket over her. Mina's asleep. I stare through the bed's side bars at the dark shape of the door. The night-shift aides make their rounds, skipping us, because of Jenny. Then everything quiets down out in the hallways, and in the room.

I wake up when the door opens, hissing softly across the floor. Then he leans back against it, pushing it most of the way closed. He stops when he sees my wheelchair. He'll know it's mine. Can he tell my eyes are open? Can he tell I'm awake? He has to, my breathing is so loud, frantic. Jenny must be waiting for him to do something. He leans over Mina. "Oh, my dear," he whispers. "How perfect this is." Is he talking to me? To Mina? Why isn't Jenny doing anything? My hand is on the cold metal of the bed rail, and I reach past it, shaking, slow, slow as in nightmares. His hands are sliding the pillow out from under her head. I scream at muscles, tendons, nerves, this one time, this one last time, to move, to hold themselves in the air, how can they not hear? He is pushing down on her now, back and elbows stiff. I see the shadow of her small body jerk once, twice. And my hand spasms, knocks one vase against another, glass shattering, and at the noise Jenny flies out of the chair. Before he can turn her arms are around him, and she drags him to the floor. I think I hear his bones break when he falls. I hope I can, over Mina's gasps and cries.

Wednesday

They come in and talk to me. They tell me he's gone. They've taken him away.

I'm still here.

JEFFERY DEAVER

The Incident of 10 November

FROM *In Sunlight or in Shadow*

Edward Hopper, *Hotel by a Railroad*, 1952

December 2, 1954

General Mikhail Tasarich, First Deputy Chairman of the Council of Ministers of the Union of Soviet Socialist Republics
Kremlin Senate, Moscow

Comrade General Tasarich:

I, Colonel Mikhail Sergeyevich Sidorov, of recent attached to the GRU, Directorate for Military Intelligence, am writing this report regarding the incident of 10 November, of this year, and the death associated therewith.

First, allow me to offer some information about myself. I will say that in my forty-eight years on this earth I have spent thirty-two of them as a soldier in the service of Our Mother-Homeland. And those have been proud years, years that I would not exchange for any sum. During the Great Patriotic War, I fought in the 62nd Army, 13th Guards Rifle Division (our motto, as you, Comrade, may recall, is "Not One Step Back!" And o, how we stayed true to that slogan!). I was privileged to serve under General Vasily Chuikov at Stalingrad, where you, of course, commanded the army that, during the glorious Operation Uranus, crushed the Romanian flank and encircled the German 6th Army (which merely months later surrendered, setting the stage for Our Mother-Homeland's victory over the Nazi Reich). I myself was wounded several times in the butchery that was the defense of Stalingrad but continued to fight, despite the wounds and hardships. For my efforts I received the Order of Bogdan Khmelnitsky, 3rd Class, and the Order of Glory, 2nd Class. And of course my unit, as yours, Comrade General, was honored with the Order of Lenin.

After the War I remained in the military and joined the GRU, since I had, I was told, a knack for the subject of intelligence, having identified and denounced a number of soldiers whose loyalty to the army and to Revolutionary ideals was questionable. Everyone I denounced admitted their crime or was found guilty by tribunals and either executed or sent east. Few GRU officers had such a record as I.

I ran several networks of spies, which were successful in halting Western attempts to infiltrate Our Mother-Homeland, and I was promoted through the GRU to my recent rank of colonel.

In March of 1951 I was given the assignment of protecting a certain individual who was deemed instrumental in Our Mother-Homeland's plans for self-defense against the imperialism of the West.

The man I am referring to was a former German scientist, Heinrich Dieter, then aged forty-seven.

Comrade Dieter was born in Obernessa, Weissenfels, the son of a professor of mathematics. His mother was a teacher of science at a boarding school near her husband's university. Comrade Dieter had one brother, his junior by three years. Comrade Dieter studied physics at the Martin Luther University of Halle-Wittenberg, which awarded him a bachelor's of science degree, and he received a master's of science in physics from Leopold Franzens University of Innsbruck. He completed his doctorate work in physics shortly thereafter at the University of Berlin. He specialized in column ionization of alpha particles. No, Comrade General, I too was not familiar with this esoteric subject, but as you will see in a moment, his discipline of study was to have quite some significant consequences.

While in school he joined the student branch of the Social Democratic Party of Germany (SPD) and the Reichsbanner Schwarz-Rot-Gold, which served as the party's paramilitary wing. But he quit these organizations after a time, as he showed little interest in politics, preferring to spend the hours in the classroom or laboratory. He was, it is asserted, part Jew, and accordingly could not join the Nazi Party. However, since he appeared apolitical and did not openly practice his religion, he was permitted to maintain his teaching and research posts. That leniency on the part of the Nazis could also be attributed to his brilliance; Albert Einstein himself said of Comrade Dieter that he had a formidable mind and was, rare among scientists, a man who could appreciate both the theoretical and the applicable aspects of physics.

When the Dieter family observed that people like themselves— intellectuals of Jewish heritage—would be at risk in Germany, they made plans to emigrate. Dieter's parents and brother (and his family) successfully traveled from Berlin to England and from there to America, but Comrade Dieter, delayed in finishing a research project, was stopped on the eve of his departure by the Gestapo, based on a professor's recommendation that he be pressed into service to assist in the war effort. Owing to his research (concerning the aforementioned "alpha particles"), Comrade Dieter was assigned to assist with the development of the most significant weapon of our century: the atomic bomb.

He was part of the second Uranverein, the Nazi uranium project, jointly run by the HWA, the Army Ordnance Office, and RFR, the Reich Research Council of the Ministry of Education. His contributions were significant, though he did not advance far in rank or salary owing to his Jewish background.

Following Our Mother-Homeland's victory over the Nazis in the Great Patriotic War, Comrade Dieter was identified as one of the Uranverein scientists by our NKVD's Alsos Project officers in Germany. After fruitful discussions with the security officers, Comrade Dieter volunteered to come to the Soviet Union and continue his research into atomic weapons—now for the benefit of Our Mother-Homeland. He stated that he considered it an honor to assist in protecting against the West's aggression and their attempts to spread the poisonous hegemony of capitalism and decadence throughout Europe, Asia, and the world.

Comrade Dieter was transported immediately to Russia and underwent a period of reeducation and indoctrination. He became a member of the Communist Party, learned to speak Russian, and was helped to understand the lessons of the Revolution and the value of the Proletariat. He fervently embraced Our Mother-Homeland's culture and people. Once this period of transition was completed he was assigned work at the All-Union Scientific Research Institute of Experimental Physics at the premier Atomograd in the nation: the closed city of Arzamas-16. It was to here that I was sent and assigned the job of protecting him.

I spent much time with Comrade Dieter and can report that he took to his work immediately, and his contributions were many, including assisting in the preparation of Our Mother-Homeland's first hydrogen bomb, detonated last August, you may recall, Comrade General. That test, the RDS-6, was a device of 400 kilotons. Comrade Dieter's team had recently been working to create a fissile device in the megaton range, as the Americans have done (though it is well known that their weapons are in all ways inferior to ours).

Like most such extranational scientists vital to our national defense, Comrade Dieter was closely watched. One of my duties was to take measure of his personal loyalty to Our Mother-Homeland and report on same to all relevant ministries. My scrupulous observations convinced me of his devotion to our cause and that his loyalty was beyond reproach.

For instance, he was, as I mention, part Jew. Now, he knew that I had denounced certain men and women in Arzamas-16 for subversive and counterrevolutionary speech and activity; every one of those happened to be, by purest coincidence, a Jew. I inquired of Comrade Dieter if he was troubled by my actions and he assured me that no, he would have done the same had anyone, friends or family, Jew or gentile, displayed even a whisper of anti-Revolutionary leaning. To prove that I harbored no ill will against the Children of David, I explained that one of my former assignments was identifying Jews as part of the ongoing Central Committee's program to resettle his people in the newly formed State of Israel as expeditiously as possible. He expressed to me his pleasure at learning this fact.

Comrade Dieter had no wife, and I would arrange "chance meetings" between him and beautiful women, with the goal that he take a Russian-born wife. (This did not occur, but he did have relations with some of them for varying lengths of time.) Each of these women reported to me in detail about their conversations, and not a single word of disloyalty ever passed Comrade Dieter's lips when speaking with them, even in moments that he believed were wholly unguarded.

Further, I can hardly count the many times when he and I would sit with a bottle of vodka, and I would regale him at length and in great detail about the philosophy of Marxist dialectic materialism, reading long passages. As his Russian was good but not perfect, I would also read to him the lengthy reports of speeches by noble Chairman Khrushchev, as they appeared in *Pravda*. He took great interest in what I read to him.

His loyalty was evident to me in one other aspect of his life: his passion for art.

A love of painting and sculpture was a tradition in his family, he explained; his brother was a professor of art history at a university in upstate New York, and that brother's daughter, Comrade Dieter's niece, is a painter (and dancer) in the city of Manhattan. When he finally received permission from the Party to correspond with his family, all his letters were carefully vetted by me to make certain that nothing impugned the state or hinted at disloyalty (much less discussed his work). The subject was exclusively his, and his family's, love of art.

He described the rousing art scene here in Our Mother-Homeland, extolling the Soviet artists who labor to further the goals of the Revolution. He wrote glowingly to his family about the "Socialist Realist" movement that has typified our culture since the days of Comrade Lenin: paintings that are not only brilliantly executed but embrace the four pillars of Our Mother-Homeland values: Party-mindedness, ideology-mindedness, class-content, and truthfulness. Among the art that he sent to his family were a postcard of a landscape by Dmitry Maevsky, another card of a thoughtful portrait by Vladimir Alexandrovich Gorb (of the famed Repin Institute of Art), and a poster announcing a forthcoming Party Congress, which Comrade Dieter himself would be attending, illustrated with the rousing *Trumpeter and Standard-bearer* by Mitrofan Grekov, a work, of course, much revered by all patriotic countrymen.

His brother in return would send postcards or small posters of paintings that he believed Comrade Dieter might enjoy and that he might use to decorate his quarters. These cards, like the letters themselves, were vetted by the GRU technical division and found to contain no secret messages, microfilm, etc., though I did not think that likely. My concern with these gifts, for concern there was, Comrade General, lay elsewhere.

You are perhaps aware of the American Central Intelligence Agency's International Organizations Division. This insidious directorate (which the GRU was the first to uncover, I must add) has in recent years attempted to use art as a weapon—by promoting the incoherent and decadent American "abstract expression-ism" to the world. This absurd defacing of canvases, by the likes of Jackson Pollock, Robert Motherwell, Willem de Kooning, and Mark Rothko, is considered by true connoisseurs of art to be sacri-lege. Had these men (and the occasional woman) committed such self-indulgence here, they would find themselves under arrest. The International Organizations Division is the CIA's pathetic attempt to proclaim that the West values freedom of expression and cre-ativity while Our Mother-Homeland does not. This is, on its face, absurd. Why, even the American president Harry Truman said of the abstract expressionist movement, "If that's art, then I'm a Hot-tentot."

But I was vastly relieved to note that Comrade Dieter's family —and obviously he—also rejected such nonsensical travesty. The paintings and sketches they sent him were realistic works that dis-played traditional composition and themes not incompatible with those of the Revolution—by such Americans as Frederick Reming-ton, George Innes, and Edward Hopper, as well as classic painters like the Italian Jacopo Vignali.

Indeed, some of the reproductions sent to Comrade Dieter were tantamount to agitprop supporting the values of Our Moth-er-Homeland! The Jerome Myers paintings, for instance, of immi-grants struggling on the streets of New York, and those of Otto Dix, the German, whose paintings mocked the decadence of the Weimar Republic.

If ever anyone seemed enamored of his adopted home, it was Comrade Dieter. No, my instincts as an intelligence officer told me that if there were any risk regarding this singular man, it would not be his loyalty but that foreign agents or counterrevolutionaries would attempt to murder him, in an effort to derail Our Moth-er-Homeland's efforts in the field of atomic weapons. Protecting him from such harm became my whole life, and I made certain he was protected at all times.

Now, having "set the stage," Comrade General Tasarich, I must turn to the unfortunate incident of 10 November of this year.

Comrade Dieter was active in the Party and attended Party Con-gresses and rallies whenever he could. These, however, were rare in the closed city of Arzamas-16 and so he would occasionally travel to larger metropolises in Russia or other nations within the Soviet Union to attend these events. One such gathering was that which

I had mentioned earlier—described in the poster illustrated by the artist Grekov: the Joint Party Congress in Berlin, scheduled for November of this year, at which First Secretary Khrushchev and East German prime minister Otto Grotewohl would speak. The Congress would celebrate East Germany's recent autonomy, and it was anticipated that plans would be announced for allegiances between the two nations. Everyone in Our Mother-Homeland was curious what direction the relationship between these former enemies would take.

I set about to make secure arrangements for the travel, contacting the MVD, Ministry of Internal Affairs, and the newly formed KGB, Committee for State Security. I wished to know if they had any intelligence of potential threats to Soviet citizens at the Congress and any word regarding risks to Comrade Dieter specifically. They said no, there was no such intelligence. Still, I proceeded as if there could well be a threat. I would not accompany him alone but would be aided by a KGB security officer, Lieutenant Nikolai Alesov. Both of us would be armed. Further, we would work closely with the Stasi (I am no fan of the East German secret police, but one can hardly argue with their—dare I say ruthless?—efficiency).

Our instructions—from both GRU command and Our Mother-Homeland state security ministers—were to insure that Comrade Dieter was at no point in danger from counterrevolutionaries or foreign agents—and from criminals too, Berlin, of course, being well known as a hotbed of illegal activity perpetrated by the Roma, Catholics, and Jews that have not been relocated.

We had additional orders too. If it turned out that Western agents or counterrevolutionaries made a move to kidnap Comrade Dieter, we were to make sure that "he was not able to supply our enemies with any classified information about the weapons program."

Our superiors did not elaborate, but it was clear what they meant.

I will be honest, Comrade General, that though I would have had some regrets, if the matter came down to it, I knew I could kill Comrade Dieter to prevent him from falling into the hands of Our Mother-Homeland's foes.

Arrangements thus made, on 9 November, the day before the Congress, we flew in a military aircraft to Warsaw and then took a train to Berlin. There, quarters had been arranged for us in Pankow, not far from Schönhausen Palace. It was a most elegant area, finer than any I had ever seen. As the conference was not until the next day, the three of us—myself, Comrade Dieter, and Comrade Security Officer Alesov—attended the ballet in the evening (an acceptable version of *Swan Lake,* not up to the standards of the Bolshoi). After the performance we dined in a French restaurant (and joked that we need not use atomic bombs on the West; it will gorge itself to death!). We had cigarettes and brandy at the hotel and then retired. Comrade Alesov and I took turns remaining awake and guarding Comrade Dieter's door. The Stasi had searched the hotel for threats and assured us that the identities of every guest checked out satisfactorily.

Indeed, no danger presented itself that night. I must say, however, that despite the absence of hostile actors I got little sleep. This was not due to my duties in safeguarding Comrade Dieter, but rather because I kept thinking this: I am in the country of men who, just a few years earlier, had so viciously slaughtered so many of my fellow soldiers and who had wounded me. And yet here we were, each embracing nearly identical ideals. Such is the universal lesson of the Revolution and the invincibility of the Proletariat. Surely Our Mother-Homeland would conquer the world and live for a thousand years!

The next morning we attended the Party Congress, which proved to be a truly rousing event! Oh, what an honor to see First Secretary Khrushchev in person, as "The Internationale" played and men and women cheered and waved crimson flags. Half of East Berlin seemed to be present! Speech after speech followed —six hours, without stop. At the conclusion, we left in rousing spirits and, accompanied by a somber, weasel-faced Stasi agent, dined at a bierhaus. We then returned to the station to await the overnight train to Warsaw, where the secret police officer bade us farewell.

This station was the scene of the incident about which I'm writing.

We were seated in the departure lounge, which was quite crowded. As we read and smoked, Comrade Dieter set down his newspaper and stood, explaining that he was going to use the toilet before the train. The KGB agent and I of course accompanied him.

As we walked toward the facilities I noted nearby a middle-aged couple. The woman was sitting with a book in her lap. She wore a rose-colored dress. A man in trousers, shirt, and waistcoat stood beside her, smoking a cigarette. He was looking out the window. Curiously, on this chill evening, neither wore a coat or hat. I reflected that there was something familiar about them, though I could hardly place what it might be.

Suddenly Comrade Dieter changed direction and walked directly toward the couple. He whispered some words to them, nodding toward myself and Comrade Alesov.

I was immediately alarmed, but before I could react, the woman lifted her book, beneath which she was hiding a pistol! She gripped the Walther and pointed it at me and Alesov as the jacketless man pulled Comrade Dieter away. In American-accented Russian, she told us to throw our weapons to the floor. Comrade Alesov and I, however, drew ours. The woman fired twice—killing Comrade Alesov and wounding me, causing my pistol to fly from my grip, and I dropped to my knees in pain.

But immediately I rose, retrieved the gun, and, preparing to shoot with my left hand, ran outside, ignoring my pain and without regard to my own personal safety. But I was too late; the agents, along with Comrade Dieter, were gone.

At the train station the Criminal Investigations Directorate of the National People's Army and the Stasi investigated, but it was only a halfhearted affair—this was a matter between the West and Russia; no East Germans were involved. Indeed, they seemed to suspect that I myself had killed Comrade Alesov, as no witnesses were willing to come forth and describe what actually happened. The Stasi offered no justification for this theory other than the incredulity that a middle-aged woman would perpetrate such a crime . . . although of course the true answer is that it is easier to arrest a bird in the hand than go tramping through the bush in search of the real perpetrator—especially when that bird is in the employ of a rival security agency. That is, myself.

After two days they concluded that I was innocent, though they treated me like the worst Nonperson imaginable! I was escorted to the Polish border and ignominiously deposited there, where I had to beg the local—and extremely uncooperative—police for transportation to Warsaw for a flight to Moscow, despite my shoving my credentials as a senior member of the Russian intelligence corps into the face of everyone in uniform!

Upon my return home, I was attended to in hospital for my gunshot wound. Once released, I was asked to prepare a statement for your Committee, Comrade General, describing my recollection of the events of 10 November.

Accordingly, I am submitting this report to you now.

It is clear to me now that the spiriting away of Comrade Dieter was an operation by the Central Intelligence Agency in Washington, D.C., and carried out with the help of Comrade Dieter's brother and niece. It seems that the family's love of art was a fabrication. The reference to such an interest in the first letter sent by Comrade Dieter to America put his family on notice that he had come upon a way to communicate clandestinely with the intelligence agencies in the United States, in hopes of effecting his escape to the West. His brother and niece were not, as it now seems, involved in the arts at all but are, in their own rights, well-established scientists.

The CIA agents contacted by Comrade Dieter's brother were, without doubt, the ones who sent him the postcards depicting the paintings I referred to above. But they were not random choices; each painting had a meaning, which Dieter was able to work out. My thinking is that the messages were along these lines:

- The painting by Jacopo Vignali, a seventeenth-century artist, of the Archangel Michael saving souls near death told him that the Americans did indeed wish to rescue him from life here in Our Mother-Homeland.
- The Frederick Remington painting called *The Trooper* depicted a man armed with a gun—meaning force would be involved in the rescue.
- The George Innes painting depicted the idyllic land of the New York valley, which is where his brother lived—the image beckoning him to join them.
- The message of "immigrating," that is, fleeing from East to West, could be found in the Jerome Myers work of the tenements of New York City.

You will recall that among the paintings that Comrade Dieter himself sent to America was the poster incorporating Grekov's painting. The point of that missive was not the illustration itself but the details of the Party Congress in East Berlin. The CIA rightly took this to mean that Comrade Dieter would be present at the event. Western agents in Berlin could easily have surveyed hotels and train ticket records and confirmed when he, and his guards, would depart from East Berlin and from which station.

The Otto Dix postcard—of scenes in Germany—was the penultimate sent to Comrade Dieter from America, and it confirmed that Berlin was in fact acceptable as the site of the contact with Western agents. The last postcard sent to Comrade Dieter was the most significant of all—the Edward Hopper painting.

This canvas was entitled *Hotel by a Railroad* and it showed two people: a middle-aged woman in a rose-colored dress, reading a book, and man without a jacket or hat, looking out the window. (This is why the couple in the station struck me as familiar; I had seen the postcard of the Hopper painting not long before.) This image informed Comrade Dieter how he might recognize the agents in East Berlin who would effect his escape, as they would be dressed in the garb of the people in Hopper's painting and affecting the same pose.

I have described how the abduction occurred. I have learned since then that, following the shooting in the station, a waiting car outside drove the two operatives and Comrade Dieter to a secret location in East Berlin, where they crossed to the West undetected. From there an American Air Force plane flew Comrade Dieter to London and then onward to the United States.

This is my recollection and assessment of the incident of 10 November 1954, Comrade General, and the events leading up to it.

I am aware of the letter from the Minister of State Security which states the KGB's position that I am solely at fault for the escape of Comrade Dieter from Our Mother-Homeland and his flight to America, as well as the death of Comrade Alesov. It is claimed that I did not appreciate Comrade Dieter's true nature: that he was not, in fact, a loyal member of the Party, nor did he feel any allegiance to Our Mother-Homeland. Rather, he was simply feigning, while spending his hours learning what he might about our atomic bomb projects and awaiting the day when an escape to the West might be feasible.

Further, the letter asserts, I did not anticipate the plot that was concocted to effect such escape.

I can say in my defense only that Comrade Dieter's subterfuge and his plan—communicating with the West through the use of artworks—were marks of genius, a strategy that I submit even the most seasoned intelligence officer, such as myself, could never discover.

Comrade Dieter was, as I say, a most singular man.

Accordingly, Comrade General Tasarich, I humbly beseech you to petition First Secretary Khrushchev, a former soldier like myself, to intervene on my behalf at my forthcoming trial and reject the KGB's recommendation that I be sentenced to an indefinite term of imprisonment in the east for my part in this tragic incident.

Whatever my fate, however, please know that my devotion to the first secretary, to the Party, and to Our Mother-Homeland is undiminished and as immortal as the ideals of the Glorious Revolution.

I remain, yours in loyalty,

Mikhail Sergeyevich Sidorov
Lubyanka Prison, Moscow

BRENDAN DuBOIS

The Man from Away

FROM *Ellery Queen Mystery Magazine*

A MONTH AFTER the incident, Amos Wilson drove two hours
from his rural home to a Barnes & Noble in Manchester, the state's
largest city. He parked his old Ford F-150 pickup truck and walked
to the front entrance, John Deere cap pulled down low on his head.
Everything around him was concrete and asphalt and roadways and
traffic lights, and the steady roar of cars and trucks, and jets coming
in overhead to land at the Manchester airport. He had to be here,
but he didn't like being here.

Inside, the store was bright and well lit, and the sheer number
of books stretching out before him overwhelmed him. Never in
his life had he seen so many books. Yet he ignored all the books
and wandered until he found what he was looking for, a shelf that
offered detailed city maps. He picked up one titled *Boston and Vicinity*. It was thick and folded out nearly as wide as he could stretch
his arms. He went out to the front counter, waited patiently until
his turn came up.

The clerk was a pretty young girl about twenty or so, with tattoos
of flowers on her neck and a pierced ring through her left nostril,
wearing a black T-shirt and blue jeans. He passed the map over.
"Ma'am, I'd like to purchase this map, but I want to make sure it's
a good one."

She smiled but looked puzzled. "I'm sorry, I don't understand
the question."

Amos prodded the map with a finger that had black dirt en-
crusted under the fingernail. "Sorry, I guess I didn't speak clearly.
You think this map has what it says? Every single street?"

"I'm sure it does," she said. "Of course, if you want to be really sure, you should just check out Google Street View. You can even see what the buildings look like."

Amos took out his wallet. "I suppose you're right, but I don't own a computer. Wouldn't even know how to use one. But I sure know how to look at maps."

A month earlier, Amos Wilson had stopped at the Leah Hardware store to pick up some washers to fix a leaking faucet. Jimmy Stark, the store's owner, greeted Amos as he made his way to the cluttered checkout.

Jimmy wore blue-jean overalls with the front bib pocket stuffed with pencils, pens, and a folding ruler. He had big ears and a big nose, black-rimmed glasses, and thick black hair parted to one side. He weighed nearly three hundred pounds and sat on a stool, and he knew where everything in the store was located down to the half-inch, which is why he was still thriving in the age of Lowe's and Home Depot superstores.

He squinted as Amos put the washers down. "Faucet problems?"

"Yep."

"At the lake house?"

"The same."

Jimmy shook his head as he rung up the purchase. "I don't know why you stick with Jennifer."

"She's my wife."

"That'll be a dollar nine cents. Amos, please, she kicked you out."

He shrugged, having heard these same words about a dozen times before. "She said she wanted to take a break."

"It's been a year."

"She might change her mind."

"No, because she doesn't like to think she's wrong. Like she made a mistake when she agreed to marry you. Amos, you're a good man, but you're gullible."

"Jimmy . . ."

With his thick fingers, Jimmy deftly put the purchase in a small paper sack. "You were the star high school quarterback, good with your hands, your dad was rich and ailing . . . and she thought when he passed on she'd be the richest gal in the county. Poor dear, she had no idea he was gonna leave his entire estate to charity."

"Not the whole thing. We get an annuity."

"Yeah, but not enough for Jennifer to live above her means. Course, now that she's in the lake house and you're in your dad's hunting cabin, I'd say she's got what she wants."

"Maybe."

"But she sure is lucky, still having you as a husband. Any other man would have filed divorce papers, would have gotten half that annuity back."

Amos picked up the bag. "Guess I'm not any other man."

Outside in the small parking lot, Amos went to one of the very few pay phones still operating in Leah. He dialed the lake-house number and Jennifer answered on the second ring.

"It's Amos," he said. "I've got the washers, I'll be over there in twenty minutes."

"You'll have to come back later," she said. "I'm having lunch with Marie and the girls. Won't be back for a couple of hours."

"I could do it while you're away."

"No offense, Amos, I don't want you at the house when I'm not there."

The phone receiver was cool in his hand. "My name's still on the deed. Still my house."

"Legally, I'm sure, but let's not make a fuss, all right? I'll see you at two p.m. Don't be early."

She hung up the phone.

Amos drove away from the lake where he had grown up, going to where he was currently hanging his hat. It was a simple one-story cottage deep in the woods, shingled roof, rough wooden sides. It was a place where Dad had taken him years back, when he had turned twelve. This was where he sipped his first beer, first stayed up past midnight, and shot his first white-tailed deer. One of Dad's cousins had presented him with a sharp knife that he had used to gut his first kill, and, years later, he still always carried that knife.

He got out of the truck, ambled over to the camp. Overhead was a mix of maples and birches. The place got its hot water and heat from propane tanks, but it was still Christly cold in the winter. Not to mention that the dirt road became a sloppy mess every mud season.

Amos took a wicker rocking chair on the creaking porch and settled in. It was a nice sunny day.

He remembered what Jennifer had said, just over a year ago.

I don't know what I want, but right now I don't want you. Amos, it's time for you to go up to your dad's place.

Are you sure?

Damn it, of course I'm sure. I'm unhappy and I don't want you here.

But what about me? My . . . happiness?

She had snorted. *It's all about you, isn't it?*

He didn't know what to say to that, so he had quietly packed up a duffel bag and driven up to this cabin, and here he remained.

Amos stayed on the porch until it was near two o'clock before leaving for the lake house.

When he walked in, Jennifer called out from the bedroom, "Damn it, Amos, I told you I wanted you to knock! I don't want you surprising me like this."

He said, "I didn't think I was surprising you. You said come back at two o'clock. It's two o'clock."

"Oh," came her voice again. "Looking for a fight, are we?"

What to say about that? He pretended not to hear her and went to the kitchen, the spare washers in one hand, his toolkit in the other. He drew out a length of paper towel and put it on the floor, so no grease or dirt from the toolkit would mark up the shiny tiles.

"Hey."

He turned around. His wife was standing there in the living room, looking right at him, and his heart went *thump-a-lump*, just like it had a number of years back when she had said yes after he first asked her out. She had on tight black Spandex shorts, black rubber boat shoes, a black sports bra, and a white baseball cap that she had pulled her blond ponytail through. She was putting lip moisturizer on and smelled of sunscreen.

"I'm going out for a paddle, work off some of that lunch. Let's go."

He put the toolkit down, followed her outside to the small lawn that bordered the lakeshore and to the tiny boathouse. She opened the door and he walked in, past the lawn mower, some piled-up lawn furniture, and other odds and ends. The light-blue kayak hung from a web cradle, and he got on one end while she got on the other.

The two of them marched in silence down to the water's edge.

Once upon a time, before his dad passed on, she'd talk about who she lunched with, whose kid was acting up, whose hubby was coming home drunk every other night. The silence stayed firm all the way to the lake. He held the kayak steady while she clambered in, and then he passed over a plastic canteen of water, her paddle, and a life preserver that was on the grass. Jennifer was an excellent swimmer, but the law was the law: there had to be a PFD aboard.

He stood back. "How long will you be gone?"

"As long as I want."

"Oh."

She adjusted her sunglasses and he paused, took a breath. "Jennifer?"

"What?" she said, staring out at the open lake, still fiddling with the sunglass cord.

"Do you think I'm gullible?"

A smile slowly spread across her face and then was just as quickly erased. She turned, and he couldn't see her eyes because of the sunglasses. "Of course not . . ."

"Oh."

She pushed off and said, "Oh, if you could. Check the refrigerator. I think I'm low on one-percent milk. Will you take care of that before you leave?"

"Sure."

He watched her paddle out to the channel leading to the main lake. Williams Lake was shaped like a pair of spectacles, two wide bodies of water separated by the channel. The only place to put in your speedboat or canoe or Jet Ski was on the north body of water, which had lots of small islands and barely concealed boulders. Most boaters preferred the south end of the lake, which was deeper and relatively empty, so they could raise hell and tow water-skiers. Which meant that there was always a steady stream of boats and such traveling through the channel.

Another memory came to him.

I can't live like this. We don't have enough money.

Yes we do, hon. The annuity pays all of our bills and I can pick up extra money doing handyman work and—

Do you think I married you because I wanted a handyman? Do you? I want more, and you can't provide it, Amos. You just can't.

But . . . I love you, Jennifer. I'll take care of you.

No, she had said. *If you really love me, you'd fight your dad's will, get the money that belongs to us. That's what you would do if you really loved me.*

Amos watched her paddle for another minute or two and then headed back to the lake house.

About two yards later there was the sudden roar of engines and the slamming sound of something being shattered.

Amos started running to shore even before he knew what was going on. There were two Jet Skis going around in circles, throwing up waves and water spouts from the exhausts. Each Jet Ski had one driver—a young guy with a PFD and wearing sunglasses—and one Jet Ski was bright red and the other was dark blue with yellow lightning bolts along the side.

One driver shouted to the other—he had a long nose and was on the Jet Ski with the lightning bolts—and then the two of them sped back down the channel, heading to the north end of Williams Lake, where the put-in was located.

They moved fast, ignoring the NO WAKE buoys, engines roaring.

Jennifer's kayak floated in the channel, overturned, split in half.

He got to the lake's edge before remembering his heavy Timberland boots. He stood on one foot while trying to get the boot off the other. Waves slapped and crisscrossed over the channel. Other residents were coming to the end of their docks. Amos worked and worked at the boots, and called out "Jennifer!"

No answer.

Boots off, he stripped off his blue jeans, knowing the lake water would make them sopping wet and heavy in seconds, slow him down. He wasn't much of a swimmer and hated going into the lake when it was cold, but he didn't hesitate. He thrashed his way in, started swimming, wearing his T-shirt, underwear, white tube socks, and nothing else.

"Jennifer!"

In his peripheral vision he saw motorboats and even two canoes coming his way. His neighbors, his friends, his townspeople.

"Jennifer!"

He reached one end of the kayak. It was smashed through, the fiberglass end as sharp as a saw. Her paddle was floating by, and her life jacket, and her water bottle. He breathed hard, swam over to the other floating part of the kayak.

She was there, tangled up in her seat, her face barely out of water. "Jennifer!"

Her eyes fluttered open. Her face was gray. Her hat was gone. Her blond hair was floating behind her like an opened Chinese fan.

"Amos . . ."

"Don't you worry, I'll get you out."

"Amos . . . I'm so cold . . . do something, will you?"

She closed her eyes. He managed to get her free, and he treaded water as he looked and looked at what had happened to her.

"Hey!" came a voice from the near canoeist. "Me and the missus, we called 911. Can we help?"

Amos took a breath, kept treading water, tried to speak plainly without choking up. "Her arm," he said. "Can you help me find her arm?"

Three days later he was at the lake house, going through his closet in the master bedroom — the smallest one, of course, since Jennifer had wanted the bigger one — and he took out a black two-piece suit, which he had only worn three times before: for his Uncle John, for Mom, and for Dad.

The funeral took place at the Congregational church, just past the town common, and a couple of friends of Jennifer set up a get-together at the American Legion Hall afterward. There was an open bar and a glass bowl with a mix of ginger ale and Hawaiian Punch, and some chicken salad and tuna salad finger sandwiches. Amos was an only child, so there wasn't much in the way of relations to talk to him, which was fine. He had a Sam Adams beer and stayed away from the sandwiches.

He hated finger sandwiches.

Amos was halfway through his second beer when Chief Bobby Makem came up to him.

"Wish I had better news, Amos, but I don't," Makem said. He was a slim fellow, with bright red hair, about five years older than Amos, married with two kids. His wife, Erin, was working the punch bowl. He had on his dark-blue police chief uniform with two stars on each side of his collar.

"I understand."

"Them fellows were from away, we're sure, but nobody remembers them much from when they put their Jet Skis in at the town beach. You know how the place gets so crowded with sunbathers and swimmers and people dropping off boats, it's like that Times Square place each New Year's."

"Yeah," Amos said.

"All we know is that they're from Massachusetts. We talked to stores up and down Route 16 near here, see if anybody remembers seeing them stopping by to pick up gas or beer, but nope, nothing."

"Sounds pretty thorough."

Chief Makem sighed, gave him a gentle slap on the shoulder. "Don't you worry none, we'll keep working this case. You can count on it."

Amos said, "I'm not going to worry about that."

At some point the air inside got stifling, so he went outside. By the rear dumpsters a few guys were hanging around, smoking, and there was Jimmy Stark from the hardware store, Bob Junson from Junson's Funeral Parlor, Trent Gage—who was in Amos's class all through twelve years of school—and a bunch of others. They nodded respectfully to him as he came over, and he said to Bob, "That was a right fine service you did, Bob. I appreciate it."

Bob had the brown eyes and saggy jowls of a bloodhound, and his black suit was finely cut. "Just so sorry I had to do it, Amos. She was too young to be taken away so quickly."

At that everybody nodded and murmured some words, and after a few minutes they went back to talking about the weather, the Red Sox, and those damn tourists. When Amos decided to step back in and thank the ladies for the spread they had put on in Jennifer's memory, Trent Gage spoke up. Trent owned a card and gift shop that was rumored to be selling a lot of nontobacco cigarettes under the table, which wasn't Amos's concern.

"Amos, you always hate to speak ill of the dead, but . . . well, I wish you the best in your new life."

Amos turned back. "What do you mean by that?"

Trent grinned at the other guys like he was looking for support. "You know . . . you're a fine fellow, Amos, but you're gullible. Jennifer just took advantage of you, always did."

"I don't know about that," he said. "She was my wife."

Trent kept on smiling. "Maybe so, but c'mon . . . she could be a bitch on wheels most times. Now that she's gone . . . well, you got a new life."

Amos strolled over and punched hard, breaking Trent Gage's nose. His right hand stung and was suddenly numb. Trent fell flat on the ground, and when he stopped moaning, Amos leaned over. "Thanks for the kind wishes."

A couple of weeks passed and Amos didn't feel right moving back into the lake house. So he stayed at the hunting camp and did a job for Paul Sytek, who needed some fine oak logs cut into four-foot lengths. He spent three weeks up there, working hard, hard enough so he could sleep well during the night. Every other day he called Chief Makem, and every other day he got the same answer. Nothing new to report.

After the third week had passed, the chief had one more thing to add.

"Amos . . . in an investigation when someone gets killed, the first forty-eight hours are the most important."

"Yeah, I've heard that."

"We've gone way beyond those forty-eight hours. I don't want to sugarcoat it none."

"I know, Chief."

"So unless we get a break in the case, a new witness, somebody confessing, I don't know how much we can do. And even if we do make some progress, I'm not sure what the operator could be charged with. Manslaughter, possibly, and leaving the scene of an accident, but even then, a crafty lawyer, he could say, *Prove it, prove the owner of that Jet Ski was the guy driving that day.*"

Amos kept his mouth shut. He could hear the chief breathing on the other end.

"So," the chief said. "That's how it is."

"Appreciate the heads-up," Amos said, and he hung up the phone.

The next day he went to the town hall, where sweet Pam Grissom, the town clerk, fussed over him and gave him copies of tax records and survey maps for free. Amos gave her his deep thanks and went to the lake house. There were some dead floral arrangements in the screened-in porch from Jennifer's school friends and the local beauty parlor.

Amos sat at the end of the dock. A beautiful day. Up a ways, some kids were screeching with joy as they jumped in the water. A man in a high-powered trout-fishing boat rumbled by, gave Amos a wave, and he waved back. A pontoon boat also slowly motored through, and a couple of bikinied cuties out front gave him a shout and a wave, and Amos blushed and lowered his head.

He studied the survey map and noted the names of everyone who lived on property abutting this channel and the north end of the lake. Lots of names. That was okay. He double-checked the list and then triple-checked the list, and then he was done.

Amos went into the lake house one last time, and took the dead floral arrangements and tossed them into the woods.

Over the next two weeks Amos patiently worked down the list of names, making sure to talk to someone from each house. At every door, porch, or dock, he would introduce himself and say, *I'm hoping you might be able to help me. I'm trying to get some information on the two Jet Skis that run down my wife and killed her. Do you remember seeing them that day?*

He got a lot of sympathetic noes, a few lunches, a couple of beers, and a dinner offer from a sweet blond divorcée who lived on Powder Mill Road—she said, *You're such a good man, Amos*—but nothing helpful. Abe Goshen, who was on his kayak that day, said he remembered seeing two fellas roar back to the beach and get their Jet Skis on a trailer attached to a big black Chevy pickup truck with Massachusetts plates, and that was that.

He also kept up working on Paul Sytek's property, cutting up lengths of aged oak, and Paul was patient when Amos didn't put in too many hours, since Paul knew what Amos was up to. Paul said he was getting along in years and couldn't move much, but he was right happy with what Amos was doing.

On the fifteenth day of knocking on doors, Ralph Moran answered at the Cooper place, a nice fella who had retired here to do photo work of the mountains, foliage, loons, moose, and other nature stuff. The Cooper place was a simple cottage that had big wide windows up front, and Amos guessed that's why the photographer had purchased it. Ralph had a thick beard and wavy brown hair, and he said, "Well, yeah, I remember those two fellas."

"Where was they?"

Ralph crossed his arms. "Not on the lake."

"Excuse me?"

Ralph motioned with his head. "They was at Pat's Convenience

Grocer, the day of . . . when it happened. They was gassing up their Jet Skis, buying beer, goofing around, making a damn nuisance of themselves."

"I see. Was Pat working that day?"

"Oh, yeah, he was."

"Did you tell Chief Makem about this?"

"No, but Pat, I ran into him a couple of days later, and he said it had all been taken care of."

"I see." Amos extended his hand, which Ralph shook. "I'm in your debt, Ralph. Tell you what, this winter I can plow out your driveway for free."

Ralph blushed. "Ah, hell, Amos, you don't have to do that."

"Sure I do." And Amos left.

That evening he parked across from Pat's Convenience Grocer on Route 16. It had four gas pumps with a metal roof over the pumps, and the place sold beer, wine, soda, and lots of other stuff. It was a good place for tourists to hit before getting to the lake.

Amos checked his watch. It was near eight p.m., right when Pat Towler closed up. He got out and walked across the road, through the empty parking lot, and right into the store. The door jingled-jangled with bells on top, and Pat was behind the counter, surrounded by racks of cigarettes and state lottery tickets. Newspaper racks were to the right, carrying the weekly *Leah News* and newspapers from away, like the *New York Times*. There were shelves with narrow aisles, carrying canned goods and paper towels and such, and coolers on the far walls held beer and sodas.

"Hey, Amos, good to see you," Pat said. "Hope you're hangin' in there okay."

Pat was about Amos's age but plump and balding, always wearing black slacks and blue shirts with his store name stitched in white over the left breast pocket.

Amos went up to the counter. "Hey, Pat, I was wonderin' if I could have a moment."

"Sure, as long as it don't get me past closing time too much. What's up?"

"I was wonderin' if Chief Makem talked to you about his investigation."

Pat nodded. "Yep. Him and a state police detective. Told 'em I didn't know anything that could help them. Sorry."

Amos said, "Thanks for giving me a moment." He turned and said, "Hey, do you have any of those mini Hershey's bars, the ones with almonds? Boy, they sure make a good late-night snack."

Pat went around the counter. "I think we might have some—"

Amos went behind Pat and kicked hard, knocking his legs out from underneath him. Pat fell hard on his back, going "Oomph!" and Amos moved quickly, closing the deadbolt on the door, flipping the OPEN sign to CLOSED, and then reaching over the counter to slap at the nearest light switches. Most of the lights in the store shut off. Pat was rolled over on his side, trying to get up, and Amos kicked him hard in the ribs. Pat yelped and Amos sat down on his chest, making Pat gasp.

"Now I'll make this quick, Pat, 'cause you've always been nice to me and sent me a fine card after Jennifer got killed," Amos said, looking down at the man's red face. "So tell me about those two fellas from away who bought gas the day they run down my wife."

Pat squirmed and started to deny stuff, and Amos gave him two healthy slaps to the face. "Now that's not going to work, Pat, so tell me what you know. Now."

Pat was snuffling snot through his nose. "They was a couple of wild bucks, they was. I think they was already drunk. I had to put one of them in his place for goofing around the tittie magazines out back."

"So why didn't you tell this to the chief?"

More blubbering. "One of the bucks drove up the next day. Said to me it was all an accident, told me his lawyer said something about me having a verbal confidentiality agreement with him. I didn't know much about that 'cept he offered me a thousand bucks to keep my mouth shut. C'mon, Amos . . . it was an accident . . . and this has been a lousy summer . . . I can use the money . . ."

Amos said, "Those bucks paid with a credit card?"

Pat tried to nod with his head flat against the tile floor.

"Then you and me, we're getting up, and you're giving me that buck's name and address."

A few minutes later, sniffling, his face red, Pat passed over the man's name and address on the back of a used lottery ticket. "You gotta see it from my point of view, Amos. That guy from away scared me."

Amos took the ticket from Pat's trembling hand. "No offense, Pat, you should be more scared of me."

*

So two hours later on the day he purchased the map, Amos was in a
city called Chelsea, northeast of Boston. He was parked illegally on
Napoli Street, next to a fire hydrant, because it was the only open
space. He was breathing hard and his legs were quivering. Never
in his life had he been in traffic like this, not ever. He had heard
stories about the madness of Massachusetts drivers and the odd
way their roads were set up, but the reality was much worse. The
other drivers raced ten or twenty miles above the speed limit, saw
yellow lights as an invitation to speed through intersections, and
YIELD was obviously meant for the other guy. The road signs made
no sense — how could a highway be both I-95 South *and* Route 128
West? — and as he got deeper into Chelsea, lots of the intersections
had no signs whatsoever.

But finally he was on the street where Tony Conrad lived, Tony
Conrad who had paid for gas for his truck and his Jet Skis. How
could anybody live like this? The homes were all two-story and
were set on lots so tiny it looked like he could stand in the front
yard, stretch both arms, and touch his neighbors' fences. Oh, yeah,
fences . . . for nearly every house on this street had a chain-link
fence, no garage — what did they do when it snowed? — and almost
every house had a barred front door and barred windows.

Imagine that, living in fear of your neighbors.

A red car quickly drove by, low-slung, with bass speakers in the
rear thumping so hard it made his windshield quiver. He waited until the car turned the corner and then shifted his truck into drive.

Time to get to work.

He found a parking spot at a nightclub two blocks away. He walked
briskly along the cracked and bumpy sidewalks, glancing left and
right, left and right, all the way back to Tony Conrad's house. He
felt alone, out of place, and underneath his barn coat he had his
knife in a leather scabbard, and at his back his 9mm Sig Sauer P229
pistol. Carrying this pistol in Massachusetts was highly illegal.

Amos didn't care.

From most of the houses came a flickering blue glow from the
television sets or loud music, all mixing in with the constant roar of
traffic. Maybe all this noise and tight quarters explained why Massachusetts drivers acted so recklessly, either on a road or on a lake,
racing fast on their Jet Skis and leaving the scene of an accident.

Maybe.

He strolled by 10 Napoli Street, saw a black Chevrolet pickup truck in the narrow driveway, backed in so its front bumper was facing out. He caught a glimpse of a Red Sox game from a television inside the house. He reached the end of the block, took a deep breath, and then walked back.

It was on the walk back that he saw the covered shape in the rear yard, near a toolshed.

He went up through the little front lawn, ducked around the side, and was in the tiny backyard. There was a tall wooden fence at the rear, the toolshed, and the tarpaulin-covered shape. He spotted wheels underneath the shape. A trailer. Amos went to the rear of the shape, tugged up the tarpaulin.

Two Jet Skis.

He took out a small flashlight, switched it on. The first Jet Ski was red, and as he pulled the tarpaulin further, he found the second one, dark blue with yellow lightning bolts. He knelt and examined them closely. The red Jet Ski looked fine. The dark blue one with lightning bolts had a series of scrapes and gouges along one side, and there were smears of light-blue paint.

The same color as Jennifer's kayak.

His chest was cold and very tight.

He put the tarpaulin back and stood up.

A man's voice called out to him. "Hey!"

Amos put his hands in his coat pockets, mouth dry, knowing how exposed he was, and started walking quickly out of the backyard.

A spotlight on the side of the house flashed on, illuminating him and everything about with a stark light. A side door slammed, footsteps echoed on the wooden steps.

"Hey!"

Men came out of the house, quickly blocking him. He looked behind him. The tall wooden fence and other chain-link fences. No escape.

There were five men, three women, bustling around, staring at him. A man with a prominent nose and short black hair strolled right up. In the glare of the spotlight, Amos instantly recognized him: the operator of the blue Jet Ski who had run down and killed Jennifer.

"Hey, what are you doing here, hunh?"

Amos looked at the men backing him up, thought through all the options, shrugged, and said, "Sorry, I was taking a leak."

Another man said, "Christ, Tony, did you just hear that?"

"Yeah," the man with the nose said. "I sure did."

Tony Conrad, then. Right before him.

Tony stepped closer. Amos could smell beer and garlic on his breath. "Who the hell are you to piss in my backyard?"

"Nobody," Amos said. "I just had to go."

"Why my backyard, then?"

"It was dark," Amos said. "I have a shy bladder."

A nearby girl laughed. Tony poked Amos's chest. "That's so much crap. Who sent you? Hunh? The DeMint brothers? They send you here?"

"I don't know anybody named DeMint," Amos said, knowing he was strong and well armed, knowing it wouldn't work here and now. "I'm from New Hampshire."

One of the men laughed, and Tony laughed this time as well. "Stupid clodhopper. What are you doing in Chelsea anyway?"

"I got lost."

"I guess the hell you did," Tony said, backing away. "Sam, Paul, Gus . . . show this out-of-towner what happens to someone who pisses in my backyard."

Amos took a deep breath, clenched his jaw, and made sure to fall to the ground and moan loudly when the first punch was thrown.

A long time later he was in his truck, lights off, engine running, the heater gently blowing air over him, letting the pain flow through him. When the guys started whaling on him, Amos had made sure to cross his legs to protect his private parts and to cover the sides of his head with his arms, shielding his ears and eyes. He yelped a lot, even when it didn't sting so much, so they thought they was hurting him something awful. At some point they got bored or tired, and they went back into the house, laughing.

Now he rested, waiting. When the pain had drifted away some, he gingerly checked everything out, determined nothing was broken, nothing was bleeding much. Just some bruises and scrapes.

All right, then. The warm heater air felt good.

Eventually he turned everything off and slept in the front seat, best he could.

Next morning when he went back to Napoli Street, a couple of folks had left to go to work, leaving a few empty spots. He parked his truck behind a Volvo that hid him pretty well. Earlier he had gotten a takeout breakfast from a nearby McDonald's and he waited. And waited.

Funny, it was almost like hunting deer, hunting a human. You had to know its territory, its turf, and its habits, and you had to get into a zone, where you were looking and waiting and listening for that flash of white among the tree trunks, the snap of a branch, the rustle of something moving slowly through leaves.

Amos sipped his coffee. Course, it was easier to hunt a human. They didn't possess the same sense of smell and sight a deer had, where the slightest motion or noise would make a deer lift its white tail and fly quickly through the woods. And a human was so big and lumbering and slow, well, in some ways it t'weren't fair, not that Amos minded.

Tony got out of his house, turned, and briefly talked to a robe-wrapped woman by the door, then went to his truck, got in, and drove off.

Amos started his own truck and started following him.

It took less than an hour for Amos to make his move. At the first traffic light he stopped two car lengths behind Tony, took out a roll of duct tape from the glove compartment, tore off four three-foot lengths of tape, which he then placed on each arm and leg. Following Tony was easier than he imagined. Back in Leah it would be impossible to do this without being noticed in about five minutes or so, 'cause the roads were so empty. But here there were stop signs, traffic lights, traffic circles, and all the squabbling traffic to keep him hidden.

Tony stopped at a store to get a newspaper, another store for coffee, and then he met up with some guys in a parking lot in front of a closed-up supermarket. The four of them stood in a circle and there was a lot of talking and waving hands.

Then there was a round of handshakes, Tony got in his truck, and Amos followed him to a tiny town park, where he took one of two empty parking spaces and got out, again talking and waving his arms, except this time it was on a cell phone. Amos cautiously parked his truck next to Tony's, left the engine running, and got out. Tony had his back to him. Amos walked up, tapped him on the shoulder. Tony turned around, and before there was a hint of recognition on his face, Amos punched him hard in the throat. Done well—while missing the chin and the upper ribs—you could drop a guy and leave him literally speechless for nearly a half hour.

Amos did it well. Tony fell back on the thin lawn, and Amos worked quickly, binding his legs and arms with the duct tape. Then he went back to his truck, worked the limp form of Tony into the passenger's seat of his Ford, fastened the seat belt, and then got in himself.

He quietly backed out and joined the crowded morning traffic.

They were nearly in New Hampshire when Tony finally got his voice back, and they had been in the Granite State for about ten minutes when Tony stopped yelling, screaming, and cursing at Amos.

Tony took a deep, rattling breath. "You're working for the De-Mint brothers, aren't you?"

"Like I told you last night, I don't know anybody named De-Mint."

"Shit, yes . . . you're the guy we tuned up last night, for pissing in my backyard."

"Have to apologize for that," Amos said, feeling relaxed, driving on back-country roads that were so familiar and friendly. "That was a lie. I wasn't urinating on your property."

"Then . . . what the hell were you doing?"

"Checking out your Jet Skis."

"Why the hell were you checking out my Jet Skis?"

Amos glanced over at him. "Really? You need to ask that question? I'm from New Hampshire and I'm checking out your Jet Skis."

Tony pondered that and then spoke carefully. "Are you a cop?"

"No," Amos said. "I'm a husband."

They drove in silence for a few minutes. Tony said, "Look, man, I'm sorry. All right? It was an accident. I panicked, I didn't know what to do, I know it was bad, leaving the scene of an accident . . . but I was scared."

Amos said, "I saw you speed away after you run down my wife. That didn't look like you was panicking. And you coming by to give a thousand dollars to Pat Towler, to keep his mouth shut, well, that was on purpose, and you sure weren't scared, were you?"

Tony tried to move in his seat, not able to do much with the seat belt and harness across him, the duct tape tight against his wrists and ankles.

"What . . . what are you going to do?"

Amos said, "You killed my wife. What do you think?"

They were about a half hour away from Leah when Tony said, "Can we reach an understanding? A . . . settlement?"

"What do you have in mind?" Amos asked.

"Some . . . compensation, for what I did. Money exchanged, you go your way, I go mine, and it's settled."

"Sounds interesting. How much money were you thinking?"

"You first."

"Nope," Amos said. "Not playing games with you. If you were serious about making an offer, you'd do that straightaway."

"Maybe . . . maybe I'm concerned you might be insulted by whatever number I mentioned."

"There's a thought," Amos said.

A while later Tony changed tactics. "When I was talking to that store owner, what's-his-name, he told me a bit about your wife. No offense, really, mister, but he told me hardly anybody in your town liked her. That she was a real bitch, and that she was taking advantage of you, kicking you out of your lake house, making you live in a shack, run all sorts of errands."

Amos kept quiet.

"So . . . really. Why all the fuss? Like I said . . . we can reach an agreement, right here and now. What do you say?"

Amos glanced down at the speedometer, was pleased to see he was traveling at exactly the posted speed limit—forty miles an hour—without losing control and speeding. That would be unwise, giving a state trooper an excuse to pull him over.

"I say this," Amos said. "For all her faults . . . Jennifer was my wife. Under God and under the law. So no matter how she treated me or how many friends she had, she was still my wife. And . . . I can't let what you did go unpunished. It ain't right. I was her husband. Taking care of her and getting justice for her, that's my responsibility. And I ain't a man to walk away from my responsibilities."

"You really believe that?" the man asked, his voice quiet.

"I do." A quick glance to him. "And if you did too, well, you wouldn't be in my truck right now, trussed up like a turkey."

As they got closer to Leah, traveling the back roads, Tony tried again. "Mister . . . please. All right. I have to pay for what I did. I get that. So pull over to a police station, or make a phone call, and I'll let myself get arrested. Hell, I'll even confess. So what do you say, mister? Okay? You do that and we'll let the cops and the courts get justice for your wife."

"Her name was Jennifer."

"All right, justice for Jennifer."

Amos waited for about thirty seconds or so. "Well, that's tempting. The problem is, though, that's what you say now. But suppose the cops, you tell them something else? That I roughed you up and kidnapped you? Then I'd be the one in trouble, not you. And even if you did let yourself get arrested, well, I'm sure all it would take would be a smart lawyer fella working on your behalf, telling the jury that you panicked, it was an accident, not to mention, hey, there's no proof you were riding the Jet Ski. Maybe you let a friend borrow it, you forgot his name, that sort of thing, gives the jurors that thing . . . yeah, reasonable doubt."

"It was an accident!"

Amos turned again to his frightened passenger. "The channel 'tween the two lakes, it's got a half-dozen orange-and-white buoys, all sayin' the same thing. NO WAKE ZONE. If you had been following those signs, you would have missed my wife. She'd still be alive. No, it was no accident, and no, I'm not gonna turn you over to the police. It's my job, my responsibility."

"That's not fair!"

"Maybe so, but it is right," Amos said.

When they got into Leah, he skirted the downtown and drove up the country road that led to Paul Sytek's place, and then he took the old logging road that headed to where he had been doing the logging and other work. The way was bumpy and rough, and soon enough he came to a clearing that he'd made with all the weeks of cutting and chopping. He parked his Ford next to a cleared area that had a nice rectangular hole dug.

Amos got out, opened the door to the other side, undid the belt, and hauled out Tony. He pushed him into the dirt hole and he fell on his face. He squirmed around like a worm and then got up, dirt smeared over his face. His lower lip was trembling. He was crying.

"Please . . . God, please . . . don't do it . . ."

Amos took out his Sig Sauer. "It's gotta be done."

"Wait! Damn it, please wait!"

Amos waited.

The man sobbed. "Back in Chelsea ... I gotta girlfriend ... Monica ... she's pregnant ... I'm gonna be a dad ... please ... I know what I deserve ... but please ... you're a guy without a wife now ... and I'm sorry, Jesus, I'm sorry ... but will you do the same to Monica? Will you? And make my boy or my girl ... grow up without a dad?"

Amos waited.

Another round of sobs, the man's taped arms before him, his legs shaking, dirt smeared all over him from where he had fallen. "Please ... I'm begging you ... if there's any mercy in you, mister ... please ... let me live ... I don't know how ... but I swear to God I'll make it right to you ... I swear on my unborn kid's life ... Honest to Christ ..."

Amos sighed.

Waited. Remembered what that cute divorcée had said, back during his search. *You're such a good man, Amos.*

Lowered the Sig Sauer.

"You sorry for what you did?"

"Oh, Christ, yes, so goddamn sorry."

"And you'll make it up to me, no matter how long it takes? Or what it takes?"

Tony nodded his head up and down, up and down. "Yes, yes, yes, I promise. Honest to God. I'll even go to the cops and confess, I promise ... just don't leave my unborn kid without a dad."

Amos put his pistol in his coat pocket.

"You figure you can climb up out of there on your own?"

It took a bit of work but Tony managed to do that, climb out of the hole, panting and breathing, and he kept on whispering, "Thank you, thank you, thank you," as Amos tore off the duct tape from his ankles and wrists.

And then Tony punched Amos hard in the gut.

Amos fell back, and Tony was on him, and in seconds Tony was standing, breathing hard, grinning, Amos's Sig Sauer in his hand.

"Man oh man, am I going to have a story to tell when I get back home. Jesus!"

Amos slowly stood up, hands empty. Tony laughed. "Man, you're one stupid piece of work, you really are. And to think I'd let some dimwit slut like Monica bear me a child . . . well, Christ, that was never going to happen. Man, but you fell for that story, didn't you?"

Amos didn't say a word. Tony's eyes flashed in anger. "Your turn to beg, mister. Your turn to cry, to have snot running down your face. C'mon! Beg!"

Amos slowly shook his head. "Sorry to say, but I don't think that's gonna make much of a difference, now, will it?"

Tony took a step forward. "First smart thing you've said all day, asshole." He raised the Sig Sauer. "You're so damn gullible."

He pulled the trigger. Nothing happened. Eyes widening, he worked the slide, pulled the trigger. Again, nothing happened. Amos reached into his coat pocket, held up a full magazine of rounds, and then put it away. Then he took out his deer knife, approached Tony.

"Yeah, well, you're not the first person to say that," Amos said.

LOREN D. ESTLEMAN

GI Jack

FROM *The Big Book of Jack the Ripper*

BURKE SAID, "What's with Mac? I offered to set him up with a redhead that rooms with a blonde I got my eye on and he said it was no go."

The detective first grade was addressing his superior, Lieutenant Max Zagreb. They were at 1300 Beaubien, Detroit Police Headquarters, in the fourth year of the Second World War. Detective Third Grade McReary was dimly visible in a far corner reading by the light of a gooseneck lamp.

Just like Lincoln, Zagreb thought. He said, "He's got ambition. He's studying for the sergeant's exam."

"What for? The higher you go, the less people you got to blame stuff on."

"Do yourself a favor. Cancel the date and spend the evening with your wife for a change."

"She'd just think I was up to something."

Zagreb found McReary immersed to his eyebrows in books piled on the desk of an officer currently ducking sniper fire on Iwo Jima. The lieutenant slid the volume off the top of a stack, a fifty-year-old chronicle of murders in both hemispheres. A puff of desiccated paper came out when he cracked it open, making him sneeze. He snapped it shut.

"You know they're not going to ask you this shit on the test. Burke and Hare? Them dumb Doras in the brass'll think it's an insurance firm."

McReary, the bottom face on the totem pole of Detroit's fabled Four Horsemen (the Detroit Racket Squad, to the uninitiated), slid his fedora back from his prematurely bald head. "Once you get started, it's hard to stop. I know the Michigan Penal Code back to front; I can ace that, but they're always looking for more. Most of these old criminal cases were cracked. If I can get a handle on how it was done, I stand to nail the orals."

"Just so long as it don't get in the way of the job. We got a line on a truckload of Australian kangaroo meat that Frankie Orr's looking to pass off as South American beef docking down in Wyandotte, tonight or tomorrow night. My money says it jumps on the side of a rationing violation." He smiled. "Jumps, get it?"

Under ordinary circumstances the junior member of the squad would chuckle at his superior's joke. He grunted only, absorbed deeply in the Crippen poisoning case.

The telephone jangled on yet another vacant desk. It was Lieutenant Osprey with Homicide.

"Yeah, Ox," Zagreb said.

"The name's Oswald. I got a streetwalker carved up like a side of beef I ain't seen since before rationing."

"Since when is a hooker murder a Racket Squad deal?"

"Look, I'm shorthanded since D-day. If you like I can tell the papers she slept with Göring. We can recant on page eight."

"Something tells me I'm not getting the full story. Oh, right: I'm talking to Ox Osprey, the cop who pled the Fifth seventeen times during the McHenry grand trial."

"So I sprang a small-time bootlegger in return for a case of good Canadian for my tenth anniversary. The head of the review board shot golf with Frankie Orr the day he suspended me. It was Orr's liquor." The homicide lieutenant dropped his voice to a whisper. Zagreb had to press the receiver tightly to his ear to catch the words.

"Listen, we got the button tight on this one. She's number three. All killed the same way: throat slit, stomach cut open, and her guts dumped alongside the body. I need the manpower before the press jumps in and takes page one away from Patton's Third Army."

"Enlighten me on how three dead hookers outscore a thousand of our boys in Europe."

"The press is sick of troop movements and how MacArthur takes his shrimp tempura. You know how they like to get their hands into a sex murder up to their elbows."

Zagreb took down the particulars, depressed the plunger, and called Sergeant Canal's home number. That month the most intimidating member of the squad was living in an apartment on Michigan Avenue directly above a barbershop whose phones never seemed to stop ringing. He owed his cheap rent to a landlord who made the very good case that a little bookmaking on the side compensated for most of his clientele taking their haircuts free courtesy of the U.S. military.

"We got a name to go with the latest stiff?" he shouted above the jangling.

The lieutenant looked at his notes. "Bette Kowalski." He spelled it. "Ox's witnesses say she pronounced it 'Betty,' like Bette Davis."

"Yeah, she was clear about that."

"You *knew* her?"

"Not in the biblical sense, if that's any of your goddamn business, Lieutenant, sir. Since she's dead, I can tell you she was a firehose of information, depending on what we had in the kitty. We dumped over three warehouses of tires, gasoline, and fresh eggs on her word alone."

"Firehoses have to be connected somewhere."

"It ain't exactly a trade secret. We could've turned him over a couple of dozen times, only we'd have spent the rest of the war finding out who took his place and how he operates. Plenty of time to crank him up to the Milan pen once we run Old Glory up Schicklgruber's ass."

"You're saying Frankie Orr's added pimping to his repertoire?"

"I don't know what that is, but if it's buying tail on the street, Frankie's the man to see." Canal cleared his throat, an operation similar to coal sliding down a chute. "I ain't saying this because I need the sleep. We need to corral these bats in broad daylight."

Zagreb had something intelligent in reply, but just then a horse came in at thirty to one and the noise level on Canal's end made conversation impossible.

For formality's sake, the entire squad convened in the Wayne County Morgue to get a look at the only real evidence in any case of homicide: the victim's body naked in a pull-out tray, clay-pale except for the blue-black smile the last person she'd known had carved under her jawbone and the black cotton cross-stitches the medical examiner had used to close the incisions he'd made to examine her entrails. She'd been basted together like a made-to-order outfit for a first fitting, and from the extent of the repair work the damage had been more than substantial. She looked very young. As many stiffs as Zagreb had seen, he never got over how the brutal act of murder returned even the most jaded victims to innocence.

"You okay?" he asked McReary. "You look a little green."

"It's the iodoform, L.T. Ma bought it by the gallon during the influenza scare in '19 and doused us all by the day."

"Garlic, me," Canal said. "I ain't just sure if the old lady meant it for the ague or vampires."

Lieutenant Osprey tipped back a flask, exposing the tender flesh under a jaw cut with a miter. He didn't offer to share it with the others. "What I think? He paid his girls on the installment plan, she preferred cash-and-carry. She beefed, he cut."

"I saw a seal blow 'Anchors Aweigh' on horns in the circus. I guess he thought that was thinking too." Burke, who had a phobia against promotion, never missed a chance to take a shot at rank, with the single exception of Lieutenant Max Zagreb.

That party fired another question at Osprey just as his neck began to redden. "What about the others?"

A dilapidated notebook came out. "One colored, semipro, the other first-generation Albanian with a solicitation record as long as Errol Flynn's dick. Three nights apart, a little over six weeks ago."

"Why the dry spell, you figure?"

"I don't know, but it's a break. The press might not make the connection after all this time, but we got to sew this one up before he puts another notch on his belt."

"He's on a cycle."

They looked at McReary, whose face had begun to show some normal color. "Some of these mass murderers go by phases of the moon or the zodiac or the anniversary of their mother's death. If we can nail it down and study the behavior of known killers, we might narrow the field of suspects."

"What the hell's Dick Tracy Junior flapping his gums about?" Osprey demanded.

Zagreb smiled patiently. "He's cramming for the sergeant's exam, picking over the lush and fascinating history of crime—got it on the brain."

"No kidding. I got my first promotion by doing my damn job."

"And got busted drinking Frankie Orr's booze," Burke said.

Osprey swung his way, fists bunched at his sides. Zagreb, standing in for the League of Nations, distracted him by pressing for more details.

The other scowled, but uncrumpled his notebook and paged back, seesawing his arm as he tried to make out his own weeks-old scrawl. The first victim, Charlotte Adams, had been discovered flayed open in an alley off Grand River in the wee hours by a beat cop. A derelict found her colleague, Maria Zogu, in a trash bin behind the Albanian restaurant where she scooped up most of her clientele. Eyewitness descriptions of companions they were with when last seen were scattered and useless.

"Canal says Kowalski pounded the pavement for Frankie Orr. What about the others?"

"Indies, by all accounts. Say, maybe there's something in that. He's nailed down the steelhaulers', garbage collectors', and launderers' unions across three counties. Maybe he's moving in on the sex trade, making an example of the holdouts."

"Then why Kowalski? She worked for him."

"She wanted out."

"Listen to the quiz kid," Burke said. "Got an answer for everything except how to close a case on his own."

Osprey wheeled on him. "You want to mix it up, Detective, there's an empty tray right next door."

Zagreb said, "Let's leave the fighting to the boys in uniform and see where it happened."

Bette Kowalski had shared a third-floor walkup on Erskine with a girl who said she worked a drill press at the Chrysler tank plant. Zagreb was inclined to believe her: she was a pudding-faced brunette who bore no resemblance at all to Rosie the Riveter. None of the swing-shift queens he'd known did.

"I worked days," she said. "That way we only had to have the one bed. That's where I found her." She pointed at a gaunt iron-framed veteran with bare springs. "I got rid of the mattress, but I'm sleeping on the couch anyway. I told the landlady I'm moving out first chance I get." She hugged herself, although the room was stuffy.

"Both doors locked, hall and street," Osprey added. "Let him in, probably. All part of the job."

Zagreb flicked his gaze at Canal, who nodded and touched the girl's arm, steering her into a corner to ask innocuous questions out of earshot of the rest of the conversation.

"She must've been a mess," Zagreb told the man from Homicide.

"If we found her on the riverfront I'd've thought she got washed up after getting chopped up by the propeller of the mail boat. Working behind closed doors, without interruption, the son of a bitch had all the time in the world."

McReary said, "Ah!"

Osprey turned his head. "You said what?"

"Just 'Ah!'"

"We'll pay Frankie a visit," Zagreb said, glancing sideways at the detective third grade.

"You need me for that?" Osprey asked.

He knew the prospect of spending time in the same room with Orr wouldn't appeal to the man who'd accepted a case of his liquor. "We're used to him, Ox. We'll take it from here."

The other was so relieved he forgot to take issue with the nickname.

"Spill it," Zagreb said. They were sitting in the 1940 Chrysler the department had issued the squad before the auto industry turned its attention from Airflow transmissions to airplanes, Burke at his station behind the wheel, the lieutenant beside him.

McReary, sharing the back seat with Canal, blushed. "Just a hunch, when you said what Ox said about the perp having more time to finish the job because he and the victim were indoors. It reminded me of something I just read. Don't know why I didn't make the connection before: prostitutes cut up and left to be found, the last the worst of all because it was done in a private apartment."

"Drop the other shoe, Baldy," Burke said. "Some of us only squeaked through high school by sitting next to the smartest kid in class."

"The Whitechapel murders, London, England, fall of 1888." He glanced around at the faces turned his way, brows lifted. "Any takers?"

"I seen a movie or two," Canal said. "Just what we needed. Didn't have enough on the burner with saboteurs, rioters, and the black market, no sir. Let's throw in Jack the Ripper Junior, just to ice the cake." He crumpled his soggy cigar into a ball and threw it out the open window.

The Negro who opened the door of Frankie Orr's forty-room house in Grosse Pointe said his employer was out.

"Where'd he be, then, Jeeves?" Canal asked. "We been to his suite in the Book-Cadillac. That butler said try here. I rolled boxcars that looked less alike."

"I can't tell you apart either," said the man, without irony. "If the police can't find him, I certainly can't."

A female voice called out behind him, sounding slightly soused. "Tell 'em to try the yacht club. They can scrape him off the hull with the barnacles."

"Who was that?" asked McReary when the paneled door shut in their faces.

"Mrs. Orr," Zagreb said. "She must've caught him squeezing one of his other tomatoes."

"Well, at least we won't be burning off gas the boys need on Okinawa." Burke turned toward the Chrysler.

The Grosse Pointe Yacht Club was just a few blocks away, a structure of Venetian design, complete with Gothic arches and a soaring bell tower, built directly into Lake St. Clair. They parked in a sandy lot off Vernier and entered the office, where a salty manager informed them Mr. Orr's boat could be found in slip nine.

The boat in the slip was a converted Great War minesweeper with *Gloria* painted on the stern. McReary said, "I thought his wife's name was Estelle."

"Gloria was his gun girl during Prohibition," Zagreb said. "She reinforced a handbag with steel so it didn't sag when he saw a cop and slipped her his rod."

"What happened to her?"

"Making flak jackets for the air corps last I heard. Ahoy the boat!"

A man dressed as a deckhand, in canvas trousers and a striped jersey with the sleeves rolled up past his swollen biceps, came to the rail carrying a Tommy gun. "Scram, bo."

Burke shielded his eyes. "That you, Rocks? I thought the warden had you working the jute mill in Jackson."

"Still would be if Mr. Orr didn't spring me legal." The machine gun lowered. "Sorry, Detective. I thought you was somebody else."

"I usually am. This is my lieutenant, Max Zagreb. You can call him Lieutenant. We're here to palaver, not pinch."

Rocks gestured with the Tommy and the Horsemen climbed a rope ladder. The boat swayed when their weight hit the deck. "She don't draw much water," Zagreb said.

"Mr. Orr replaced the brass with aluminum. Put in four Rolls-

Royce engines so he could outrun the coast guard with a thousand gallons of Old Log Cabin in the hull."

"Rocks left out the part about me giving up running contraband after repeal." The new voice belonged to a slender man whose black hair gleamed at the temples under the sweatband of a yachting cap with an anchor embroidered on it in gold thread. He wore a double-breasted blazer, white duck trousers, gum soles, and a silk ascot tucked into the open collar of his shirt.

"Throat sore, Frankie?" Zagreb snatched the weapon from the deckhand and thrust it at Burke, who took it. "Ever hear of the Sullivan Act?"

Orr said, "Rocks is in the naval reserve. He's licensed to carry it in case we run into a U-boat."

Canal grinned around a fresh cigar. "G'wan with you. The service don't take ex-cons."

"They're less picky in the merchant marines. Let's go in the saloon."

"Salon," corrected Rocks. "You told me to remind you, boss."

"It's Captain when we're on the water. Go swab the deck or something while I speak with these gentlemen."

They descended a gangway into a wide cabin containing a chrome bar and an evenly tanned blonde standing behind it in a white sharkskin swimsuit. "Cocktail?"

The visitors ordered bourbon all around except for McReary, who asked for a Vernors. She mixed, served, and exited the cabin when Orr jerked his chin toward the gangway. Zagreb caught Burke admiring the creamy band of untanned skin where fabric met flesh. "Down, boy." He stirred his glass with a finger and sucked it. "Trouble at home, skipper?"

Orr frowned. "I guess you seen Estelle. She's got a private dick watching the hotel, so I have to smuggle in my hobbies in a dinghy on the Canadian side of the lake."

Canal said, "Try keeping your dinghy at home."

The lieutenant said, "You're mellowing. In the old days you'd drop a snooper out in the middle tied to a Chevy short block."

"Not that I ever done anything like that, but the agency's run by a retired police inspector. You cops hang together a lot tighter than the Purple Gang ever did."

"We're like the Masons that way. Hear what happened to Bette Kowalski?"

"I don't know no one by that name."

Zagreb wobbled good bourbon around his mouth and swallowed. "It gets old: you play dumb, we get tough, you call your mouthpiece ship-to-shore, we stuff you in a torpedo tube and blow you to Windsor. Why not take it easy on our lumbago and you can play hockey some other time?"

"The *Gloria*'s a minesweeper, not a destroyer. She ain't got torpedo tubes. Okay, okay," Orr said when Canal set down his glass and started his way. "I just want you to understand I don't run whores. The Kowalski dame kept her ear to the ground and told me when one of my joints had to stand for a raid. It gave me time to sacrifice a couple of slot machines and keep my best dealers out of the can."

Zagreb said, "She was your department pipeline?"

"Double agent." Canal spat a soggy piece of tobacco into an ice bucket. "You're saying my snitch was two-timing me with the mob and the whole damn Vice Squad?"

"Not the whole squad; just Sergeant Coopersmith. He pinched her in front of God and everybody whenever he wanted scuttlebutt from the street, and after she made bail she slipped me what she overheard at headquarters. I never paid for nothing else, and if she put out for Coop or didn't, she never said boo either way. So you can see I had as much to lose as anybody when she opened her door to that butcher," he finished.

"Not as much as her." McReary's straw gurgled. He got rid of the ginger ale bottle. "When'd you see her last?"

"The night before her roommate found her gutted like a goose. I asked her wasn't it about time the cops swept her off the street again and she said, 'Right after I do my part for the boys in the service.'"

"What'd she mean by that?" Zagreb asked.

Capped teeth flashed white in the gangster's olive-hued face. "I'm just guessing, but I don't think she was planning to serve coffee and doughnuts at the USO."

Zagreb studied him over his half-raised drink. "On the level, she took a serviceman back to her room that night?"

"Bette made Kate Smith look like Tokyo Rose. She bought bonds, donated to the scrap drive, and offered a discount every time she sat under the apple tree with a GI."

"Thanks, Frankie," the lieutenant said. "Just to show our heart's in the right place, we'll forget about that shipment of kangaroo meat on its way to Wyandotte. We'll even throw in whatever you got stashed in their pouches."

Orr flushed high on his cheekbones. "How the hell—? Oh," he said, resuming his customary calm. "I hope you boys don't bury her on Zug Island with the other unclaimed stiffs. That was a doozy of a going-away present she gave you."

Back on deck, Burke returned the Thompson to Rocks. "Next time take the safety off, mug. Them underwater krauts never put theirs on."

Back at 1300, Burke poured two fingers of Four Roses into a Dixie cup. "I ain't George M. Cohan, but nobody's going to sell me one of our troops is slashing hookers."

McReary gave up on the book he was studying. "One of the theories about the Ripper was he served in India or Afghanistan. Hand-to-hand combat can do things to a man."

Canal said, "Seems to me we paid this bill off last July during the riots. Two nutcase killers in one year?"

McReary said, "This is different. That screwball Kilroy thought he was helping the war effort by slicing up ration-stamp hoarders. He only wore a uniform to get in the door."

"I'd buy that this time around too. The Quartermaster Corps has got too much on its hands to keep track of what happens to its laundry."

The lieutenant was restless. He'd tried sitting and straddling a number of vacant chairs like Goldilocks and wound up pacing the squad room chain-smoking Chesterfields. "We're wasting time trying to talk ourselves out of thinking he's a GI when we ought to be considering what if he is. Ox told us it'd been six weeks since the first two killings. Don't that suggest something?"

"He's on a cycle, like I said," McReary reminded him. "We just got to—" He looked up, color flooding his face.

Zagreb nodded. "Basic training's six weeks. Suppose he threw himself a little call-up party, or enlisted before the investigation turned on him. Now he's out on leave."

Canal, fogging the outside air with one of his nickel stogies, slid off the windowsill. Plaster fell from the ceiling when his clodhoppers hit the floor. "We need a date on that second killing, then call the War Department to see who signed up in any of the services during the next month."

"Six weeks," Zagreb said, "to be sure. You take it."

"Give that to the kid, Zag. He's good on the horn."

"He's better with girls his age. Mac, you're going back to talk to the roommate, and if you come out without a line on just what uniform Bette's last john had on, you got about as much chance of making sergeant as Sad Sack."

"But she said she didn't see anything."

"That's what she thinks. We need to narrow the suspects to one branch of the service. If this son of a bitch ships out before we ID him, he'll be spilling civilian blood all over Europe and the Philippines."

The roommate's name was Jill Wheeler. Her landlady told McReary she was working, but that she usually returned home just after the five o'clock whistle.

Waiting for her at the bus stop on the corner, he caught himself humming "The Five O'Clock Whistle Never Blew." He liked jive music okay, but the way the lyrics wormed their way into his brain shoved out everything important.

She alighted behind a stout woman in a babushka and woolen topcoat that made his own skin prickle in the heat, a dead duck swinging by its neck in one fist; Polish-populated Hamtramck was still the best place to procure quality poultry under rationing. By contrast, Jill Wheeler looked as fresh as Deanna Durbin. Her round face with its clear complexion, black hair cut in a bob, brimmed hat, summer dress, and chunky heels made a refreshing change from the world represented by her dead roommate.

She stopped before the man touching his hat, gripping her handbag tightly. "I know you."

He introduced himself, steeling himself for the back-and-forth: "One or two more questions."

"I've told you everything I know."

"Just for the record, miss."

With that behind them, he escorted her back to her room. There, with the door left open to appease the landlady, she assured him repeatedly that she knew nothing about Bette Kowalski's last rendezvous. (She actually used the word; he suspected she'd sat through *Algiers* at least twice.) At length he turned toward the door, putting on his hat. Taking it off in a young lady's presence to expose his bare scalp had been a major contribution to the cause of

justice. "If you remember anything else, please call me at headquarters. Daniel J. McReary, detective third grade."

"I can't think what that would be. All I know is she said she
hoped she'd make some dogface wag its tail."

He paused in the midst of smoothing the brim. "When'd she
say that?"

"I don't know; just before I left for my shift, I suppose. Yes, I was
on my way out the door. Is it important?"

"Probably not. But thank you." Lieutenant Zagreb had told him
again and again never to let a witness know she'd put you on to
something good. "Otherwise they'll start making things up just to
get you to pat 'em on the head."

*The fog didn't roll, didn't creep; the poets who wrote that had never visited
London in the autumn. It spread like sludge from the harbor, yellow as
piss and soggy as a snot rag, so thick round your ankles you swore you'd
stepped into a bucket of dead squid. On the cobblestone streets, sound carried
through it as across a lake; the poets were dead wrong about that as well,
claiming it muffled noise when in fact Big Ben's iron bell rang from a mile
down the Thames fit to burst your eardrums.*

*Example: the squeak of a hinge, and a gush of tinny music, cut short
abruptly by the clap of a door shutting against it, then the sole of a
shoe scraping the pavement, sounding as close as if it were his own, but
sharper; a narrow heel attached to a small foot, a fact confirmed by a
puff of cheap scent. A woman, and one who doused herself, advertising
her availability like a cat in heat. He felt the gorge of blood rising to his
face; but he suppressed his rage, or more accurately channeled it toward
the business at hand. He stepped from the doorway neighboring the public
house, the fumes of ale and vomit and urine mingling with the fog as he
passed the hellish place, fixing his gaze on snatches of tawdry satin and
dyed feathers glimpsed between wisps of mist, but relying as fully on smell
and sound; groping, as he closed the distance, for the handle of the knife
on his belt . . .*

McReary started awake. Having found Zagreb absent, he'd sat at
the desk he'd commandeered for his studies to wait, and didn't
know he'd drifted off until the squad room door closed, shaking
him out of his dream.

"You're an angel when you sleep." The lieutenant sat on a corner of the desk unoccupied by books and hung a cigarette on his

lower lip. "You know, studying all night every night's no good if you doze off during the test."

"Sorry, L.T. I got something from the roommate."

"Too soon. Probably just a bladder infection."

"What? Oh." He blushed. "Does the ribbing stop when I make sergeant?"

"Not unless we bring in a kid younger than you. What'd you get?"

"Just something that came out when I'd finished asking questions." He told him what Jill Wheeler had said.

"Sure you heard her right?"

"Sure I'm sure. Think it's anything?"

Canal came in just then and read their faces. "We take Berlin?"

"Close. The Kowalski dame as much as told her roommate her john was a dogface."

"That's army, ain't it?"

"I think so. Don't Burke have a brother or something in the army?"

"Brother-in-law," said Burke, entering. "Dumb as a box of Lux. He's a cinch to make general."

"Ship out yet?"

"I wish. Dumb cluck's still parking on my couch."

"Ring him up."

The detective snatched up a candlestick phone and dialed. "Me, Sadie. Roy in? Imagine that. Put him on. No, I'm not looking to bust his butt, just ask him a question. Well, sure I have. Didn't I ask him just this morning when's he going to start paying rent?" He pressed the mouthpiece to his chest. "I tell you, if I hadn't knocked her up—Roy?" He leaned forward. "You ever hear anyone in basic call a guy with the navy or Marines a dogface?" He listened. "Okay." He pegged the earpiece. "Sailors are gobs, Marines leathernecks or jarheads. Dogfaces are army buck privates. Always."

"Gimme that phone." Zagreb asked the long-distance operator for the War Department. While he was waiting, McReary said, "L.T., what's it mean when a cop dreams he's a perp?"

"It means he's got the makings of a good detective."

The news from Washington was disheartening at first. During the six weeks following the murder of Maria Zogu, the second victim, 166 men were recruited into the army from the Detroit area. Many phone calls later determined the following:

Thirty-four with the paratroopers had been shipped overseas directly after basic training, that service having suffered heavy casualties during the push toward Germany.

Twenty-three were discharged for unfitness or insubordination.

Sixteen of those were tracked down and their movements accounted for the night Bette Kowalski was murdered.

The remaining seven were interviewed and eliminated as likely suspects.

Three died during training, one from incaution during a drill involving live rounds, one from cerebral hemorrhage after a brawl in the PX, one from Spanish influenza.

Eighteen soldiers who'd been exposed to the stricken man were in quarantine at the time of the last murder.

The squad tabled six who supplied sound alibis for at least one of the first two killings.

Little by little, with help from Osprey's Homicide detail, the uniform division, and reserves, most of the eighty-plus men left fell away, leaving just four: a handy number for the Four Horsemen to interview separately.

"What we got?" Zagreb asked when they reunited at 1300.

Canal passed an unlit cigar under his nose and made the same face the others usually made when he lit one. "My guy's eighteen going on eleven. Tried every whistle stop between here and his hometown in Texas before he found a recruiting sergeant blind enough to accept the date of birth he gave. He's a shrimp. Bette had muscles on her muscles from pounding the pavement and smacking around deadbeats. She'd've took him three falls out of three."

Burke said, "Mine took a swing at me when I told him what I was looking into. I knocked him flat, frisked him and the dump he lives in. If he's our guy, he sure cleans up after himself. He's in holding downstairs."

"We'll take turns," Zagreb said. "Mac?"

McReary got out his notebook. "Lives in Dearborn. With his mother, the landlord says. Both out; she cooks in the bomber plant in Willow Run, gets off at midnight. My guess is he's sowing some oats before he ships out. The landlord wouldn't let me check out the apartment. Should we get a warrant?"

"Not yet." Zagreb looked at his watch. "Twenty to twelve. We'll try schmoozing Mom when she comes home."

"What about yours, Zag?" Canal asked.

"Halfway to Honolulu on a troop ship. If we turn anything up on a search warrant we can tip off the MPs, though I'd sure hate to dump it in somebody else's lap."

Burke grinned at McReary. "Slap on the Old Spice, Junior. If you can Romeo a jane like Bette's roomie, the old lady on Dearborn's a fish in a barrel."

"Mrs. Corbett?" Zagreb took off his hat.

"Miss. I went back to my maiden name after my husband left me. For a tramp," she added, pinching her nostrils.

The woman who'd opened the door had a slight middle-aged spread but was still attractive. A lock of strawberry-blond hair had strayed from the red bandanna she wore tied around her head. The lieutenant had to admit she resembled Rosie the Riveter, even if her skills with a stove surpassed those with a jackhammer. She smelled not unpleasantly of hot grease.

After the pleasantries, she let the squad into a tidy living room with a fake fireplace above which hung a period photograph in a matted frame of a man in his thirties who parted his hair in the middle and wore a trim mustache.

"My great-great-uncle Boston," she said. "He's the man who shot John Wilkes Booth."

Zagreb nodded. "Good for him. Lincoln's my favorite president."

As the others took seats on slightly worn mohair cushions, their lieutenant went through all the motions, assuring their hostess that her son wasn't in trouble, just that they wanted to speak with him in connection with an investigation.

"Leonard should be back any time," she said. "He's to report for duty at eight a.m. By this time next week he'll be in England. I'm hoping he'll find the time to visit family. His great-great-great-uncle was born there." The cheerful glitter in her pale-brown eyes fell short of dissembling the concern behind them.

McReary noted it. "He's your only child?"

"Yes."

"Then I'm sure he'll be especially careful."

"You're very kind."

Burke, not kind, asked if she knew where Leonard was on the night of the date Bette Kowalski was killed.

"Was it a weeknight?"

"Wednesday." Zagreb cut his eyes Burke's way, registering disapproval.

"I wouldn't know, then. I'd have been at work. He may have stayed home, or he may have gone out for a beer with friends. That's what he went out for tonight—he's throwing himself a sort of going-away party." Once again concern clouded the glitter in her eyes.

Canal fumbled at the pocket containing his cigars but refrained from taking one out. "Could we see his room?"

"Oh, I don't know. He's a very private person. He won't even let me go in to clean."

"We won't disturb anything." McReary looked sincere.

"I'm afraid he keeps it locked."

"No problem, ma'am." Canal took out a small leather case, displaying a collection of picks and skeleton keys.

The room was upstairs, with a yellow tin sign tacked to the door reading:

FIRING RANGE
AUTHORIZED PERSONNEL ONLY

Mrs. Corbett's smile was nervous. "Leonard's little joke. He bought it in the army surplus store. He's always bringing home odd bits."

Five minutes, three keys, and two picks later, the sergeant got off his knees and twisted the knob. Artfully the four men arranged themselves between the woman and the door and drew their revolvers, shielding the maneuver from her line of sight with their bodies. They sprang in single file and spread out inside the room; holstered their weapons when it proved to be unoccupied.

"Holy—"

"Mackerel," Zagreb interrupted Burke.

It was a small room with a single bed, a writing table, and a wooden chair. A Class-A army uniform in an open dry cleaner's bag hung in a closet without a door. A metal bookrack beside the desk contained rows of worn books: *The Lodger, The Curse of Mitre Square,* several titled *Jack the Ripper.* A corkboard mounted above the table was plastered with black-and-white and sepia photographs, most of them clipped from newspapers and magazines, showing narrow cobblestone alleys, a stately building captioned NEW SCOTLAND

YARD, and shots taken from dozens of angles of obviously dead women, some of them naked, exposing ghastly slashes imperfectly stitched.

Mrs. Corbett gasped in the hallway. Zagreb jerked his chin at Canal, standing nearest the door. He eased it shut and leaned his back against it.

"I've seen these," McReary said. "There's Annie Chapman, Catherine Eddowes, Elizabeth Stride." He indicated the grisliest image of all, a skilled artist's sketch. "Mary Kelly, the Ripper's last known victim. Ring a bell?"

"He cut up Bette Kowalski the same way," Canal said.

A black satchel, like the kind doctors carried, stood open on the table. It was old and cracked. Zagreb reached inside and began taking out the contents: stethoscope, glass medicine bottles, scalpels, a gadget resembling a brace and bit—what some people called a hand drill. He held up the last item. "You're the big reader, Mac. This looks like it belongs in a carpenter's toolbox."

"Trepan." McReary paled. "They don't make 'em anymore. Forensic surgeons used it to bore holes in skulls, looking for bullets and such. It's an autopsy kit, L.T."

"None of these scalpels looks big enough for the murder weapon."

"There should be a postmortem knife in the bag." The detective third grade spread his hands a foot apart. "About yay long. The experts figured that's what the Ripper used."

Zagreb rummaged further, then picked up the bag and dumped it upside down onto the table. No such instrument made its appearance.

Mrs. Corbett had no idea where her son had gone to celebrate his last night as a civilian. Zagreb borrowed her phone and described Leonard Corbett from a recent photo supplied by his agitated mother, showing a bland-faced young man in his uniform. Minutes later they were driving with the two-way radio turned up full blast.

"Any cars in the vicinity of Woodward and Parsons," crackled the dispatcher's voice. "Suspect seen near the Paradise Theatre. Consider him armed and extremely dangerous."

"That place draws almost as many hookers as jazz buffs," Zagreb said.

Burke flipped on the siren and hit the gas.

The street in front of the popular swing club was a sea of department vehicles, marked and unmarked. Spotting a uniformed officer on the sidewalk holding his sidearm, Zagreb rolled down the window and flashed his shield.

The patrolman skipped the preliminaries. "Someone just ducked down that alley." He pointed with his weapon.

They left the Chrysler at the curb. At the lieutenant's instructions, McReary and Canal circled the building on the corner to come in from the other end. Zagreb and Burke gave them two minutes, then entered from the Woodward Avenue side. All four had their weapons out.

Crossing a dark doorway, McReary glimpsed a movement in the shadows. He touched Burke's arm. Burke nodded and leveled his revolver on the doorway as his partner entered. The deep passage was black as a shroud. He felt for the door. A hinge squeaked and it swung open at his touch.

A long hallway with a checkerboard floor showed barely in the dim light of a wall sconce. The far end was in deep shadow. He crept forward.

The man at the far end of the hall came to a locked door. He turned and pressed his back to it, holding his breath. Three yards away, visible in the lighted section, a man with a gun was approaching, wearing a dark suit and a light-colored hat. He himself was secure in the blackness, as if he were enveloped in thick fog. The man creeping his way wore shoes appropriate to someone who habitually carried a gun, but he could hear the slight squish of the rubber soles as he advanced, smell the crisp odor of spice-based aftershave. That was another advantage, his heightened senses. But he would have to move fast and strike surely; this was no tart, her brains dulled by liquor and the plague her kind had brought upon itself.

Closer now. He could almost reach out and touch the man. He drew the knife from his belt and sprang . . .

Suddenly the shadow at the end of the hall coagulated into something blacker, a distinct shape dressed all in dark clothing. Fabric rustled; the light behind McReary drew a bright line down a length of steel. He raised his piece and fired. Something stung his wrist, something hot splashed onto his hand. An evil stench of singed cloth filled his nostrils; the muzzle flare had set the man's coat on fire.

He kept jerking the trigger, emptying the chamber. Something heavy piled into him. Automatically he threw his arms around it, supporting the dead man entirely.

It was only after he let go and the man slid into a heap at his feet that he realized his wrist was bleeding.

Daniel J. McReary entered the squad room. From habit he reached for his sidearm, intending to lay it on the desk still stacked with books, then remembered. Pending the results of the routine shooting investigation, he'd been relieved of his weapon and assigned to desk duty.

He brightened when Lieutenant Zagreb came in. Flicking the hand belonging to the bandaged wrist at the book on top of the stack, he said, "I've been reading."

"What else is new?"

"It's about the Lincoln assassination. I got interested after Mrs. Corbett told us she was related to the man who killed John Wilkes Booth. This Boston Corbett was a piece of work: born in England under Queen Victoria, with all that entails. He was so mortified after going to bed with a prostitute he castrated himself."

Burke, cleaning his revolver at a nearby desk, dropped it on the blotter. "Holy—"

"Shit," Canal finished. "A thing like that can make a man surly."

"Do tell." McReary opened the book to the page he'd marked. "Says here twenty years after he shot Booth they stuck him in a loony bin for pulling a gun in the Kansas House of Representatives, but he escaped in 1888 and was never heard from since. That's the year the Ripper killings took place. What are the odds Corbett went back home and . . . ?"

"You think Leonard knew about that?" Burke picked up his revolver and blew through the barrel.

"You should write a book," Zagreb said.

"Not me. I'm through with 'em." He slammed the volume shut and tossed it aside.

The lieutenant lifted his eyebrows. "You failed the sergeant's exam?"

"I fell asleep."

PETER FERRY

Ike, Sharon, and Me

FROM *Fifth Wednesday*

I TAUGHT IN a little school out on the prairie among the lakes for four years until I turned twenty-six and was free of the draft. I lived in a garage apartment in town and sometimes drank beer in the Blue Moon Tap on my old paper route where Ike's father used to spend his Friday nights. According to Greg, he quit drinking when Ike died. I hung out with Greg and his wife, Alice, until they divorced, and then I hung out with Greg, who was now a full-fledged reporter on the *Courier*. I thought often about Ike. I sometimes thought about the summer I'd spent in Europe and Morocco, but as if it were a movie I'd seen or a book I'd read. I'd found my way across one continent, an ocean, another continent, and into a third and all the way back. I was capable. I could do things. I could handle things. Sometimes I was even tempted to think that I could handle anything, but that seemed a bit too much like hubris, so I settled for "things." Besides, I did not want to tempt fate. I could take care of myself, and that, I slowly, sadly began to conclude, was more than Ike could do. He'd been twenty-one when he'd stopped getting older and I hadn't, and more and more he seemed to me like a boy, a lost boy, and I, well, I seemed to me a little less lost, at least back then.

During my third year of teaching, Sharon Novak was hired at my school, although I didn't recognize her at first because her name had changed. Greg told me the story. After the fire that burned her house to the ground and in which Ike, who lived next door, had perished and she and her children had nearly perished, there had been some unspecified problems with the insurance and also some questions about smoke detectors: Had they been operational? Had they failed? Why hadn't they awakened the family? Or had they perhaps awakened the children? They didn't remember. Before any of this was settled, the Novaks left town. People did not know it at the time, but they did not leave together. Sharon and the kids went to Champaign-Urbana, where she began work on a master's degree. Charles, who was a chemical engineer, left town with his lab technician to work for Dow Chemical in Midland, Michigan. It turned out that they had been having an affair. In the divorce that ensued, Sharon appeared to have gotten everything. Charles got the lab technician, but not for long. Within two years she was back in town. At about the same time, Sharon, now using her maiden name, Postlewaite, came back too. She bought a big house and took the teaching job that probably couldn't pay her mortgage if she had one. And she looked different. Her hair was short, stylish, and streaked. Her wardrobe, which had once consisted of cotton dresses and gym shoes, was now made up of turtlenecks, tailored slacks, and clogs, and perhaps it was just these cosmetic changes, but she now seemed a little less resigned and world-weary. Still, I knew it was she the day I saw her walking away from me down the school hallway with that loose-limbed, swaying gait that Ike had so admired. *Damn,* I thought, *what's she doing here?*

I guess I'd begun to feel a certain ownership of my job. For one thing, we had a lot of turnover, so in two years I'd accrued some seniority and been given some out-of-classroom responsibility. For another, I wasn't as bad a teacher as I'd feared I'd be. Of course, I had been at first. That first year I made a lot of mistakes. Every night when I got home, I was absolutely exhausted, and by April first I was pretty much out of gas. The next year was better, and by the time Sharon Postlewaite showed up, I was even feeling competent. And while I soon knew who she was, I didn't think she knew who I was, and for quite a while I kept it that way. I did not know how much she knew about Ike, about his creepy obsession with her and her family, about the night of the fire, and I never wanted to be in a position of having or needing to tell her any of it. Then there was the fact that I knew more about her than I was comfortable with or than she could ever know I knew. No, best to keep her at a distance. I nodded in the hall, never said more than "Hi" or "Thanks" or "You're welcome." I sat on the opposite side of the coffee room or cafeteria or teachers' meeting. But I did keep an eye on her.

When the moment and angle were right, I sometimes watched her grading papers, legs crossed, even twined, coffee cup in one hand, red pen in the other, undisturbed by the clatter around her. Perhaps undisturbable.

In the meantime I helped coach boys' basketball, played church league basketball myself in the winter and city park softball in the spring. I drank beer and ate pizza with old high school friends, once in a while had a date of sorts—even ending up in the sack a couple of times—and made plans with Greg, who was still licking his wounds from the divorce, to take a long car trip that summer. Then one day in late May, Sharon Postlewaite and I found ourselves walking together down the empty hallway after school and really couldn't avoid some kind of conversation without its being awkward and obvious.

"Your kids squirrelly, Bill?" she asked me. I was surprised she knew my name.

"Oh yeah, especially with the heat."

"Got plans for the summer?"

"Going camping with a friend. Grand Tetons."

We had reached her classroom, and she was turning in. "You're Ike Lowell's friend, aren't you?"

"Yes."

"Thought so."

I was kind of stunned. I wondered how she knew and how long she had known. That evening she knocked on my door with a bottle of wine in her hand. "Wanna get drunk?" she asked.

Sharon Postlewaite was the same kind of lover as she was hall walker or paper grader: easy, undistracted, languorous. She was not in a hurry. She closed her eyes and smiled. She made little noises. "Hmmm." "Ah." "Yes." There were no gymnastics or weight-lifting involved. I remember wanting a cigarette afterward and asking her, "Do you smoke?"

"I don't know," she said. "I never looked." Then she laughed. It was an old joke, but it surprised and delighted me. She wasn't regretting what we had done as I guess I assumed she would.

"Do you want a cigarette, smart aleck?"

"Sure."

"May I ask you something? How did you know that I was Ike Lowell's friend?"

"Used to see you over there. Coming and going." That really

surprised me. I think I'd only visited Ike about three times after he came home from Vietnam, and usually after dark. "Speaking of going." She sat up on the edge of the bed and began to dress. It was a lovely thing to watch: effortless grace. The slipping on of the panties, the hooking of the bra with arched shoulders, the pulling over the head of the top, the shaking out of the hair.

"You have to go?" I very much wanted her to stay longer. All I could think of was that it was Friday night and that I'd love to make love to her again; I'd love to make love to her all night long.

She lowered her chin, raised her brow, looked at me, and said, "I have children to get to bed."

"Well," I said, remembering her invitation to "get drunk," "you okay to drive?"

She laughed at that, took my face in her two hands, kissed me deeply, and whispered, "It was a euphemism. I'm fine."

Every day after that until the end of school, it was as if that night had never happened. She never glanced my way or touched my arm to get my attention or spoke my Christian name. On the last day of school, she didn't linger by her car as I was walking to mine or say "Have a good summer" or "Have a nice trip," so I could only conclude that it had been a one-shot deal or perhaps even a disappointment. Driving west, then lying awake in my sleeping bag, I asked myself many questions: Had I been too eager? Too aggressive? Not aggressive enough? Too unimaginative? Too focused on my own pleasure? Had she driven home that night shaking her head and rolling her eyes? Had she since knocked on someone else's door with a bottle of wine? Was she doing that now, even as I lay there in that tent listening to Greg snore?

At other times I thought, *What the hell do I care? I got a free roll in the hay; she's an old woman.* I imagined being out to dinner with her somewhere and people glancing at us. Mother? No. Wife? No. Sister? Cousin? Aunt?

When I got home, I started driving by her house until one day there she was in the driveway. I honked and waved, and she waved back, but she didn't come around, not for a month, not until I'd pretty much given up hope. When she did, she was again carrying a bottle of wine. She held it up. "Wanna fuck?" she asked.

Women like Sharon Postlewaite didn't say things like that. Not then. Not yet. Not unless they were trying to impress or unless they were very unusual, and Sharon didn't seem interested in impressing anyone about anything. It occurred to me that once again Ike had found something interesting in someone that the rest of us had missed altogether.

That night when she was standing there slipping on and buttoning her blouse, she said, "I can't get away very often," answering all my questions at once. That was the last I saw of her until we returned to school. Then it was the same old thing, not so much as a glance. I started driving past her house again. I even worked up the nerve to call her once.

"Sharon?" I said.

"Sorry. Not interested," she said, and hung up. I stayed away.

Then in October I was called into the principal's office one day, and Sharon was sitting there. *Oh shit,* I thought. *I'm about to get fired. I'm about to be accused of harassment and shamed right out of town and into the army and Vietnam. Maybe I'm about to be arrested. Have I done something illegal?*

"Mrs. Postlewaite," the principal said—for he called all women of a certain age "Mrs."—"Mrs. Postlewaite would like to put on a play, and, well, we were wondering if you might like to help her." He explained that the school had never produced a play before, sounding as if he was not at all sure it should try it now, and Sharon said that she'd never directed one but had studied drama and directing in college. "Pretty rusty. I could use some help."

I said I hadn't done any drama since high school.

Sharon said that two heads would be better than one, and I thought of her holding my face and running her tongue into my mouth.

The principal said that I'd have to give up coaching basketball as if he hoped I'd say I couldn't or wouldn't and the whole thing would go away. I asked if I could sleep on it, because I didn't want to jump too quickly, and the next day it was the principal rather than Sharon to whom I said yes, so I was a little surprised when she knocked on my door that night and held up a bottle of wine. "Celebrate?"

"Is that a euphemism?"

"Of course."

The play was *A Christmas Carol,* which, with its chains and ghosts and crippled kid and corny sentiment, was perfect for a junior high school. And of course every theatrical kid in the school tried out. We had lots of histrionic girls and sensitive boys, many tears and scenes and tantrums, but we also had a great deal of fun. We assembled every day after school in the auditorium. Boys would be chasing each other around. Girls would be practicing their lines or consoling one of their number who was weeping. The shop class would be measuring and sawing and hammering. The art class would be painting. I always seemed to get there first and Sharon would then come in and sit in the row behind me. One day when I was tired of turning around, I said, "Why don't you sit up here?"

"I prefer to sit here."

"Why?"

"So I can look at you." I think it may have been the only time that she said something I thought sweet and vulnerable.

Sharon had sketched out a rehearsal schedule, but neither of us really had any idea what we were doing, so we were scared to death of not being ready on time. This justified more after-hours sessions at my apartment and toward the end a couple of long Sunday afternoons. These in turn involved very little Charles Dickens but a good deal of luxuriating in bed, drinking champagne, eating strawberries, listening to Johnny Mathis, reading *The Tropic of Cancer* and *Lady Chatterley's Lover* out loud, and doing things with and to each other that I'd only dreamed about. I did not know where Sharon had learned about these things, but it seemed unlikely from or with Charles Novak, who seemed to me an engineer in every sense of the word.

Now I probably don't need to tell you that I fall in love a lot, nor that I was falling in love with Sharon Postlewaite. I began to fantasize a future for us. I began to do things like suggest plays we might do the next year, even though I'd made it very clear that as soon as I turned twenty-six in June, I was resigning and getting out of town as fast as I could. I began to mention things we might do together, books we might read, trips we might take, and the more I did these things, the more conflicted I felt. This was, after all, the woman with whom Ike had been in love. I kept thinking of an old English folk song about sleeping with a dead man's girl. And what about Sharon? Didn't she have a right to know of Ike's infatuation with her even if it shocked her, even if it horrified her, even if it made her look anew at me and run the other way? It was this last thing that kept me from saying anything for a long time.

The play was just awful, and everyone loved it, but then it was over and then there was Christmas, and when that was over too,

Sharon and I found it hard to go back to the way things had been. There were fewer reasons to get together and less to talk about when we did. With the dull, cold days of winter, the wind seemed to go out of our sails, and I felt her slipping away. I guess I felt that if I could get her attention again, if I could create some of the drama and electricity we'd had before, I could get her back. That's why I decided to tell her about Ike. It wasn't to memorialize him or to protect her. It was to take a chance that just might make me seem daring and noble and heroic. The truth is, the more I loved Sharon and the more desperate I felt about her, the angrier I got at Ike for having hurt her, for having sent her world spinning out of control, for leaving her sitting as she was that evening smoking and staring out the window at the rain or maybe at nothing. I guess I was practicing chivalry of a rather fractured, latter-day, and self-serving sort. "He spent hours watching you from his bedroom window. He spent days and weeks watching you. He knew what you put in your coffee, what books you were reading, what laundry detergent you used, what cereal your kids ate, what station you listened to on the car radio. He knew everything about you. He watched you dress and undress." I went on and on. All this time she sat looking out the window. "I think it's fair to say Ike Lowell was totally obsessed with you," I concluded.

She lit another cigarette and smoked most of it. Just before she spoke, I realized that it was her own reflection in the window she was looking at, not the rain. "In a way," she said, "it was like being in a movie, someone else's movie. Probably a French movie—you know, one in which nothing happens. People wash dishes and you watch them wash dishes, but because you're watching, well, it's somehow different. I'd hang my wash out. I'd stand barefoot with my feet apart and my back arched and the breeze in my hair—my hair was longer then—and I'd wonder what I'd look like from up there in his window."

"Wait a minute—you mean you knew he was watching you?"

"Of course I knew. Don't you always know when someone's watching you? Like when you used to watch me across the coffee room at school. You don't think I just knocked on your door with a bottle of wine that first time by chance, do you?"

I didn't answer, and she smiled at me as she might a child. "Of course I knew. I always knew. Sometimes I'd even create little dramas. Tearful phone calls with no one on the other end of the line.

Head in hand. Sometimes I'd put on a record and imagine it a soundtrack. I'd do the dishes to it or chop vegetables or paint my toenails. Sometimes I'd dust or vacuum to the music and kind of dance around. Sometimes I'd sing. Sometimes I wrote love letters to no one. Sometimes I had sexy phone conversations with someone or other. Maybe Ike Lowell. Who knows. Sometimes," she said, raising her brow and watching me now, "sometimes I touched myself."

I was flabbergasted. Ike hadn't been imagining things. It was all true.

"It was very flattering, you see. Charles had lost interest in me. I had lost interest in me. My life as anything but a mother was pretty much over. I probably would have spent the rest of it taking care of the children and having what Charles thought of as sex once a week and forgiving him his peccadilloes, of which, by the way, there were more than one, and waiting to die unless I didn't wait. A life of shit. Ugh. Then Ike came along and put me in his movie and I was a star." She laughed at herself. "Ridiculous, right? Still . . ."

"What I'm trying to say is that Ike Lowell was in love with you."

"I know," she said brightly. "And I was in love with him. I was in love with Ike Lowell. In fact, I think it fair to say that he was the love of my life." That pierced my heart, because it so obviously meant that I was not.

"Tell me, did you . . . did you ever . . . ?"

"Never. I only really ever had a glimpse of him once or twice. The only mental images I had of him I got from the library. High school yearbooks. Old newspapers. Sports stuff mostly, when he was much younger, and while I didn't really know what he looked like now, I knew he didn't look like that. But that was it. I never touched him, never talked to him, never even met him. Except of course . . . and what a way to meet. Talk about a movie. I mean, he saves my life and then sacrifices his, all in about, what, two minutes? I mean, who could live up to that?" This time the challenge to me was more direct and the answer to her question was obvious. Perhaps that's why in this whole sordid mess, it's the next moment that I'm a little bit proud of. It's the one in which I did *not* tell Sharon Postlewaite that Ike had set the fire that burned her house and almost killed her. I'd intended to. That was to be my coup de grâce, but I didn't do it. I didn't do it, and this time it truly was a noble thing, if only slightly. The woman was in love, and so what if it was an illusion?

Isn't all love to some extent? Isn't it what we insist upon, force into existence, make a mountain of a molehill of only because we need it so badly? Let her have her love; denying it was not going to give me mine.

That spring I took up running. It helped me pass the evenings as they grew lighter, and it was better than passing them on a barstool watching baseball on TV. It also allowed me to feel good about myself, something I needed, even if I did put a cigarette behind my ear to smoke at the end, and it gave me time to think; I also needed that. One of the things I thought about was my relationships with women. They weren't turning out very well. They all seemed to end at the lolling-about-and-fucking-six-ways-from-Sunday stage. I thought I might be ready for the how-are-we-going-to-pay-these-bills stage or maybe even the I-think-I-have-a-lump-in-my-breast stage. I wanted something more serious and important, but I didn't know how to get it.

Sharon and I weren't quite finished. We had two more encounters. The first of these was just going through the motions, as if we'd lost something in the bedclothes. The second, her bottle was nearly empty when she showed up, and it was only then that I began to think that maybe she too was a little desperate and trying to salvage something. She stood in the middle of the room and pulled her sweater over her head, messing her hair and losing her balance so that she stumbled. I'd never been so drawn to her nor certain that I should not be.

"You know what?" I lied. "I'm sick as a dog. You don't want to get anywhere near me." I drove her back to her house in her car and walked home. We both knew that it was over even though apparently neither of us wanted it to be. Funny how that works. I've known a couple women who I liked so much I wished I could love, and a couple more I liked so little that I wished I didn't.

The other thing I thought a lot about on my runs was Ike. He'd done it again. He'd stolen my girlfriend and left me standing there watching them walk away, just like in sixth grade. "I'm jealous of a dead man," I told Greg. "What the hell did he have?"

"I wish I knew." Greg's former wife, Alice, had taken up with a somewhat older guy who had some money. They had opened a bar and restaurant together, something she and Greg had often dreamed of doing, and it was all the rage. Greg couldn't go there, and I didn't because of him. Part of the reason was that I kept

seeing parallels to my own situation; it was I, after all, who had
cuckolded Ike.

Greg and I sat in the Blue Moon at the bar or at Office Billiards
or on one particularly bleak evening in the bowling alley drinking
beer and feeling sorry for ourselves. "I think this guy must have a
big wanger. Alice would love that. Did Ike have a big wanger?"

"Not particularly. Average size."

"Course Sharon wouldn't have known that anyway, would she?
That wasn't it, then."

No, what it was was ease. It was certainty and confidence, not
in himself but in you. Ike believed in people, just about everyone
but himself. That's what it had been with me from the beginning.
He believed that I had saved his life, that I could and would and
did save his life one snowy morning when we were kids and I had
come along on my sled and quite inadvertently knocked him out
of the way of a skidding car. He believed in the inherent goodness
of people. He believed in me and Greg and whatever scrawny girl
he had his arm around and every black guy from the rural South
in Vietnam and Sharon Novak. He believed in us so fiercely that it
changed us. It changed us all. And any disappointment he ever felt
took the form of concern. "I'm worried about you, Bill," he said in
high school. "We gotta get you laid," or later, "I'm worried about
you; you take things too seriously," or when I didn't anymore, "Isn't
anything serious to you?" But it was always because you weren't living up to your own high standard, and he needed us to. Ike Lowell
needed us to.

That's what I thought about it until I let myself remember the
unsavory fact that Ike had started the fire that burned Sharon Postlewaite's house, and then I didn't know what to think. Ike was
angry. He was suffering from shell shock. Maybe he thought he
was running into battle when he ran into that burning house. Ike
was delusional. Ike was hallucinating. Worst-case scenario, things
got out of hand. He set the fire so he could save Sharon from her
dull life and bad marriage, so he could save the kids, whisk them
all away to live happily ever after and escape his demons in the
process. He would put the fire out, be a hero, and step out of the
shadows like Boo Radley. Okay, misguided and dangerous and desperate, but well-intentioned. No evil or malice involved. And after
all, they all had gotten out. No harm came to anyone but himself.

That's how I thought about it until Charles Novak died. One

morning there was just a little notice in the office at school saying that Sharon would be away for a few days because of "a death in the family." The secretary told me about it. "Carbon monoxide poisoning, I guess. Colleague came to pick him up to go to the airport. Couldn't rouse him. Found him inside."

That changed everything. Sure, Charles Novak had been a bum, but now he was a dead bum, and Ike was the reason why. If Ike hadn't started that fire, the chances were good that Sharon and Ike's infatuation would have faded or passed. After all, isn't that what happens to infatuation? Isn't that what had happened to hers and mine? Ike would have slowly gotten better. Sharon would have realized it was all a fantasy; I thought of a couple of those that I'd had that were as titillating and intense as any of my real-life experiences and a good bit more. Charles's affair would have ended as it in fact did. Maybe he and Sharon would have gotten some counseling. Probably they would have settled down and grown old together; Sharon said as much herself. Not perfect, but then, what is that isn't a wet dream or some other fantasy? At least the kids would have a father. At least Charles and Sharon wouldn't have ended up alone. At least Charles would be alive.

But he wasn't alive, and what had only been theoretical now became real. Ike had claimed his first true victim. And while I did not want the reason to be either my anger with Ike or my jealousy of him, I was also no longer comfortable with my secret. Sharon had to know the truth. She had a right to know, and I had a duty to tell her.

Sharon's house was dark for four days. Then I waited two more and called. "Can I come by? I need to tell you something."

We sat at a picnic table in the backyard while the kids watched TV inside. We could see the flickering images. There was no wine. "I got what I'm about to tell you from Greg," I said. "He helped to write the story at the *Courier;* he was on the inside." I told her about the mysterious substance the fire marshal had discovered, the FBI lab report, the top-secret designation. I told her that the only conclusion anyone could reach was that somehow Ike had brought the stuff home from Vietnam and used it to start the fire. I told her that Ike had no longer been the carefree boy whose photographs she'd seen in yearbooks and newspapers, that he'd lost forty pounds and was weak and washed out, that he was frightened and damaged. I described how he had trouble making eye contact, how his hand

shook, how he couldn't sleep and had nightmares. Some of this I
exaggerated. The point I wanted to pound home when I started I
now felt I should soften, but then it occurred to me that if I made
Ike out to be too crazy, Sharon might think that I was saying that
she was crazy too. It also occurred to me that maybe I *was* saying
that, that maybe I wanted her to be, that I at least didn't mind
thinking of her as pathetic and lonely.

Sharon Postlewaite listened passively to all this as the evening
grew dark around us. Occasionally she lit a cigarette and turned
her head to blow the smoke away. When I finished, we sat quietly
for a while. Then she asked, "That everything?"

"I think so. I'm sorry."

"You know that stuff, the accelerant that you talked about?"

"Yes."

"It's called DP123."

"It is? How do you know that?" I thought perhaps there were
things Greg hadn't told me, maybe things he didn't know himself.
"I mean . . ."

"I know because Charles invented it. He was the head of the
team that developed it, but it was his baby."

"You're kidding."

"No, Charles was a very brilliant man. He had a brilliant mind,
but up until very recently I thought he was a psychopath. I thought
he'd tried to kill us all. You see, Ike didn't set that fire. Charles did."

"Charles? He was out of town."

"Charles was an engineer, Bill. Charles was a genius. He could
set up a timer to turn the furnace on when we were away from
home or preheat the oven. Did you ever see our Christmas lights?
All on timers. And remote controls. Charles had a squabble with
our neighbor one time. He got even by rigging his garage door so
it would go up in the middle of the night. He used to lie in bed and
laugh. That was Charles.

"You see, he'd fallen in love with this little lab tech and wanted
to run away with her, wanted to fuck himself to death. I knew all
about it. We were in the way. We were a problem, and he was a
problem solver. Voilà. He set that fire to kill us all."

"Now wait a minute . . . what are you saying . . . I mean, is all of
this just pure speculation, because if . . ."

"Not at all. I can prove it. I proved it to Charles. That's how I got
the divorce settlement I did. I put everything in a sealed file and gave

it to my attorney and told him to take it to the FBI if anything happened to me. Then I confronted Charles. I said I didn't know how he did it but I knew that he did it. He buckled like that. So you see, your friend Ike is off the hook, and so are you. Okay?" She watched me and nodded. "Listen, I should get these kids to bed. Okay?"

"Wait a minute," I said. "You said you thought he was a psychopath until recently. What changed?"

"Oh," she said, "Charles's death was no accident either. Of that I'm sure. As I say, he was a brilliant engineer. He would never, ever have died of carbon monoxide poisoning unless he wanted to. He had sensors everywhere. He was phobic about both fumes and smoke. Scared to death of dying in his sleep. So Charles must have wanted to die, which means that he must have felt remorse for what he did or tried to do, which means he wasn't a psychopath. Plus he left the door unlocked and set it up so he'd be found quickly so he wouldn't blow up the whole neighborhood. No, I really don't think he was a psychopath after all."

"But if he wanted to die, why not just kill himself? Why fake it?"

"Insurance. Charles always provided for us very well. He prided himself on it. I'm about to be a wealthy woman, Bill. Again." She smiled, then crossed the yard and patio and disappeared into the house.

I lit another cigarette. I lit several more. I watched until the lights went out on the first floor and then one by one on the second floor until there was just one and then it went out too. I sat there trying to figure this thing out. Who really set that fire? Could Ike have actually smuggled that stuff into the country? Would the Charles Novak I knew about try to kill his own children? And if he truly wasn't a psychopath, was someone? Was Sharon, for God's sake? There was something unsettling about the dispassion with which she'd described everything. Could she have somehow started that fire?

She'd said that she always knew when she was being watched. Did she know it now? And didn't that mean that she was also always watching? Might she be up there at this very moment standing in the shadows and peering through the venetian blinds?

When I'd smoked my last cigarette, I put it out right on the picnic table and left. In June when I turned twenty-six, I left my job. In August when my lease was up, I left town. In a way I've been leaving ever since, and I don't think that I'm finished leaving even now. Not quite yet.

Lovers and Thieves

FROM *Alfred Hitchcock Mystery Magazine*

IT WAS THE kind of rain favored by lovers and thieves. A misty November rain. The kind that hangs low, veil-like, obscuring the dark, desperate world beneath it. The kind that sends lovers into their bedrooms and thieves into the night.

I was more like the thief, waiting outside the Bon Vivant on La Brea, a tired, three-story stucco apartment building with a name more festive than its architecture. Waiting inside my gunmetal-gray 1934 DeSoto Airflow Coupe.

It wasn't where I wanted to be. It wasn't where a PI makes any real money in this town. That kind of dough—the kind I never seemed to have—was found up in the Hollywood Hills, where the famous and the desperate-to-be-famous always managed to find trouble where trouble shouldn't be found.

But at the Bon Vivant, trouble came in the form of two lovers, a midlevel oil executive, Frank "Mac" McKenzie, and his youthful secretary, Teresa Vail. She lived in Apartment 311. The one on the top floor, right side, on the corner. The one with the lights still on at one-fifteen in the morning.

It wasn't that Mac's wife cared all that much. Alice McKenzie just needed divorce-court evidence so that she could squeeze the most out of her philandering husband.

She'd squeezed plenty out of me, talking me down to $50 a day and no expenses. I'd been no match for her the minute she'd walked into my office. I'd needed the work. Even though it was only fourteen months since V-J Day and the subsequent end to gasoline rationing, keeping the twelve-year-old DeSoto in fuel—and run-ning—wasn't cheap.

I'd been tailing Mac around ten p.m. when he'd pulled his cream-colored Buick Roadmaster to the curb a block past the Bon Vivant. He'd walked in fast, his shoulders hunched against the rain, carrying a small black Gladstone bag. A change of clothes, maybe, or a gift for his concubine.

I'd waited over three hours since then, only seeing a handful of people enter or leave the building. The first a happy man whistling a happy tune on his way out at ten forty-five. Whistling, that is, until he saw me, which made him pull his hat lower and hurry on, glanc-ing back a couple of times as if I might be tailing him instead of Mac McKenzie. Which confirmed something I already knew: that everyone in this town was guilty of something.

At eleven I saw two young women in their twenties scurry inside, looking guilty of little more than believing in the future. In who they still could be.

And at one, a middle-aged couple in a drunken argument, both guilty as sin of who they'd become.

That was it. In three hours. Three hours I'd never get back. Three hours that had turned my mood from gray to black.

That's when I decided it was time to move things along. Time to go in, get a shot of Mac *in flagrante delicto,* then run like hell. If all went well, I'd be home and in bed by two.

The Bon Vivant was horseshoe-shaped, with its opening toward the street, but in the dark, oppressive drizzle it didn't feel terribly lucky. I crossed the damp courtyard and walked inside. Passed the bank of mail slots, including the one with Teresa Vail's name on it. Followed the worn floral carpeting to the stairs and up to the third floor. Found Apartment 311 and gave the knob a quiet turn. It wasn't locked.

I edged the door open. Held my AGFA Readyset Special camera in front of me like a gun. Kept my finger on its red shutter-but-ton trigger, ready-set to immortalize Mac McKenzie's infidelity in a flash of exposed silver.

All the lights were on in the living room, an average space dec-orated with above-average furniture. Despite her age, Teresa Vail had taste. Not a thing that didn't belong. Not a thing out of place.

Except for the man on the couch pitched sideways against the armrest with the ruby face and the cloth-covered extension cord wrapped around his neck.

And the young woman slumped against his shoulder with the .22 in her hand and the bullet hole under her chin.

Outside, a misty rain still veiled the sins of a desperate city. But inside Apartment 311, those sins were in full view, embodied in two dead lovers and the blood-red echoes they'd left behind.

I was leaning against the jamb in the opening to the bedroom, smoking a cigarette, counting the black shoe marks on the bedroom door, waiting for the cops to cut me loose. Twenty-eight lines and smudges a foot above the wood floor. I pictured Mac carrying Teresa in his arms and kicking the bedroom door open on his way to violating the Sixth Commandment.

Pictured that up until Teresa Vail's mother walked in. As a cynical private eye, it's easy to forget about the humanity that props up each life. A humanity that seems at its purest—its most sincere —when someone dies. Having seen hundreds of dead bodies from Anzio to Dachau as a rifleman-turned-medic in the war, I'd developed a certain indifference to the fate of others. A certain hardness to their trauma and pain. Enough, at least, to get me through the endless nightmare of battle.

But seeing the mother of the young woman burst through the open doorway, push past the policemen milling about and the coroner taking still lifes of the bodies, and hearing the chilling, feral howl that rose from her soul when she saw her daughter, made me swallow hard. She would have thrown herself on her daughter's body if an alert cop hadn't stepped in front of her and gripped her shoulders, keeping her from disturbing the crime scene. She struggled but soon collapsed, borne down by the invisible weight of death. A weight that would, as I'd learned from the war, press down on her for years to come. If not forever.

My client, on the other hand, showed no signs of heartbreak. Alice McKenzie—fortyish with unnaturally black hair and the swollen face of an aspiring alcoholic—strode through the door in a brown slack suit with a cigarette between her fingers and lipstick on her teeth. She reacted like a foreman who finds the crew lying down on the job. Wide stance, hands on hips, lips pressed into a thin, derisive line.

"That s.o.b.," she said.

Unlike Teresa's mother, Alice was childless. And now husbandless, but with an inheritance instead of a divorce. Assuming, of course, that she hadn't murdered him, which had crossed my mind as I'd begun to wonder how she'd known to show up at the interloper's apartment at this late hour.

I sidled over to the detective in charge, who stood by the front door like a groomsman, his hands clasped behind his back. His name was Beaumont. I knew him from a prior case. We'd parted from that case like an old vaudeville team, sick to death of each other's act. "Who called the wife?" I said.

Beaumont wore a brown hat and brown suit that looked like they'd been up all night. He kept a stony face, but his eyes took on a blue twinkle as they stared past me at the commotion that follows in the wake of violent death. The commotion that paid for his tired suit and the mortgage on his house. "Dunno, Nash. I hear she's your client. Why don't you ask her?"

"How about the mother?"

"Dunno about her either. Maybe they're both fortunetellers, like Doreena on the Santa Monica Pier." He let the hint of a smile nuzzle his lips. Then he raised an eyebrow and turned his sights on me. "What I wanna know, Nash, is how you knew to be here. Square in the middle of a murder-suicide."

"I was watching the place, trying to get some black-and-white evidence for my client. But when McKenzie didn't come out, I decided to come in. This is what I found."

"You're a helluva PI," he said, with more twinkles in his eyes. "Always one step behind."

I twinkled my eyes back at him. "But always one step ahead of you." Then I took several steps over to Alice. With her feet planted on the wood floor, she looked more in charge than Beaumont.

"Alice," I said with a nod.

"You found them?" Her skepticism was as subtle as the lipstick on her teeth.

"I'm a full-service PI," I said. "Who called you?"

She turned her head toward me, took a pull on her cigarette, then exhaled. Her eyes narrowed behind the smoke that drifted from her lips. "A friend."

"What's his name?"

Her eyes turned steely. She dropped the cigarette on the varnished floor and stepped it out. "You can go now, Mr. Nash. I don't

need your help anymore. Send me a bill." Then she spun and
walked toward the door. She paused just long enough to give Teresa Vail's mother a dismissive look and to tell Beaumont that if he
needed anything more she was in the telephone book under Mr.
Frank "Mac" McKenzie.

After Alice left Teresa Vail's apartment, I took a moment to
gather up my camera and my hat from an accent chair and, with
Beaumont's blessing, made my way out of the apartment. In the
hall I passed a Rita Hayworth redhead with her face buried in her
hands, crouching with her back against the wall, struggling to com-
pose herself. I almost stopped, but the wall of indifference rose up
and without a second thought I took the stairs to the back door of
the Bon Vivant.

Once outside I followed the alley to the corner of the building,
then crept up the narrow sidewalk between the Bon Vivant and a
long hedge. I stopped in the shadows of the walkway not far from
the street. From there I could see Alice standing at the curb near
the no-parking zone, where two vacant patrol cars sat with their
lights off.

The misty rain made the world feel small, intimate, cold. But
Alice seemed unaware of the dismal weather, her gaze distant, as if
she'd forgotten where she'd parked her car but was in no hurry to
remember. She glanced back at the courtyard and the front door to
the Bon Vivant. Looked up at the windows to No. 311.

I thought it might be a moment of weakness for Alice, a long,
last look toward the man she had once loved. But then a dark Packard, wipers thumping, rolled to a stop in front of her. She slipped
between the two empty prowlers and into the passenger side of the
sedan. All I could see of the driver was the silhouette of a fedora.

They drove off down the veiled darkness of La Brea, passing under the streetlamps, gliding like a blackened ghost in and out of
the falling pools of light.

As I drove back to my apartment on Hollywood Boulevard, I
thought about the case Alice McKenzie had just fired me from.
Thought about it free of charge, just like most things I thought
about these days. Thought about what I'd seen when I'd discovered
the bodies.

Teresa had worn a gray pleated skirt and a pink wool pullover
sweater—pink except for a scarlet cascade of blood at the collar.

A pink ribbon held back her dark-brown hair in a ponytail. Her perfume was the expensive kind, not too sweet, and the makeup on her midtwenties face was flawless. She was the picture of vibrant youth. As vibrant as youth can look when the animation of the soul is gone.

Mac had been dressed for a night on the town in a light-blue herringbone coat and pleated slacks and black-and-white wingtip shoes that needed a polish on the heels. His blue-black hair was slick with tonic and shaped as neatly as a mannequin's. He was short and carried none of the extra pounds that seemed to come with age. He looked as trim as a varsity rower.

The only thing out of place on him—other than the extension cord around his neck and the deep red coloring of his face—was the crop of medals pinned in random spots on his jacket. A World War II Victory Medal on the lapel. An army Good Conduct Medal on a lower pocket. An American Campaign Medal on the shoulder. A Combat Infantry Badge on the collar. A Purple Heart through a buttonhole. A European–African–Middle Eastern Campaign Medal, pierced by two bronze battle stars and a bronze arrowhead, near a cuff. And, sticking out of the upper left pocket like a red-and-blue pocket square, the Bronze Star.

I'd never seen medals displayed on civilian clothes before, or in such a careless way, but maybe Mac had been a proud veteran. VFW type. There were millions of them around these days. Or maybe his medals had given Teresa a sexual thrill. Maybe his heroism was what had blinded her to the twenty years that separated their births.

Whatever the case, they'd been two people dressed for a night out that had never come. And from the looks of it, hadn't done anything more physical than sit on the couch and listen to *The Adventures of Ellery Queen* on the radio.

But something about the whole picture hadn't added up. Something that had drawn me to their hands. Made me smell them. Both of his carried a hint of soap, both of hers the muskiness of sweaty skin. None of them had smelled of gunpowder, not even the one—hers—holding the .22 that had sent the bullet up under her chin.

Detective Beaumont saw it as a murder-suicide. I was seeing something else.

Then again, what did I care? I was off the clock. Common sense said there'd be no payment for anything else I did on this case and

to keep the DeSoto aimed for home. To let Beaumont and his un-
derlings deal with it.

I couldn't have agreed more.

Until I made an impulsive U-turn in the middle of Hollywood
Boulevard, the DeSoto's tires hissing as they pivoted on the wet,
black, shimmering pavement.

When I pulled to a stop at the curb in front of a small bungalow a
block off Fairfax, Teresa Vail's mother was being helped out of a
dark-green prewar Dodge parked in the driveway. She stumbled
toward the door, propped up by a woman nearly a foot taller than
her. The same woman I'd seen crouched in the hallway of the Bon
Vivant. The Rita Hayworth redhead.

I checked my watch. Almost three a.m. The rain had stopped,
leaving in its wake a cold, surly dampness. The redhead, still holding Teresa's mother with one arm, was struggling to find a key in
her purse. I hurried up the driveway.

"Can I help?"

The redhead looked back at me, wary, protective. "Who are you?"

I stopped a dozen feet from them and raised my hands. "Darrow Nash. I was at Teresa's apartment. I wanted to see if Mrs. Vail
needed anything."

"I've got it covered." The redhead turned away and continued
to dig in the purse as Mrs. Vail moaned at her side. The purse fell
and its contents spilled out onto the front step. Curses spilled out
of the redhead.

I helped gather up the debris, then used the key that I'd picked
up off the step to unlock the front door. The redhead led Mrs. Vail
inside and straight down a hall. I wiped my feet on the rug by the
front door and waited. To the left lay the living room, a small space
stuffed with a sofa and a pair of chairs and a trio of burning lights.
It looked like a room that had been left in a hurry, and smelled like
a room that was beginning to sour. But what captured my attention
stood between two double-hung windows: a liquor table holding a
quartet of upside-down tumblers and a bottle of Jameson.

A couple of minutes later the redhead came back up the hallway, her head down, her hands buried in the pockets of her tan
raincoat. She looked up, saw me standing in the living room, and
gasped, a hand shooting up to cover her heart. Irritation flooded
her words. "What are you still doing here?"

"I was the one who found Teresa."

"That doesn't give you the right to barge in here."

"I'm the one who let you in."

She gazed at the two tumblers of Jameson I held in my hands. Finally said, "Are you with the police?"

"No. I'm Darrow Nash. A private detective."

"Then why should I let you stay?"

I offered her one of the drinks. "You probably shouldn't."

She stared at me. Seemed to assess my face, studying it for clues. Then she shrugged off her coat, tossed it over the back of the sofa, and kicked her shoes toward the door. She took the drink from my hand. "You win, Darrow Nash."

"Nobody wins tonight," I said.

She dropped into one of the stuffed chairs and took something between a sip and a gulp. Held the side of the glass against her forehead. Leaned into it. Her silk burgundy blouse, open at the neck in a *V,* gave me a glimpse of the dark depths between her breasts. Later I noticed her dark gray skirt.

"How's Mrs. Vail?"

Her eyes brushed me off. "How do you think?"

"I'd say terrible."

"Brilliant deduction, Holmes," she said, tilting her drink in a salute. "She fell asleep the minute her head hit the pillow."

"Is she your mother?"

"Clara? No. Teresa and I aren't sisters. We're . . ." She paused, looked away, rubbed her eyes. "We were friends from work."

"But you live here, right?"

She nodded. "Just until I find some work. Cattle calls don't pay the rent. Teresa and I used to be in the secretarial pool together at Standard Oil." Something about my silence made her add, "I wasn't fired. I quit."

"Why?"

She started to speak but caught herself. Her eyes narrowed. "Not that it's any of your business." She waited. Finally said, "My boss wanted more from me than I was willing to give."

"Who was your boss?"

"Paul Devore." Just saying his name made her clench her jaw. "Teresa helped me stand up to him. She . . ." Then the tears came, filling her eyes, spilling down her cheeks. Quiet tears, unaccompanied by sobs or anguished moans. The ones that look like they hurt the most.

I filled the void the best I could. "If it helps, I don't think she killed herself."

Her swollen eyes widened and locked on mine. She hesitated, as if too many words had come to mind and she couldn't decide which ones to use. She didn't have to.

"There's no way on God's green earth," said a voice from down the hall, a voice both fragile and firm, "that Teresa would ever kill herself." Mrs. Vail stopped at the edge of the hallway, one hand pressed for support against the wall. "She was too strong to do that."

The redhead stood up. "Clara, I told you to get some sleep."

It seemed to take herculean effort for Mrs. Vail to turn her gaze on her housemate. "My daughter is dead, Eileen. I can do whatever I like."

She hauled her eyes back over to me. "Teresa would never take her own life, sir. Never." It came out stronger than before, over-whelming whatever had been fragile. But the effort used up what strength she had left. Her knees buckled and she slumped to the floor, sobbing. Eileen and I each took an arm and helped her back to her bedroom. The light was off, but I got a picture of it from the smell of lingering perfume and the profound lack of a male presence. A room that had seen its share of tears and loneliness over the years. With many more to come.

Eileen and I returned to the main room and took long sips of our drinks. I felt nauseous from the perfume and the air of death in the house, but I needed to know more. I looked at Eileen. She seemed exhausted, distracted.

"Cattle calls?" I said. "You're an actress?"

"Aspiring." She wrapped the word in a thin sheen of bitterness. "Which means 'unemployed.'"

Looking at Eileen, I thought of Rita Hayworth in *The Lady in Question*, the innocent, melancholy defendant.

"How long had Teresa been seeing Mac?"

She let out a short burst of air, a cheap substitute for a laugh. "Teresa and Mac? You're not much of a private eye, are you?"

"He brought a Gladstone bag with him like he might be spending the night."

The thought made her smile. "Not a chance. She was his secretary and they were friendly, but he wasn't the dating type, if you know what I mean. And he wasn't particularly good-looking. Teresa felt sorry for him, married to that bitch of a woman. Living behind that kind of a lie."

Something dawned on me. Something that should have crossed my mind earlier. "Why did you move in here with Mrs. Vail? Why not with Teresa at the Bon Vivant?"

Eileen cocked her head and looked at me like I was a sap. "Teresa didn't live there. She lived here. That was Mac's apartment."

"But the mail slot has Teresa's name on it."

"She did that for him. He wanted a place where he could be himself and be free of that nasty woman."

I nodded, trying to hide the fact that I'd been surprised by the information. "What do you think happened?"

"Murder-suicide. What else?"

"Most murder-suicides come from romances gone bad. But you said they were just friends."

She stared at me for a moment, mulling over my reasoning, then seemed to give up, her only response a self-conscious sip of her drink.

"How did you and Mrs. Vail know to go to the apartment?"

She took another sip before answering. "Paul Devore called me."

"How did he know about it?"

"I didn't think to ask," she said, glancing away. "I wanted off the phone as fast as possible."

"Did Devore and Mac know each other?"

"Yes. I guess you could call them rivals. Paul always envied Mac's success with the company. Before the war, Mac had even beaten Paul out of a couple of promotions." She paused and her eyes widened. "Maybe Paul was the one who killed them. Maybe that's how he knew about it."

We looked at each other, considering the possibility. But then her eyes eased from thoughtful into purposeful. She stood up and stretched. My eyes wandered off on their own to see what that stretch did to her curves. It didn't hurt them at all. Rita Hayworth in *Cover Girl*, the sexy showgirl. I set my empty glass on an end table.

Eileen did the same, her eyes now deep and dangerous.

I gave her a long look. A very long look. "I better get going. Thanks for talking." I moved to the front door, but fought every step. I was surprised by how much I liked this Rita Hayworth redhead. Liked her toughness. Her ease. Her complexity.

When I turned back to her, she had followed me to the door. "What did you say your name was?"

I fingered an information card out of my suit coat and gave it to her. "Darrow Nash."

"Eileen Burnham."

"Thanks for not kicking me out earlier, Eileen Burnham."

"Thanks for the drink, Darrow Nash. Is it too late for a second?"

"I'll take a rain check on that."

"It's raining now."

I knew what a second would mean. Saw it in her eyes. Felt it in my blood. And it wasn't what you should be doing on a night like this. A night when a friend is dead and the mother of that friend is sleeping in the next room.

"That card I gave you has a telephone number on it," I said. "If after a week or so you find yourself wondering about me, try that number. Won't cost you a thing. It's a local call."

She didn't smile. Just kept staring at me with those deep, dangerous eyes. Eyes that I felt following me all the way back to my car.

Mac and Alice McKenzie lived on a quiet, unlighted street in Burbank in the heart of the San Fernando Valley, bounded by the Santa Monica Mountains to the south and the San Gabriels to the north. A flat basin in the middle of mountain ranges, like the bottom of a petri dish where, particularly in the entertainment business, everyone seemed to be under a microscope.

It was raining again.

The house, one story of faux-Spanish stucco, was dark. I looked at my watch. It was just after four a.m. Either Alice and her boyfriend were home and asleep already or they hadn't come back to Alice's house at all. The one-lane driveway was empty.

I knocked on the front door a couple of times, rang the bell a few more. No answer. Tried the knob. Locked. Tried the back door to the patio. Locked. Tried the hairpin I kept in my coat pocket. Unlocked.

I left the lights off as I stepped into the kitchen. Switched on my flashlight. Moved to the living room. Found nothing but the casual disarray of everyday life.

Moved down the hall to the bedrooms. All the doors were open and all the beds were made. It didn't take long to see that Alice and Mac didn't sleep together. Alice, of course, had the larger bedroom, Mac the smaller one.

I wasn't sure what I was looking for, so I started with Mac's closet. Found half a dozen pairs of hard shoes, a dozen wool suits, two dozen dress shirts, three dozen ties. Nothing out of the ordinary for a middle-aged oil executive. His dresser wasn't much different, though I learned his hair tonic was Lucky Tiger and his aftershave was Yardley. The drawers held undershirts, silk socks, boxers, pocket squares, and a handful of neatly folded sweaters. The common denominator was quality. All of his clothes were very expensive and very new.

The same wasn't true in Mac's desk. I found it in another bedroom, which had been turned into a study. The top of the desk was covered by a writing blotter and anchored at the two outer corners by a fluorescent lamp and by something that was no longer there. Something that had sat on that corner long enough to have left a faint outline in the dust. Just enough dust to betray a rectangle.

The drawers of the desk were filled with a hodgepodge of pens and pencils and old financial detritus: receipts, bank statements, bills. I flipped quickly through some documents but couldn't find any life insurance policies that might betray a million-dollar motive.

The right-hand middle drawer held several small rectangular boxes. Inside the boxes were stacks of canceled checks. I was about to close the drawer when I noticed that its interior seemed shorter than it should.

I reached a hand in and touched the back panel. There was a space at the top of the panel for a finger to gain purchase. When I pulled on it, the panel fell forward. Behind it in the secret space was another small rectangular box and a letter-sized envelope folded in half.

I opened the box expecting to find more canceled checks but instead found several matchbooks from a place called The Roaring 20s. Inside the matchbooks were handwritten first names and telephone numbers.

Lying in the box beneath all the matchbooks were a dozen black-and-white photographs, the kind with thick white borders. Different names were written on the backs of the photographs, names that were the same as those in the matchbooks. Men's names. And in each of the pictures Mac was with a different man. All of the men were naked. Doing the kinds of things people do when they're naked.

Better divorce photographs than I could have ever taken at the Bon Vivant.

The flash of headlights swung across the rain-streaked window to the study like a lighthouse beam through the mist. I thought about trying to hide or to make a break for the back door, but my old DeSoto was parked down the street. Alice knew it was mine.

Instead, as I heard the car pull to a stop in the driveway, I tucked the small box back into its hiding place in the desk and replaced the fake drawer wall. I slipped the pictures and the envelope into the inside pocket of my suit coat.

In the living room I turned on a lamp, aimed a flower-patterned wing chair toward the front door, and took a seat. Crossed my legs. Used one hand to prop up my chin. Used the other to keep my .38 company inside the pocket of my raincoat.

The front door opened. Alice, still in her brown slack suit, led the way, the keys jangling in her hand. She stopped when she saw me. Took up the foreman pose she'd displayed at the Bon Vivant, feet planted, hands on hips, flint in her eyes. "I thought I made it clear you were fired."

"You did," I said. "I'm off the clock."

A man came through the door behind her wearing a navy-blue suit and hat with water droplets on the shoulders and crown. He bore a slight limp that I recognized from the war—I'd treated several GIs for the same wound. He wasn't tall but had a certain sense of size about him. Probably from his ego, because he came at me with the misplaced confidence of a rookie cop.

He grabbed my lapels and hoisted me from the chair. "Time to go, pal."

"Not just yet, pal," I said, and kneed him in a place a knee is never welcome. He doubled over and dropped face-first onto the floor. I left the gun in my coat pocket and pulled his right arm behind him, resting the offending knee in the middle of his back. I leveraged his arm up until he yelped.

I glanced up at Alice. "Introductions?"

She looked disgusted with both of us. "Darrow Nash. Paul Devore."

I gave his arm another twist, and he yelped again. "Pleased to meet you, Paul."

"You're hurting me."

"Tell Mr. Devore," I said to Alice, "that I'll let him up if he stops playing a tough guy."

"He won't do anything."

I eased off his arm and used my knee on his back to push myself up to my feet. He yelped again but remained on the floor, squirming, finally able to wallow in the pain in his groin now that the pain in his arm and back had subsided.

I dipped my hand into my raincoat pocket and kept it there. I trusted Alice, but not Devore.

"How did you get in?" she said as she pulled a pack from her purse and shook a cigarette between her lips.

"I carry a master key shaped like a hairpin."

She didn't seem to care, as she snapped her lighter shut and blew a cloud of smoke toward the ceiling. It swirled over us, between us, like silent blue worry. "What do you want?"

"I want to know why you went to the apartment tonight."

She glanced down at the man on the floor between us. "Paul took me there."

I hoisted Devore to his feet and settled him into the flowered chair he'd pulled me out of. His hat had fallen off, exposing the smooth curvature of his head through thinning black hair. An oversized grimace exposed tiny fractures around his eyes.

"Why did you take Alice to the apartment?"

He squeezed the words out through exaggerated pain. "I wanted her to see Mac's home away from home. I didn't know he was dead."

"But you knew it was Mac's place and not Teresa Vail's." It wasn't a question.

His eyes shifting away from me was as good as a nod.

I turned to Alice. "Did you know it was Mac's?"

She looked off through the walls toward a spot somewhere beyond the Santa Monicas. Somewhere closer to La Brea. Took a long drag on her cigarette, let the smoke out with the words. "No. I figured on the nights he didn't come home he'd found some bimbo to put him up." Her eyes came back to me with a darker tint. "I didn't know his affairs were month-to-month."

I studied her. Realized that she had no idea who Mac McKenzie really was.

I turned back to Devore. "How did you know about the apartment?"

"None of your damn business."

I didn't have to threaten him. Alice did it for me. She wanted to know too. "Answer him."

"My secretary called me tonight and told me."

"What's her name?"

"Eileen Burnham."

"Don't you mean your former secretary?"

His focus sharpened on me. "How do you know that?"

"I'm good at what I do." I gestured toward Alice. "Why don't you tell her why Eileen quit."

He took a quick, panicked glance at Alice. Her gaze narrowed into a hard stare. Then she stuffed out her cigarette in an ashtray and folded her arms.

I didn't have a warm spot in my heart for Alice. Had never liked that kind of cynicism in a woman. But I hated guys like Paul Devore. Guys with moneyed egos and bankrupt character. Guys who used their positions of authority to get what they wanted, not through persuasion but through force. I answered for him.

"Paul here likes his secretaries to take more from him than just dictation."

Alice eyed Devore like a hammer eyes a nail. Devore verbally backpedaled in the chair. "It was before I met you, honey."

Nobody in the room believed that.

I watched Alice, waiting for the anger inside her to show itself in something specific, in either her words or her fists. Devore was watching for the same thing. Instead the anger melted into disillusionment. As if her expectations had been met. Expectations she'd been hoping would be proven wrong. She moved to a window and lit another cigarette.

"Get out of here, Paul," she said, her voice low, resigned. "And don't come back."

He jumped to his feet. "But I love you."

Nobody in the room believed that either.

I steered him toward the front door, noticing his limp again. "Beat it, Devore. She's done with you. Alice doesn't go for cowards."

The guilty verdict in his eyes was followed by an embarrassed rage that sent him out the door, hobbling toward his Packard. A rage still evident as he backed wildly out of the driveway and sped off into the night.

Alice stood fingering the cigarette close to her lips as she stared into a darkness that illuminated her reflection in the window.

I stepped up beside her. "You're better off without him."

She turned her head and gave me a long look. I hesitated, surprised for a moment by what I saw, what I hadn't noticed before. That her eyes—blue eyes that had once been so cynical—possessed a raw humanity. A tender loneliness.

"You'll find someone," I said. And I meant it.

She stared at me. Took a deep pull on her cigarette. Then looked away and exhaled, the smoke obscuring her image in the window.

As I closed the front door behind me, I marveled at how somebody so hard-edged could be so vulnerable. But sometimes, I guess, the deepest truths can conjure up the greatest facades.

At five a.m. outside the Bon Vivant there was no external evidence that two people had suffered tragic deaths inside. No ambulances. No cop cars. All that was left in the wake of the murderous violence was the pregnant, drizzling darkness just before another dawn.

I'd stopped by hoping to catch Beaumont still on the job. I wanted to give him the envelope I'd found in the secret compartment inside Mac's desk, proof that this wasn't a simple murder-suicide.

After leaving Alice's house, I'd sat in my car and looked through the envelope's contents. It held three short, cryptic notes, each typewritten on small pieces of white paper: I'M WATCHING YOU and DOES YOUR WIFE KNOW? and DOES YOUR BOSS KNOW?

The fourth note got to the point:

I KNOW WHAT YOU ARE. I KNOW WHO YOU ENTERTAIN AT THE BON VIVANT. IF YOU DON'T WANT ALICE AND EVERYONE AT STANDARD OIL TO KNOW TOO IT WILL COST YOU $50,000. IF YOU AREN'T AT THE APARTMENT ON SUNDAY NIGHT AT 10:00 WITH THE CASH BY MONDAY MORNING YOUR CAREER AND YOUR MARRIAGE WILL BE OVER.

My guess was that tonight had been the Sunday night for the meeting. And I'd noticed when I'd followed Mac there that he had rushed into the Bon Vivant just before ten carrying a small Glad-

stone bag. At the time I hadn't given it much thought. I had just
assumed it held a change of clothes or a present for someone. But
it might have contained something else. Something dangerous,
like a gun. Or something worse, like money.

And during my time inside the apartment, I hadn't seen the
cops tag it as evidence. I needed to know if it was still in there. And
what, if anything, it still contained.

As I walked through the courtyard to the front door, lights had
come on in the windows of a handful of apartments, but not the
one with Teresa Vail's name on it. When I reached 311 there was
no indication that the cops cared about this case anymore. No post-
ings to keep out. No police tape. To them, it was a murder-suicide.
Case closed.

Then I heard a muffled noise through the paneled wood door. I
pulled the .38 from my raincoat pocket.

I examined the lock on the door. No evidence of tampering. I
tried the knob. No resistance. The cops would have at least locked
it when they'd left. Whoever was inside had used a key.

I felt my heart clench. The feeling that comes with news I don't
want to hear. Or don't want to believe.

I stepped inside and closed the door. The living room was dark,
but a flashlight beam danced against the walls in the bedroom.
I turned on the lamp next to the couch where Mac and Teresa
had died, casting the room in a tepid yellow glow. But not tepid
enough to soften the poignancy of the bloodstains left behind on
the couch.

I heard the flashlight click off, leaving the bedroom buried in
darkness.

"It's me," I said into a silence both sharp and airless. "Darrow
Nash."

No sound. Then a form in an overcoat stepped into the open
doorway.

"You work long hours for a PI."

"I work as long as it takes," I said.

"As long as it takes for what?"

"For the truth."

No response. Just a long, wary stare. Deep and dangerous.

"How's Mrs. Vail?" I said.

"Asleep."

"What brings you back here?"

Eileen rolled her shoulders and lolled her head as if to stretch. "I couldn't sleep there. I was too upset." She set the flashlight on a small table by the bedroom door and opened her tan overcoat. She still wore the burgundy blouse, the one with the open-neck *V* that ended where her cleavage started. Her Rita Hayworth hair rested on her shoulders.

"If you were looking for sleep, why did you bring a flashlight?"

She took several slow steps out of the bedroom, the fingers of her left hand caressing the skin that led down into the deep cleft between her breasts. Her right hand was tucked into her raincoat pocket. I didn't trust either hand. Or what either one was suggesting.

"I wanted to collect some of Teresa's things." She stopped six feet away from me. "I was hoping I'd see you again. Maybe collect on that rain check."

Rita Hayworth in *Blood and Sand*. The sultry temptress.

I took a deep breath and let out a long sigh. "Whose idea was it?"

She cocked her head and pasted on a quizzical look. "Whose idea was what?"

I gestured toward the bloodstained couch. "This."

She shrugged. "How would I know? It was a murder-suicide."

"If that's true, why didn't Teresa just shoot Mac, then shoot herself? Why go to the trouble of strangling him first?"

She watched me, her hands frozen in place, one at her chest, the other in her pocket.

"There was no gunpowder on Teresa's skin," I said, holding her gaze. "I smelled her hands. Someone else put that bullet in her head."

Eileen's face seemed thinner than earlier in the night. And older. "Maybe we should sit down and discuss this. I know where we might be more comfortable." Then she walked back into the bedroom and hit the wall switch, filling the room with a milky luminescence from the ceiling light. She sat on the edge of the double bed and crossed her legs.

I stopped in the doorway. It was the same room from the pictures Mac had hidden in his desk at the house. The bed, made with military precision, was covered in a bright red satin spread. The dresser drawers were closed. The closet door was open.

Eileen let an idle hand play back and forth across the silky covering. "Sit by me."

I made no movement toward the bed.

"Here's what I think," I said. "You and Teresa were extorting money from Mac. You found out he preferred the company of men and used it to try to get fifty thousand dollars out of him. He was supposed to meet you here tonight to give you the money."

She tried on a look of skepticism. It didn't fit. Even she knew that, so she tried on something else. "Mac shot Teresa."

I looked down, shaking my head. Caught sight of the black marks on the bedroom door, a foot above the floor. The marks I'd been counting as I'd been waiting earlier in the night for Beaumont to release me. All twenty-eight of them. Some of them thin, curved lines. Some of them dense smudges.

And I remembered Mac's shoes. Black-and-white wingtips that had needed polishing. Not on the toes but on the heels.

A burst of clarity shot through me. I looked up at Eileen. "Mac didn't kill Teresa. He couldn't have, because he was already dead."

Eileen rose to her feet. Stared down at the bottom of the bedroom door, at the collection of black scars.

"Mac's shoes were scuffed on the heels," I said. "He died hanging from this door. My guess is the extension cord was tied to the knob on the other side and draped over the top. But for some reason his neck didn't break. He struggled, then eventually suffocated. Which leaves only one person who could have shot Teresa. You."

"I would never do that." She said it with icy confidence, but I sensed a weakening. Her act wasn't working on me like she'd thought it would.

"Tell me what happened."

She stared at me, her face a pallid mask. Stared so long that I began to wonder if she was going to say anything at all. "No one was supposed to die."

"Was it Teresa's idea?"

Eileen nodded. "She'd helped Mac get the apartment, but when she found out he only had men over here, she saw an opportunity. She didn't think he'd be man enough to fight our demands." Her eyes narrowed and she shook her head. "But neither of us thought he was the kind of guy who would kill himself."

"Why not?"

"Mac seemed okay with his . . . with himself. And he was a war hero. All those medals. I never even knew he'd been in the war. He never talked about it."

"Why would you get involved?"

"I don't know. Easy money, I guess. I figured if I had enough cash I could quit looking for a day job and start going to more auditions."

"Then why did you shoot Teresa?"

Eileen's eyes grew wide and pleading. "I didn't mean to. I was . . ." She glanced away for a moment, then looked out of the bedroom toward the living room. Toward the couch. "When we walked in at eleven and saw Mac hanging from the door . . ."

"Eleven? Weren't you supposed to meet him at ten?"

"No, the note said eleven. So when we saw him hanging from the door, Teresa pulled out her gun, thinking it was some sort of a setup. But when she realized he was dead, she went crazy. Screaming and crying, shouting that he wasn't supposed to kill himself. I knew she had to quiet down or someone would come to the door. She was waving the gun around and I was afraid it would go off, so I grabbed it from her. She tried to take it back. We struggled. It went off."

She hesitated, replaying the scene in her head. "Then Teresa fell onto the couch." Eileen looked down and her tears fell silently onto the carpet.

"And you moved Mac's body there to make it look like a murder-suicide. Did he leave a note?"

"I don't know." She paused, glanced around. "I don't think so. I guess I was so shocked that he'd done it I didn't even think about a note."

"Did you call Paul Devore?"

"No." It came out sharp, angry. Honest.

"Why'd you come back with Mrs. Vail?"

She sighed. "I thought it would give me an alibi."

"And why come back now when you knew there was no money?"

She shrugged, resigned, nearly drained of life. "When you mentioned the bag at the house, I thought maybe I was wrong. That there might still be some money in it."

"Did you find the bag?"

She gestured with her head toward the closet. "Just now. The only thing in it was an empty leather jewelry box."

The box that was missing from the corner of Mac's desk at home. The box in which he must have kept his medals.

It all made sense.

Still, I couldn't shake the fact that the times didn't add up. Eileen said that she and Teresa were supposed to meet Mac at eleven. But the extortion letter from Mac's desk said to meet at ten. And when I'd been waiting outside the Bon Vivant I'd seen Mac go in at ten and two women—Eileen Burnham and Teresa Vail as it turns out—enter at eleven. Mac had died in that hour. But by whose hand? His own or someone else's?

Eileen took a long, slow breath. Finally looked up at me. The tears had left faint tracks in her makeup. She pulled a gun from her coat pocket. A .38. Aimed it at the general area of my heart.

Rita Hayworth in *Gilda*. The femme fatale.

She stared at me until tears began to well in her eyes. It looked like remorse, but I wasn't sure if it was for what she had done or for what she was about to do.

"I don't want to kill you," she said. "But I don't want to go to prison either."

"You should put that away. Someone could get hurt."

Her gaze drifted over my shoulder into the living room again. This time her eyes grew wide.

"He's right, Eileen," said a voice from behind me. "Drop the gun." Then a chuckle. "Nice job, Nash. I heard the whole thing. She's the killer. You might be a decent PI after all."

I turned to see the self-satisfied mug of Paul Devore, and the accusatory barrel of his revolver aimed past me at Eileen.

He stood near the bloody couch as he punched a gesture toward her with the gun. "Mac killed himself and you killed Teresa. Isn't that right, doll?"

Eileen bore the stricken look of someone whose secret is out, but she didn't respond.

"Why are you here, Devore?" I said.

"I followed you," he said, glancing at me. "I was going to pay you back for what you did to me at Alice's. But when I heard Eileen's confession, I decided you needed my help."

"Sticking up for me like you stuck up for the men in your platoon?"

He looked offended. I immediately felt better about myself. "Look, Nash, it's five in the morning. You turned Alice against me. Just be happy I'm here to save your ass."

I almost said something glib. But then it struck me. First as a hunch, then as a flood of certainty. "You never cared about Alice, Paul. You just wanted her to be your alibi."

"That's absurd." He tried to mean it, but the phony outrage died somewhere in the space between us.

"Not really," I said as I moved out of the doorway and into the living room, away from both Eileen and Devore.

I needed some space in case what I was about to say inspired a gun to go off. Including the one that I pulled from my coat pocket as I turned near the windows. I aimed it at Devore. Eileen, her gun also aimed at Devore, stepped into the doorway. Devore smirked when he saw my .38 but kept his gun aimed at Eileen. There was a ten-foot triangle between the three of us.

"The extortion play on Mac," I said, "was your idea, Paul. Teresa told you about Mac's visitors here and you saw an opportunity."

"*You* were behind it?" Eileen took a step toward Devore, the shock on her face as real as the gun in her hand.

"You didn't know that?" I said.

She shook her head. "Teresa knew how much I hated this bastard. She said it was her idea but that she didn't want to come here alone."

Devore didn't respond, but his eyes had narrowed.

"What Teresa didn't know," I said, "was that Paul here was going to set you and Teresa up to take the fall at eleven o'clock for his extortion and murder of Mac at ten. Paul would get the money and you and Teresa would do the time."

Devore tried to laugh. He wasn't the actor that Eileen was. "You can't prove any of that."

"Actually, I can." I patted my jacket where the inside breast pocket was. "I have the note you sent to Mac. It said to meet here at ten. But Eileen told me that they were supposed to meet Mac at eleven." I glanced to Eileen. "Who decided on eleven?"

Eileen kept her eyes and her gun on Devore. "He did. And he said he'd take care of sending a note to Mac."

I nodded at Devore. "So you told them eleven, but you told Mac ten. That gave you an hour to get the money, kill Mac, and make it look like a suicide. A gun would have been too loud, so you choked him with the cord until he passed out, then you strung him up so that Teresa and Eileen wouldn't suspect you of murdering him and taking all the money. They would think that he had simply killed himself because of the extortion letter. That sound about right?"

"You've really lost it, Nash." He kept his gun aimed at Eileen. "She killed Teresa and Mac killed himself."

"I saw you leave at ten forty-five." Devore had been the man whistling a happy tune. The one who had seen me. Who had pulled his hat low. Who I'd assumed was guilty of something. "You were going to call the police so that they would get here just after Teresa and Eileen showed up at eleven. But you saw me outside sitting in my car and you got nervous. You were worried I could place you at the scene, so you didn't call the cops."

Devore looked ashen in the yellow light of the room.

"You were the one who pinned those medals all over his coat," I said. "Was that your way of mocking him, Devore? Did those medals make you jealous? Make you face your own cowardice?"

He turned his gun toward me and took a hobbled step. "I saw action, Nash."

"Where? Behind the Fort Bragg Officers' Club?"

"Iwo." His face wrenched into a phony rage that almost gave cover for the blush that had spread across his cheeks and the beads of sweat that had popped up on his forehead.

"Do you have a Combat Infantry Badge that will back that up? Or just a dishonorable discharge?"

The fake rage turned real. "You think pinning a medal on somebody makes them a hero?"

"No. But it says they've got more inside them than guys like you. Those heroes were just as scared as you, only they knew their buddies were depending on them. You've never cared about anybody but yourself. Mac was more of a man than you are."

Devore was breathing heavy, drawing in air in big, noisy wheezes, but his response came out breathless. "That's what Mac said. You know what I said? 'Medals or no medals, do you think Standard Oil is going to promote you when they find out you're a queerie?'"

"What did he say to that?"

Devore paused. Seemed to stop functioning. He was looking at me, but his eyes went flat. Like they'd stopped seeing what was in front of him. When he spoke, his voice was as flat as his eyes. "He said, 'I'll just tell them about my war record. And if that's not enough, then I'll tell them about yours.'"

Mac McKenzie had recognized the limp too. Had known what it meant. Had known that with all the veterans who were back running the business world, being a coward on the battlefield could be just as fatal to a career as being a homosexual.

"That's when you killed him," I said.

Devore's stillness didn't change. "We were in the kitchen. He bent down to put the box of medals back in his bag. I grabbed the extension cord and started to choke him. He passed out."

Suddenly his eyes focused and he was back with us in the apartment. "I really don't remember much after that."

"You don't remember hanging Mac from the door with the cord while he was still alive? Don't remember him kicking his heels against the door, struggling to breathe? Or pinning the medals to his jacket?"

"Those goddamned medals," he said. "They looked ridiculous on his herringbone coat." I expected him to smile, but he'd turned cold. Bloodless. "Killing him was better than any money." He aimed his gun at my head. "And killing you will be just as good. You and Mac are the same. You've probably got a shoebox full of medals too. I hear they gave them out like candy."

"Only in the air force," I said. He didn't laugh. Not even a smile. That proved he'd never been infantry.

"You think you're pretty funny, Nash, but the joke's on you."

Eileen took a slow step forward. "You're wrong, Paul," she said.

Devore swung his gun toward her. "You stay where you are."

"Yeah," I said. "Stay where you are." I needed to keep Devore's attention on me.

But she took another slow step toward him. "You killed Mac, Paul. And because of that"—her voice hitched and tears began spilling down her cheeks—"I killed Teresa."

Devore tried to take a step back but bumped into the bloodstained couch. "I said stay where you are."

Another step forward. "You're an evil man, Paul." The tears still fell, but her voice grew stronger as she spoke. "You've hurt so many people. When will it stop?"

Devore was panicked now. She was only a few feet from him. He looked cornered. Scared.

Both guns exploded.

Eileen staggered and fell to the carpet. Devore tumbled over the back of the couch, his feet swinging sideways, knocking the lamp off the end table. The bulb flared as it hit the floor, went black as it shattered. The only light now angled in through the bedroom door.

I checked Devore first. He was the real threat.

But not anymore. His eyes and mouth were open, frozen in a look of perplexed fear. His forehead was open as well, the wake of her bullet having left behind a black, viscous hole. A hole that seemed to have sucked the life out of everything within reach. Including me.

I didn't miss the irony of it all. Devore had tried to run away from a violent death in the war by shooting himself in the foot. But Death had shadowed him back across the ocean, through his convalescence, through his dishonorable discharge, through his repetitive, calculating days at Standard Oil, into Apartment 311 of the Bon Vivant on La Brea. Had shadowed him like a thief determined to take what he valued most.

Eileen was moaning. She was on her back near the doorway to the bedroom. Devore's bullet had left a crimson bloom on the lapel of her raincoat, on the upper part of her left breast. Her breathing was shallow.

I lifted her left shoulder and felt her back for the exit wound. Pulled my hand away covered in bright red blood and bits of snow-white bone.

I ran to the bathroom, grabbed the towels off the rack. Found a pair of scissors in a kitchen drawer. As I pulled her raincoat away from the wound, her eyes opened. She whispered, "Am I going to die?"

I felt the indifference I'd cultivated in the war falter and tears sneak into my eyes. Whispered back, "I've seen worse." The only thing I could say that I was sure of. I focused on the wound, the only honest thing in the room.

Air wheezed in and out of the hole. The sucking chest wound I'd seen countless times on the battlefield. I tore the towels into dressings and packed them over both wounds, front and back, then cut large pieces from the raincoat and placed those over the dressings. Used my tie and strips cut from her coat to bind the bandages to her body. Then I had her lie on her left side.

Truth is, I didn't know if she would make it. She'd lost a lot of blood and splinters of bone could have nicked her heart. It would come down to those things that go beyond blood and bone. Like determination. Or purpose. Or the will to live. I had no idea if she possessed any of those things. Had no idea who she really was at heart.

Other than an actress.

I could hear murmuring in the hallway, tenants who had heard the gunshots but were too scared to investigate. I started for the telephone.

"I'm sorry," she whispered. Sweat had seeped onto her forehead and upper lip. Shock beginning to set in.

I came back and knelt beside her. "Sorry for what?"

"For the lies I told you."

"No confessions right now. You need to get to a hospital."

"Was I convincing?"

I brushed back her hair, caressed her cheek. "Perfectly."

She tried to smile. "The role of my life."

It wasn't long after that night at the Bon Vivant that I pulled my own army dress uniform from the closet and laid it on the bed. I hadn't taken any real time to look at it in the fifteen months since I'd come back from Europe, but its familiarity immediately aroused a well-worn dread.

The forest-green four-pocket coat still bore the insignias, bars, and medals I'd been awarded over the course of the war. There were a lot of them, a few more than Mac McKenzie had earned, but that didn't matter to me. Some men were proud of their accomplishments overseas. I wasn't. I was no hero. If there had been a way to escape the war that wouldn't have required a bullet in the foot or a dishonorable discharge, I'd have taken it. I only kept moving forward because I realized that the only honest way back led in front of me. Every step I took was one step closer to home—no matter which direction that step had led.

Like everyone else who'd served in every branch of the service, I'd been trying to hide my fear. And ever since I'd come home, trying to hide the truth I'd seen. About war. About death. About me.

The insignias, bars, and medals merely supplied the gilt of heroism to the endless guilt of the facade I wore.

That I wear.

An actor in my own right. The role of *my* life. One that never seems to end.

*

Eileen Burnham survived, but I haven't seen her since that night.

The police kept a close eye on both of us as they investigated the crime. And I did my best to cooperate, including turning over the extortion letter to Beaumont the morning Eileen had gone to the hospital. He and the prosecutor, William Reinhardt, a hollow-eyed man with no hair and two chins, both believed that Mac had been entertaining women at the apartment and that that was the basis for the extortion attempt. I let them think that.

Neither of them saw the pictures of Mac with other men. I'd kept them in my coat pocket until I was able to go home and burn them. Did I destroy evidence? Sure. Did I care? Not a damn. The extortion letter was enough. Mac McKenzie didn't die because of his lust for men. He died because of Paul Devore's greed. And which has done more harm in this world?

No charges were filed against Eileen, and after a brief flurry of lurid articles in the newspapers, the case faded away. Somehow Reinhardt must have bought her claims that her involvement in the extortion plan was limited, her shooting of Teresa was an accident, and her killing of Paul Devore was self-defense. He also must have bought my explanation of how Paul Devore had murdered Mac McKenzie and my corroboration of Eileen's version of her actions.

But I'm still not sure if I believe her.

There's a part of me—the PI part—that thinks that it really was the role of her life. That she intended all along to kill Teresa and keep the money—if there had been any—for herself. And that killing Paul Devore had been an unexpected bonus.

But there's another part of me—the man in me—that wants to believe her. Wants to believe that it was all a tragic accident and that her interest in me had been real. The same part of me that remembers her looks and smarts, her toughness and complexity. The same part of me that, every time it rains, thinks of lovers and thieves and wonders which of the two Eileen Burnham might be.

Or if—like all the rest of us—she's both.

CRAIG JOHNSON

Land of the Blind

FROM *The Strand Magazine*

IT'S THE LAST thing you want to hear in law enforcement and certainly the last thing you want to hear on Christmas Eve, just as you're finishing up payroll and heading out the office door.

"Where?" I asked.

My deputy, Double Tough, leaned against the doorway and held said door open with one hand. The mottled skin of his face was highlighted by the haloed glow of the Christmas lights, which he had hung above the main entrance of the old Carnegie Library that served as the office of the Absaroka County Sheriff's Department.

"Near Story."

I stuffed the small red leather-bound copy of *A Christmas Carol,* which had been a gift from my father, under my arm and handed him his check. "That's Sheridan County."

He stuffed the envelope in his back pocket. "Not exactly—just south, near the fish hatchery."

I stepped out into the frigid air, flipped up the collar of my old horsehide jacket, and pulled my hat down against the wind. I let the door skip closed behind us and locked it as I hurried toward his unit, yanked open the door, and climbed inside. "Wait, there's a hostage situation at the fish hatchery?"

"Nope, at the church just next door—the Congregational Baptist."

I noticed the crucifix hanging from his rearview mirror and made the connection. Since the fire that had cost him his eye, Double Tough had gone through something of a religious reawakening and had been auditioning churches around the area in search of the right theological fit. "Did you try that one?"

"I did, but they were a little too fire-and-brimstone for me." He fired up the Chevrolet and glanced over his shoulder, checking for traffic even though the street was vacant, before pulling out and hitting his lights and siren.

An Appalachian by birth, the energy worker had followed the methane gas boom that had sprung up in the Powder River, but when it had faded a couple of years ago, he'd pinned on one of my stars. "I would've thought with your background that would've been right down your alley."

He reached up and touched the melted skin at his jawline. "I figure I been singed enough for one lifetime." He smiled, but I wasn't sure if it was the real eye or the glass one that glanced at me. He navigated onto the interstate highway, and nailing the accelerator, he slid slightly before getting the Suburban straightened out. "The Highway Patrol and Jim Persil are on-scene. You know, that new sheriff from over in Sheridan."

I fastened my seatbelt, a bit disgruntled—Christmas not being my best season. "So why do they need us?"

He smiled again. "It's your county, Bossman."

The newly elected neighboring sheriff was young and had been genuinely concerned about not overstepping his jurisdiction, so circumspect in fact that he'd become something of a pain in the butt. "Okay, give me the lowdown."

"Christmas Eve service at the church had just begun when they had this kid come in, twenties, wearin' nuthin' but a pair of tighty-whities with a nine-millimeter tucked in the waistband. He grabs this poor woman from the front row and drags her up on the altar and says he's going to shoot her for all our sins. I guess the preacher tried to step in and got a round through his hand for his trouble."

I rested a palm on the red leather volume that I had set on the center console. "Men's courses will foreshadow certain ends, to which, if persevered in, they must lead . . ."

He nodded toward the copy of *A Christmas Carol.* "You still reading that book every Christmas?"

"Yep, you?"

"Me what?"

I noticed he canted his face to one side as he drove, giving his live eye an advantage, so I was pretty sure the right one was real. "Reading?"

"Yeah." Double Tough had, along with his religious redemption, taken up reading again, something he'd abandoned years ago. "That book you gave me, the Davis Grubb."

Thinking a geographical advantage might help the man along, I'd loaned him a stack of Appalachian literature from my office bookshelves, including Grubb, Jesse Stuart, and Wendell Berry. "*Night of the Hunter?*"

"Nope, the other one."

As we drove, I looked out over the pristine, smooth surface of Lake DeSmet, covered with a sheet, blanket, and comforter of a fourteen-inch snow. "*Fool's Parade.*"

He nodded and then glanced at me again, and I still wasn't quite sure with which eye. "You give me that book because the guy had a glass eye?"

"No."

He nodded, taking the exit to the little town of Story, Wyoming, and drawled "Good."

It was a cop convention. The Sheridan County sheriff had set up a command center, and the HPs had covered the periphery with halo-gen emergency lights focused on the church with an honest-to-good-ness sniper on top of one of the nearest vehicles, a large black step-van with the Highway Patrol insignia emblazoned on the side.

The newly minted neighboring sheriff explained, "The HP's Rapid Response Team was up here from Cheyenne having a train-ing session with our SWAT at the shooting club in Sheridan and were all loaded up to go home when we got the call, so they all tagged along."

I glanced around at all the armed men in camouflage, looking more like an occupying army than a police force. "Don't these peo-ple have homes? It's Christmas Eve, for goodness' sake."

He shrugged. "I guess everybody's bored." I looked back at the Congregational Baptist church, looking like a Currier & Ives, the snow curling off the edges of the roof and steeple, the stained glass windows glowing warmly, as Persil rolled out a floor plan of the church on the tailgate of one of his trucks. "The stained glass is playing hell with the sniper—he can't get a laser dot on the kid."

"Does he have a name?"

"The sniper?"

"The kid."

"Sam Erlanger, recent parolee with a substance abuse problem, Bolivian black tar heroin being the substance of choice as of late, but who knows what he's on tonight. We've had him inside a few times. The last time he was in, the churches were offering Bible classes to the inmates, and he got all Old Testament on us. Got released a couple of weeks ago." He pointed to a spot on the plan as he unclipped a handheld radio and laid it on the corner as a paperweight. "There's a back door on the right side of the altar where we can get in behind him, but it might be safer just to let the sniper take the shot, stained window be damned."

I looked at the scroll of paper rolled out on the sheet metal. "Where in the world did you get a floor plan of the church this fast?"

He gestured to where I assumed the wounded preacher was being attended to in the nearby EMT van. "The minister had it in his car; I guess they're planning an expansion."

"Has anybody gone in there to talk with him?"

"The preacher?"

"The guy in his underwear." I glanced at the church. "Fruit of the Loom."

Persil looked at me as if the answer should have been obvious. "No. I mean, the last one that tried to talk to him got a hole shot in his hand."

"What's the hostage's name?"

"Daniela Breese."

I made the mental note. "Anybody else in the church?"

"Yeah, about a half-dozen in the pews who were too far from the door to make an escape. All the rest checked out when he started talking human sacrifice for the holidays."

I pulled out my .45, sliding the mechanism and dropping a round in the pipe before flicking on the safety and returning it to my holster, which I left unsnapped. "All right, please tell the sniper not to shoot me."

"You're going in there?"

I started off toward the main doors of the church when I noticed Double Tough falling in behind me. "Where do you think you're going?"

He was checking his .40 as his face rose from under his cowboy hat. "Bossman, if he decides it's better to give than to receive with that nine-millimeter, another couple of rounds might be handy."

As I pushed down the clasp on the heavy door, I could hear someone from inside talking in a low slur, almost as if hypnotized. Sam Erlanger was deep into a one-sided tête-à-tête with God, his voice dulled, his conversation meandering. "As you come to him, a living stone rejected by men but in the sight of God . . ."

Pushing the door the rest of the way open, I held it and, taking in the scene in front of me, rested the web of my thumb on my Colt. Through the vestibule, still loaded with the hats, coats, and galoshes of the faithful who had rapidly retreated, I could see down the main aisle where the heads of those who had not been able to escape popped up now and again, looking toward the simple white cloth-covered altar where Sam Erlanger held Daniela Breese by her hair with a gun to her head.

The woman wasn't moving and her eyes were closed, but she was breathing. Erlanger was breathing too, as his emaciated muscles contracted against themselves. Continually wetting his lips with a darting tongue, he slowly slung his glance around the room, his deadened eyes looking everywhere and seeing nothing. "Behold, I am laying in Zion a stone, a cornerstone chosen and precious."

There were no doorways into the main part of the church other than the one point-blank in front of us, so attempting to enter without his noticing wasn't much of an option. Figuring we'd at least have some semblance of surprise if one of us lingered in the entryway out of sight, I motioned for Double Tough to move to the right. I walked into the nave, carefully leaving the door slightly ajar for my deputy and in case any of the other hostages could find the courage to beat a hasty exit.

He droned on. "Ah, sinful nation . . . They have forsaken the Lord, they have despised the Holy One of Israel, and they are utterly estranged."

"Amen."

His head rose slowly and he looked at the ceiling, but failing in seeing his God, he allowed his eyes to slip to me, standing in the center aisle with my hands on my hips.

"Hi, Sam."

He slowly focused, raising a cheap Hi-Point semiautomatic from

Daniela's head and pointing it directly at me. "Stay where you are or I'll kill you."

I tipped my hat back, making sure he could see that I didn't have a weapon in my hands. "I wouldn't do that if I were you."

His face split in a creeping, sick smile, his skin flushed and his nose running freely. "You aren't me." The grin widened to where I could see his black teeth. "I'm chosen."

Over the years you get a feeling in these situations, an idea of how they're going to play out—and I was getting a bad one on this. It was the certainty that was disconcerting, a snakelike stillness that led me to believe that it was a heroin cocktail that Sam was on —both shaken and stirred.

"He speaks to me."

I started down the aisle but stopped when he forced the muzzle against Daniela's head again, his dark eyes flicking away for the briefest of instants.

"Don't you hear him?" The smile was still there as his face caught the light from the emergency halogens that shone through the stained glass. "He says that I have to make a sacrifice for this country. We've lost our way and the only way it can be redeemed is with blood." He wiped his nose with his gun hand but then pushed the weapon back against the woman's head. "He's talking to us now . . ."

Watching his finger tighten on the trigger, I turned slightly to the right to hide the movement and dropped my hand to my side-arm. The angle was bad, and I was going to have to clear almost up to my shoulder before firing, but I didn't see anything else for it.

"I hear his voice!"

I froze and slowly turned my head to the left, where I could see that Double Tough, having moved along the far wall for a better position, was holding both his hands out so that Erlanger could see he meant no harm.

"I hear him, brother!" The undisputable zeal in my deputy's voice must've been acquired over the years in his fundamentalist upbringing. Erlanger didn't move, but his hooded eyes opened a bit as Double Tough continued to advance, shouting his testament as he came. "Out of the heavens he let you hear his voice to discipline you, and on earth he let you see his great fire."

When DT was within twenty feet, the addict pulled the 9mm away from the young woman's head and shakily directed it in my deputy's general direction. "You . . . You need to stop where you are."

Double Tough swung his arms wide and spun in a circle, all the time looking up at the ceiling and ignoring the gun pointed at him. "Is that you, Lord?" He stopped spinning, faced Erlanger, and stared at the peak of the church, the mottling of his skin looking like a caul. "You can hear him too, brother, can't you?"

The addict began nodding his head and looking up at the same spot. "I do hear him." The semiautomatic dropped a little, now wavering between Double Tough and me as he glanced my way. "I do!"

DT's head snapped back up toward the ceiling, and his face turned back and forth before he cupped a hand to his ear. "How have we offended thee, Lord?"

Erlanger actually moved forward, forgetting his hostage in his eagerness to receive the message. He repeated, "How have we offended thee?"

My deputy crept a little closer with his hand still at his ear, now only ten feet away from the deeply disturbed man. "You demand a sacrifice?"

Erlanger beamed as his eyes cast about, and he cried out in triumph, once again placing the muzzle of the Hi-Point against Daniela's head. "I told you, I told you all!"

"No. Wait, brother. Wait!" Double Tough's hand shot out. "He demands a different sort of sacrifice . . ." The same hand returned to his ear, and his face rose to the rafters. "What can we do to remove the offense?" He stood there motionless for a moment, and I even found myself leaning forward along with Erlanger to hear what my deputy might say next. "And if thine eye offend thee, pluck it out?"

Erlanger didn't move.

Agonizingly, DT reached up and began prying at his face, screaming as his voice rebounded against the confines of the church walls. He thrashed against the banister that separated him from the altar and turned away, caterwauling, and finally plucking the furious bright eye from his face, he held it heavenward. "Here it is, Lord!"

He turned slowly, revealing the empty socket in his damaged face as Erlanger stood straight with his rotten mouth hanging open, his head shaking back and forth.

"Here, take it! It's seen enough of this world's woes and mischiefs!" Double Tough lowered the ghastly trophy, and examining it with the remaining eye before looking skyward, he stumbled forward until he was within arm's reach of Erlanger. "What's that, Lord?"

By this time the drug addict was shaking and had completely forgotten his hostage and scrambled backward against the pulpit.

"It is better for thee to enter into life with one eye rather than having two eyes to be cast into hellfire?" DT's hand thrust forward, giving Erlanger a closer look at the dislocated orb as he held the vivid eye out to the addict until it seemed to loom larger and larger. "Brother, he wants you to have it!"

Dropping the gun, Erlanger turned and tripped over the stairs in search of the back door, finally finding it, and clawed at the knob as Double Tough casually threw a leg over the banister and moved steadily toward him with the proffered offering. "Wait, he wants you to have it!"

Turning to look at his tormentor, the addict wailed and pressed his back against the door, sliding down it, leaving a grease mark as he sank. Finally, as my deputy was only inches from reaching him, he screamed, managed to get to his feet to yank the door open, and disappeared into the snowy night, his terrified cries trailing after him.

Double Tough stepped toward the doorway and watched the mostly naked man through the skimming flakes. "Say what you want about those heroin addicts, they can really move when they want to." He continued to peer into the darkness where outside we could hear shouting as the assembled manpower moved in and apprehended the culprit. It was then that DT turned, popped the orb into his mouth for lubrication, swished it around, and then, spitting it out, tipped his head back, thumbed a lid up, and redeposited the glass eye.

He turned and winked at me. "God bless us, every one."

WILLIAM KENT KRUEGER

The Painted Smile

FROM *Echoes of Sherlock Holmes*

HE WAS AN odd child to begin with. After he received the book as
a Christmas present, things only got worse. Eventually his aunt was
beside herself and sought my help.

I have an office in Saint Paul, in a building that was grand about
the time Dillinger was big news. It's long been in need of a facelift.
One of the things I like about it is that I can see the Mississippi
River from my window. Another is that I can afford the rent.

Although she'd called ahead and had explained the situation,
when she brought in the boy, I was still surprised. He was small,
even for a ten-year-old. But his eyes were sharp and quick, darting
like bees around the room, taking in everything. I welcomed the
woman and her nephew, shook their hands, and we sat in the comfortable easy chairs I use during my sessions.

"So, Oliver," I said. "I'm very curious about your costume."

"My name is Sherlock. And this is not a costume."

"Your aunt has told me that your birth certificate reads Oliver
Wendell Holmes. You were named after the great Supreme Court
justice."

"I prefer Sherlock."

"All right. For now. Tell me about your attire. That hat is pretty
striking, and your cape as well. Tweed, yes? How did you manage
to come by them?"

"I made them myself."

I looked to his aunt.

She nodded. "He taught himself to use my sewing machine. And
he does a fine stitch by hand too."

In our initial phone conversation, she'd told me her nephew had been tested in school and had demonstrated an IQ of 170. I'm generally leery of quantifications of this kind, but it was clear the boy was gifted.

"When did you become Sherlock Holmes?"

"I've always been Sherlock Holmes. I just didn't realize it until I received the volume of Conan Doyle at Christmas."

"Always?"

"Just as you've always been Watson."

"But I'm not. You know that. My name is simply Watt."

"Are you not the son of Watt, therefore Watt's son?"

"Clever," I admitted with a smile.

"I'm not crazy, Watson," he said quite calmly. "Not delusional. I'm well aware that Sherlock Holmes is a literary fiction. I'm simply the mental and emotional incarnation of that fictional construct, the confirmation that the literary may sometimes, indeed, reflect a concrete reality. The name Sherlock feels suited to me. But all this is something my aunt has difficulty accepting. I understand."

"You get made fun of," his aunt said to him, a situation that clearly caused her distress. "The other kids at school pick on you. Doesn't that bother you?"

"I'm the object of ridicule because they're not comfortable with who they are. They work hard at creating just the right image, and I threaten that. It's the same with adults. If you weren't so insecure in your own circumstances, Aunt Louise, you would see me for who I am instead of who you want me to be."

"That's a rather harsh judgment, Oliver," I said.

"Sherlock," he reminded me. "And I would say the same about you, Watson."

"Oh?"

"Your office is on the third floor of a building that houses enterprises of a less than robust nature. Your shelves are full of books on psychology that haven't been read in a good long while. You spend a lot of time sitting at your desk and staring at the river, wishing that instead of becoming a child psychologist you'd gone to sea. You've recently separated from your wife. Or perhaps divorced. And you'd like desperately to find a woman who understands you."

"I beg your pardon?"

"The building speaks for itself," he explained. "The dust on your shelves is evidence that you seldom reference your reference mate-

rials. You've arranged your office so that the best view—the river
—is in front of you, and only a very dedicated individual wouldn't
be constantly seduced by that wistful scene. Your walls are filled
with photographs and paintings of great ships at sea. Your left ring
finger still bears a strip of skin much paler than the area around it,
indicating that until very recently you wore a wedding band. And
in your wastebasket is the latest issue of *City Pages* folded to the
personal ads section."

Though I was shaken by the accuracy of his observations, I did
my best not to show it. From that point on, I conducted a fairly
standard intake interview. The boy's parents were deceased, killed
two years earlier when their car slid off an icy road while they were
returning from a New Year's Eve party. His parents had both been
successful attorneys.

At the end, I spoke with his aunt alone. I told her I thought I
could help the boy, but that it might take some time. She agreed to
bring him back for sessions twice a week.

I walked her out of my office to where the boy sat waiting in the
hallway. I explained what his aunt and I had decided. He didn't
seem upset in the least. I bid them goodbye, and the woman started
away. But the boy held back and, before catching up with his aunt,
whispered something to me in a grave voice.

I returned to my office and stood at the window, looking down at
the street, watching them get into the woman's old sedan and drive
away. The whole time, the final words the boy had spoken to me
ran through my head: *One thing you should know, Watson. Moriarty
is here.*

I'm a bit of a dreamer. That's why my wife left me. Well, one of the
reasons. And so, truthfully, I was inclined to be sympathetic toward
Oliver Holmes, who, like me, and despite his protestations to the
contrary, was someone wanting to be someone else. I found myself looking forward to our next visit three days later. When Oliver
showed up, his aunt simply dropped him off, saying she would be
back in an hour. She had errands to run.

We sat in my office, and I asked how his days had gone since I
last saw him.

He cut to the chase. "I've been worried about Moriarty."

"Tell me about him."

"You know who he is, Watson."

"I've read my Conan Doyle," I said.

"Then you understand the evil he's capable of."

"Is this really Moriarty or another instance of some kind of—what did you call it? 'A concrete reflection of a literary reality'?"

"Moriarty is not the source of all evil, Watson. But his malicious intent here is quite real."

"So he's up to something?"

"What a stupid question, Watson. Of course he's up to something. The real question is what?"

"You've seen him, then?"

"Of course."

"Can you describe him to me?"

"I've never seen him except in disguise."

"If he was in disguise and you've never seen him otherwise, how do you know it was him?"

"A wolf may don sheep's clothing, but he still behaves like a wolf."

I sat back and considered the boy.

"Do you play chess?" I finally asked.

"Of course. Since I was four."

"Care to play a game?"

"On my aunt's nickel? Isn't that a bit unfair to her, Watson?"

"Tell you what. I give every client one free session. We'll count this as your free one."

He shrugged, a very boylike gesture, and I went to a cabinet and brought out my chess set.

"Carved alabaster," he said, clearly impressed. "Roman motif."

"I take my chess seriously."

We set up the board and played for half an hour to a stalemate. I was impressed with how well he conducted himself. I'm no slouch, and he kept me on my toes. Mostly, however, it afforded me an opportunity to observe his thinking. He was aggressive, too much so, I thought. He didn't consider his defense as carefully as he should have in order to anticipate the danger inherent in some of his bolder moves. He was smart, beyond smart, but he was still a child. I could tell it irritated him that he didn't win.

"Tell me more about Moriarty," I said.

"I believe he killed my parents." It was an astounding statement, but he spoke it as a simple truth.

"Your aunt told me they died in an automobile accident."

"Moriarty was behind it."

"To what end?"

"I don't know. Ever since I realized he was here, I've been observing him. I haven't quite deciphered the pattern of his actions."

"Observing him how?"

"How does one normally observe, Watson? I've been following him."

This alarmed me, though I tried not to show it. His brashness, if what he told me was true, was the kind of heedless aggression I'd seen in his chess play. Though I didn't believe in Moriarty, whatever the boy was up to wasn't healthy.

A knock at the door ended our session. His aunt entered the office.

"Could I speak with you alone?" I asked.

"I'm in a bit of a hurry," she said. "Perhaps next time. Come on, Oliver. We've got to run."

When they'd gone, I was left with a profound sense of uneasiness. Whatever was going on, I couldn't help thinking that the boy was heading somewhere dangerous, dangerous to him and perhaps to others. Frankly, I wasn't sure what to do except bide my time until our next visit.

"Would you care to see him, Watson?" the boy asked. "Moriarty."

His aunt had dropped him at the door to the building, and he'd come up alone. He'd insisted on a chess rematch, and while we'd played I'd probed him more about his obsession with that fictional villain.

"I'd like that," I said.

"Meet me at six this evening at the corner of Seventh and Randolph."

"I beg your pardon?"

"Do you want to see Moriarty or not?"

"I do."

"Then meet me."

"I'll have to discuss this with your aunt."

"No."

"Oliver—"

"Sherlock, damn you!"

"Oliver," I replied firmly, "there are lines I won't cross. I can't connive with you behind your aunt's back."

"I'll make a deal with you, Watson," the boy said, having calmed himself. "Meet me tonight, this one time. If you're not convinced that there's danger afoot and that Moriarty is the source, I won't insist anymore that you call me Sherlock."

I considered his proposal and decided there was nothing to lose. I certainly didn't believe in Moriarty, and so this might be a way to crack through the boy's wall of resistance.

"Six," I agreed.

He was there to meet me and got into my car when I pulled to the curb. He directed me a couple of blocks away to an apartment building in a working-class section with a view of the old brewery. We parked well back from the entrance, sandwiched inconspicuously between two other cars.

"What exactly are we watching for?" I asked.

"At six-fifteen you'll see."

I talked with him while we waited, asked him about his aunt.

"She's a bit dull," he said. "Not like my mom and dad were. She feels trapped, but I believe she does her best."

"Trapped?"

"In her life, in her marriage."

"She's married?" This was a piece of new information. His aunt had said nothing during the intake interview, and the boy had been silent on the subject until now.

"Of course. I assumed you saw the ring." He frowned at me. "Really, Watson, you need to pay closer attention to the details."

"Tell me about your uncle."

"He drives a semi truck. He's gone most days of the week, but usually makes it home for the weekends. It's better when he's not around. He's got a mean streak in him." He glanced at his watch. "She should be coming out any minute now."

There she was, right on time, pushing out the front door of the apartment building at six-fifteen sharp. She crossed the street and got into the old sedan I'd seen her driving before.

"Follow her," the boy said.

I pulled out and stayed behind her for the next ten minutes.

"Now watch," the boy said. "This is where it gets interesting."

The street ran past a large entertainment center called Palladium Pizza. On the big sign out front was a neon Ferris wheel and below that a lit marquee that proclaimed FOOD, FUN, AND GAMES FOR THE WHOLE FAMILY. The parking lot was quite full. The place was clearly a popular enterprise. The boy's aunt pulled into the lot and parked. I pulled in too but stayed well away. She left the sedan, glanced at her watch, then stood looking expectantly toward the double glass doors of the establishment.

Lo and behold, a clown appeared. He wore a big red wig and his nose was tipped with a little red ball. His clothes were a ridiculous burlesque of elegant evening wear, complete with a large fake flower on his lapel that I was certain shot water. The shoes on his feet were a dozen sizes too big. His mouth was elongated with red face paint into a perpetual and I thought rather frightening grin. He approached the woman. To my amazement, they kissed.

"Who's that?" I asked. But no sooner had I spoken than the light dawned. "Moriarty."

The boy gave a single, solemn nod. "Moriarty."

They walked arm in arm to a van at the other end of the parking lot. The vehicle was decorated with brightly colored balloon decals, and floating among them were the words "Marco the Magnificent: Magic and Buffoonery for All Ages." They got in, the van pulled onto the street, and it quickly disappeared amid the traffic.

"Your aunt is having an affair with a clown?"

"With Moriarty," the boy said.

"Your uncle doesn't know?"

"Clueless."

"Okay," I said. "If this is Moriarty, what's he up to?"

"That's the question, isn't it, Watson? I hope to have an answer soon."

He continued to stare down the street where his aunt and the clown had gone.

"Did you see his face? The painted smile? Such a grotesque mockery of goodwill." His eyes narrowed in a determined way and he said grimly, "Pure Moriarty."

When his aunt dropped him off for his next session, I caught her before she rushed away and asked to speak with her privately a moment. She seemed a bit put out, but stepped into my office while Oliver waited outside.

"You're seeing someone," I said.

She was clearly startled. "What do you mean?"

"Marco the Magnificent."

"How—" she started, then her eyes shifted to the office door.

"Oliver." She looked at me again, and I could see that she was try-ing to decide on a course of action. She finally settled on what seemed to me the truth.

"I don't love my husband anymore. Morrie makes me feel spe-cial. Makes me feel young. Makes me laugh."

"Morrie? That's his name?"

"Morris Peterson."

"When did Morrie enter your life?"

"A while ago."

"Could you be more specific?"

"Just before Christmas."

"About the time you gave Oliver the volume of Conan Doyle stories. Look, I believe your nephew is threatened by Morrie. He's lost his parents. I think he might be afraid of losing you too. You're all the family he has now."

"He's never said anything."

"You're having an affair. What could he say? But it comes out in this fantasy of his that he's Sherlock Holmes. He uses it to justify his feeling of being threatened. And also, I believe, as a way of trying to have some control over the situation."

She looked again at the door, beyond which her nephew sat, a lonely, orphaned boy dressed in a deerstalker hat and matching cape. I saw the pain in her eyes. But I went on, laying it all out for her.

"Although your nephew claims to understand that he is not in fact Sherlock Holmes, I think that deep down he really believes he is. He's not just emulating that literary creation, he sees himself as the flesh-and-blood incarnation. He can rationalize it all he wants, but he's not acting truly rational."

"And I'm responsible?"

"No. Or at least, not entirely. But your current situation certainly isn't helping."

"So you're saying I have to break it off with Morrie? That will fix Oliver?"

"It's not a question of fixing. Oliver's not a broken machine. He's simply a child, brilliant but lost."

She looked truly lost herself, and I could tell that pushing her at this point would do no good.

"Take some time to think it over," I advised. "But not too long. In the meantime, I'll work with Oliver and do what I can to help him face the truth of the situation."

"He can't tell my husband," she said, and now her eyes bloomed with fear. "He would kill me."

"I'll talk to him," I promised.

When she'd gone, I called the boy into my office and we sat together.

I said, "Moriarty isn't his real name, you know. His name is Morris Peterson."

"That's simply an alias," the boy said. "He's using a name similar to his own. A common ploy. Look, Watson, I know the true nature of his interest now."

I thought I had a pretty good idea of the true nature of his interest myself. The boy's aunt was a woman desperate for attention. She wanted to feel loved, young, special. And she would probably do almost anything to please the man who made her feel that way. Even a clown.

"You know, of course, about sexual attraction, Oliver."

"Sherlock," he said in an icy tone. "My name is Sherlock." He took a moment to settle himself, then said, "Of course I know that sex is a part of his attraction. Will you just listen to me for a moment, Watson? Let me explain everything to you."

"You?" I said evenly, after he'd laid it all out for me. "He's after you?"

"I present a threat to him. And a challenge. I'm the only person alive who is his intellectual equal and moral opposite."

"And you believe he wants to do you harm?"

"Not just harm, Watson. He wants me dead."

And there it was, the full manifestation of his delusion. Against my best judgment, I'd come to care about the boy, and this paranoia troubled me greatly.

"I can see that you don't believe me," Oliver said. "Just listen to me for a moment, Watson. Moriarty is in fact a fugitive on the run. He has warrants for his arrest in California, Oregon, and Colorado. Any other common criminal would have been taken into custody, but Moriarty is not your common criminal."

"Warrants for what?"

"Theft, fraud, and one for a particularly nasty incident in Denver."

"How do you know this?"

"Because of the greatest boon to the modern detective, Watson. The Internet. You know the game of poker?"

"Of course."

"An experienced poker player watches for what's called a tell, an unconscious gesture that gives another player away in the heat of betting. Moriarty has a tell."

"And what would that be?"

"The clown costume. It's an unusual disguise, to say the least. But it's clearly one he's comfortable with. I merely did an Internet search for crimes that involved clowns. I came across a case in California several years ago. A clown who called himself Professor Perplexing. He traveled with a small circus as one of their sideshow offerings. He entertained the children with his clown antics and their parents by appearing to read their minds. He also managed to read their credit cards and charged up a hefty sum. He skipped just ahead of the police. According to the circus folks, Professor Perplexing's real name was Martin Petters.

"The next case I found was in Portland. A clown working for a nonprofit called Smile A Day. The organization provided entertainment for nursing homes and senior residential facilities. In addition to offering the old people a few laughs, he offered to invest their savings. Again, he left town just before the police caught up with him. The nonprofit reported his name was Mark Patterson.

"Finally Denver. A little over a year ago. A man working for a service that provided entertainment at children's parties was accused of molesting a child during one of these parties. He vanished immediately thereafter. His name, according to the service, was Milton Parks."

"That's quite a leap from Denver to the Twin Cities."

"There's one more connection, Watson. Moriarty, or Parks, as he was calling himself then, was involved with a widow. Before he fled town, he'd stolen much of the money she'd received from her husband's life insurance." Oliver counted off on his fingers. "M. Petters. M. Patterson. M. Parks. And now Morris Peterson. All Moriarty."

"I still don't understand why he would want you dead."

"The insurance money that came from my parents' deaths is quite a tidy sum—over a million dollars. My aunt isn't just my legal guardian. In the event of my death, she inherits the money. If Moriarty gets rid of me, he not only eliminates his greatest foe, but all that money becomes available to him."

"There's your uncle," I said. "He's an obstacle."

"If she doesn't divorce him, I suspect Moriarty will find a way to deal with him too."

"Why would a villain as brilliant as Moriarty stoop to such petty crimes? Even a million dollars, I imagine, would be a paltry sum in his view. If he is Moriarty, why hasn't he set his sights on grander schemes?"

Young Holmes seemed not at all perplexed by the question. "I've wondered that myself, Watson. But I believe he's simply been biding his time."

"Until what?"

"Until he could get to me. When I'm out of the way, who's to stop him from whatever grander design he has in mind? Something needs to be done about Moriarty, Watson, and soon."

I realized the boy's delusional behavior had taken a sudden, more troubling turn. "You wouldn't act on this belief, would you?"

"I already have, my dear fellow."

Alarm bells went off.

"What have you done, Oliver?"

He gave me an exasperated look and wouldn't reply.

"Sherlock," I said. "What have you done?"

"I've simply set the wheels in motion, Watson. Moriarty's own inertia will carry him to his just end."

"Indulge me. What exactly do you mean?"

"Reichenbach Falls," the boy said.

"Where Holmes and Moriarty struggle?"

"More importantly, where Moriarty falls to his death."

"But Holmes falls to his death there too."

The boy arched an eyebrow. "Does he?"

"There is no Reichenbach Falls in Minnesota."

"No, Watson, there is not." He gave me a smile, but so tinged with sadness that it nearly broke my heart.

Our time was up, and a knock came at the door. I desperately wanted to speak with the boy's aunt alone, but when I opened up, a man stood there. Big, bearded, wearing a ball cap with PETER-BILT across the crown. He looked quite put out. "I've come for my nephew."

"Uncle Walter?" the boy said at my back. "Where's Aunt Louise?"

"She's too upset to drive. So I'm here to get you."

"What's wrong?" I asked.

"Family business," Uncle Walter said to me, much on the surly side. "Come on, Ollie. Let's go."

I knelt at the door and looked into the boy's face. "Promise me you won't do anything until I've had a chance to talk to your aunt."

"It's too late, Watson. The great mechanism of fate has been set in motion." He put a hand on my shoulder. "It's all right, dear friend. I can take care of this."

I was overcome with a deep concern for the boy. I knew that despite his intellect—or maybe because of it—he was living a profound delusion, one that seemed more and more to promise harm to himself and to another.

Because I had a session immediately afterward, it was quite a while before I could sit down uninterrupted at my computer. I conducted an Internet search in the same way that I imagined young Holmes had. It took me no time at all to find the story he'd referenced in our session about one Milton Parks, still wanted in Denver, Colorado, on a charge of fraud stemming from the scamming of a widowed woman and also a charge of child molestation. I found a picture of him in the clown costume he'd worn while working at children's parties, a costume very similar to the one I'd seen Morris Peterson wearing. I could find no photograph showing me what he looked like without face paint and ridiculous clothing. In short order, I also found the other incidents the boy had referenced, in Portland and California. But still no photographs of what Moriarty looked like beneath the face paint.

And that's when I caught myself. I'd begun to think of the clown as Moriarty.

I drove to the building where Oliver lived with his aunt and uncle. I buzzed their apartment. A moment later I heard the gruff voice of Uncle Walter through the speaker in the entryway.

"I need to speak with Oliver's aunt," I said.

"It'll have to wait."

"It's rather important," I said. "It's about Oliver's safety."

"A little late for that," he said.

"I beg your pardon?"

"Ollie's gone. Run away, looks like."

Reichenbach Falls. There was nothing like that in the Twin Cities or anywhere near. But there was a rather famous waterfall in a park across the river in Minneapolis: Minnehaha Falls. It was a thin prospect, but the only one I had.

It was nearing dark when I arrived at the park, and I was greeted with an amazing sight. Near the falls stood a pavilion with a bustling restaurant and outdoor patio. The pavilion was surrounded by tall trees, and on the grass between the trees a multitude of colorful tents had been set up. A huge banner strung between two of the trees declared SOUTH MINNEAPOLIS NEIGHBORHOOD CIRCUS. Temporary floodlights lit the scene. Carnival music blared. On a little stage, a man in a jester's costume was juggling swords. A tightrope hung a few feet off the ground, and a young woman dressed as a ballerina and carrying a parasol balanced precariously on the line. In front of the tents, local hawkers called to the milling crowd to come inside and see the wonders of two-headed snakes and dogs who did tricks and yogis who could turn themselves into pretzels. There were games of all kinds, and the air was redolent with the smell of cotton candy and mini-doughnuts, and children ran to and fro trailing balloons on long strings. And everywhere there were clowns.

I made my way among the confusion of bodies to the bridge above Minnehaha Creek and its waterfall. We'd had a wet spring. The creek was full, and the water swept in a roaring torrent over the edge of the falls. Laughing children half climbed the stone walls that edged the bridge. Their parents called harsh warnings to them or pulled them back. The bridge was lit with glaring streetlamps that had come on with the dark, and the people on it cast shadows so that it seemed as if the bridge was populated by two species, one of flesh and the other of black silhouettes.

I couldn't see Oliver anywhere, nor could I see a clown that looked like the one I'd seen coming from Palladium Pizza. But I knew Moriarty had used different costumes in the past, so God only knew how he might have been dressed that night. I searched desperately, overwhelmed with a mounting sense of dread.

A scream shot like a rocket above the chaos of sounds around me. It came from the other end of the bridge. The scream of a child. I turned and pushed through the crowd in that direction. Another scream, and my heart raced as the crowd parted before me. I came at last to a place where a little boy stood near a clown who knelt with a huge boa constrictor draped over his shoulders.

"He won't bite," the clown assured the boy. "But he might swallow you."

The clown leaned nearer, with the snake's head in his hand. The boy screamed again and danced back, but it was clear he was delighted.

The crowd had formed a little circle and was focused on the boy and the snake. That's when I caught sight of Oliver Wendell Holmes. He was standing off the bridge, in the shadows next to a tree near the edge of the chasm where the creek ran and fell fifty feet to the rocks below. He wore the deerstalker hat and the cape of his own making. He was alone, and I was washed in a great relief.

Then, from behind the tree next to Holmes, the clown emerged, with that grotesque grin painted on his face, that cruel mockery of good intent.

"Oliver!" I cried.

But at that same moment, the boy near the snake screamed again, and the crowd roared with laughter and gave their applause, and my desperate cry was lost.

I watched helplessly as the clown reached out and little Holmes turned suddenly to face him. The clown grasped the boy and shoved him toward the edge of the precipice. Oliver in turn grabbed the clown, and in the next instant, my heart broke as I watched them tumble together over the edge of the precipice.

"Oliver!" I cried again, though I knew it was hopeless. Absolutely hopeless.

I shoved my way across the bridge and off the path to the tree where the boy and the clown had fallen. I knelt, leaned over the edge, and looked down at the bottom of the chasm. The streetlamps on the bridge lit the scene below with a raw glare, and I saw the body of the clown sprawled on the rocks where the water crashed and ran on. But I saw no sign of Oliver.

"I could use a hand, Watson."

The voice startled me. In disbelief, I stared below where young Holmes hung upside down, flat against the chasm wall, his right ankle secured with a rope that, as I followed it, I could see was tied to the base of the tree. I drew him up quickly. When I'd pulled him to safety, I couldn't help myself. I took him firmly into my arms and hugged him dearly.

"Please, Watson, a little decorum," Holmes whispered into my ear.

*

"I took his number off my aunt's cell phone and called him," the boy explained to me as we stood on the bridge with the rest of the crowd and watched the body being dealt with below. We'd talked with several policemen already and were waiting for a detective who was supposed to arrive soon to take our official statements.

"I told him I knew who he was and that I wanted to meet him here, and that if he didn't come I would tell my aunt exactly who he was, and I would inform the police as well."

"You knew about this neighborhood circus?"

He looked at me with disappointment. "I never do anything without knowing everything in advance. I was certain Moriarty would feel quite comfortable in this setting. Bold and, I speculated, reckless."

"Why didn't he just skip town?"

"Because I'm Holmes and he was Moriarty. Just as I thought, he couldn't resist the confrontation. A simple push, that was all he thought it would take. But because I'd anticipated his move and held to him, my own weight carried him over the edge along with me."

"Except that you had the rope around your ankle."

"Yes."

"Why didn't you just talk to the police?"

"He was a clever fellow. He slipped them in California and Portland and Denver. There was no reason to believe he couldn't slip them here. No, Watson, this was something I had to take care of myself."

The detective finally arrived, a tall fellow in an ill-fitting brown suit. "We've called your aunt and uncle," he informed the boy. "When they get here, we'll all sit down together and talk."

"May I stay with him?" I asked.

"For now," the detective agreed.

I looked at Holmes. The crowd had cleared away from him but still stared, as if he was just another of the oddities of the evening. He was a lonely boy, with no friends. But I thought he needed one. Didn't everybody, even the most brilliant and solitary among us?

"When this is all over, I'll still expect to see you in my office on Thursday," I said, then added with a gentle and genuine smile, "my dear Sherlock."

K. McGEE

Dot Rat

FROM *Mystery Weekly Magazine*

WHEN HELEN WAS young and couldn't sleep she'd conjure a comforting circle of people she loved, but now most of them were gone and instead she spent her white nights watching an endless loop of losses and regrets jumping a fence like cartoon sheep. At three-thirty, she gave up and rose from bed.

The house was cold, and she turned up the thermostat and then stood in the kitchen waiting for the kettle to boil and staring out the window into the backyard. A streetlight threw her garden in shadows. Against the white fence was an unfamiliar silhouette. Like furniture that assumes the shapes of monsters in the dark, she was sure the shadow would resolve itself if she looked at it long enough. Had she left the wheelbarrow outside? But she knew she hadn't. And then, just as the kettle let out a sharp whistle, the dark shape against her fence moved.

"Cass?" she called, turning the burner off. Her voice sounded weak in the quiet. She listened for the taps of her Staffordshire terrier's nails on the floor. Maybe it was Cass out by the fence. She'd left the doggie door open. But the shape looked too big, and besides, would Cass stay out there in the cold alone?

"Cass?" she called again, but still nothing. Which wasn't right. Even from a deep sleep, Cass came running at the sound of her name.

Helen grabbed a heavy metal flashlight and moved to the back door. She hesitated for a moment. The neighborhood had seen its share of problems, but none lately. And whatever lurked back there had breached her fence and come into her yard. She couldn't allow that.

She opened the door and walked past overgrown tomato plants and a row of cabbages toward the fence. When she was a few yards away, she turned on the flashlight and pointed. Two sets of eyes shone in the beam. A boy, leaning against the fence, arms around Cass.

Helen bent over and whispered, "Who are you?"

"I'm not doing nothing. Just resting."

Cass whined and the boy released her. She moved to Helen, tail wagging, and then back to the boy, as if to ease an introduction. Helen started to tell him the fence was there for a reason, but the boy stood and Helen got a shock. His head barely came to her waist.

"Too cold out here to rest. Come inside." Helen patted her thigh twice for Cass to follow and turned to the house. She listened for sounds behind her, half expecting to hear light, rapid footsteps in retreat. That would be best. He should be home, with his own people. But when she climbed the porch stairs to the back door and turned, the boy was a few steps behind, next to Cass. She opened the door and waited while dog and then boy entered.

Inside he stood next to the door, visibly shivering and taking in his surroundings as if trying to decide whether to stay or flee.

"I was just making tea," she said. "Would you like something hot?"

"You got coffee?"

"Regular?"

"Yes, ma'am."

She moved to the kitchen and reached for the bag of decaf. She wasn't going to give a child real coffee. After she made it, she added plenty of cream and sugar and carried it to the low table in the parlor along with her cup of tea.

"Here you go," she said, gesturing to the sofa. "Have a seat."

The boy hadn't moved from his place by the door, but now he stepped toward her. Cass looped from her to the boy, leading him into the parlor.

Helen drank her tea in silence, watching him out of the corner of her eye. He held the mug with two hands, drank his coffee eagerly, and looked at the bookshelves. His hair was light brown and clung to his head like a cap, his eyes hazel.

"You got a lot of books," he said as he put the empty mug down.

"You like books?"

He answered with a shrug that could have meant yes, no, or undecided.

"Who's that?" He pointed to a framed photograph on the table next to him.

The couple seemed like strangers, her face unlined, her hair dark against the white veil, Sean's wide, pale Irish face so earnest. "That's my wedding photo," she said.

The boy studied it, his face serious. "Is he sleeping?"

"You could say that. Sean died fifteen years ago." She didn't like to think about Sean's death. "Would you like more coffee?"

"Yes, please."

She took his mug to the kitchen and refilled it. When she returned, his head was thrown back, his eyes shut and mouth open. Cass lay on the sofa next to him, her head in his lap.

Helen set the coffee down and looked him over. Even if he was small for his age, he couldn't be more than ten. What was he doing out at night? He looked too thin, there was dirt under his nails and grime on his neck, and he smelled like Cass when she needed a bath. Was he homeless? Or just a fellow insomniac from the neighborhood? Helen didn't recognize him, but then, she didn't pay much attention to kids on the street. She should call the police, but Cass seemed to know this boy. And what he needed most at the moment was rest. Besides, Helen didn't trust police. She was used to handling her own problems.

She took a heavy blue blanket from the closet—one that held up in the washing machine—and dropped it over the boy. She was tempted to remove his shoes, but decided it would only wake him. Plus she didn't relish getting close to his filthy socks. Just as well the sofa was already the color of dirt. She took *The Brothers Karamazov* from the shelves and retreated to her bedroom to read, but instead she slept.

When she woke at eight, the blanket was folded on the sofa, the coffee mug empty, and the boy gone. Cass slinked off the sofa sheepishly, sniffed at the blanket, and followed Helen into the kitchen. Helen laundered the blanket in hot water with extra bleach, thinking about lice. That night she drifted to the back door several times, checking for the boy, but Cass stayed inside and there were no mysterious shadows along the fence. After two more nights, Helen decided to forget about him.

There was a string of warm days, too warm for October in Massachusetts, and between her shifts at the library Helen worked furiously to harvest the last of her tomatoes, beans, and cabbages and put the beds to sleep for the winter. Pulling up roots and spreading layers of compost was a big job, and she slept well.

Two weeks after the first time she saw the boy, Helen rose at seven to a cold morning, made herself coffee, and discovered him asleep on the sofa, Cass stretched next to him. He wore a different T-shirt, and he seemed about as dirty, not worse, so maybe he wasn't homeless. She checked the back door; still locked. He must have crawled through Cass's doggie door. She checked her purse. Cash and credit cards were where they belonged. But then, if he were breaking in to steal, presumably he wouldn't stick around for a nap.

She returned to the kitchen. She didn't care for breakfast herself. Just a cup of coffee or two was enough in the morning. She knew nothing about children. Would the boy eat eggs, and how would he want them? And how many? He was small, but he was growing. She decided on three, scrambled with cheese—the way Sean had liked them—and two pieces of toast.

He stirred on the sofa as she set the plate on the table, and then stood so quickly he startled Cass, who scrambled off the sofa and let out a muffled bark of protest.

"Come have breakfast," she said, going back to the kitchen for the coffee.

He stepped toward the table. "What time is it?"

"Seven-twenty."

"I have to go to school."

"No time for breakfast?"

He glanced at the plate and then at the back door.

She pointed. "The bathroom's that way, first door, if you want to wash your hands."

He looked toward the hall, forehead creased. She sat and sipped her coffee, waiting for him to decide, but then lost patience. "Go on. The eggs are getting cold."

When he returned from the bathroom, he took a seat and ate as if he'd entered a race, head down, scooping his food. Nobody had bothered to teach him table manners.

"I'm Helen, by the way. What's your name?"

He answered without pausing to swallow.

"Andy?" It was hard to hear around the eggs and toast, but he nodded in response.

"You must live quite close, Andy."

He nodded again, drank the rest of his coffee, and set the mug down with finality. Then he stood. "Thank you. I have to go to school."

"Right. See you some other time, Andy."

He stopped at the back door, a hand on the knob, and without turning said, "I didn't think you'd mind."

"No," she said, "I don't seem to."

And then he was gone. After she cleared up the dishes, she went to the kitchen desk and looked at the calendar. It was marked with her work hours at the library, where she volunteered twice a week, a dentist appointment, nothing else. Both times Andy had come in from the cold on Wednesday nights. Maybe there was something that happened at his house on Wednesdays. Maybe not. Twice wasn't a pattern. At least she'd learned a few things this time: he lived in the neighborhood, he went to school, and his name was Andy. Also, he was hungry.

She decided if Andy came back she'd have to call the police. She ran through a list of the old contacts in the Boston Police Department and wondered how many were still around. The kid was in some kind of trouble, and she'd learned a long time ago not to go borrowing trouble. Life brought enough. And she didn't know anything about kids. "It's none of my affair," she muttered. That decided, she locked her purse in her bedroom dresser at night, and she left the blue blanket and an old pillow on the sofa. No reason for him to be cold all night, even if she'd be turning him over to the police in the morning.

The next time she saw Andy was at sunset on Sunday. He sat leaning against the fence, petting Cass. There was something awkward in his movements, and when she crossed the yard she could see he had a bloody lip and a welt under one eye. He nodded at her and kept stroking Cass.

"You want to come in and feed her?" she asked.

He got up slowly. "Sure."

She gave him Cass's bowl and showed him the kibble and measuring cup. "Just one. She eats twice a day, and we don't want her getting fat."

"Okay. And she needs water."

"Right."

He filled the bowls and stood watching Cass eat. "She's a pit bull, isn't she?" he said.

"Staffordshire terrier."

"What's the difference?"

"Attitude."

He nodded like it was the answer he expected.

"You been in an accident?" she said.

"Nah, just Uncle Jake. Best to stay out of his way when he has an appointment with Mr. Jameson."

He used the phrase like he'd heard it a hundred times, *I've got an appointment with Mr. Jameson.*

"Is that who you live with? Your uncle?"

He nodded. "Uncle Jake's all I got."

That sounded memorized as well. *I'm all you've got, kid. You better get lost now. I've got an appointment with Mr. Jameson.* She was beginning to dislike Uncle Jake, a man who routinely drank so much Irish whiskey he would beat a small child. Not that it was any of her business.

"You have time for a bath before we eat dinner."

"A bath?" He looked at her like she'd offered to saw off a limb.

"You know how to draw a bath, don't you?"

"I'm almost ten!"

"How long until you are ten?"

He slid a gaze to her and away and shrugged his shoulders with the eloquence of an old man.

"Best to stay clean when you've got cuts and scrapes, unless you want to be dealing with a nasty infection and pus and unsightly scars." She paused to see if he was going to challenge this, but he seemed suitably impressed. "Use plenty of soap and shampoo. And toss your clothes in the hall. They look like they could stand running through the laundry."

He shook his head. "I can't eat dinner bare naked."

"You can borrow one of Sean's old shirts."

He stood frowning at her, probably trying to think of another objection.

"Go on, now. I've got to get dinner."

"Yes, ma'am." He turned and trudged toward the bathroom, Cass at his heels.

When he came out Sean's red flannel shirt hung to his pale calves and she got her first look at the boy under the dirt. He had a bruise on his temple and there were probably others beneath the shirt. His hair had a wave and was going to be blond when it dried.

Without being asked he came to the table and took the same seat he'd used for breakfast. Helen had made spaghetti and meatballs as well as steaming beans and cabbage from her garden. She set a full plate in front of him, along with a glass of milk. He ate with the same concentration as before, but at a more leisurely pace.

"Those came from the yard," she said as he ate a forkful of beans.

He froze, staring at his plate, then looked up at her with a smile of disbelief. "No suh!"

"What do you think the back garden's for?"

He shook his head and resumed eating. After dinner, she had him dry while she washed. They returned to the parlor, where he looked around thoroughly and finally asked, "You don't have a TV."

Helen had a television in her bedroom, along with a shelf of DVDs, most of them movies made long before Andy was born. But she didn't want him in her bedroom.

"I usually read at night," she said.

Andy looked at her for a moment and then gazed at Cass, no doubt pitying any dog that had to live without a television.

"Do you read, Andy?"

He nodded. "Course. I'm almost ten."

"Right. Well . . . you can read . . ." Her shelves were full of hard-back copies of classics bought at used bookstores over a lifetime, all in good condition. The Limited Editions Club and Heritage Club books were her favorites. She liked the slipcases and the illustrations. She didn't have children's books. What would a boy Andy's age want to read? Maybe he'd like *The Three Musketeers*? *Huckleberry Finn*? Did kids like Twain? Would he know how to treat a good hardback? She looked at her shelves and then remembered a boxed set she bought years ago. It was on the bottom shelf under a thick layer of dust. She pulled out the first of four books and handed it to him. "You can try this one."

He looked at it. "*The Hobbit*?"

"You read it already?"

"No, ma'am."

"You don't need glasses, do you?"

"No."

"Well then." Helen read *The Red and the Black* in her easy chair while Andy read on the sofa next to Cass. She wasn't sure if he liked the book, but he turned the pages at regular if somewhat lengthy intervals, so she assumed he was getting through it.

She left once to put his clothes in the dryer and again to take them out and fold them. Andy kept reading. At nine o'clock she noticed his head starting to bob over the pages.

"I'm ready to sleep now," she said, standing up. "Good night, Andy."

"Good night," he said, his voice sleepy. "Thanks for the spa- ghetti."

She nodded and went into her bedroom, frowning because she didn't have a toothbrush for him and then thinking about the phone call she'd have to make in the morning. He obviously needed a new home, someone to feed him and take care of him, but it wasn't going to be her. He needed a mother, not a grand- mother. She dozed off thinking about how she'd explain Andy to the cops, and how she'd explain the cops to Andy.

Perhaps it was the prospect of police in the morning that dis- rupted her sleep. She woke at one and read for a few hours be- fore going back to sleep, and when she woke again, it was after eight. She had lost the habit of using an alarm clock, and as she rose she realized she'd probably lost her chance to deal with Andy. Sure enough, he was already gone, *The Hobbit* returned to its place on the bottom shelf, the blanket, pillow, and shirt forming a neat stack at one end of the sofa. She looked down at the blanket, glad she wouldn't have to wash it this time. Was Andy's neatness nor- mal? Weren't young boys usually messy? She went to the back door to lock it after him, but it was already locked. He must have left through the doggie door. She felt a surge of emotion, something like regret or pity, and turned swiftly to go to the kitchen. "It's not your problem. He's not even family," she muttered as she made coffee. But she knew this time she couldn't just forget him. She'd fed him, and like any stray, he would return for more.

After her shift at the library she stopped at the bakery and then walked down the block and around the corner to visit Sylvia, one of the few remaining neighbors who'd been around as long as Helen. Sylvia lived on the top floor of a three-decker, and when she opened the apartment door at the top of the stairs, Helen thought she saw a flash of alarm. Then Sylvia's gaze landed on the box of cookies in Helen's hands. "Come on in. How are you, Helen?"

Sylvia was about Helen's age, early seventies, but unlike Helen she'd grown very fat and moved slowly. The house was still as clean as ever, though, the windows sparkling, the tables and shelves dust-free. In the front parlor a faded brown recliner faced the window overlooking the street, venetian blinds drawn up to let in the daylight.

"I'll just make some coffee to go with these," Sylvia said, retreating to the kitchen with the pink box.

Helen listened to her move around as she watched the street in front of the house.

"Oh, you brought the macaroons!"

"Those still your favorite?"

"Oh yes, but I don't get down there very often anymore. Lovely." Sylvia moved into the parlor, all smiles now, carrying a tray with a plate of macaroons and two coffee cups. Helen stood. "You need some help?"

"No. I'm a little slow these days, but I'm not feeble." Sylvia set the tray down on the coffee table, turned the brown chair around to face her, and sat in it. Then she leaned forward and took a cookie.

Helen picked up the coffee and sipped. "You still make the best coffee."

Sylvia nodded. "I grind the beans every morning. Marie says it's a waste of time, but you can taste the difference, can't you?"

Marie was Sylvia's oldest, a sensible girl. Helen agreed with her about grinding beans. The last thing she wanted first thing in the morning was noise and mess. "Listen, Sylvia, I met a boy the other day, someone from the neighborhood. Name is Andy. About ten or so? Thought you might know him."

"White boy? Fair hair?"

"Sounds like him."

Sylvia nodded. "Sure, I know him." She set her foot down and pushed on the floor to turn her chair toward the window. "See that building across the street? Not the Miller house, the yellow one next to it. That's where Andy lives, in the first-floor apartment. But he's eight, not ten."

Like much of Dorchester, the neighborhood was crowded with flat-roofed, narrow, three-story houses, a separate apartment on each floor. Built in the late 1800s to house immigrants, recently many three-deckers in the area had been stripped of ugly aluminum siding and painted in contrasting colors. The yellow building Andy lived in still wore old, scaly-looking siding.

"Andy's in third grade," Sylvia said. "Miss Evanston's class. My grandson William's in the same class."

Sylvia had about a dozen grandchildren, and Helen would hear all about their clever remarks and accomplishments before she left. She didn't mind. She wasn't in a great rush to get home, though Cass would be eager to get her afternoon walk. Sometimes Helen lay in bed at night and tried to recall the moment when her days had changed from too full to too empty. After Sean's death she'd been busier than ever, what with taking over the business. It was when she'd passed the business to Micky that life had slowed down, but that had been gradual. Her sister filled her time with church, but Helen had lost her faith while still young and wasn't enough of a hypocrite to get religion now that she needed something to do. No, organic gardening was her only religion, reading her vocation, and on many days Cass her only contact.

"He lives with his uncle," Sylvia said, still looking out the window. "No parents in the picture. The uncle is hardly much of a family for the boy. Well, you can see how it is."

If a yard was a measure of a first-floor tenant, Jake was a miserable failure. The flowerbeds were empty, the privet hedge overgrown, and the rosebush next to the front steps dead.

"Is he gone a lot?" Helen asked.

Sylvia snorted. "No, he's always home. The Sczeiwskys still live on the second floor, and there's a Vietnamese family on the third. Say what you will, those people work. They're always gone. But Jake rarely stirs before noon. No real job, except . . . once a week, like clockwork, he gets a visit."

"A visit?"

Sylvia nodded slowly, her eyes on the offending building. "A black Mercedes pulls up, the passenger gets out, takes a big suitcase out of the trunk, and carries it in the house. About a half hour later, he comes out, puts the suitcase back in the trunk, and off they go. Every week, Wednesday at nine, like clockwork."

"Nine at night?"

"That's right. I doubt Jake's up before noon."

"What do the men look like?"

"I don't get much of a look at the driver. The one who gets out wears a leather jacket, fur collar. Had to guess, I'd say Russian. Something about his clothes and the way he moves . . . I'd be surprised if he was raised here."

"What about Jake?"

"Oh, he's not foreign. In the summer I hear him yelling at Andy;

his voice comes right through my window. He's always sending the boy out on errands, all kinds of hours. You can bet he's cooking up some kind of drug in there. Well, what else would he be doing? I expect the building to blow up one of these days. Just hope he doesn't take the whole block with him."

Sylvia swiveled her chair to face Helen, her back to the window, and for a moment seemed nervous, as though she'd just remembered it was Helen she was addressing. Then she reached for another macaroon. "My Marie brought William by the other day. I do believe he's the smartest of the grandkids."

Helen changed her walking route to pass Andy's house. Sylvia was almost always sitting at the front window, and she'd wave as they walked by. During one of her walks, just as she came up to Andy's house, a beat-up Chevy Impala pulled to the curb, and out came Andy and a heavy, dark-haired man of about forty. The man had thick brows, hairy forearms, and he needed a shave. So this was Jake. Helen had imagined a thin fair man, someone like Andy. Jake carried a cardboard box full of liquor bottles and moved like he'd helped himself to one of the bottles in the car. Andy glanced in her direction, froze for a moment, and then took a step toward Cass, who was straining at her leash and whining.

Jake kicked Andy in the seat, and he staggered forward to stay afoot. "Where you think you're going, stupid? Don't you know what that is? That's a fuckin' pit bull. Bitch will tear your arm right off. Get in the fucking house." He said "focking" and ran his words together, typical Dorchester accent, but if he'd been a Dot rat, Helen didn't recognize him. Maybe he was from Southie.

Andy turned to the house, walking stiffly, his eyes on the ground in front of him. Jake growled "Get the fucking door!" when they reached the porch.

Neither of them acknowledged Helen with so much as a nod. As she finished the walk, she replayed the scene. Had Andy been ashamed of her? Maybe he'd been ashamed of his uncle. Or maybe he'd been afraid. Jake hadn't even seen her. There were a few advantages to being old, and one of them was invisibility. She could probably walk past Uncle Jake a dozen times and he still wouldn't recognize her, would never register more than generic "old woman." He might recognize Cass, though.

After the walk she fed Cass and then instead of fixing her own dinner, she sat at the kitchen desk and stared out the window as the day faded. Finally she sighed, reached for the phone, and dialed a number she knew by heart.

"Dot Vending," a deep voice rumbled.

They were supposed to say "Dorchester Vending Machines and Trucking." So much for best business practices. "Is Micky around?" she asked.

"Who wants to know?"

"Helen McKinnon."

"Oh, er, yes, ma'am," the man said, his voice moving up an octave. "Hold on, please."

Helen smiled at the change of tone and waited.

"Aunt Helen?" Micky sounded equal parts surprised and wary, like he was afraid she was going to scold him.

"Micky. You doing any business in my neighborhood?"

There was a pause, Micky pondering territory before answering. "Nah. I mean, we got some action on Dot Ave and further west, but nothing in your parish. Why? What have you seen?"

This time it was Helen who took a moment. Information was currency in their line of work; once you let it out, you couldn't put it back. Not that she was in that line anymore. Still, the instinct for discretion hadn't faded.

"Aunt Helen? You got some kind of trouble?"

"No trouble. Just curious." Helen hung up to the sound of Micky asking another question. She needed time to think.

Helen decided to sleep on it for a few days, but Wednesday evening she couldn't focus on her book. At 8:50 she picked up Cass's leash and took her out. The block was quiet, Sylvia's window dim and the blind down to close out prying eyes, but Helen thought she was probably watching through the slats. A black Mercedes stood at the curb outside Andy's building, and Helen approached from Sylvia's side of the street, moving slowly so she could get a look at the driver. The car was parked under a streetlight. As she drew close she wasn't surprised to see the driver watching her and Cass. He was probably bored. What did surprise her was that his glance didn't move past them after a few seconds. It stayed with her, the angle of his big, square head changing to follow them as they moved. Even from forty feet away, she could feel a challenge in that stare. He thought this was his street, his block, and Helen, who had lived here all her life, was the trespasser. She wasn't invisible, his gaze said, and she wasn't safe looking in his direction.

Helen picked up her pace and turned the corner, relief mixing with outrage as she moved out of sight. She walked through the dark streets for a long time, automatically sticking to a safe route, the good blocks of Dorchester, while thinking about the man in the Mercedes and Jake. When she returned to the house, she discovered Andy on the sofa, under the blue blanket, already asleep. *The Hobbit* rested open on his chest. He'd removed his shoes and set them on the floor near the end of the sofa, where he could jump into them in the morning.

Helen put the book on the coffee table and went to bed, setting her alarm for 6:30. She read for several hours, occasionally letting thoughts of the man in the Mercedes intrude.

The next morning she asked Andy a few questions as he shoveled in his eggs. Yes, he ran errands for Uncle Jake, "carrying things," and the territory of his travels encompassed much of Dorchester, including parts Helen wouldn't send Cass into. All she got out of him about the Wednesday visitors was, "Jake don't like 'em to see me, says they steal boys." When asked about Jake's activities in their home, Andy became evasive and ate faster, so she dropped it. It wasn't like she needed confirmation.

That week Helen found herself noticing children more than usual. On her walks, in the library, at the Stop and Shop, she noticed how loud and demanding they were, how often they laughed and cried and yelled, how mobile their faces were. She noticed their backpacks and wondered why Andy didn't have one. She observed their puffy coats and gaudy shoes and crisp haircuts. She picked up an extra toothbrush and left it in its cellophane wrapper next to the sink.

Wednesday morning she woke with a sense of decision. She opened the bottom drawer of her dresser and removed her heavy black handbag with the long shoulder strap. Then she pulled the false back out of the drawer and reached through to remove two neat packs of $100 bills. She stuck them in the bag. At noon she went for a walk without Cass, and instead of passing Sylvia's house, she cut through the yard to the back of Andy's building. She rang the buzzer to the first-floor apartment several times before a disgruntled Jake appeared.

"Who the hell are you?" he asked, blinking out at her as if the daylight hurt his eyes.

"I'm here to discuss Andy."

"You from the social services? You people are supposed to call first. I warned you last time." He shook his head and glared at her, but when she opened the screen and moved into the building, he backed up, then moved quickly into the apartment to close the door to the kitchen. He waved her into the parlor, where the scent of beer and garbage lingered. The small room held no books, no pictures or decorative items of any kind, but was crowded by a too-large sofa, a black leather recliner, and a large flat-screen TV. A stack of pizza boxes stood on the floor next to the recliner, the top one full of cigarette butts, and an olive-colored shag carpet that belonged in the seventies was littered with crumpled fast-food bags and empty Budweiser cans. A half-empty bottle of Jameson Irish Whiskey lay on the sofa.

"What's it this time?" he asked, sounding impatient. "His teacher complain about bruises again? The kid's clumsy, what can I do?"

"I'm not from social services. I'm a friend of Andy's. I live in the neighborhood."

He stared at her for a moment, his face showing confusion and then disbelief. "Look, lady, you're not the social services, you can move your ass out of here!"

"I think you should let me have him. You're not doing a good job of caring for the boy. I can meet him outside his school today and let him know he's going to stay with me from now on."

"Let you have him? Let you have him?" He put a hand on her shoulder and she got a blast of rotting teeth, tobacco, and stale whiskey. She stepped away to escape the stench and realized it was a mistake. He'd assume he could bully her.

"Jesus Christ, who the fuck you think you are, coming in here and telling me to give up my own kid?"

"My name is Helen McKinnon." She said her name slowly, watching for recognition. She believed in giving a man a fair chance, even contemptible scum like Jake. The McKinnon crew wasn't exactly the Winter Hill Gang, but it still ran Dorchester. If the boy was local, he should know the name. "And I don't think Andy is your kid. Is he?"

He flinched and then his face blanched. "Look, his cunt of a mother was a junkie. I may not be blood, but I'm all he's got. She's probably dead by now anyway."

"That doesn't mean you're the best man to raise the boy."

"We're doing fine. And who the hell do you think you are, coming in here like you own the world?"

"I'm prepared to make you a deal."

That stopped him. Helen released the snap on her handbag and reached inside. Jake leered at the bag. Whatever he was doing for the Russians couldn't require much intelligence, she decided. He hadn't the slightest chance in a game of poker.

"What kind of deal?"

"I'm willing to pay," she said, pulling out a form she'd found at the library. "You sign this guardianship form, I'll give you ten thousand dollars."

"You brought the money with ya?" he asked, his tone casual as he shifted closer.

"You'll have to sign the agreement." She handed him the paper.

He glared at it and shook his head. "Maybe I'll just take the money and throw your scrawny, wrinkled ass out of here. Give up Andy, just when he's starting to be useful? You know what raising a kid costs?"

He shoved her against the wall, gripped her throat, and leaned in, staring into her eyes as if hoping to see panic. He didn't notice her hand dip into her bag as she struggled for breath. Her fingers found the familiar cold shape, fitted around it, adjusted the angle, and squeezed. The gun made a loud bang and the pressure on her neck ceased. Jake looked confused as his gaze fell to her bag and then to the red spot spreading on his stomach. Then he dropped.

Helen stood and listened to his moans for a moment, then went and peered through the kitchen door. On the counter were rows of small, neat packages containing white powder. She'd have to call Micky as soon as she got home, so he'd have time to clean things up. By the time the Russians arrived, Jake and the drugs would be gone, along with some of Jake's things. They wouldn't find any witnesses in this neighborhood, and they sure as hell wouldn't call the cops.

Helen moved back to Jake and looked down at him. He made a weak coughing sound and stared up at her, moving his mouth like he was trying to deliver an important message.

"Don't worry about Andy," she said. "I'll meet him at the school."

JOYCE CAROL OATES

The Woman in the Window

FROM *One Story*

Edward Hopper, *Eleven A.M.*, 1926

BENEATH THE CUSHION of the plush blue chair she has hidden it.
Almost shyly her fingers grope for it, then recoil as if it were burning hot.
No! None of this will happen, don't be ridiculous.

It is eleven a.m. He has promised to meet her in this room in which it is always eleven a.m.
She's doing what she does best: waiting.
In fact, she is waiting for him in the way that he prefers: naked. Yet wearing shoes.
Nude, he calls it. Not *naked.*
("Naked" is a coarse word! He's a gentleman and he feels revulsion for vulgarity. Any sort of crude word, mannerism—in a woman.)
She understands. She herself disapproves of women uttering profanities.
Only when she's alone would she utter even a mild profanity —*Damn! God damn. Oh hell . . .*
Only if she were very upset. Only if her heart were broken.
He can say anything he likes. It's a masculine prerogative to say the coarsest cruelest words uttered with a laugh—as a man will do.
Though he might also murmur *Jesus!*
Not profanity but an expression of awe. Sometimes.
Jesus! You are beautiful.

*

Is she beautiful? She smiles to think so.

She is *the woman in the window*. In the wan light of an autumn morning in New York City.

In the plush blue chair, waiting. Eleven a.m.

Sleepless through much of the night and in the early morning soaking in her bath preparing herself for *him*.

Rubbing lotion onto her body: breasts, belly, hips, buttocks.

Such soft skin. Amazing . . . His voice catches in his throat.

At first he scarcely dares touch her. But only at first.

It is a solemn ritual, creamy-white lotion smelling of faint gardenias rubbed into her skin.

In a trance like a woman in a dream rubbing lotion into her skin, for she is terrified of her skin drying out in the radiator-heat, arid airlessness of The Maguire (as it is called) — the brownstone apartment building at Tenth Avenue and Twenty-Third where she lives.

From the street The Maguire is a dignified-looking older building, but inside it is really just *old*.

Like the wallpaper in this room, and the dull-green carpet, and the plush blue chair — *old*.

Dry heat! Sometimes she wakes in the night scarcely able to breathe and her throat dry as ashes.

She has seen the dried-out skin of older women. Some of them not so very old, in their sixties, even younger. Papery-thin skin, desiccated as a snake's husk of a skin, a maze of fine white wrinkles, terrible to behold.

Her own mother. Her grandmother.

Telling herself don't be silly, it will never happen to *her*.

She wonders how old his wife is. He is a gentleman, he will not speak of his wife. She dares not ask. She dares not even hint. His face flushes with indignation, his wide dark nostrils like holes in his face pinch as if he has smelled a bad odor. Very quiet, very stiff he becomes, a sign of danger so she knows to retreat.

Yet thinking, gloating, *His wife is not young. She is not so beautiful as I am. When he sees her, he thinks of me.*

(But is this true? The past half year, since the previous winter, since the long break over Christmas when they were apart — *she* was in the city; *he* was away with his family in some undisclosed place, very likely Bermuda for his face and hands were tanned when he returned — she has not been so certain.)

She has never been to Bermuda, or any tropical place. If *he* does not take her, it is not likely that she will ever go.

Instead, she is trapped here in this room. Where it is always eleven a.m. Sometimes it feels to her as if she is trapped in this chair, in the window gazing out with great yearning at—what?

An apartment building like the building in which she lives. A narrow shaft of sky. Light that appears fading already at eleven a.m.

Damned tired of the plush blue chair that is beginning to fray.

Damned tired of the bed (he'd chosen) that is a double bed, with a headboard.

Her previous bed, in her previous living quarters on East Eighth Street, in a fifth-floor walkup single room, had been a single bed, of course. A girl's bed too small, too narrow, too insubstantial for *him*.

The girth, the weight of *him*—he is two hundred pounds at least. *All muscle,* he likes to say. (Joking.) And she murmurs in response *Yes.*

If she rolls her eyes, he does not see.

She has come to hate her entrapment here. Where it is always eleven a.m. and she is always waiting for *him*.

The more she thinks about it, the more her hatred roils like smoldering heat about to burst into flame.

She hates him. For trapping her here.

For treating her like dirt.

Worse than dirt, something stuck on the sole of his shoe he tries to scrape off with that priggish look in his face that makes her want to murder him.

Next time you touch me! You will regret it.

Except: at work, at the office—she's envied.

The other secretaries know she lives in The Maguire, for she'd brought one of them to see it once.

Such a pleasure it was, to see the look in Molly's eyes!

And it is true—this is a very nice place really. Far nicer than anything she could afford on her secretary's salary.

Except she has no kitchen, only just a hot plate in a corner alcove, and so it is difficult for her to prepare food for herself. Dependent on eating at the automat on Twenty-First and Sixth or else (but this is never more than once a week, at the most) when *he* takes her out to dinner.

(Even then, she has to take care. Nothing so disgusting as seeing a female *who eats like a horse,* he has said.)

She does have a tiny bathroom. The first private bathroom she's ever had in her life.

He pays most of the rent. She has not asked him, he volunteers to give her cash unbidden, as if each time he has just thought of it.

My beautiful girl! Please don't say a word, you will break the spell and ruin everything.

What's the time? Eleven a.m.

He will be late coming to her. Always he is late coming to her.

At the corner of Lexington and Thirty-Seventh. Headed south.

The one with the dark fedora, camel's hair coat. Whistling thinly through his teeth. Not a tall man, though he gives that impression. Not a large man, but he won't give way if there's another pedestrian in his path.

Excuse me, mister! Look where the hell you're going.

Doesn't break his stride. Only partially conscious of his surroundings.

Face shut up tight. Jaws clenched.

Murder rushing to happen.

The woman in the window, he likes to imagine her.

He has stood on the sidewalk three floors below. He has counted the windows of the brownstone. Knows which one is *hers.*

After dark, the lighted interior reflected against the blind makes of the blind a translucent skin.

When he leaves her. Or before he comes to her.

It is less frequent that he comes to her by day. His days are taken up with work, family. His days are what is *known.*

Nighttime there is another self. Unpeeling his tight clothes: coat, trousers, white cotton dress shirt, belt, necktie, socks and shoes.

But now the woman has Thursdays off, late mornings at The Maguire are convenient.

Late mornings shifting into afternoon. Late afternoon, and early evening.

He calls home, leaves a message with the maid — *Unavoidable delay at office. Don't wait dinner.*

In fact it is the contemplation of the woman in the window he likes best, for in his imagination this girl never utters a vulgar remark or makes a vulgar mannerism. Never says a banal or stupid or predictable thing. His sensitive nerves are offended by (for instance) a female shrugging her shoulders, as a man might do; or trying to make a joke, or a sarcastic remark. He hates a female *grinning*.

Worst of all, crossing her (bare) legs so that the thighs thicken, bulge. Hard-muscled legs with soft downy hairs, repulsive to behold.

The shades must be drawn. Tight.

Shadows, not sunlight. Why darkness is best.

Lie still. Don't move. Don't speak. Just—don't.

It's a long way from when she'd moved to the city from Hackensack needing to breathe.

She'd never looked back. Sure they called her selfish, cruel. What the hell, the use they'd have made of her, she'd be sucked dry by now like bone marrow.

Saying it was sin. Her Polish grandmother angrily rattling her rosary, praying aloud.

Who the hell cares! Leave me alone.

First job was file clerk at Trinity Trust down on Wall Street. Wasted three years of her young life waiting for her boss, Mr. Broderick, to leave his (invalid) wife and (emotionally unstable) adolescent daughter, and wouldn't you think a smart girl like her would know better?

Second job also file clerk, but then she'd been promoted to Mr. Castle's secretarial staff at Lyman Typewriters on West Fourteenth. The least the old buzzard could do for her, and she'd have done a lot better except for fat-face Stella Czechi intruding where she wasn't wanted.

One day she'd come close to pushing Stella Czechi into the elevator shaft when the elevator was broken. The doors clanked opened onto a terrifying drafty cavern where dusty-oily cords hung twisted like ugly thick black snakes. Stella gave a little scream and stepped back, and she'd actually grabbed Stella's hand, the two of them so frightened— *Oh my God, there's no elevator! We almost got killed.*

Later she would wish she'd pushed Stella. Guessing Stella was wishing she'd pushed *her*.

Third job, Tvek Realtors & Insurance in the Flatiron Building and she's Mr. Tvek's private secretary— *What would I do without you, my dear one?*

As long as Tvek pays her decent. And *he* doesn't let her down like last Christmas, she'd wanted to die.

It is eleven a.m. Will this be the morning? She is trembling with excitement, dread.

Wanting badly to hurt him. Punish!

That morning after her bath she'd watched with fascination as her fingers lifted the sewing shears out of the bureau drawer. Watched her fingers test the sharpness of the points: very sharp, icepick-sharp.

Watched her hand pushing the shears beneath the cushion of the blue plush chair by the window.

It is not the first time she has hidden the sewing shears beneath the cushion. It is not the first time she has wished him *dead*.

Once she hid the shears beneath her pillow on the bed.

Another time, in the drawer of the bedside table.

How she has hated him, and yet—she has not (yet) summoned the courage, or the desperation, to kill him.

(For is not "kill" a terrifying word? If you *kill*, you become a *killer*.)

(Better to think of punishment, exacting justice. When there is no other recourse but the sewing shears.)

She has never hurt anyone in her life! Even as a child she didn't hit or wrestle with other children, or at least not often. Or at least that she remembers.

He is the oppressor. *He* has murdered her dreams.

He must be punished before he leaves her.

Each time she has hidden the shears she has come a little closer (she thinks) to the time when she will use them. Just *stab, stab, stab* in the way he pounds himself into her, her body, using her body, his face contorted and ugly, terrible to behold.

The act that is unthinkable as it is irrevocable.

The shears are much stronger than an ordinary pair of scissors, as they are slightly larger.

The shears once belonged to her mother, who'd been a quite skilled seamstress. In the Polish community in Hackensack, her mother was most admired.

She tries to sew too. Though she is less skilled than her mother.

Needing to mend her clothes—hems of dresses, underwear, even stockings. And it is calming to the nerves, like knitting, crocheting, even typing when there is no time pressure.

Except— *You did a dandy job with these letters, my dear! But I'm afraid not "perfect"—you will have to do them over.*

Sometimes she hates Mr. Tvek as much as she hates *him*.

Under duress she can grip the shears firmly, she is sure. She has been a typist since the age of fifteen, and she believes that it is because of this skill that her fingers have grown not only strong but unerring.

Of course, she understands: a man could slap the shears out of her hand in a single gesture. If he sees what she is doing, before the icepick-sharp points stabs into his flesh.

She must strike him swiftly and she must strike him in the throat. The "carotid artery"—she knows what this is.

Not the heart, she doesn't know where the heart might be, exactly. Protected by ribs. The torso is large, bulky—too much fat. She could not hope to pierce the heart with the shears in a single swift blow.

Even the back, where the flesh is less thick, would be intimidating to her. She has a nightmare vision of the points of the shears stuck in the man's back, not deep enough to kill him, only just wound him, blood streaming everywhere as he flails his arms and bellows in rage and pain . . .

Therefore, the neck. The throat.

In the throat, the male is as vulnerable as the female.

Once the sharp points of the shears pierce his skin, puncture the artery, there will be no turning back for either of them.

Eleven a.m.

Light rap of his knuckles on the door. *Hel-lo.*

.Turning of the key. And then—

Shutting the door behind him. Approaching her.

Staring at her with eyes like ants running over her (nude) body.

It is a scene in a movie: that look of desire in a man's face. A kind of hunger, greed.

(Should she speak to him? Often at such times he seems scarcely to hear her words, so engrossed in what he sees.)

(Maybe better to say nothing. So he can't wince at her nasal New Jersey accent, tell her *Shhh!*)

Last winter after that bad quarrel she'd tried to bar him from the apartment. Tried to barricade the door by dragging a chair in front of it, but (of course) he pushed his way in by brute strength.

It is childish, futile to try to bar the man. He has his own key, of course.

Following which she was punished. Severely.

Thrown onto the bed and her face pressed into a pillow, scarcely could she breathe, her cries muffled, begging for him not to kill her as her back, hips, buttocks were soundly beaten with his fists.

And then, her legs roughly parted.

Just a taste of what I will do to you if you—ever—try—this—again. Dirty Polack!

Of course they'd made up.

Each time, they'd made up.

He had punished her by not calling, staying away. But eventually he'd returned, as she'd known he would.

Bringing her a dozen red roses. A bottle of his favorite Scotch whisky.

She'd taken him back, it might be said.

She'd had no choice. It might be said.

No! None of this will happen, don't be ridiculous.

She is frightened but she is thrilled.

She is thrilled but she is frightened.

At eleven a.m. she will see him at the door to the bedroom, as he pockets his key. Staring at her so intently she feels the power of being, if only for these fleeting moments, female.

That look of desire in the man's face. The clutch of the mouth like a pike's mouth.

The look of possession as he thinks, *Mine.*

By this time she will have changed her shoes. Of course.

As in a movie scene, it is imperative that the woman be wearing not the plain black flat-heeled shoes she wears for comfort when she is alone but a pair of glamorous sexy high-heeled shoes which the man has purchased for her.

(Though it is risky to appear together in public in such a way, the man quite enjoys taking the girl to several Fifth Avenue stores for the purchase of shoes. In her closet are at least a dozen pairs of expensive shoes he has bought for her, high-heeled, painful to wear but undeniably glamorous. Gorgeous crocodile-skin shoes he'd bought her for her last birthday, last month. He insists she wear high-heeled shoes even if it's just when they're alone together in her apartment.)

(Especially high heels when she's *nude*.)

Seeing that look in the man's eyes thinking, *Of course he loves me. That is the face of love.*

Waiting for him to arrive. And what time is it? Eleven a.m.

If he truly loves her he will bring flowers.

To make it up to you, honey. For last night.

He has said to her that of all the females he has known, she is the only one who seems to be happy in her body.

Happy in her body. This is good to hear!

He means, she guesses, adult females. Little girls are quite happy in their bodies when they are little/young enough.

So unhappy. Or—happy . . .

I mean, I am happy.

In my body I am happy.

I am happy when I am with you.

And so when he steps into the room she will smile happily at him. She will lift her arms to him as if she does not hate him and wish him dead.

She will feel the weight of her breasts as she raises her arms. She will see his eyes fasten greedily on her breasts.

She will not scream at him, *Why the hell didn't you come last night like you promised? Goddamn bastard, you can't treat me like shit on your shoe!*

Will not scream at him, *D'you think I will just take it—this shit of yours? D'you think I am like your damn wife, just lay there and take it, d'you think a woman has no way of hitting back? No way of revenge?*

A weapon of revenge. Not a male weapon but a female weapon: sewing shears.

It is appropriate that the sewing shears had once belonged to her mother. Though her mother never used the shears as she might have wished.

If she can grasp the shears firmly in her hand, her strong right hand, if she can direct the blow, if she can strike without flinching.

If she is that kind of woman.

Except: she isn't that kind of woman. She is a *romantic-minded girl* to whom a man might bring a dozen red roses, a box of expensive chocolates, articles of (silky, intimate) clothing. Expensive high-heeled shoes.

A woman who sings and hums "Tea for two, and two for tea, you for me and me for you, alone . . ."

Eleven a.m. He will be late!

Goddamn, he hates this. *He is always late.*

At the corner of Lexington and Thirty-First turning west on Thirty-First and so to Fifth Avenue. And then south.

Headed south into a less dazzling Manhattan.

He lives at Seventy-Second and Madison: Upper East Side.

She lives in a pretty good neighborhood (he thinks) — for her.

Pretty damn good for a little Polack secretary from Hackensack, New Jersey.

Tempted to stop for a drink. That bar on Eighth Avenue.

Except it's not yet eleven a.m. Too early to drink!

Noon is the earliest. You have to have preserve standards.

Noon could mean lunch. Customary to have drinks at a business lunch. A cocktail to start. A cocktail to continue. A cocktail to conclude. But he draws the line at drinking during the midday when he will take a cab to his office, far downtown on Chambers Street.

His excuse is a dental appointment in midtown. Unavoidable!

Of course five p.m. is a respectful hour for a drink. Almost, a drink at five p.m. might be considered the "first drink of the day," since it has been a long time since lunch.

Five p.m. drinks are "drinks before dinner." Dinner at eight p.m., if not later.

Wondering if he should make a little detour before going to her place. Liquor store, bottle of Scotch whisky. The bottle he'd brought to her place last week is probably almost empty.

(Sure, the woman drinks in secret. Sitting in the window, drink in hand. Doesn't want him to know. How in hell could he not know? Deceitful little bitch.)

There's a place on Ninth. Shamrock Inn. He can stop there.

Looks forward to drinking with her. One thing you can say about the little Polack, she's a good drinking companion, and drinking deflects most needs to talk.

Unless she drinks too much. Last thing he wants to hear from her is complaints, accusations.

Last thing he wants to see is her face pouty and sulky and not so good-looking. Sharp creases in her forehead like a forecast of how she'll look in another ten years, or less.

It isn't fair! You don't call when you promise! You don't show up when you promise! Tell me you love me but—

Many times he has heard these words that are beginning to bore him.

Many times he has appeared to be listening but is scarcely aware which of them is berating him: the girl in the window or the wife.

To the woman in the window he has learned to say, *Sure I love you. That's enough, now.*

To the wife he has learned to say, *You know I have work to do. I work damn hard. Who the hell pays for all this?*

His life is complicated. That is actually true. He is not deceiving the woman. He is not deceiving the wife.

(Well—maybe he is deceiving the wife.)

(Maybe he is deceiving the woman.)

(But women expect to be deceived, don't they? Deception is the terms of the sex contract.)

In fact he'd told the little Polack secretary (warned her) at the outset, almost two years ago now (Jesus! That long, no wonder he's getting to feel trapped, claustrophobic), *I love my family. My obligations to my family come first.*

(Fact is, he's getting tired of this one. Bored. She talks too much even when she isn't talking, he can hear her *thinking.* Her breasts are heavy, beginning to droop. Flaccid skin at her belly. Thinking sometimes when they're in bed together he'd like to settle his hands around her throat and just start squeezing.)

(How much of a struggle would she put up? She's not a small woman but *he's* strong.)

(The French girl he'd had a "tussle" with—that was the word he'd given the transaction—had put up quite a struggle, like a fox or a mink or a weasel, but that was wartime, in Paris, people were desperate then, even a girl that young and starved-looking like a rat. *Aidez-moi! Aidez-moi!* But there'd been no one.)

(Hard to take any of them seriously when they're chattering away in some damn language like a parrot or a hyena. Worse when they screamed.)

Set out late from his apartment that morning. Goddamn, he resents his goddamn wife, suspicious of him for no reason.

Hadn't he stayed home the night before? Hadn't he disappointed the girl? All because of the wife.

Stiff and cold-silent the wife. God, how she bores him!

Her suspicions bore him. Her hurt feelings bore him. Her dull repressed anger bores him. Worst of all, her boredom bores him.

He has imagined his wife dead many times, of course. How long have they been married, twenty years, twenty-three years, he'd believed he was lucky marrying the daughter of a well-to-do stockbroker, except the stockbroker wasn't that well-to-do and within a few years he wasn't a stockbroker any longer but a bankrupt. Asking to borrow money from *him*.

Also, the wife's looks are gone. Melted look of a female of a certain age. Face sags, body sags. He has fantasized his wife dying (in an accident: not his fault) and the insurance policy paying off: $40,000 free and clear. So he'd be free to marry the other one.

Except: does he want to marry *her*?

God! Feeling the need for a drink.

It is eleven a.m. Goddamn bastard will be late again.

After the insult and injury of the previous night!

If he is late, it will happen. She will stab, stab, stab until he has bled out. She feels a wave of relief; finally it has been decided for her.

Checks the sewing shears, hidden beneath the cushion. Something surprising, unnerving—the blades of the shears seem to be a faint, faded red. From cutting red cloth? But she doesn't remember using the shears to cut red cloth.

Must be the light from the window passing through the gauze curtains.

Something consoling in the touch of the shears.

She wouldn't want a knife from the kitchen—no. Nothing like a butcher knife. Such a weapon would be premeditated, while a pair of sewing shears is something a woman might pick up by chance, frightened for her life.

He threatened me. He began to beat me. Strangle me. He'd warned me many times in one of his moods he would murder me.

It was in defense of my life. God help me! I had no choice.

Hears herself laugh aloud. Rehearsing her lines like an actress about to step out onto the bright-lit stage.

Might've been an actress, if her damn mother hadn't sent her right to secretarial school. She's as good-looking as most of the actresses on Broadway.

He'd told her so. Brought her a dozen blood-red roses first time he came to take her out.

Except they hadn't gone out. Spent the night in her fifth-floor walkup, East Eighth Street.

(She misses that sometimes. Lower East Side, where she'd had friends and people who knew her, on the street.)

Strange to be naked, that is *nude*, yet wearing shoes.

Time for her to squeeze her (bare) feet into high heels.

Like a dancer. Girlie-dancer they are called. Stag parties exclusively for men. She'd heard of girls who danced at these parties. Danced *nude*. Made more in a single night's work than she made in two weeks as a secretary.

"Nude" is a fancy word. Hoity-toity like an artist-word.

What she has not wanted to see: her body isn't a girl's body any longer. At a distance (maybe) on the street she can fool the casual eye, but not up close.

Dreads to see in the mirror a fleshy aging body like her mother's.

And her posture in the damned chair, when she's alone—leaning forward, arms on knees, staring out the window into a narrow shaft of sunshine between buildings—makes her belly bulge, soft belly-fat.

A shock, first time she'd noticed. Just by accident glancing in a mirror.

Not a sign of getting older. Just putting on weight.

For your birthday, sweetheart. Is it—thirty-two?

She'd blushed; yes, it is thirty-two.

Not meeting his eye. Pretending she was eager to unwrap the present. (By the size of the box, weight of what's inside, she guesses it's another pair of goddamn high-heeled shoes.) Heart beating rapidly in a delirium of dread.

If he knew. Thirty-nine.

That was last year. The next birthday is rushing at her.

Hates him, wishes he were dead.

Except she would never see him again. Except the wife would collect the insurance.

She does not want to kill him, however. She is not the type to hurt anyone.

In fact she wants to kill him. She has no choice, he will be leaving her soon. She will never see him again and she will have nothing.

When she is alone she understands this. Which is why she has hidden the sewing shears beneath the cushion for the final time.

She will claim that he began to abuse her, he threatened to kill her, closing his fingers around her throat so she had no choice but to grope for the shears and stab him in desperation, repeatedly, unable to breathe and unable to call for help until his heavy body slipped from her, twitching and spurting blood, onto the green rectangle of light in the carpet.

His age is beyond forty-nine, she's sure.

Glanced at his ID once. Riffling through his wallet while he slept open-mouthed, wetly snoring. Sound like a rhinoceros snorting. She'd been stunned to see his young photograph—taken when he'd been younger than she is right now—dark-haired, thick dark-haired, and eyes boring into the camera, so intense. In his U.S. Army uniform, so handsome!

She'd thought, *Where is this man? I could have loved this man.*

Now when they make love she detaches herself from the situation to imagine him as he'd been, young. *Him,* she could have felt something for.

Having to pretend too much. That's tiring.

Like the pretense she is *happy in her body.*

Like the pretense she is *happy when he shows up.*

No other secretary in her office could afford an apartment in this building. True.

Damn apartment she'd thought was so special at first now she hates. *He* helps with expenses. Counting out bills like he's cautious not to be overpaying.

This should tide you over, sweetheart. Give yourself a treat.

She thanks him. She is the good girl thanking *him.*

Give yourself a *treat!* With the money he gives her, a few tens, a rare twenty! God, she hates him.

Her fingers tremble, gripping the shears. Just the feel of the shears.

Never dared tell him how she has come to hate this apartment. Meeting in the elevators old women, some of them with walkers, eyeing her. Older couples, eyeing her. Unfriendly. Suspicious. How's a secretary from New Jersey afford The Maguire?

Dim-lit on the third floor like a low-level region of the soul into which light doesn't penetrate. Soft-shabby furniture and mattress already beginning to sag like those bodies in dreams we feel but don't see. But she keeps the damn bed made every day whether anyone except her sees.

He doesn't like disorder. *He'd* told her how he'd learned to make a proper bed in the U.S. Army in 1917.

The trick is, he says, you make the bed as soon as you get up.

Pull the sheets tight. Tuck in corners—tight. No wrinkles! Smooth with the edge of your hand! Again.

First lieutenant, he'd been. Rank when discharged. Holds himself like a soldier, stiff backbone like maybe he is feeling pain—arthritis? Shrapnel?

She has wondered—*Has he killed? Shot, bayoneted? With his bare hands?*

What she can't forgive: the way he detaches himself from her as soon as it's over.

Sticky skin, hairy legs, patches of scratchy hair on his shoulders, chest, belly. She'd like him to hold her and they could drift into sleep together, but rarely this happens. Hates feeling the nerves twitching in his legs. Hates sensing how he is smelling her. How he'd like to leap from her as soon as he comes, the bastard.

A man is crazy wanting to make love, then abruptly it's over— *he's* inside his head, and *she's* inside hers.

The night before waiting for him to call to explain when he didn't show up. From eight p.m. until midnight she'd waited, rationing whisky-and-water to calm her nerves. Considering the sharp-tipped shears she might use against herself one day.

In those hours sick with hating him and hating herself, and yet —the leap of hope when the phone finally rang.

Unavoidable, crisis at home. Sorry.

Now it is eleven a.m. Waiting for him to rap on the door.

She knows he will be late. He is always late.

She is becoming very agitated. But: too early to drink.

Even to calm her nerves too early to drink.

Imagines she hears footsteps. Sound of the elevator door opening, closing. Light rap of his knuckles on the door just before he
unlocks it.

Eagerly he will step inside, come to the door of the bedroom
—see her in the chair awaiting him . . .

The (nude) woman in the window. Awaiting him.

That look in his face. Though she hates him, she craves that look
in his face.

A man's desire is sincere enough. Can't be faked. (She wants to
think this.) She does not want to think that the man's desire for her
might be as fraudulent as her desire for him, but if this is so, why'd
he see her at all?

He does love her. He loves something he sees in her.

Thirty-one years old, he thinks she is. No—thirty-two.

And his wife is ten, twelve years older at least. Like Mr. Broderick's wife, this one is something of an *invalid.*

Pretty damned suspicious. Every wife you hear of is an *invalid.*

How they avoid sex, she supposes. Once they are married, once
they have children, that's enough. Sex is something the man has to
do elsewhere.

What time is it? Eleven a.m.

He is late. Of course he is late.

After the humiliation of last night, when she had not eaten
all day anticipating a nice dinner at Delmonico's. And he never
showed up, and his call was a feeble excuse.

Yet in the past he has behaved unpredictably. She'd thought that
he was through with her, she'd seen disgust in his face, nothing so
sincere as disgust in a man's face; and yet—he'd called her, after a
week, ten days.

Or he'd showed up at the apartment. Knocking on the door
before inserting the key.

And almost in his face a look of anger, resentment.

Couldn't keep away.

God, I'm crazy for you.

In the mirror she likes to examine herself if the light isn't too
bright. Mirror to avoid is the bathroom mirror unprotected and
raw lit by daylight, but the bureau mirror is softer, more forgiving.
Bureau mirror is the woman she *is.*

Actually she looks (she thinks) younger than thirty-two.

Much younger than thirty-nine!

A girl's pouty face, full lips, red-lipstick lips. Sulky brunette still damned good-looking and *he* knows it, *he* has seen men on the street and in restaurants following her with their eyes, undressing her with their eyes, this is exciting to him (she knows), though if she seems to react, if she glances around, he will become angry —at *her.*

What a man wants, she thinks, is a woman whom other men want, but the woman *must not seem to seek out this attention or even be aware of it.*

She would never bleach her hair blond, she exults in her brunette beauty, knowing it is more real, earthier. Nothing phony, synthetic, showy about *her.*

Next birthday, forty. Maybe she will kill herself.

Though it's eleven a.m. he has stopped for a drink at the Shamrock. Vodka on the rocks. Just one.

Excited thinking about the sulky-faced woman waiting for him: in the blue plush chair, at the window, nude except for high-heeled shoes.

Full lips, lipstick-red. Heavy-lidded eyes. A head of thick hair, just slightly coarse. And hairs elsewhere on her body that arouse him.

Slight disgust, yet arousal.

Yet he's late, why is that? Something seems to be pulling at him, holding him back. Another vodka?

Staring at his watch thinking, *If I am not with her by eleven-fifteen it will mean it's over.*

A flood of relief, never having to see her again!

Never the risk of losing his control with her, hurting her.

Never the risk she will provoke him into a *tussle.*

She's thinking she will give the bastard ten more minutes.

If he arrives after eleven-fifteen it is over between them.

Her fingers grope for the shears beneath the cushion. There!

She has no intention of stabbing him—of course. Not here in her room, not where he'd bleed onto the blue plush chair and the green carpet and she would never be able to remove the stains even if she could argue (she could argue) that he'd tried to kill her, more than once in his strenuous lovemaking he'd closed his fingers around her throat, she'd begun to protest *Please don't, hey you are hurting me* but he'd seemed scarcely to hear, in a delirium of sexual rapacity, pounding his heavy body into her like a jackhammer.

You have no right to treat me like that. I am not a whore, I am not your pathetic wife. If you insult me I will kill you—I will kill you to save my own life.

Last spring for instance when he'd come to take her out to Delmonico's but seeing her he'd gotten excited, clumsy bastard knocking over the bedside lamp and in the dim-lit room they'd made love in her bed and never got out until too late for supper and she'd overheard him afterward on the phone *explaining*—in the bathroom stepping out of the shower she'd listened at the door fascinated, furious—the sound of a man's voice when he is *explaining to a wife* is so callow, so craven, she's sick with contempt recalling.

Yet *he* says he has left his family, he loves *her.*

Runs his hands over her body like a blind man trying to see. And the radiance in his face that's pitted and scarred, he needs her in the way a starving man needs food. *Die without you. Don't leave me.*

Well, she loves him! She guesses.

Eleven a.m. He is crossing the street at Ninth and Twenty-Fourth. Gusts of wind blow grit into his eyes. The vodka is coursing along his veins.

Feels determined: if she stares at him with that reproachful pouty expression he will slap her face and if she begins to cry he will close his fingers around her throat and squeeze, squeeze.

She has not threatened to speak to his wife. As her predecessor had done, to her regret. Yet he imagines that she is rehearsing such a confrontation.

Mrs. ——? You don't know me but I know you. I am the woman your husband loves.

He has told her it isn't what she thinks. Isn't his family that keeps him from loving her all he could love her but his life he'd never told anyone about in the war, in the infantry, in France. What crept like paralysis through him.

Things that had happened to him, and things that he'd witnessed, and (a few) things that he'd perpetrated himself with his own hands. And if they'd been drinking this look would come into his face of sorrow, horror. A sickness of regret she did not want to understand. And she'd taken his hands that had killed (she supposed) (but only in wartime) and kissed them, and brought them against her breasts that were aching like the breasts of a young mother ravenous to give suck, and sustenance.

And she said, *No. That is your old life.*

I am your new life.

He has entered the foyer. At last!

It is eleven a.m.—he is not late after all. His heart is pounding in his chest.

Waves of adrenaline as he has not felt since the war.

On Ninth Avenue he purchased a bottle of whisky, and from a street vendor he purchased a bouquet of one dozen blood-red roses.

For the woman in the window. *Kill or be killed.*

Soon as he unlocks the door, soon as he sees her, he will know what it is he will do to her.

Eleven a.m. In the plush blue chair in the window the woman is waiting nude, except for her high-heeled shoes. Another time she checks the shears hidden beneath the cushion, which feel strangely warm to her touch, even damp.

Stares out the window at a narrow patch of sky. Almost she is at peace. She is prepared. She waits.

STEVEN POPKES

The Sweet Warm Earth

FROM *Fantasy and Science Fiction*

IN THE SUMMER of 1961, I was working for Bernie McLaughlin and the Charlestown mob up in Boston. I wasn't important, you understand. I was an enforcer. I made sure debts got paid.

That Labor Day, when Georgie McLaughlin felt up Bobo Petricone's girlfriend and was beaten half to death by the Winter Hill Gang, I got nervous. When Bernie couldn't get satisfaction and was caught trying to put a bomb in Buddy McLean's car, I knew the time had come to move on.

I called my cousin Joey in Santa Monica and he said, *Larry, come on out here. I'll take care of you.*

So I loaded up my car and drove west before the gang war started. I made it to Los Angeles by the beginning of October. Just as well. McLean shot Bernie full of holes by the end of the month.

I didn't care. California was like in the movies.

First thing I noticed was the *light*, a golden syrup poured over everything. People glowed. The colors of the buildings, the trees, the cars—everything looked lit from inside, shining through like the way flame shines through the wax of a candle. I never knew until then how dull and ugly it was back east.

It was warm—I mean, even the dirt was warm. Even in the dead heat of a Boston summer you could still feel winter underneath. Heck, in the middle of every August there always came a day or a week when you could feel October rolling toward you. Summer was something temporary. Something chancy. Maybe it would come this year. Maybe it wouldn't. No one was going to tell you.

But here there was no hunching your shoulders against the cold, no ice on the trees, no hiding from the snow. Here the air smelled like summer all the time and winter was something that happened somewhere else.

And the women. I mean, it's not like they were naked, but you needed no special instructions to know what was underneath. They were all tall, beautiful, and walking like they knew exactly who they were, what they could do, and who was in charge.

I decided then and there: I was *never* going to leave.

Joey got me a job with the DeSimone outfit watching the Los Alamitos track.

It was my job to keep an eye on the horses and the bettors to make sure that everything we didn't control was on the up-and-up. Los Alamitos was a fairly honest track. Our outfit didn't fix it. I was there to make sure nobody else did either. I didn't work for DeSimone directly, of course. Joey and I both worked for a soldier named Alfredo Paretti.

Mind you, this was back in the days of the Mickey Mouse Mafia. Mickey Cohen was already in jail. Simone Scozzari was losing his deportation appeal. Frank DeSimone didn't have good control of things. He was just a whipping boy for Chicago and New York. DeSimone's weakness didn't make my job any easier. There were always two-bit attempts to drug this horse or hobble that one. Not what you would call a glamorous job. Even so, it was better than waiting for the shoe to drop up in Boston. And as November rolled around and I remembered the miserable rains that always settled in by Thanksgiving, I felt like kissing the warm Los Angeles earth.

Sure, I'd seen horses. In the circus or driving past farms where they were standing in a field staring at nothing in particular. The Boston cops even had a horse patrol.

None of that prepared me for the horses of Los Alamitos.

They were big—their shoulders were as high as my head. Their bodies were marked by muscles defined as carefully and precisely as if they were professional bodybuilders. They watched you.

I'd played the dogs in Boston for years, so I thought I was knowledgeable about racing animals. But these were thousand-pound beasts ridden by humans no bigger than monkeys. The first time they roared past me at the fence, I cheered.

So: it was a beautiful day in early 1962 and I was sitting just outside the barn entrance, reading a week-old *Boston Herald*, smoking

a Chesterfield. Big Teamsters strike up in Boston and it looked like
the old Winter Hill Gang was in the thick of it. Just marking time
until Buddy McLean got out of jail. Again, I was ready to kiss the
sweet earth.

This tiny old guy strolled in and showed me his pass. I'm not the
biggest man in the world but I sure towered over him. I mean, he
barely came up to my chest—I've seen bigger jockeys. I nodded
like I'd checked him out and went back to my paper, but I kept
an eye on him. He went up to I'm a Nobody—a big black mare,
seven to one in the third race—and started talking to her. Nothing
important, just asking her how she was feeling and was she going
to win or place?

That made me watch him even more closely. I marked that big
nose and deep grooves in his face—like the old Italians I used to
know. I thought, *If he's connected, I'll have to be careful.* Those guys
back east weren't always polite.

Then he reached out and scratched behind the horse's ears and
I was up and over to him.

"Sorry," I said. "Can't touch the horses."

He started. Then looked guilty. "Just scratching an itch. She
asked."

"Yeah. Right. No touching."

He nodded and bowed slightly to me in that old-world way I
hadn't seen since I left Boston. I got to say, it charmed me.

"Antonio Bernardi," he said. "Sorry to break the rules."

"Larry Mulcahey. It's all right." I felt a rare need to explain. "We
have to protect the animals. Some folks might do something to rig
the race."

Antonio nodded. "I understand completely." He walked around,
continuing to talk to the horses. I leaned against the door and let
him, but watching. Then he tipped his hat to me and left. I went
back to the *Herald*.

Come the third race, I stood and watched from the fence. I'm a
Nobody tore up the outside, cut to center, and placed third. Four-
to-one payout. I went to the windows and waited. Sure enough, old
Antonio picked up his winnings from the window and caught a bus.
I cut in line past the dirty looks and asked the clerk what Antonio
took home.

"Forty bucks," he said.

"Thanks." I wandered back to the stables, thinking. Forty bucks isn't a lot of money, but it's more than dinner and a cup of coffee. I'm a Nobody was back in her stall and the jockey was there.

I came up beside him. "You had a good run?"

"You bet!" The jockey grinned, real excited. "Who knew the nag had it in her?"

I reached up and scratched behind her ear like I'd seen Antonio do. She pulled her head back and glared at me.

"She don't like that sort of thing," said the jockey. "She's real particular about her ears."

"Yeah." I didn't feel anything like a needle mark, but I'm not a vet. The horse wasn't shaking or anything. Antonio hadn't slipped her a goofball.

"Particular," I said. "Some girls, eh?"

The jockey laughed.

I asked the window guard about Antonio. "The old guy?" he told me. "He's been coming here for years. Likes horses."

The next day I planted myself in front of the barn like it was my favorite place to be. Antonio arrived in the morning. This time I made a show of checking his pass, to see if he got irritated or tried to get something past me. But he just played the innocent old man. Maybe that's exactly what he was.

"Your horse came in yesterday," I said.

"Sometimes they do me a favor. Keeps me in vino."

"Where are you from?"

He picked up immediately on the question. "Siena. Greatest town for horses in all of Italy. I came over after the war. Ever been?"

"No."

"You should have gone before the war. Beautiful. Now, not so good."

"Pretty rough over there?"

"Terrible. You would not believe."

I nodded, dropped my cigarette, and ground it out. "You know, Antonio, I have to watch the horses."

"Yes. It is an important job."

"I suppose. If somebody were to slip them a needle, I'd have to hurt them."

His face went stern. "Absolutely."

I let him go and he walked around talking to the horses again. Sure enough, he took home sixty bucks. I lit another Chesterfield, thinking.

Watching the track wasn't my only responsibility. Sometimes I had to look out for DeSimone's or Paretti's interests. Say somebody wanted to take home more than they could from the windows. Say somebody made a bet on credit to somebody in the organization. It was my job to keep everybody honest—not that much different from Boston. It didn't happen often. Most people were smart enough not to cross us or were able to offer up something else in trade.

But not everybody's that smart. The day after I talked to Bernardi I got a call from Joey that I needed to visit a Harry Cohen —no relation to Mickey. I checked that first thing. Big guy. Used to be a boxer. I visited him at a gym down on Figueroa where he worked out to keep his hand in.

Harry was no stranger to debt collection. He used to work for Paretti but got out of the business to become a long-distance trucker. My visit to the gym was a sort of professional courtesy. I wanted him to get the message that I was serious but not a fanatic or anything. I wanted repayment of the debt without trouble.

Harry figured out who I was soon as I came through the door. This was not brilliant detective work; I was the only one in a suit in the middle of a bunch of guys wearing boxing trunks and sweatshirts.

He stood up, a head taller than me. I kept my hands in my pockets; I had a blackjack ready and my piece shouldered and loose. I wasn't about to give up home-court advantage without equalizers. I'm peaceful, not stupid.

"Paretti sent you?"

I nodded. "Got twelve hundred?"

He laughed. "Do I look like I'm good for that kind of money?"

"You got paid from Hamm Trucking this morning," I said. "A couple of hundred from that would be a gesture of good faith."

He laughed again, ugly. I figured I was about thirty seconds from having to prove my point.

He sneered at me. "How about I send you out of here in pieces as a gesture of my own?"

I whipped around, blackjack in my left hand, and caught some mug across the temple. I kept turning, pulling out my piece with my other hand, and it was in Harry's face as he started to move toward me.

"Not a good plan, Harry." My piece was an old army .45 from the thirties: so big it hypnotized people. Harry stared down the muzzle, cross-eyed. I heard movement behind me and pulled the hammer back. "Not good at all."

Harry waved someone off I couldn't see. "That could have gone better."

"You get paid every week," I said. "Two hundred now isn't going to break you. Then we figure out a payment plan. It's a good deal and leaves your parts intact. Otherwise it'll be messy. Of course, I'm from Boston. We're used to messy up there."

"Okay," he said sullenly.

I slipped around him so I was covering his back. Then I pushed him away. We were the center of attention. "Get it."

He walked off slowly. The other boxers were watching me. Two of them were in the ring, hot and full of red meat. They'd have taken me on if they thought they had half a chance.

I sat in a chair, my back to the wall. These guys were small change. Dinner fighters. Not good enough to do more than entertain half-drunk Mexicans on a Saturday night. They thought they were tough. I sighed a little, thinking of Buddy taking down Bernie in broad daylight. I hoped Harry was smarter than he looked.

Harry came back and my estimation of him went up a couple of points. He handed me a crisp set of bills: two hundred bucks plus an extra twenty.

I held the bills for a moment. Why didn't people do what they were told? "That's more than I said."

"It's a gesture of good faith."

It was an excuse. An opportunity to be insulted. A chance grab at control. I handed him back the twenty. "I appreciate the gesture, but I said two. You give me a hundred a week through June and we're square. You miss a payment and I take a piece of your right hand or maybe an ear. You miss a second payment and I'll have to justify taking a loss. Understand?"

"I understand."

Maybe he understood.

I started to get up and with a roar he took a swing at me.

Maybe not.

I caught his fist in my hand and bent the wrist until it was just short of breaking. He gasped and dropped to his knees: that or lose the wrist. I leaned down and spoke slowly and clearly, as if he were three. "I don't bluff and I don't argue. If you don't like the deal I can always burn down your house, slaughter your wife, and fuck your sweet little daughter, all in front of you. Then gouge out your eyes with a grapefruit spoon so it's the last thing you ever see. Your call."

He gasped from the pain. "Sorry, man. Don't break it. I can't drive with a broken hand. I can't work the shift lever."

I let him go. "Next week."

I walked out into the sunshine. Next to my car, I lit a cigarette and took a deep breath. Stupid people pissed me off. Guys pounding their chests and pretending they're chewing the thighbone of an ox—none of it meant a thing. Of course, dealing with stupid people was part of the job. If they weren't stupid, they wouldn't borrow money from a shark like Paretti. What level of stupidity is it to welsh on the payback and then threaten someone like me? Paretti wanted the money. He didn't want broken bones and dead boxers. But if broken bones and dead boxers were the price required to keep the status quo, he was willing to pay it. Stupid not to see that.

Back at the track I watched Bernardi for a week or so. He never bet enough to shift the odds, but he always won something.

It put me in a funny position. By now I was pretty sure he wasn't connected; just an old Italian guy going to the track on his own. Although a string of luck like this was suspicious. I could have asked Joey about him, or Paretti. But that would have made him something to be dealt with. As long as he wasn't officially a problem I could ignore him. Then again, if it turned out later he was a problem I had already known about and *didn't* act on, I could be out of a job. Or worse.

I was waiting when he showed up.

"Mr. Mulcahey," he said.

"Mr. Bernardi," I responded. "I'm thinking I may have to keep you out of the barn."

He looked startled. "Why?"

I took a drag on my cigarette. "You've been winning—"

"Only small amounts!"

I nodded. "You're doing something to the horses. It's fixing the races. I can't have that."

He spread his hands. "I fix *nothing*. I merely encourage them as you would encourage a friend to do his best. Besides, I only work the small races. The tryouts and jockey starters. Nothing important to Mr. DeSimone."

I noticed he mentioned DeSimone. "Yeah. There were no needles or pills. I would have had to hurt you for that."

"Of course!"

"What are you doing, Mr. Bernardi?"

He hesitated for a minute.

I sighed. I don't like hurting old people. Leaves a bad taste in my mouth.

"I talk to them," he said finally.

"Yeah. Right."

"No. Truly. When I was a boy, I lived in Dormelletto, near the mountains. My father worked for the great Federico Tesio. I was born in the stables. I learned the smell of horses before I learned to nurse. I myself helped train Nearco, the greatest thoroughbred champion that ever lived!"

"Who is Federico Tesio?"

He gave me a withering glare, and then his expression softened like a mother who's lost her temper with her idiot son and thought better of it.

It made me laugh out loud. "Okay. You talk to the horses."

He held up his finger. "Only if they're willing to listen. I find out which horse is most excited for the day. I talk to them. They pass the time with me—I admit that sometimes a horse might take such pleasure in the conversation he runs more strongly. But I have done nothing to him."

"No drugs. No touching."

He drew himself up to his full height—maybe five feet. "Never," he pronounced.

I thought about it for a minute. "Okay. But if you touch the horses—"

He shook his head violently. "Never!" He watched me for a moment. "You should meet them."

"The horses? They're just horses."

"Not so." He pointed to a brown gelding in the far stall.

"Consider Fraidy Cat. He has a terrible crush on one particular jockey named Phillip. Loves the man. Would take him as a mare if only he could but instead must satisfy himself by running his heart out for him. Or consider Island Queen. She is the sworn enemy of Pale Pauline."

"Which one is she?"

"She's not here today. Don't bet on Island Queen. She never performs well unless Pale Pauline is racing against her. Then the two will try to murder one another."

"Why?"

"Who can know? They're horses. They feel what they feel. They do what they do. Whatever hopes and dreams they have are the hopes and dreams of horses, not people."

"What about that one?" I pointed to a pale gray mare.

He didn't speak for a moment. Then: "That is White Glory. I don't know her. She is quiet about herself and speaks only of the farm she has left behind. She is very sad."

I laughed. "You're so full of it, it's entertaining just to listen."

Antonio was at the track nearly every day, and there weren't many other people I could talk to. Jockeys are about as dull as they come, and I didn't see Joey that often; he was too busy. Any conversation with Mr. Paretti was over the phone and pure business. There were other soldiers I talked with every now and then: Go get this bag and deliver it to this guy. Pick up this car and take it down to niggertown and leave it but take the license, registration, and identification number. Go get this guy and bring him over to this address. You don't have to stay if you don't want to.

The soldiers were duller than the jockeys.

Not that the guys I left up in Boston were any better, but their topics of conversation were more interesting. We might talk about family back in Ireland or how the British and the IRA were trying to blow each other up. We had pools on the next likely spot the IRA might attack. Won some of them, too. And Boston politics were downright fun to watch—Los Angeles politics consists of one dumb guy arguing with another dumb guy, both of them crowded off the front page by which movie stars were sleeping together. I mean, I wouldn't read about Elizabeth Taylor even if she were caught screwing a goat.

Okay. Maybe a goat.

I liked Antonio. He was pleasant and smart—he knew the difference between a simple dirty joke and a really rough one and when to tell which. He had been around the old country and had the stories to show for it. He liked beer and Italian wine and he had some Italian magic with fish that came deep from the dark heart of Tuscany. I can't say we ever became friends exactly, but we enjoyed each other's company. We talked about everything, and when we exhausted normal conversation we came back to the horses. Always he spoke of the horses: this one's triumph, that one's tragedy, the loss of that one's friend or this one's unrequited love.

Then Mr. Paretti told me to take care of a Leo Bernardi by the end of the week.

I didn't look him up immediately. Instead I waited at the stables for Antonio. Los Angeles wasn't so big that the name Bernardi was all that common. I decided to brace him about it. Family members can be fair game when you're collecting a debt.

His face fell when he saw me. "I am in trouble?"

And like that I decided against it. "No. Just something on my mind."

He put both hands on my elbows. "You are troubled, Larry."

I shook my head and disentangled his hands carefully. "No." Besides, I thought, it wouldn't be professional.

Leo liked to hang out in a bar down in Long Beach. He must have known he was marked. No one can be that stupid. But he was still in the same place, sprawled over two stools at the end of the counter and joking with the waitress. He was pretty lit when I arrived.

I looked around. The floor was sticky and there was a doorway obscured by a black curtain. Had to be hookers or stag films. The place stank of rotten sawdust and old beer. There were a dozen men at the counter and a few filling out the tables and chairs but little or no conversation. A stage occupied one end of the room, but there was nothing happening and I got the impression nothing had happened for some time. The only rough character tended the bar and ignored everyone except me. We sparked on each other, neither wanting difficulties where there didn't need to be any. He checked out the rest of the room and settled on Leo instantly, then moved away to the far side of the bar to watch.

I sat down close enough to Leo that he had to move his legs. I gave him an insulting once-over and he snarled something at me.

I tried to look small and weak to invite attack as I snarled something back, mentioning his mother. He roared up off his stool and
I slammed my elbow into his gut and got out of the way as he puked
all over the bar. I grabbed him in an armlock and dropped a fifty to
cover the mess. Seconds later, Leo was on the sidewalk, under my
control, and still emptying out.

He blearily looked up at me and I took that to mean he was
done. I clipped him on the back of the head and he went limp
enough to fit into the trunk.

I'd booked a room at a motel a few miles out of town across the
highway from a training track—one of those no-questions-asked
sort of places.

Antonio pulled in right behind me.

I got out of the car slowly, watching him. I had figured him un-
connected. Was I wrong? "What are you doing here, Antonio?"

"I followed you."

"I didn't know you had a car."

Antonio glanced at my trunk. Thumped it. There was no sound.

I lit my cigarette. "Who's Leo Bernardi?"

He swore softly in Italian. "My brother's boy. He and I came over
together, but we didn't see things the same way. You ever get involved in one of those family fights like in the old country?"

I shook my head.

He looked off at the track. Some two-year-olds were working out,
running short sprints and then walking off the sweat. You could
hear the trainers and the jockeys planning strategy.

Antonio turned back to me. "Back home you had family everywhere. Your sister married some guy you didn't like or your uncle
had a wife nobody could stand. Angry words were said and thereafter the guy or the wife wouldn't be spoken to. For a while. But
the family was always there. That wife's brother might be the local
butcher. Were you going to quit eating meat? Or the guy married
to your sister was part of the family that ran the dairy farm. Were
you going to stop eating cheese or drinking milk? Eventually the
families would force people to be at least cordial to one another.
Otherwise the town would fall apart."

He shrugged. "Here it is different. Family isn't everywhere—
people are in different towns, different cities, different states. If
you don't like the butcher, you can go down the street to another

one. If you don't like the cheese, buy somewhere else or eat that health-food crap. If you don't like what someone says to you, this is America, right? You tell him to buzz off." Antonio shook his head. "My brother was a bum. I didn't like him and told him so and that's the last I see of him. He runs off and I hear nothing until the boy's mother dies of emphysema four years ago. My brother is nowhere to be found but he left her with a boy, now a man. The bum could be dead for all I know or care. I only know about any of this because she's on her deathbed and wants me to look out for my nephew, named after my bum brother. She dies. But my brother lives on in his son. Leo is a gambler. He's a drinker. He chases after women. He is too lazy for work and too stupid to make crime pay. A year ago he disappears and today you have him."

"Are you telling me you knew this day would come?"

"That Leo would fall afoul of one of you people? That was a certainty. That it would be you in particular? No. That is mere coincidence. I never expected to hear of it beforehand but only to learn his fate in the papers. How bad is it?"

"Bad," I said. "Eight thousand with the vig. Paretti wants this resolved by the end of the week. No payment plan. No options. Maybe he pissed off Paretti or Paretti wants to make an example of him. Or maybe Paretti's strapped for cash and needs to call in every marker he can."

He didn't say anything for a long moment. "Allow me to accompany you. Perhaps I can be persuasive."

"You stay here. I'll call you if I need you."

Leo came around as I dragged him up the stairs.

"What the hell?" he yelled as I slammed him into a chair.

"I work for Paretti." I pulled over another chair and sat across from him.

He blanched and didn't say anything.

"Eight thousand dollars?" I said. "Ring any bells?"

"I haven't got that kind of money." He stared back at me, sullen.

"Can you get it?"

"I don't know where."

"Would you be able to figure that out minus a couple of fingers? Or an eye?"

He kept quiet, just glared at me.

I shook my head. "Tough guy. I know all about tough guys. All bluster and beef. If you're tough enough, you can stand anything. If you're angry enough, you can overcome anything. Nothing but blind faith." I leaned forward. "You want to know the truth? If I chop off your legs and arms and pull out your tongue, you're just the toughest guy in the cripple ward lying in your own shit. Is that what you want? Paretti gave me the green light, anything I want to do. So either you give me the money or all you're good for is holding down a rubber sheet. Which is it going to be?"

I could see I got to him. Now came stage two: the lying. I never liked this part—it was a natural follow-on from the tough-guy stage. *My sister's sick. My mother is dying. I haven't got the money.*

The lies would come thick and fast. Until I passed through this stage I couldn't get to the begging. That was when I'd find out where his money was. Not that he had enough—I knew that right off. If I hadn't already come into this knowing it, I could have guessed by the desperate pitch of his bravado. Harry Cohen could pay Paretti back and was fighting to keep the money. Leo Bernardi couldn't and was fighting to keep me from finding out. I could tell the difference.

"Okay. I got the money. Not *on* me, of course. But stashed. I was holding on to it—"

I took my cigarette, grabbed his knee, and stubbed it out on his thigh. Leo screamed.

"Leo," I said gently. "You give me every dime you have. Every penny. I want your bank accounts. I want the deed to your car. I want your shirt and your shoes. Then, if I think it's enough, I might let you keep something. Otherwise I'll take everything you have, including your body. When I'm done, you won't even be able to beg me to die."

The light dawned. Then he looked over my shoulder and hope came back. "Uncle Tony!"

I shook my head. I didn't turn around. "You were supposed to stay in your car."

"Uncle Tony. This guy's going to hurt me—"

"Shut up, Leo. You're an idiot." Antonio searched Leo's face, then turned to me. "Eight thousand, you said?"

"That covers it."

"I'm good for it, Uncle Antonio! Honest."

Antonio stared at him like a bug. "Shut up." He rubbed his face. "He's my brother's boy."

"You have eight grand?"

Antonio shook his head. "No. But I know how to get it."

He stood at the door of the stables for a long time. He looked at me, pain lining the wrinkles on his face. "What can I do? He's my brother's boy."

I shrugged and didn't say anything. What did I know about it?

He went in and wandered from one horse to another and then stopped. I could see him through the door talking with one particular horse.

Afterward we went up to the betting window and he put down a thousand on I'm a Nobody to win. Thirteen to one.

Then we went down to the fence to watch.

We sat through two races before ours came up. I'm a Nobody was dancing in the stall. Then came the bell.

I'm a Nobody tore out ahead in the first few seconds and stayed there, running hard, strides out and in. I remembered the track back east. Dogs run like that. He came by, eyes wild and the whites showing, mouth open and slavering, sweat splattering us as he passed. He whipped by and a moment later came the rest of them.

"He can't keep that up, can he?" I asked.

Antonio shrugged. "Who can say?"

I'm a Nobody didn't flag on the far turn. Coming back on the far side, I could see his sides heaving. Something dark was hanging from his mouth, but he didn't waver. He roared through the home stretch and crossed the finish line. Kept going until he passed the stalls. Passed the gates. Until he reached us. Then he stopped, breath ragged and deep. The jockey was pale and frozen, staring not at us but at the horse.

Then, like some great oak, I'm a Nobody wavered, caught himself, and fell on his side. The jockey rolled off to his knees. He held the horse's head and murmured to him. I'm a Nobody snorted, blood coming from his mouth, and stopped breathing. Everything was silent for a few seconds.

At that point, the crowd around us roared and moved forward. "Come on. We have to get out of here." I jumped the fence onto the track and pulled Antonio over. We ran through the mud until the crowd thinned. I climbed back over and hauled him across.

"First the window," he said.

We took just enough time for Antonio to claim his winnings.

Then out of the park and into my car. Down Katella and over to a bar I knew on Cerritos. I hustled him inside and toward a dark booth at the back.

Antonio said nothing. He pulled out the money and retrieved a thousand, then gave me the rest.

"That's too much."

"Yes." He fell silent.

I ordered us a couple of beers. I sipped mine. Antonio left his untouched. Once or twice tears welled up and fell on his cheeks. His expression didn't change and he didn't wipe them off.

Finally he roused himself. "Larry? Can you drive me home?"

I could. He lived in a tiny bungalow a few miles away. He shook my hand in a formal way and walked slowly up the path and inside his house without looking back.

The total had been $13,000. Minus Antonio's seed money and what Leo owed Paretti, I had $4,000 left. I put it in a coffee can in my apartment.

Antonio didn't come back to the track, and after a couple of weeks I looked him up. He was gone. I put out a couple of feelers—not enough to attract much attention. I didn't want anybody taking too much interest in the old man. He'd sold the bungalow for cash and left town. One guy said he went back to Italy. Another thought he'd gone to Atlanta—why, he couldn't say. Why would anybody voluntarily go to Atlanta?

I didn't ask Leo. I didn't want to see him.

Six months passed.

Once I'd delivered the money to Paretti, the word had gone out: Leo was a bad risk. Nothing personal, you understand. Just business. Unless you seriously want to make an example of someone, it doesn't make sense to get into the same position twice. Apparently some bookie in Santa Monica didn't get the message. Leo ran up a quick $3,000 note before he was found out. Then, of course, he tried to skip town and Paretti called me.

I could have paid it off. I had Antonio's money. But I kept thinking of I'm a Nobody, dying in front of us. It felt like a promise.

So I went looking for Leo.

The papers loved the "brutality" of the crime, and I took a quiet trip up north to Crescent City for a while.

I rented a little house on the ocean end of A Street. I drank coffee and read the paper for nearly a year. I joined a little boxing club on the other side of town to keep my hand in. Nothing much —maybe half a dozen of us taking out our boredom on each other. I bought a boat and learned how to fish in the deep blue sea.

Back east, Buddy McLean got out of jail and the war started up in earnest. It was the weekly Irish slaughter.

I went back to work in '63—just after Kennedy got shot. De-Simone was on shaky ground with the organization. Joe Bonanno put DeSimone on a death list but didn't carry it out. DeSimone got pretty crazy at that point, so we all kept our heads down to avoid any shrapnel. The paranoia must have killed him in the end; he died of a heart attack in '67 and Nick Licata took over. We all breathed easier.

Then Alfredo Paretti retired and Joey and I both wanted his job. I took Joey out on my boat and came back alone. He'd done right by me so I made it quick. He thought I'd agreed to let him have the job. He never had a chance to regret it.

That's where I've stayed: lower management. High enough I don't have to do the heavy lifting but low enough not to be a target.

I still read the news from back east, where winter is close to the bone and the alleys stink of garbage. The names change in the Irish mob, but they manage to keep enough blood in the streets to stay the same.

Sometimes I go to the track. I don't bet but I like watching the sweaty grace of the horses. I think of Antonio often. It's not the same without him.

But the horses are beautiful. The weather is picture-perfect every day and everybody is tanned and smiling. Antonio's money remains in the same old coffee can.

I still kiss the sweet warm earth of California.

WILLIAM SOLDAN

All Things Come Around

FROM *Thuglit*

IT'S GETTING LATE, and Travis Hayes can't think straight with all the noise. Cody's screams have reached an unbearable pitch by the time the traffic on I-680 slows to a crawl, then stops. An accident. Tractor-trailer jackknifed on the ice. Half a dozen other vehicles lost control trying to avoid collision. A few have gone off the road, partially buried in the snowdrifts along the freeway. Several more have accordioned into one another like a twisted metal centipede. Behind him, impatient motorists lay on their horns and his son shrieks in his car seat. The boy is cutting molars and having a hell of a time of it. *No one ever tells you,* Travis thinks. *No one ever sits you down and prepares you for these things.*

"It's okay, buddy." He reaches back, offers Cody the soft, circular teething ring from the diaper bag on the passenger seat. Cody flails, slaps it away. His pudgy little face is ember-red and shiny with snot and tears.

Travis checks the traffic ahead of him—still not moving. Three lanes at a standstill, everyone with their blinkers on, trying to merge but getting nowhere. "Come on, come on," he mutters, "move your asses."

The digital display on the dash of the Honda reads 9:07 p.m. They left Travis's mother's place in Columbus at about five-thirty. He wanted to avoid rush hour but hadn't been quick enough. And now this. They should have been home nearly an hour ago.

Cody continues to scream, a wet staccato that makes Travis feel as hopeless as ever.

He finally pulls out the small tube of benzocaine he picked up at the CVS yesterday when the homeopathic teething tablets and clove oil that Emma packed in his overnight bag weren't working. Emma's big on organic food and natural medicine, especially when it comes to their child. Normally Travis is all for it, and he does his best to respect her wishes. But he refuses to let his son suffer.

"What she doesn't know won't hurt her, right, pal?" He squeezes a dab of the benzocaine on the tip of his index finger, then checks the road again. Still no movement.

Travis puts the car in park and turns to Cody. His son's arms flail once more as he reaches toward him, but Travis gets the finger in his mouth, and the screams turn to garbles as Travis works the clear gel into Cody's swollen gums.

"Shhh, it's all—" he begins as Cody's razor-sharp incisors clamp down in the groove of Travis's first knuckle. He yells, yanks his hand back. Cody's pitch climbs several octaves, and Travis hears something crackle in his right ear. "No, no, shhh. It's okay, shhh," he says in vain.

He doesn't hear the phone in his coat pocket over the chaos both inside and outside the car, but Travis always keeps his cell set to vibrate when it rings, so he feels it going off. He looks at the caller ID. Emma wondering where they are.

He answers, "Hey, babe." His voice is louder than normal.

"Where are you? Is everything okay? What's wrong with Cody?"

As much as he loves her, he wishes he hadn't answered. She's just one more noise right now. It makes him feel bad to think this way, but sometimes she can be a bit much. And he's got enough on his mind right now.

"There was an accident," he says, but before he can finish she interrupts with a litany of frantic questions.

He waits for a gap and jumps in. "Honey, it's fine. We're fine. A truck went off the road. We're stuck in traffic and waiting to get around it."

She calms down. "But I can hear Cody."

"His gums are just sore," he says.

"Did you try the teething tablets, or the—"

Though he feels a twinge of guilt, he cuts her off and says, "Way ahead of you. In fact, I think he's starting to feel better, actually." This much at least is true. The medicine is working and Cody's fit has begun to subside. "I've got the last bottle of milk ready to go for him too."

She asks him how much longer he thinks they'll be.

"We're about twenty minutes out," he says. "We'll be home as soon as these damn cars start moving again."

"I hope it's soon. I made tofu for dinner."

"Yum."

"Ha-ha, funny man."

Cody's breaths come out in short, quick bursts, but his crying has stopped. Travis opens the cooler compartment of the diaper bag and removes a bottle of milk while Emma continues to talk. When he offers the bottle, Cody takes it.

"Uh-huh," he tells her. "Love you too, babe. See you soon."

After he hangs up and returns the phone to his pocket, Travis tunes the radio to a classical station and examines the deep red indentation on the knuckle of his index finger where Cody bit him. Didn't break the skin, but hurts like hell.

The clock now reads 9:32 p.m. Cody has finished his bottle in record time and is fighting sleep, a battle he ultimately loses two minutes later when a small opening appears up ahead, just before the pileup. An exit ramp. Several cars maneuver along the rumble strip in the breakdown lane, and Travis falls in behind them. He follows the ramp's sharp curve as it straightens out into a two-lane residential street. A block farther, he comes to an intersection and stops at a red light.

Relieved to be moving again, but with a head still reeling from Cody's meltdown, he isn't initially aware of where he is. As he sits waiting for the light to change, however, bad memories gather around the car like stray dogs, and Travis suddenly knows all too well.

It's been years since he's been on the South Side, much less on Glenwood. He considers turning right and getting back on the freeway, sitting in traffic as long as it takes. But his temples are still throbbing, and when he imagines Cody waking up, freaking out again, he thinks better of it.

The light turns green. Travis hangs a left.

He's at the bottom end of the avenue, and it's a slow climb on the icy asphalt. He looks out at deserted lots and ruined buildings, nail salon neons and barred windows.

The neighborhood is how he remembers it. A few more vacancies. A few more boarded-up homes. But otherwise the same. Still the type of area many people won't wander around during the day, never mind when the sun goes down. Drive-throughs perch on corners every couple blocks or so, nuclei around which the populace darts and dashes at all hours, buying beer and loose cigarettes. The Foster Theater continues to defy time, dirty yellow bulbs illuminating its wedge-shaped marquee—ADULT FILMS XXX—in a stubborn revolt against the World Wide Web.

He spent many days and nights here. Up and down the hill. In and out of condemned houses on shady side streets. Breaden. Delason. Overlook and Evergreen. All the time running.

At another red light, Travis watches bangers in spoke-rimmed Caddies fuel up at the Gas Mart near Princeton, feels the bass from their sound systems in his bones. A deep vibration. Cody stirs, then settles. A faint whistle escapes his nose as he breathes.

Not a day has gone by over the last four and a half years that he hasn't been reminded of just how lucky he is. To have Emma and Cody. To have placed one unsure foot in front of the other until, at last, he was no longer a part of that world. This world.

Emma never knew the other Travis, and never will if he can help it. He was a year out of treatment when he met her at the health-food store where she works. He came in looking for something to help him sleep. She was out of his league but helpful, and she laughed at one of his unfunny jokes. He'd researched various supplements online—milk thistle, 5-hydroxytryptophan, melatonin, GABA, passionflower tea—things shown to promote detoxification, relaxation, and elevated mood. After a few weeks of visiting the store, he asked her out and she said yes. He took it for a fluke, but she went out with him a second time, a third. By the time it occurred to him that he hadn't thought about his old life in a long while, they'd been together for going on a year and had a kid on the way. It seemed impossible, and he began to wonder when he'd wake up from it all. He still wonders.

"Things sure turned out for the better, huh, buddy?" he says, and glances in the rearview to check on the boy, whose head is lolled to the side like a fragile flower. He passes beneath one of the sodium streetlamps, and Travis notices a glimmer of spittle running from the corner of Cody's mouth. Travis smiles.

The weather is frigid, just above freezing, so besides the gas station, there are few people on the streets. Two dark shapes lurk to Travis's right in the doorway of the old Park Hotel, smoking cigarettes and giving him the stink eye. One steps out from the shadowy alcove and moves toward the passenger window, hinging at the waist to look inside. Travis feels that feeling again, the one that always preceded a terrible decision. Tightening throughout his body. Sweaty palms and rising pulse.

The light changes, and Travis thinks, *Not tonight, fellas.*

The tires of his Honda spin on the slick blacktop before they bite. As he passes a Family Dollar with its metal security doors rolled down and a fenced-in car lot, he looks back and sees the guy raise his arms, as if to say, *What the fuck?* A moment later the man drops his hands and turns back to his dark shelter as Travis crests a hump in the road.

Since first turning onto the avenue, his gut has been a tight knot of nerves. The closer he gets to being out of the neighborhood, however, the better he feels. His heart rate returns to its normal cadence, and the knot begins to loosen.

He's about to pat himself on the back, tell himself *Good job,* but as the street curves past a block of dilapidated brick duplexes and a Baptist church, that old voice returns. The one that used to bark at him from the depths whenever he was attempting to act in his own best interest. The one that visited him every night as he sweated it out in County, during the late hours in the halfway house, and as he white-knuckled it through meetings that first year. One negative affirmation after another.

Don't fool yourself, kid. It's just the same resolution all these miserable fuckers make when they hear the gavel fall. When they run out of cash and run out of credit. Next it's vow to walk the righteous path, find Jesus. All that happy shit. Give it up, kid. You can pretend, but people don't change.

He doesn't get into the usual dialogue with it, doesn't argue and doesn't deny, just turns up the radio a few clicks and drives a little faster.

A hard bend in the road and he's no longer on the avenue but on Midlothian Boulevard. The dividing line between where people want to be and where they don't. Ahead, the luminous sign of Popeyes Chicken & Biscuits springs into view.

He's more or less succeeded in embracing healthy living, but now that his gut has untangled, he's hungry, and the rationalization comes easy: he's been a good boy—a little fried food won't kill him.

See, you're still the same.

The sign grows larger as he gets closer, closer to being farther from that world again.

The same as you always were.

He turns into the Popeyes parking lot.

The same as you'll always be.

"The truck stop is a far cry from the farmers' market," Emma said the first time she and Travis went away for the weekend.

They'd stopped to get gas and stretch their legs. She had packed a cooler with healthy snacks—fruits, vegetables, hummus, bottles of spring water. When Travis came out of the store with a bag of Doritos and a Monster energy drink, Emma started in with that tone she adopts when "educating" people about the horrors of the food industry. "That stuff is packed with preservatives and artificial colors," she told him. "If you can't pronounce the ingredients, it's pretty much poison."

He's since memorized her rhetoric, parroted from Netflix documentaries and the *Huffington Post.*

Trans fats and processed sugar are the real terrorists in this country.

Margarine is only one molecule away from plastic.

Wheat has us hooked like heroin.

Travis often wants to laugh when she goes on a rant. He wants to tell her that we also share roughly 80 percent of our genetic makeup with cows, that everything is only one molecule away from something else, and that when it comes to comparing wheat to heroin, she hasn't got a damn clue. But he doesn't. He's afraid a certain door will open, that certain truths might step through. So he chants his mantra instead: What she doesn't know won't hurt her.

So far, it's been enough.

The tinny voice coming through the speaker reads back his order, and Travis pulls up to the window. A pretty black girl wearing a visor and headset takes his money, tells him they just dropped a fresh batch of chicken and it's going to be a few minutes. He can see that she's pregnant, and when she spots Cody sleeping in the car seat, she makes small talk.

"Aw, he's cute," she says. "How old?"

"Just about a year and a half," he says, then nods toward her bump. "How far along?"

"I could pop before your order's up." She laughs as another car pulls up to the speaker behind him, then closes the pickup window and begins talking into the mouthpiece of her headset.

A few minutes turn into a few more, and the girl pokes her head back out the window, says it's going to be a bit longer. She apologizes and tells him he can pull up, that someone will bring it out to him when it's ready.

"I'll try to toss in a little something extra," she says, and smiles toward Cody again. "Take care of that little cutie-pie."

He smiles, then pulls out of line and into a parking spot.

It soon becomes apparent to Travis that the discrepancy between the concept of "fast" food and the actual speed with which it's delivered is yet another reason he doesn't miss eating the stuff. He looks at the car's digital clock. Thirteen minutes. He's been waiting for thirteen minutes. It's been just over half an hour since he got off the phone with Emma. They should have been home by now. She'll be calling again soon.

Part of him thinks, *Screw it, just go.* But he's paid for it, so now he's committed, invested in the situation. All in.

The dilemma now is whether to go in and get his food or go in and get his money back. He figures he'll decide by the time he gets to the counter.

But then there's the issue of Cody. He reaches back and brushes the boy's shaggy bangs out of his face. Should he wake him up after the ordeal of getting him calmed down? He looks at the restaurant. The register is within view. He thinks, *Don't even.* Then, *It won't take but a minute.*

He tucks Cody's baby blanket around him and considers leaving the car running with the heat on.

What if someone jumps in and drives off?

Won't happen.

But it could.

Come on.

Inside, the smells of fryer grease and spices make him both queasy and ravenous. But ravenous wins, and he decides that he still wants the food. He walks to the counter. When the guy in the batter-stained polo shirt hands him his bag of chicken and fries, Travis's stomach begins to grumble and flip, similar to the way it would before he used to shoot up or hit the pipe. The thought unsettles him, but only for a moment before someone says his name.

"Yo, Travis."

He's halfway out the door and freezes. It's finally happened. He's always known he might eventually cross paths with someone he used to run with, or, worse yet, someone he burned. Eventually all things come around. As he turns toward the voice, puts a face to it, he discovers it's the latter.

"Where you been?" The guy stands up from a table where three other guys remain seated and eating. His words come out slightly muddled as he speaks through the sparkle of his platinum grill. "I been lookin' for you for a long time."

His name is Q. One among many of Travis's dealers before everything changed. As with most of the guys from whom Travis scored, Q let him open up a line of credit because Travis always made good and was a steady customer. But when Travis was ordered to six months in rehab in lieu of jail time for a botched robbery, he got it in his head to go out in style. His initial plan was to rip off every dealer that would front him. Cut ties. A little insurance policy for when he got out, something to guarantee he wouldn't come back around. But Q was the only one he could track down that would let him owe. Travis took him for a bundle of dope and then some.

He plays it cool. "Q, what's up, man? I've been plannin' on hittin' you up."

"Uh-huh." He steps closer to Travis, his hands in the pockets of his puffy coat.

"Things have just been crazy lately. You hear I got locked up?"

Q cocks an incredulous eye. "Yeah?"

"Right after I saw you last. I just got out a few months back. They got me checking in and pissing in a cup every week."

"You bit down in Belmont?"

Travis has never done time in the joint. His minor offenses have never landed him past County. But he's known enough guys who have gone down for long stretches in places like Lucasville and Mansfield and Belmont to talk the talk. Still, he hopes this conversation ends sooner than later.

"Yeah, it's another world down there, man," Travis says.

Q smiles and his teeth glint like foil. "Fuckin' gladiator school," he says. "You got your stripes now."

Travis thinks for a moment that this might be as far as it goes, but he knows better. There is no statute of limitations on the street. He just wonders how long Q wants to catch up beforehand.

As it happens, not long.

Q's grin levels out. "So you got me?"

Travis is coiled inside like a rusty spring. He glances out at the car and sees the top of Cody's head, thinks of running. Bad idea. Even if he could make it to the car before Q or one of the other three guys caught him in the parking lot, what then? Q has put holes in people, at least three bodies from what Travis has heard.

You fucked up, kid.

He's got no choice but to make good. He does a quick mental calculation. Two grand and change in the bank. About ninety bucks in his wallet. Emma will want to know where the money went, but he'll worry about that later.

"We can head over there real quick." Travis points with his clutched bag of food toward the ATM at the Home Savings and Loan across the street.

"All right," Q says, and nods. He leans in to whisper something to his boys. They wipe their greasy mouths and stand up.

When they get outside, Travis starts walking toward his car.

"Nope," Q says as his boys walk up on Travis and grab his arms. "You ridin' over with us."

The coil inside him continues to tighten. "Come on, Q, my kid's in the car, man. I can't just leave him in there."

"Since when you got a kid?"

"Since just before I went downstate."

"How old?"

"About eighteen months." He's already said it before he realizes his mistake.

It's been over four years since they've seen each other, and right now Q's face appears to be working out the math. After a moment, he seems to settle on a number, realizes things don't add up.

"That means you was still on the street for a long time before you went to the joint."

Caught in the lie, Travis goes blank.

"Shit, it don't matter," Q says. He removes a hand from his coat pocket and gestures toward the car. "You left him in there already."

"At least let me check on him first."

Q nods to go ahead, and his boys release Travis's arms.

He opens the back door and leans in. Cody hasn't budged. He kisses the top of his son's head, checks to make sure he's covered and warm. "I'll be right back, buddy," he says. Cody lets out a soft sigh. Travis thinks, *I'm so sorry*, then shuts the door and bites back the tears.

They get into the Escalade that's parked a few spots down. The drive across the street seems to stretch out forever. Travis feels caged, wedged between two of them in the back seat. No one speaks.

When they pull up beside the ATM and let him out, Q gets out with him. He stands with his hands still sunk into the pockets of his puffy coat. Travis puts his bank card into the machine.

At the fifty-cents-on-the-dollar rate Q always charged him on his fronts, the three hundred Travis had been into him for automatically doubled.

"So it's six, right?" Travis says before punching in the numbers.

"Plus interest."

Shit. He hasn't accounted for what Q might tack on for him being MIA all this time. In the corporate world it's called "delinquency." In Q's world it's called "lucky you're still breathing."

"Yeah," Travis says. "So where's that put me?"

Q takes a moment to consider it. "I always liked you, Travis. Let's make it a straight G and we good."

Travis feels himself wince. As good of a liar as he can be, he'll never be able to explain such a large withdrawal to Emma. He'll have to come clean with her.

"I can do that," Travis says.

As he starts typing in the amount, Q says, "You look like you got your shit together, Trav. Joint musta done you some good . . . if you went to the joint."

Travis is about to respond when the words appear on the screen: CANNOT EXCEED $300 WITHDRAWAL FROM ATM IN 24-HOUR PERIOD.

His heart seizes in his chest. His stomach jumps and falls flat.

No. No no no.

He turns to Q. "It won't let me take out more than three hundred. I have to go into the bank. And it's closed till the morning."

"Travis, Travis, that's no good." Q's hand moves in his pocket, and Travis thinks, *It's all over.*

His thoughts grope one another, trying to construct a solution, a way out of this. He's about to give up when he remembers—a kid named Mickey. Young. New to it and going hard like he had something to prove. Lifted his old man's card. They ran into the same problem and discovered by sheer chance they could go to multiple ATMs and take out more money. They skated around town hitting different machines. Three days and three grand later, the account was frozen. Fun while it lasted.

"Wait, wait," Travis says. "I can hit a few more ATMs and get the rest. I've done it before."

Q looks at him with that cocked, incredulous eye, then motions for Travis to get in the truck.

There are two other banks and a corner store within eyeshot of Popeyes. As they drive him to each one, Travis feels his phone blowing up in his pocket. Emma. He ignores it and keeps his eyes on the Honda. He pictures Cody inside and prays he's still asleep.

He pays Q his $1,000, and they drive him back to his car. Only when they get there, they keep going. Toward the back of the restaurant. They've barely said a word the entire time, which unsettles him. They stop next to the dumpster. This part of the lot is in the building's shadow, and he can no longer see the Honda. They let him out.

"Look, Q," Travis says, standing outside the SUV's passenger window, still holding his bag of chicken and fries. "I never meant to do you like that. I was just out of commission, you know?"

"We cool," Q says. He smiles again, flashing platinum.

Travis nods and turns to walk back. He gets within sight of the car, then hears, "Yo, Travis."

He turns around and sees the pistol in Q's hand. Smile gone.

Everything stops.

Travis steps outside himself, watches from beside himself yet somehow still inside himself as the Glock chamber glides and snaps back and the muzzle blooming spits whipcracks of light—and the him he stepped out of takes them one-two sledgehammers and a wrecking ball in a chest flood of molten feeling . . .

Smell of gunpowder and scorched rubber.

Taillights.

Ears ringing and body . . .

. . . falling.

The cold pavement reaches through his back and steals his breath. Sounds swim through his head—voices, distant cars. Is that Cody? He can't move his body. He thinks again, *You fucked up, kid.*

Thinks, *It won't take but a minute.* Thinks, *I'm so sorry.* He sees the car, a blur with windows of reflected light. He moves his lips to speak, but only gasps. There's no one there to hear him anyway. In the dark. His pounding heart is the only sound now. He turns his head, watches his breath rise like smoke. A moment or a lifetime, he doesn't know which, and the stars begin to come unglued. No, not stars, he thinks as they melt against his face. Snow.

He sees this all before returning to himself, no longer both inside and outside but only inside himself. He stares into the barrel of the gun, several feet away yet gaping with its cold finality. He has time, Q has given him that much. Time to think of all he'll miss, of all he wishes he would have said and done and done differently. So many things, differently.

He closes his eyes and sees Cody's face.

Please forgive me.

Then there's the dry-fire click of an empty chamber. Travis opens his eyes.

Q still has the gun raised, but again he's smiling. A chrome flicker. "Bang," he says, and he and his boys begin to laugh. When the laughing stops, Q says, "You," and wags the Glock at him. "You better remember this."

The window of the Escalade goes up, and they drive off.

On the way back to the car, Travis stops, bends over, and dry heaves, but nothing comes out. He realizes he's still clutching the bag of food and drops it on the ground behind the car.

When he opens the passenger-side rear door to check on Cody, the boy is awake and looking up at him, his chin spittle-slick. He looks happy. Travis unbuckles him, holds him, presses his numb face against his son's warm one, kisses him on the eyes. Cody says, "Da-dee," and pats Travis on the cheek with his soft little hand. "Dadee da-dee." It's not the first time Cody has spoken, but it could be for all it makes him feel.

When his phone goes off again, he hesitates before answering.

Don't say anything.

What about the money? I'll have to explain.

You'll think of something.

He thumbs the screen. He hears Emma's voice but not her words.

You'll think of something.

"It's all over now," he says. "We're on our way."

He hangs up and puts Cody back in his car seat. As he backs the car out of the parking spot, he feels the tires crunch over the greasy sack of chicken and fries. Driving out of the lot, he sees it there in the side-view mirror, and for a brief moment he sees himself lying on the cold ground beside it.

The Process Is a Process All Its Own

FROM *Conjunctions*

I have this thing I do because the thing reminds me of you know. You use these little deals, like the hearing-aid batteries that go into that thing deaf guys put in their shirt pockets, the thing with the wires that come out. You dump these batteries out of the pack and swish them around in three to four inches of water. Little bubbles begin to come up: in fact, little bubbles show up almost immediately. Why, I don't know, but they do. Maybe for reasons we will get into later. The batteries rest like little machine turds down there on the bottom of your ashtray or whatever. (I use an ashtray mainly.) Then what you do is, you sniff the bubbles.

Huh.

If you push your head right down next to the water, the bubbles open up right under your nose. Which is the point here, O Unseen. They give off this strange little smell. Those bubbles from Rayovac hearing-aid batteries smell like what happens when you shove your nose right into the middle of an old dictionary, the gutter where the two pages come together, and inhale. That's the smell you get from the bubbles out of hearing-aid batteries.

If the odor you get from the bubbles from hearing-aid batteries has anything in common with the odor you get from thrusting your nose deep into the seam of an open dictionary, particularly a dictionary of some vintage, then it cannot be inaccurate to say that the odor must be that of words. One comes across the odors of words in many, many contexts, and the odors of words are usually the same from one context to another. Only the strongest, most distinctly individuated, if that's a word, of individuals can control the colorations of the words that pass through them.

Nothing in this situation is odd, actually, odd given that we are dealing with words. Words are produced within the medium of air, and balloons and other empty spaces that produce bubbles do so because they themselves are filled with air. Air itself must be thought to be laden with words, to be word packed, word jammed. In fact, words tumble out of every orifice, panting to be born, screaming against the resistant membrane, trying their best to . . . Here's the deal. Words have plans. Ambitions. Goals. They are always trying to veer around us & zoom away. They wish to leave us in an abysmal darkness. You can think what you like about this.

Try the following experiment. Choose any old balloon you happen to see lying by the side of the path in a public park, even a balloon that may have been blown up for a child's birthday. (But make sure it's a *balloon* balloon, or you might not like the results!) When you thrust these poor old things underwater, pierce their hides with your knife, your hatpin, whatever, and then inhale the fragrance of the hazy penumbra substance that escapes into the water and bursts above it in bubble form, nine times out of ten, five out of six anyhow, there may be heard the off-key delivery of birthday songs, the chanting of inane good wishes, on top of these frequent invocations of the birthday child's name, and distributed through all of the intermediate spaces the names of his wretched friends and, guess what, lists of the silly birthday presents given and acquired on this date. *And* this tired, tired smell. All this verbal information can be detected within the exhalations to be had from these semideflated pastel-colored balloons. Once you really commit to this process, pretty much the same goes for gadgets like tape recorders, typewriters, old over-under cameras, headphones, microphones, everything like that. Once they have been plunged underwater and agitated crushed berated abused destroyed, one can detect beneath the more prominent odors of distressed metal, rubber, and plastic the ambitious stench of words that once passed through these various windows.

To a casual observer, dear little friend, all of the above may seem overspecialized, in fact obsessive. I can scarcely pretend that I am a casual onlooker. To illustrate the exact nature of my function, which at the moment I am perhaps a bit reluctant to do, I might allude to the properties of another set of bubbles and the nature of the inhalations contained within, which is to say, getting at last to the point, well, *one* of my points, the bubbles found in blood. Blood is particularly given to the formation of bubbles. Those with the stomach to lean over bubbles of blood and inhale their messages will find that they have in the process acquired a complex detailed subtle record of the life from which that blood emerged. It is one of the most delicate and moving instances of information transmission that I can imagine. It is certainly one of the most beautiful experiences that I have ever known—the catching of the deep, particular inflections within the bubbles of blood that issue from the human throat. Voices contain smells: all human structures carry—on their backs sides bellies feet cocks pussies scalps —stinks and perfumes. We cannot escape into any goddamn odor-free realm. Any such realm should scare us right out of our you know. Odors fasten us to our common world. Rot, fragrance, bud, and bloom exude the physical aura of the process that animates them. It does not take a scientist to detect a verbal motion, a verbal smell, within the bubbles of blood of a recently deceased beast or human. There is, however, perhaps only one given my particular history who may with a reasonably good assurance of being believed claim that when words are detected within the blood of human beings they generally have an English smell. It is the odor, and I understand that what I am telling you might seem arbitrary, of fish-and-chip shops on barren High Streets, of overcooked roast beefs, of limp, glistening "chips," of blank-eyed mackerel reeking on the departing tide, of dull seaweed and wet wool, of humid beards, of crap Virginia tobacco, of damp hair, likewise of cheap cologne and hair oil, also of flowers sold three days past their prime in Covent Garden, also of similar flowers wilting in the hair of neglected women—all of these structures are to be detected in the bubbles that form when blood is released from *any* human being, cart man, prince regent, or vicious greedy poxy trollop.

Those kinds of people I was talking about before, they do not produce these English smells. With them, it's all different, you don't know what you're going to hear. Fortunately they are very few in number.

Am I being fanciful? All right, perhaps I'm being fanciful. And yet what I tell you is on the nose. Most of the time, an English accent is what you get. What's more, it's usually a Cockney accent—turns out words are blue-collar guys.

I don't want you to think that I mess around smelling blood bubbles, for God's sake. Nobody has that much time. Time is a luxury. And what human beings do with luxuries is very much their own business, thank you very much.

—*T.H., June 1958*

A man named Tillman Hayward wrote these words in a Hardy & Badgett leather-bound notebook, five by four inches, with pale-blue lined paper. He had purchased the notebook, along with three others like it, on sale for $9.95 at Ballantine and Scarneccia, a high-end stationery store in Columbus, Ohio. He "lived" in Columbus. His real life took place elsewhere.

Tillman Hayward, "Tilly," did not work in Columbus. He earned his reasonably substantial salary as a property manager in

Columbus, but his real work—his "work"—was done elsewhere. This separation was self-protective.

He was writing with a German-made mechanical pencil purchased for $8.99 at the same store. Faber-Castell, its manufacturer, described it as a "propelling pencil." He liked the word "propelling": to propel sounded madly up-to-date. A propeller-pencil. (It, the word, not the pencil, smelled a great deal of Elmer's Glue.)

Tilly Hayward had been married for nine years to a blond woman named Charlotte, née Sullivan. Tilly and Charlotte had produced three blond daughters, each of them the replica of both her mother and her sisters. They looked like triplicates born in different years. These perfect girls were named Edith, Hannah, and Faith. The Hayward family lived in one of the apartment buildings owned by Charlotte's father, Daniel Sullivan, a flinty Irish immigrant in a flat cap, who had never known a moment's warmth or sentimentality. Tilly's job was to oversee the properties, keep them in satisfactory condition, check out whatever new might come on the market, and to make sure the rents came in. He deployed a full range of subcontractors to deal with the tenants' demands. With his father-in-law's approval, Tilly also had taken it upon himself to search for other properties to add to his holdings. He had convinced his father-in-law that the city of Milwaukee, his birthplace, was an excellent location for the long-planned expansion of the Sullivan company. Six or seven times a year, sometimes way more than that, Tilly either drove, took the train, or flew to Milwaukee (the handsome General Mitchell Field, where his tricky old dad used to take the kids to watch the planes take off and land). There, he sometimes stayed with his brother, Bobby, and Bobby's wife, Mags, in the old brown-and-yellow duplex on West Forty-Fourth Street, where Bobby, Tilly, and their sister, Margaret (later Margot), had been born and raised. At other times he planted himself in hotels, not always under his real name. "Jesse Unruh" and "Joe Ball" spent a few days at the Pfister, "Leslie Ervin" at the funkier, less expensive Plaza. Although Tilly appeared to be, and sometimes actually was, dedicated in his search for commercial properties, he had as yet to purchase a single one of these buildings for the Sullivan real estate empire.

It was in Milwaukee and under conditions of rigorous secrecy that Tilly's real "work" was carried out.

Tilly Hayward was one of those men in possession of two lives. Either he was a dark, disturbing criminal sociopath who wore a more conventional person around him like a perfectly fitted suit of clothing, or he was a conventional person who within himself concealed a being like a wild animal. Tillman's response to his duality was not simple. He wondered sometimes if he were really a person at all. Perhaps he had originated on some faraway star — or in some other, far-distant time. Often, he felt *other*.

Many of the words whose odors Tillman caught as they emerged reeked of death and corruption. There were some words that almost always stank of the graveyard, of death and corpses. (These were words such as "happiness," "fulfillment," "satisfaction," "pleasure," also "joy.") Tillman understood that these words smelled foul because the things they referred to were false.

In Tilly's sensitive nostrils, the word "job" often smelled like fresh vomit. People who spoke of their jobs evoked entire butcher shops filled with rotting meat. Tilly knew that if he ever permitted himself to speak in mixed company, away from his family, of the job he did for Sullivan Real Estate Holdings, the same terrible stench would attach itself to his vocabulary. Therefore he never did speak of these matters except to his wife, who either did not notice the stinks that accompanied these words or, having grown accustomed to them during childhood, pretended that she did not. Words like "sorrow," "unhappiness," "grief," these words that should have carried perhaps the worst stenches of all, did not actually smell so bad — more like rotting flowers than rotting meat, as though what had once been fresh about them was not so very distant. When Tilly went out in search of the people whom he dealt with as part of his real "work," he deliberately sought women who uttered the foulest words of all. He had an unerring instinct for women whose vocabularies betrayed a deep intrinsic falsity. He often thought that other people could do the same. He thought that a kind of politeness kept other people from speaking of this power, so out of uncharacteristic politeness he himself remained silent about it. There were times when he wondered if he alone could detect the odors that clung to the spoken words, but if that were true, and the power only his, he could never figure out what to do with it. Apart from being perhaps another indication of his status as an alien from a sphere far different, the power seemed a mere frivolity: like so much else, it had no relevance beyond its own borders.

Funny thing: the word "remorse" actually smelled pretty good, on the whole. The word "remorse" tended to smell like wood shavings and sunburned lawns; at its worst it smelled of anthills, or something sort of like anthills, sand dunes, Indian burial mounds. He never objected to the smell of the word "remorse." In fact, rather to his surprise, Tilly tended to like it a lot. It was a pity that the word was heard so seldom in the course of ordinary conversation.

Tilly, of course, tended not to have ordinary conversations.

In October of 1958 Tilly once again found himself in Milwaukee. He had come not in pursuit of one or more of his many private obsessions, but because he had a genuine interest in a real estate property. Two years before, Tilly had acquired a real estate license. It had required considerable effort, but he managed to pass the qualifying exams on his first attempt. He wanted to be able to justify his trips out of town, especially those to Milwaukee, on commercial grounds. Now he had come to inspect a building, a four-story, mixed-use building on Welles Street. Its only problem was its single tenant: a sixty-five-year-old woman who had once worked for the mayor and for the past six years of her life had claimed to be dying from cardiomyopathy. Tilly had come to see if it might be possible to resolve this tenancy problem by means of certain efficient measures never to be revealed. Yet when he looked at it again, the building had become far less attractive—he saw the old lady, intractable, seated on her unclean old sofa, skinny arms extended as if for hundreds of feet, and chose not to negotiate in any way.

Late in the afternoon of the same day, Tilly decided to take a walk through downtown Milwaukee. He wanted to uncoil, perhaps also to allow passage into the attentive atmosphere of some portion of his rabid, prancing inner self. Around the corner on Wisconsin Avenue stood the vast stone structure of the Central Milwaukee Library, and across the avenue from this big, dark building was a bookstore called Mannheim's.

Tilly had no interest in these buildings and could imagine no circumstance that would persuade him to enter either one. No sooner had he become conscious of this fact than he took note of someone, a young woman, who had no problem being in both. Through the slightly sunken and recessed front door of Mannheim's she floated, unencumbered by handbag, not to mention doubt, fear, depression, or any other conventional female disorder —perhaps thirty yards away, and already, instantly upon her entrance into his frame, rivetingly, infuriatingly attractive.

The girl was in her midtwenties, and perhaps five and a half feet tall, with dark brown hair and long blue eyes in a decisive little face with a flexible red mouth. She wore a green cardigan sweater and a khaki skirt. Her hair had been cut unusually short, to almost the length of a boy's hair, though no one could mistake her for a boy. He liked her suntanned fox face and her twinned immediate air of independence and intelligence. The girl glanced at him, and before continuing on displayed perhaps a flicker of rote, species-reproductive interest. (Tilly had long felt that women capable of bearing children came to all-but-instantaneous decisions about their willingness to do so with the men they met.)

She went up the stairs to the sidewalk, moved across the cement, and with a side-to-side flick of her eyes jumped down into the traffic moving north and south on busy Wisconsin Avenue. Delightful little twirls of her hands directed the cars that coursed around her, also to dismiss the few drivers who tried to flirt with her. It was like watching someone conducting an orchestra that moved around the room. She looked so valiant as she dodged through the fluid traffic. Who was this girl: her whole life long, had she never been afraid of anything? At first not entirely aware of what he was doing, Tilly began to move more quickly up the block.

The young woman reached the near curb and flowed safely onto the sidewalk. Without the renewed glance he felt he rather deserved, she sped across the pavement and proceeded up the wide stone path to the Central Library's massive front doors. Tilly began walking a little faster, then realized that she would be inside the building before he had even reached the pathway. He suffered a quick, hell-lit vision of the library's interior as a mazy series of tobacco-colored corridors connected by random staircases and dim, flickering bulbs.

Once he got through the main door, he looked both left and right in search of the girl, then straight ahead down the empty central hallway. At the end of the hallway stood a wide glass door, closed. Black letters painted on the pebbled glass said FICTION. This was almost certainly where she had gone. She was imaginative, she was interested in literature: when the moment came, she'd have things to say, she would be able to speak up. Tilly enjoyed flashes of spirit in his playmates.

At the you know. During the. Maybe. If not then, what a pity, never.

Tilly strode through the glass door into the fiction room. The girl could have been bent over a book at one of the wide tables or hidden behind some of the open shelves at the edges of the room. He did a quick scan of the tables and saw only the usual library riffraff, then moved toward the shelves. His heart began to beat a little more quickly.

Tilly could taste blood; he could already catch the meat-sack stench of "please" and "mercy" as they slid through the girl's sweetheart lips. Better than a meal to a hungry man, the you know . . . except the you know *was* a meal, finer than a T-bone fresh from the slaughterhouse and butchered on the spot . . .

Tilly stopped moving, closed his eyes, and touched his tongue to the center of his upper lip. He made himself breathe softly and evenly. There was no point in letting his emotions ride him like a pony.

Twice he wandered through the three stacks of books on the fiction floor, going in one end and out the other, along the way peering over the cityscape tops of the books to see if his target was drifting down the other side. Within a couple of minutes he had looked everywhere, yet had somehow failed to locate the girl. Girl walks into room, girl disappears. This was a red-line disappointment, a tremble, a shake-and-quiver. Already Tilly had begun to feel that this girl should have had some special place in his grand scheme—that if she were granted such a place, a perfection of the sort he had seldom known would have taken hold. The grand scheme itself borrowed its shape from those who contributed to it —the girls whose lives were demanded—and for that reason at the moment of his fruitless search the floating girl felt like an essential aspect of his life in Milwaukee. He needed her. The surprise of real fulfillment could be found only in what would happen after he managed to talk her into his "special place" out in the far western suburbs.

After something like fifteen minutes, Tilly finally admitted to himself that somehow she had managed to escape from the fiction room. Baffling; impossible. He had kept his eye on the door the whole time he'd been in the room. Two people, both now bent over their reading, had entered, and only three people had left—a pair of emaciated women in their fifties and a slender Negro girl with glossy little curls in her hair.

For a moment Tilly considered racing out and following the

wide central hallway wherever it went. He saw, as if arrayed before him on a desktop, pictures of frantic Tillman Hayward charging into rooms where quiet people dozed over books or newspapers. No part of balance and restitution could be found in the images strewn across the desk. Something told him—everything told him! —that none of these people half asleep under the library lamps could be his girl.

He had lost her for good. This wonderful young woman would never be permitted to fulfill her role in the grand design of Tillman Hayward's extraordinary life. For both of them, what a tragic diminution. Tilly spun around and dropped himself into an empty chair. None of the pig-ignorant people reading their trashy books even bothered to glance at him. He continued to try to force calm upon himself, to take control of his emotions. Tilly feared that he might have to go outside, prop his hands on his knees, and inhale deeply to find calm. Eventually his body began to relax.

The girl was gone. There was nothing to be done for it. It would always be as if he had never seen her. For the rest of his life he would have to act as though he had never sensed the possibilities with which this young woman, so alive with possibility, had presented him. Tilly knew himself to be a supreme compartmentalizer, and he did not doubt his power to squeeze the girl down into a little drawer in his mind, and there quite nearly to forget her.

Two nights later, he had planned to get some rest before going back to Columbus, but the idea of Mags and Bob sitting in their miserable living room thinking God knows what and remembering too much of what he might have said made him edgy. Probably he should never have given that *True Detective* to poor little Keith. It was like a secret handshake he could not as yet acknowledge. It was like saying, *This is my work, and I want you to admire my achievement, but it is still too soon for you and me to really talk about it. But you're beginning to understand, aren't you?* Because that was true: the kid was beginning to put things together.

Tilly tried stretching out on the bed and sort of reading his book, which was a novel based on the career of Caryl Chessman, the Red Light Bandit, who had been sentenced to execution in the gas chamber at San Quentin. Tilly loved the book. He thought it made Chessman seem at least a little sympathetic. Yet his attempt at reading did not go well. The image of Bob and Mags seated stiffly before their television, and that of Keith doing God knew what with *True Detective* in his bedroom, kept dragging his concentration away from the page. Finally he decided: one last night, maybe one last girl. Good old Caryl kept himself in the game, you had to give him that.

He checked his inner weather. A sullen little flame of pure desire had flared into being at the prospect of going out on the hunt one last time. He tucked the book beneath his pillow, took his second-favorite knife from its hiding place, then put it back. He would play it All or Nothing: if he could coax a girl out to his special place in the suburbs, he would use his favorite knife, which was stashed in a drawer out there; if he failed, there'd be one less corpse in the world. All or Nothing always made his mouth fizz. He lifted his overcoat off the hook on the back of the door and slipped his arms into the sleeves on the short distance to the living room.

That coat fit him like another skin. When he moved, it moved with him. (Such sensations were another benefit of All or Nothing.)

"Why do you do that, Tilly?" Mags asked.

"Do what?"

"That thing you just did. That . . . shimmy."

"Shimmy," a word he seldom used, stank of celery.

"I have no idea how to shimmy, sorry."

"But you are obviously going out. Aren't you?"

"Oh, Mags," sighed Bob.

"Last-minute look at a property. I shouldn't be superlate, but don't wait up for me."

"Where would this property be, Tilly, exactly?"

He grinned at her. "It's on North Avenue, way east, past that French restaurant over there. The next block."

"Is it nice?"

"Exactly my question. Be good now, you two."

"What time is your train tomorrow?"

"Eleven in the morning. I won't be home until midnight, probably."

When he got outside and began walking down the street to his rented car through the cool air, he felt himself turning into his other, deeper self. It had been months since he had last been in Lou's Rendezvous.

Formerly an unrepentant dive, Lou's had recently become

a college joint with an overlay of old-time neighborhood pond scum. Ever optimistic about the possibility of having sex with these good-looking youngsters, the old-timers kept jamming quarters into the jukebox and playing "Great Balls of Fire" and "All I Have to Do Is Dream of You." That the neighborhood characters never got disgusting made for a loose, lively crowd. Supposedly a businessman from Chicago, a man who had been at Lou's several times before, the Ladykiller dressed well, he was relaxed and good-looking. Knew how to make a person laugh. The man wandered in and out, had a few drinks, talked to this one and that one, whispered into a few ears. Some thought his name was Mac, maybe Mark. Like a single flower in a pretty vase, the girl from the library was parked at the corner of the bar. Her name was Lori Terry. She called him Mike and slipped out of the bar with him before anyone had time to notice.

So not Nothing. All. A final present from the city of Milwaukee.

After he had driven west some fifteen minutes she asked, "So where are we going anyhow, Mike?" (Young avocado, peppermint.)

Like very few people he had observed, Lori Terry had the gift of imbuing words and even whole sentences with fragrances all her own. His nephew had a touch of this ability too.

"This place a little way out of town," he said.

"Sounds romantic. Is it romantic?" She'd had perhaps two or three drinks too many. ("Romantic" kind of hovered over a blocked drain.)

"I think it is, yes." He smiled at her. "Tonight wasn't the first time I've ever seen you, you know. I was in the library this morning. I saw you walk from Fiction right through into Biography."

"Why didn't you say hello?"

"You were too fast for me. Peeled right out of there."

"Must have made quite the impression." (Some lively pepperminty thing here, like gum, only not really.)

"I looked at you, and I thought, *That girl could change my life.*"

"Well, maybe I will. Maybe you'll change mine. Look what we're doing! Nobody ever takes me out of town."

"I'll try to make the trip extra-memorable."

"Actually, isn't it a little late for going out of town?"

"Lori, are you worried about sleep? Because I'll make sure you get enough sleep."

"Promise?" This word floated on a bed of fat green olives.

He promised her all the sleep she was going to need.

Trouble started twenty minutes later, when he pulled up into the weedy dirt driveway. As she stared first at the unpromising little tavern next to his actual building, then at him, disbelief widened her eyes. "This place isn't even open!" (Rancid milk.)

"Not that one, no," said the Ladykiller, now nearly on the verge of laughter. "The other one."

She swiveled her head and took in the old storehouse with the ghostlike word clinging to a front window. "Goods?" she asked. "If you tell me that's the name of the place, you're fulla shit." (Gunmetal, silver polish.)

"That's not a name, it's a disguise."

"Are you really sure about this?"

"Do you think I brought you all the way out here by mistake?" He opened his door, leaned toward her, and smiled. "Come on, you'll see."

"What is this, an after-hours joint? Like a club?" With a gathering, slow-moving reluctance, she swung the door open on a dissipating cloud of rainwater and fried onions and moved one leg out of the car.

"Private club." He moved gracefully around the hood and took her hand to ease her delivery from the car. The temperature of his resolve was doing that thing of turning hot as lava, then as cold as the flanks of a glacier, then back again, in about a second and a half. "Just for us, tonight."

"Jesus, you can do that?"

"You wait," he said, and searched his pocket for the magic key. It glided into the lock and struck home with the usual heavy-duty sound effects.

"Maybe we should both wait." (Chalk-dusty blackboard.)

He gave her an over-the-shoulder glance of rueful, ironic mock regret. "Wait? I'll get you back into town in plenty of time."

"We just met. You want me to follow you into this old building, and it's already past twelve . . ."

"You don't trust me?" Now he was frankly pouting. "And after all we've meant to each other."

"I was just thinking my father would be really suspicious right now."

"Isn't that part of the whole point about me, Lori? That your father wouldn't like me?"

She laughed. "You may be right."

"All right then." He opened the door onto an absolute darkness. "Just give me a sec. It's one flight down."

"A basement? I'm not so . . ."

"That's how they keep the place private. Wait, I'll get the light."

He disappeared inside and a moment later flipped a switch. Watery illumination revealed floorboards with a sweeping, half-visible grain. She heard the turning of another vaultlike lock. He again appeared in the doorway, took her hand, and with only a minimum of pressure urged her into the building. Shivering in the sudden cold, she glanced around at the barren cell-like room she had entered. It seemed to be perfectly empty and perfectly clean. He was drawing her toward a door that opened onto a rectangle of greater brightness. It gradually revealed the flat, dimpled platform and gray descending handrail of a metal staircase. No noise came from the dark realm beyond the circle of light at the bottom of the steps.

"Ladies first," he said, and she had reached the fifth step down before she realized that he had blocked any possibility of escape. She turned to look at him over her shoulder, and received, as if in payment, a smile of utmost white seductiveness. "I know, it looks like no one's here. Works in our favor, actually. We'll have the whole place to ourselves. Do anything we like, absolutely everything."

"Wait a second," she said. "I want to have a good time, Mike, but absolutely everything is not in the picture, do you hear me?" What he had here, Till realized, was a clear, straightforward case of a specific fragrance emerging from a sentence as a whole, instead of blooming into the foreground of a lot of other, lesser smells. And in this case, the fragrance was that of a fresh fruit salad, heavy on the melons but with clean, ringing top notes of lime, just now liberated from the grocer's wrapping. Dazzled, he felt momentarily off-balance, as if his weight were on the wrong foot.

"Loud and clear. I don't have those kinds of designs on you."

"You don't?" In spite of everything, it was a kind of shock. He could smell it too: the fruit salad had been topped with a layer of thin, dark German pumpernickel. From *two words.* He was going to kill this wonderful girl, but part of him wished he could eat her too.

"Just wait at the bottom of the stairs. There's another door, and I have to get the light."

The habit of obedience rooted her to the floor as he squeezed past and pushed a third key into a third lock. Again Lori took in the heaviness of the mechanism, the thunk of precision-made machinery falling into place. Whatever made Mike happy, he had taken pains to keep it safe. Mike grasped her elbow and drew her after him into the dark room. The door closed heavily behind her, and Mike said, "Okay, Lori, take a gander at my sandbox, my pride and joy."

He flipped up a switch and in the sudden glare of illumination she heard him relocking the door. In all the sparkle and shine she thought for a moment that she was actually looking at a metal sandbox. When her vision cleared, she glanced over her shoulder to see him tucking a key into his pocket.

"Oh my God," she said, and stepped away from him through a briefly hovering cloud of old saddles and baseball mitts.

"Lori Terry. Here you are."

"You're him."

"I am?"

"You're the Ladykiller guy. Goddamn." (Concrete sidewalks. Steel girders, plus maple syrup. She imprinted *her own* odors upon the words that issued from her, and she had the strength of character to shape entire utterances within that framework. He was still reeling.)

He spread his arms and summoned a handsome smile. "Like what I've done with the place?"

"I'd like you to take me home, please."

He stepped toward her. "In all honesty, Lori, this could go either way. Whichever path you choose, you're gonna end up in the same place. That's the deal here."

She moved about three inches backward, slowly. "You like blowjobs, Mike? I'll make you come like a fire hose." (Oh, exquisite, in fact almost *painfully* exquisite: when she must have been dropping into terror like a dead bird, her sentences came swaddled in clove, and ginger, and yet again the kind of maple syrup that came from trees bleeding into pails way up in Vermont and Maine, that area.)

"I always come like a fire hose. Of course, most of my partners aren't alive anymore. I like it that way. Come to think of it, they probably do too."

"You think a woman would have to be dead to enjoy making love to you? Let me prove how wrong you are."

He was inching toward her, but the distance between them remained constant.

"You're an unusual girl, Lori."

"What makes me 'unusual'?" (Marshmallow and chocolate: s'mores!)

"You're not cowering on the floor. Or sniveling. All the other girls—"

She took one fast step backward, spun around, and sprinted toward the center of the room. Amused by this display of nerve, he lunged for her playfully and almost deliberately missed. Lori ran around to the other side of the second steel table and leaned on it with stiff arms, her eyes and mouth open, watching him closely, ready to flee in any direction. For a couple of seconds only, she glanced into the corners of the shiny basement.

"To get out, you need my keys," he said. "Which means you ain't gonna get out. So are you going to make a break for it or wait for me to come get you? I recommend the second one. It's not in your best interest to piss me off, I promise you." From across the room, he gave her the openhearted gift of a wide, very nearly genuine smile.

She kept watching him with the close, steady attention of a sailor regarding an unpredictable sea. On every second inhalation, she bent her elbows and leaned forward.

"Because right at this moment? Right at this moment, I admire the hell out of you. All kinds of reasons, honest to God."

He waited for her to break for either the right or the left side of the metal table so that he could at last close the distance between them and finish the gesture he had begun at Lou's Rendezvous, but she did not move. She kept on leaning forward and pushing back.

"You remind me of something I can't really remember. That fubar enough for you? Doozy of a story. About someone who won't stay dead but doesn't live." He lifted his arms, palms up, and all but uttered an involuntary sigh. "People keep telling me this shit, like they want me to remember! My brother, that stupid Henry James story . . . It's no good. It doesn't actually *mean* anything . . . but shouldn't it mean *everything*? A person who won't stay dead? Plus . . . someone else, a boy? An *old* boy?"

He shook his head as though to clear it. "Say something. Say anything. I love what happens when you talk."

"Oh?" Not enough to be measured: something about peanuts in a roaster . . . peanuts rolling in an oiled pan . . .

"You know how words have these smells? Like 'paycheck' always smells like a dirty men's room? You know what I'm talking about, yeah?"

"You smell what I'm saying?" Without relaxing her attention, Lori leaned forward and narrowed her eyes. "How would you de-scribe the smell of what I'm saying now?"

"Like butter, salt, and caramel sauce. Honest to God. You're amazing."

Lori exhaled and straightened her arms, pushing herself back. "You're a crazy piece of shit."

The Ladykiller kept looking at her steadily, almost not blinking, waiting for her to move to the right or the left. He told himself, *This resurrection stuff is all bullshit to lull her into breaking away from the autopsy table.*

Unless . . .

Something dark, something unstable flickered in his mind and memory and vanished back into the purely dark and fathomless realm where so much of the Ladykiller was rooted. Once again he shook his head, this time to rid himself of the terror and misery that had so briefly shone forth, and after that briefest possible mo-ment of disconnection saw that Lori had not after all been waiting to bolt from the table. Instead she had jerked open the drawer and snatched out a knife with a curved blade and a fat leather handle wrapped in layers of sweat- and dirt-stained tape. He loved that knife. Looking at it, you would be so distracted by its ugliness that you'd never notice how sharp it was. You wouldn't fear what it could do until it was already too late.

"Oh, that old thing," he said. "What are you going to do, open a beer can?"

"I'll open you right up unless you toss me those keys." (The worse it got, the better it smelled: a bank of tiger lilies, the open window of a country kitchen.)

He pulled himself back into focus. "Jeez, you could have picked up one of the scalpels. Then I might be scared."

"You want me to swap it for a scalpel? It must be really lethal."

"*You'll* never find out," he said, and began slowly to move toward her again, holding out his hands as if in supplication.

"No matter what happens, I'm glad I'm not you." (Dishwashing liquid in a soapy sink, a wealth of lemon-scented bubbles: in his humble opinion, one of the world's greatest odors.)

Lori Terry moved back a single step and assumed a firmer grip on the ugly handle. She was holding it the right way, he noticed, sharp side up.

"You're a funny little thing." He straightened up, laughed, and wagged an index finger at her. "You have to admit, that is pretty droll."

"You have the emptiest, ugliest life I can imagine. You look like you'd be so much fun, but really you're as boring as a cockroach —the rest of your life is a disguise for what you do in this miserable room. Everything else is just a performance. Can't you see how disgusting that is?" This whole statement emerged clothed in a slowly turning haze of perfumed girl neck gradually melting to a smellscape of haystacks drying in a sunstruck field. This was terrible, somehow shaming.

"I thought I heard you trying to talk me into a blowjob."

"That's when I was scared. I'm not afraid of you anymore." (Spinach, creamed, in a steakhouse.)

"Oh, come on." He moved across the room on a slanting line, trying to back her into a corner. "I know you're scared."

"I was afraid when I thought I had a chance to get out of this cockroach parlor. But I really don't, do I? I'm going to die here. At best, I'll cut you up a little bit. Then you'll kill me, and it'll all be over. You, however, will have to go on being a miserable, fucked-up creep with a horrible, depressing life." (Who knew what that was —horses? A rich man's stables?)

"At least I'll have a life," he said, and felt that he had yielded some obscure concession, or told her absolutely the wrong thing.

"Sure. A terrible one, and you'll still be incredibly creepy." (Astonishingly, this came out in a sunny ripple of clean laundry drying on a line.)

"I believe you might be starting to piss me off."

"Wouldn't that be a fucking shame." An idea of some kind moved into her eyes. "You thought I might change your life? I think you were right, I think I will change your life. Only right now you have no idea how that'll happen. But it'll be a surprise, that I can tell you."

Amazed, he said, "You think you're better than me?" (*And you just said four or five sentences that smelled like cloves and vetiver.*)

"You're a disgusting person, and I'm a good one."

She feinted and jabbed with the curved blade. It was enough to push him backward.

"I see you're afraid of this knife."

He licked his lips, wishing he were holding a baseball bat, or maybe a truncheon, a thing you could swing, hard, to knock in the side of someone's head. Then, before he could think about what he was going to do, he ducked left and immediately swerved to his right. Having succeeded in faking her off-balance, the Ladykiller rushed forward, furious and exulting, eager to finish off this mouthy bitch.

Before he could get a proper grip on her, Lori surprised him by jumping left and slashing at him. The blade, which had been fabricated by a long-dead craftsman in Arkansas and honed and honed again a thousand times on wet Arkansas stone, opened the sleeve of his nice tweed jacket and continued on to slice through the midriff of his blue broadcloth shirt. In the second and a half it took him to let go of her shoulder and anchor his hand on her wrist, blood soaked through the fine fabric of the shirt and began to ooze downward along a straight horizontal axis. As soon as he noticed that the growing bloodstain had immediately begun to spread and widen, he heard blood splashing steadily onto the floor, looked for the source, and witnessed a fat red stream gliding through the slashed fabric on his sleeve.

"Damn you." He jerked her forward and threw her to the ground. "What am I supposed to do now? Hell!"

She looked up at him from the floor. Crimson stains and spatters blossomed on her opened skirt and splayed legs. "The sight of your own blood throws you into a panic," she said. "Figures, I guess." (Tomato soup, no surprise, with garlic. Was she actually controlling the smells she sent out?)

"You *hurt* me!" He kicked her in the hip.

"Okay, you hurt me back. Now we're even," she said. "If you give me the keys, I'll bandage you up. You could bleed to death, you know. I think you ought to be aware of—"

Both her words and the renewed smell of laundry drying in sunshine on a backyard clothesline caused rage to flare through all the empty spaces in his head and body. He bent over, ripped the knife from her loose hand, and with a single sweep of his arm cut so deeply through her throat that he all but decapitated her. A jet of blood shot from the long wound, soaking his chest before he could dodge out of the way. Lori Terry jittered a moment and was dead.

"Bitch, bitch, damn bitch," he said. "Fuck this shit—I'm bleeding to death here!"

He trotted across the room to a pair of sinks, stripping off his jacket as he went and leaving bloody footprints in his wake. Though his wounds bled freely, and when first exposed seemed life-threatening, a matter that made him feel queasy and lightheaded, soon he was winding bands of tape around a fat pad of gauze on his arm. The long cut on his stomach proved less dangerous but harder to stanch. While simultaneously stretching toward his spine with one hand and groping with the other, he found himself wishing that Lori had not been such a colossal bitch as to make him kill her before she could help him wrap the long bandage around the middle of his body. Of course, had she not been such an unfeeling bitch, she would have obliged him by curling up in whimpering terror even before he explained in free-spending detail precisely what he was going to do to her. The tramp had escaped the punishment she had craved, down there at the dark center of her heart. She got to fulfill her goal, but she had cheated herself of most of the journey toward it! And cheated him of being her guide!

While he was mopping the floor with a mixture of bleach and soapy water, the Ladykiller remembered his admiration of Lori Terry—the respect she had evoked in him by being uncowed. Instead of bursting into tears and falling down she had offered him a blowjob! He had approved the tilt of her chin, the steadiness of her voice. Also the resolute, undaunted look in her eyes. And the odors, the odors, the odors, in their unfathomable unhurried march. In farewell to her spirit, he dropped to his knees at the edge of her pooled blood, pursed his lips, and forcefully expelled air, but although he managed to create a row of sturdy little ripples, for only the second or at a stretch maybe third time in his life as the Ladykiller he failed to raise up even a single bubble. He nearly moaned in frustration, but held back: she had refused to speak in Cockney, she had held to her dignity.

For the first time in his long career, the Ladykiller came close to regretting an obligatory murder, but this approach to remorse withered and died before the memory of her ugly dismissal of his life. Why, he wondered, should a sustained, lifelong performance be *disgusting*? Couldn't the cow see how interesting, how clever, his whole splendid balancing act had been? After this consoling reflection, his pain, which had been quietly pulsing away, throbbed within his lower abdomen and left forearm. This was a sharp reminder of her treachery. When the floor shone like the surface of a pond, he rinsed and stowed the mop, reverently washed the curved knife in a sink, and approached the long, cold table where Lori Terry's naked body, already cleansed and readied, awaited the final rites.

Two hours later, with everything—tables, walls, floor, switches, the dismembered body—rescrubbed and doused yet again in bleach, he stacked Lori's remains in a cardboard steamer trunk: feet and calves; thighs; pelvis; female organs from which his traces had been washed; liver, heart, lungs, stomach, and spleen in one bag, the long silver ropes of her intestines in another; hands and forearms; upper arms; rib cage; spine; shoulders; and as in life the open-eyed head atop all in a swirl of bleached hair. At the end she had smelled of nothing but washed corpse. He locked the trunk, lugged it up the stairs, dragged it to his car, and with considerable effort wedged it into the car's trunk.

On his journey back into the city, he found that the care he had given her body, the thorough cleansing, the equally thorough separation of part from part, its arrangement within its conveyance, brought back to him now the respect he had learned to feel for her once the final key had turned in his serial locks. For respect it had been, greater and more valuable than admiration. Lori Terry had displayed none of the terror she, no less than his other victims, felt when she saw the pickle she was in: instead she had fought him from the beginning, with, he saw now, offers of sex that had actually promised something else altogether. She had wanted him exposed and vulnerable, she had wanted him open to pain, *in* grave pain—she had intended to put him in agony. It was true, he had to admire the bitch.

A momentary vision of the dismembered body arrayed like an unfolding blossom in the cardboard trunk popped like a flashbulb in his mind. He heard words begin to flow through his throat before he realized that he was talking out loud—talking to Lori Terry.

As he spoke, he had been removing the girl's remains from the cardboard trunk and placing them this way and that on the cobblestones of backstreet downtown Milwaukee. It took a while to get them right. By the time he was satisfied, gray, early light had begun to wash across the cobbles and the garbage cans behind the clubs. Lori Terry's porcelain face gazed up at him like a bust in a museum. Then he was gone, yessir, the Ladykiller was right straight outta there, clean as a you-know-what and on to pastures new.

WALLACE STROBY

Night Run

FROM *The Highway Kind*

LATER, KIRWAN WOULD think about how it started, when he might have stopped it. What he could have done differently. But by then it didn't matter.

He'd just crossed the Georgia-Florida line on I-95, running south, the lights of Jacksonville in the far distance ahead. Two a.m. and his eyes watery, his legs jumpy. The Volvo had nearly 300,000 miles on it, and its suspension was shot. Every pothole or patch of uneven blacktop jolted his spine.

Still, he felt himself drifting, eyelids heavy. He'd need to sleep soon but wanted to make it as far south as he could. The meeting at Marco Landscaping, to show them the new brick samples, was at ten a.m., and New Smyrna Beach was still about a hundred miles away. He'd give it another hour on the road, then find a motel.

He thought of Lois Pettimore, Marco's accountant. She'd be at the meeting. The same perfume as always, her blouse open one button too deep, with a glimpse of black lace beneath. Sometimes in their office he'd notice her watching him, but he never knew how to respond. He'd look away, his face flushed, then flee as soon as he had their order sheets and contracts.

At the last meeting, two weeks ago, she'd handed him an invoice, let her nails brush the back of his wrist. He'd seen then that her wedding band was gone, only a faint white line left where it had been. He wondered if the imminent divorce she always managed to bring up in conversation had gone through.

His right front tire crossed onto the shoulder, hit gravel. The noise and vibration snapped him awake. He sat up straighter and steered back into his lane, the momentary burst of adrenaline clearing his mind. *That was stupid,* he thought, *dangerous. Stay alert.*

Powering down the window to let in the night air, he caught the rotten-egg-and-sulfur smell of the nearby swamp. Trees and wetlands on both sides of the highway here. Even at this hour, the air was warmer than when he'd stopped in Roanoke for dinner eight hours ago.

A car flew by in the far left lane, a blur of taillights as it passed. The speed limit for this stretch of interstate was seventy, and Kirwan kept the Volvo at a safe sixty-five, let the other vehicles pass him.

He turned on the radio, scanned stations. Somewhere south of Charleston, the all-news station he'd been listening to had dissolved into static. Now he got only snatches of rap, country music, preachers. Nothing coming in strong. *Get that satellite radio set up,* he thought. *Do yourself a favor. Or at least get the CD player fixed.*

He drove a thousand miles a week, and sometimes during thunderstorms he would pick up faraway AM stations, the signal bouncing off the clouds. Once, near Atlanta, he'd gotten a talk station out of Fort Wayne, Indiana, crystal-clear for a solid half hour before the storm passed.

No such luck tonight. More static; then, near the end of the dial, someone speaking rapid French. A Haitian station out of Miami. He switched over to FM, finally got a country tune he recognized. He left it there, settled back.

Sometimes at night, when the danger of falling asleep at the wheel was strongest, when he felt himself starting to dream, he'd turn off the headlights, the road going black in front of him. The jolt of adrenaline and panic that followed would wake him up, keep him going for another half hour. He'd leave the lights off for only a few seconds, but it was enough.

There was a guardrail on the right now, and the lane seemed to narrow. He signaled, even though there were no other cars around, started to move into the near left lane, heard the sharp bleat of a horn.

He jerked the Volvo back into the right lane, saw the single headlight to his left. A motorcycle had come out of the blind spot there. Had he missed it in the rearview? Had he even checked the mirror before changing lanes? He wasn't sure.

He turned off the radio, wanted to call out *Sorry,* realized how stupid that would sound. He slowed, waited for the motorcycle to pass. Instead it came abreast of him, hung there. He could hear the rider shouting. Kirwan kept his eyes forward. He couldn't make out the words, but his face grew hot.

He slowed to fifty-five, but the bike stayed with him. He looked then. It was a big Harley with extended front forks, black all around, dual silver exhausts. The rider had a beard and mustache, wore a leather jacket and jeans with a wallet chain. No helmet.

Kirwan faced front again. *Don't look. It'll just aggravate the situation.*

The biker was still shouting. Kirwan looked in the rearview, hoping to see a vehicle coming up from behind that would force the bike to speed up or pass him. Only darkness back there. They were alone on the road.

The yelling stopped. He chanced a look, saw the biker's right hand leave the throttle and come up, middle finger extended. Kirwan shook his head, faced front again. *Just go,* he thought. *I'm sorry about what happened, but it's over now. Just go.*

The bike surged past him, engine growling, went up two car lengths, and swept into his lane. His headlights lit the back of it, the pale-gray Georgia plate, and then the bike slowed and the Volvo was almost on top of it. Kirwan hit the brake, and the Volvo slewed to the right, the front fender inches from the guardrail. The boxed samples in the rear cargo area slid across the floor, bumped into the wall. He straightened the wheel, got centered in the lane once more. The biker twisted around in the headlights, grinning, gave him the finger again, then sped up.

Kirwan felt a rush of anger. Without thinking, he hit the gas, closed the space between them. The motorcycle glided easily back into the left lane, the rider gesturing to Kirwan as if inviting him to pass. When he didn't, the rider looked at him, grinned, and shrugged. A tractor-trailer came up in the far left lane, rumbled past them, disappeared over the rise ahead.

Kirwan knew this part of 95 — no exits for at least another few miles. He could pull over, hope the biker kept going, but there wasn't much shoulder here. It would be dangerous to stop.

The biker slowed until they were even again, then pointed at him. Kirwan tried to ignore him, kept the speedometer at sixty. It was no use speeding up or slowing down. The motorcycle would stay with him. He just had to wait until the biker lost interest, sped off.

More shouting. He started to power up the window, saw the motorcycle ease ahead of him. The biker's right arm flashed out, and something clicked against the windshield, flew off. Kirwan jerked his head back, saw the tiny chip in the glass. A coin, maybe. Something too small to do much damage, but enough to mark the glass, get his attention. The bike slowed, and they were side by side again. Kirwan turned to look at him then and saw the gun.

It was a dark automatic. The biker pointed it at him through the half-open window, not shouting now. The gun was steady.

Kirwan stood on the brake. The Volvo's tires screamed, and its rear end slid to the left, the wagon going into a skid. He panicked, fought the wheel, and pumped the brake, trying to remember what he'd learned— *turn in the direction of the skid. Don't lock the brakes.* The front end of the wagon swung from right to left and back again, headlights illuminating the guardrail, the trees beyond, the roadway, then the guardrail again. The sample boxes thudded into the back of the rear seat.

He steered onto the shoulder, gravel rattling against the undercarriage. He braked steadily, avoiding the guardrail, and the wagon came to a stop, bucked forward slightly, settled back, and was still.

A cloud of dust rose in his headlights. He jammed the console gearshift into park, gripped the wheel, tried to slow his breathing. His knuckles were white.

When the dust cleared, he saw the motorcycle. It had pulled onto the shoulder three car lengths ahead. The rider was looking back at him.

Kirwan felt the sharp stab of fear. He waited for the rider to get off, come back toward him, the gun out. For a moment, crazily, he considered shifting back into drive, hitting the gas, plowing into the bike. Decided that's what he would do if the rider came at him with the gun. *Could he do that? Run a man over, maybe kill him?*

But the biker stayed where he was, boots on the gravel, balancing the bike under him. No sign of the gun. Kirwan wondered if he'd imagined it, if his fear and the night had colluded to make him see something that wasn't there. Or had the gun just gone back into wherever he'd pulled it from? Maybe the biker had brought it out only to scare him, make him overreact and oversteer, wreck the Volvo on his own.

The biker watched him as if waiting to see what he would do. Kirwan didn't move, kept his hands tight on the wheel. The biker grinned, faced forward again. He steered back onto the roadway, gave the Harley gas. His taillights climbed the rise and vanished.

Breathe, Kirwan told himself, *breathe*. His neck and shoulders were rigid. He could feel a vessel throb in his left temple. What now? Get off at the next exit, find a town, a police station, report what happened? Even if he did, he had no proof except the chip in the windshield, which could have come from a small rock, a piece of gravel. And the Harley had been moving fast. They'd never catch up with the biker, and what if they did? Down here, like as not, the gun would be legal—if there even was a gun. It would be Kirwan's word against his. No witnesses.

His cell phone was in the console cup holder. He could call 911, give a description of the biker, have the dispatcher alert the highway patrol. But he'd already forgotten the plate number. A *G*, maybe an *X* after that, but that was all he had. And calling it in might mean more questions, a report, hours spent in a station house or trooper barracks. And if they caught the biker, Kirwan would have to face him again, the man who'd pointed a gun at him, nearly run him off the road.

Cars passed. When his breathing was back to normal, he powered the window shut, put on his blinker. He shifted into drive, waited until the road was clear, then steered into the lane, gave the Volvo gas.

He would have to get the alignment checked, the tires as well. The Volvo had lost its grip on the road for a moment, and that had frightened him almost as much as the gun—the sense of powerlessness, of being out of control. He'd find a garage in New Smyrna tomorrow, right after the meeting; he wouldn't put it off. Get the windshield fixed too, before the chip turned into a crack.

Back up to sixty, keeping it steady there. Any cars that came up behind would pass him, give him space. And with every minute the biker would be farther ahead, farther away from him. Kirwan breathed in deep, then exhaled. He turned the radio back on, the same country station.

After a while he realized he had to urinate. He tried to ignore it at first, but the pressure in his bladder grew. He didn't want to stop, wanted to keep going, make up the time he'd lost. But now there was a twinge of pain, and he knew he couldn't wait until he found a motel.

There were exits ahead now, motels and mammoth gas stations

right off the roadway, their signs raised on poles so they'd be seen from a distance. He took the exit for I-10. At the end of the ramp, signs pointed left and right, logos showing what gas and food were available in either direction, how far they were. It made no difference. The restaurants would be mostly fast-food joints, and some of them would be closed at this hour. If nothing else, he'd top off the tank at a gas station, find a restroom.

He turned right, the road here leading away from the highway. A mile ahead he saw the lights of a truck stop and diner, a Days Inn adjoining them. He thought about checking in, but it was too early still, and he was wired, wouldn't sleep. He decided to keep driving for a bit longer before he found a place to stay. Then a quick breakfast in the morning and on to New Smyrna. He thought of Lois, her perfume.

He signaled, even though there was no one behind him, pulled into the diner lot. And there, parked alongside an idling tractor-trailer, was the Harley. Kirwan felt his stomach tighten, and for a moment he thought his bladder would let go. He pulled the Volvo beneath a tree on the edge of the lot, out of the light wash from the big pole lamps, killed the engine and headlights.

Half a dozen cars here, and just the one tractor-trailer. Through the big diner windows he could see people sitting at booths, two men at the counter beyond. No sign of the biker.

Was it the same motorcycle? He looked at it again, unsure now. It seemed to be black, like the other one, but that might be a trick of the light. It had the same extended front end, and he could see the Harley insignia on the gas tank, so that much was the same. But he couldn't be sure.

Turn around. Get back on the road, then onto the highway. Find another diner or truck stop, another bathroom. Drive away.

Inside the diner, a door swung open, gave a glimpse of a white-tiled hallway, where the restrooms and trucker showers would be. The biker stepped out, went to the counter. He looked older in the bright interior lights, gray in his hair and beard. He spoke to the waitress there, his back to the window.

When he came out the front door, he was carrying a Styrofoam cup of coffee. He spit on the ground, looked around the lot.

Kirwan slid lower in his seat. The biker glanced in his direction, then away. He set the cup atop a metal trash can, put both hands on the small of his back and stretched, then reached inside the jacket. *He's going for the gun.*

The hand came out with a pack of cigarettes. Kirwan wondered again if the gun had been his imagination, his fatigue, his fear.

The biker lit the cigarette with a plastic lighter, put the pack away, blew out smoke. He was standing in the direct light fall from the windows now, and Kirwan could see the glint of a diamond stud in his right ear. He hadn't noticed that before. Was it even the same man?

The biker went over to the Harley, opened the right saddlebag. He crouched, looked inside, moved something around, fastened the flap again. He retrieved his coffee, walked around the bike as if checking for damage, the cup in his left hand.

He looked out at the road for a while, smoking and drinking coffee, then flicked the cigarette away. It landed sparking on the blacktop. Straddling the bike, he took a last pull at the cup, pitched it toward the trash can. It fell short, splashed on the sidewalk, sprayed coffee on the door of an SUV parked there. Then he rose in the seat, came down hard, kick-started the engine. It roared into life. The people inside the diner looked out. He sat back, revved the engine, still in neutral, as if enjoying the attention. The heavy throb of the exhaust seemed to fill the night.

He wheeled the Harley around toward the road. Would he go left, back to the lights of I-95? Or right and farther west into unbroken darkness? In that direction, I-10 would eventually take him to Tallahassee, Kirwan knew, but there was a lot of nothing between here and there, mostly sugarcane and swamp.

Kirwan started his engine. *Drive away,* he thought once more. *You'll never see him again. Your business, your life, is down the road. Places you need to be, people to see. Commitments and responsibilities.*

Still, a sourness burned in his stomach. The biker had laughed about what he'd done, and now he was riding off as if nothing had happened. He'd laugh again when he told the story later of how he'd put the fear of death into a middle-aged man in a station wagon.

The Harley pulled out of the lot, back tire spraying gravel. He turned right, as Kirwan had somehow known he would.

Headlights off, Kirwan followed.

*

No lights on this stretch of road, no moon above, but the Harley was easy to follow. Twice cars coming in the opposite direction flashed their high beams at Kirwan, letting him know his lights were off. But the biker didn't seem to notice. The Harley kept at a steady speed, didn't try to race ahead, lose him. *He doesn't know I'm here.*

He powered down the window, could hear the deep growl of the Harley's engine. The swamp smell was strong, and a low mist hung over the roadway, was swept under the front tires as he drove. The urge to urinate was gone.

Houses started to pop up, most of them dark. Concrete and stucco, bare yards. The road began to run parallel to a canal, the Harley's headlamp reflected in the water.

Past the houses and into tall sugarcane now. In the Harley's headlamp, Kirwan caught glimpses of dirt roads that ran off the highway. The Harley slowed, as if the rider was watching for an upcoming turn. Kirwan slowed with it. *He's almost there, wherever he's going. You'll lose him. And maybe that's a good thing.*

An intersection ahead, with a blinking yellow light in all four directions. The Harley blew through it without slowing. Kirwan did the same. The road began to curve gradually to the right. Ahead, lit by a single pole light, a concrete bridge spanned the canal.

Pull over. Let him go. Put your headlights on, turn around. You're in the middle of nowhere, and you're losing time. Don't be stupid.

The Harley slowed, rider and machine leaning to the right as they followed the curve of the road. Kirwan floored the gas pedal.

The Volvo leaped forward, faster than he'd expected, closed on the Harley in an instant. The bike had almost reached the bridge when the rider shifted in his seat, looked back, saw him for the first time. Kirwan hit the headlights, gave him the brights, barely thirty feet between them.

The biker was still turned in his seat when the Harley reached the bridge. Kirwan saw it as if in slow motion—the biker looking forward at the last moment, the bike coming in too sharp, the angle wrong. Then the front tire hit the abutment and the rider was catapulted into the darkness, the bike somersaulting after him, end over end, off the bridge and onto the ground below.

Kirwan's foot moved from gas pedal to brake, stomped down hard. The Volvo shimmied as it had before, slewed to the right, the samples thumping into the seatback. The tires squealed, dug in, and the Volvo came to a shuddering stop just short of the bridge.

He reversed onto the shoulder, shifted into park, and listened. All he could hear over his engine noise was crickets. He switched on the hazards. Didn't want another car to come speeding along, rear-end him in the darkness.

He got out, left the door ajar. There were bits of metal and broken glass on the bridge, a single skid mark. He walked up the shoulder, hazards clicking behind him, the headlights throwing his shadow long on the pavement.

At the bridge, he looked down. The ground sloped steeply to the edge of the canal. The bike was about fifteen feet away, had ripped a hole through the foliage. The rear tire was spinning slowly. From somewhere in the darkness came a moan.

He went back to the car, opened the glove box, took out the plastic flashlight, looked at the phone on the console.

Back at the bridge, he switched on the flashlight. The bright narrow beam leaped out, starkly lit the grass below. Torn-up earth down there. The bike had tumbled at least once before coming to rest in the trees.

He aimed the light toward it. It lay on its right side, the forks bent back and twisted, the front tire gone. The left saddlebag had been thrown open and its contents—clothes mostly—littered the grass. The air smelled of gasoline.

The moaning again. He picked his way carefully down the slope, shoes sinking in the damp earth. Playing the light along the edge of the canal, he followed the noise.

The biker lay on a wide flat stone below the bridge. He was on his left side, and there was blood on his face. Kirwan walked toward him, watching where he put his feet, not wanting to slip and fall.

The biker's right boot was scraping uselessly against the stone. His left boot was missing, and the leg there was bent at a right angle away from his body. He'd dragged himself onto the rock, left a smear of dark blood and mud on the stone to mark his passage.

Kirwan shone the light in his face. The biker raised his right hand, let it fall. His left arm was trapped beneath him.

The gun. Watch for the gun.

He came closer. The biker was hyperventilating like a wounded animal, chest rising and falling. His left eye was swollen shut. He raised his arm again, weakly.

He doesn't recognize me. Doesn't know what happened.

Kirwan came closer, shone the light up and down the biker's body, then around it. No gun.

"Help . . . help me." The voice was a hoarse whisper. In the darkness, something splashed in the canal, swam away.

Kirwan squatted. "You don't know who I am, do you?"

The biker tried to shift onto his back, gasped.

"Remember me?" Kirwan said.

He turned the flashlight toward himself, holding it low so the biker could see his face. The good eye narrowed into a squint. He shook his head.

A big leather wallet was on the ground a few feet away, had come free from its chain. Kirwan tucked the flashlight in his armpit, picked up the wallet, unsnapped and opened it. In one pocket were three hundred-dollar bills and six twenties. In another was a laminated Georgia driver's license with the biker's picture. His name was Miles Hanson, and he was sixty-one years old.

Hanson coughed, and Kirwan looked back at him. The biker raised his head, spit a blot of blood onto the stone. "Keep it, man . . . it's all yours. Just help me." The voice still weak.

Kirwan closed the wallet, set it on a rock.

"Hurry up, man. I think I got something broken inside."

"My cell phone's in the car. I'll call 911."

He started up the slope, then stopped, looked back down. Hanson was watching him. He saw the glimmer of the diamond stud, remembered the grin, the middle finger, the chip in the windshield.

He went back down the slope, set the flashlight in the grass.

"What are you doing?" Hanson said.

Kirwan crouched, gripped the back of the man's leather jacket with both hands. Hanson swatted at him with his good arm, but there was nothing behind it. Kirwan took a breath, straightened up so as not to pull a muscle, then jerked the jacket up, pushed, and tumbled Hanson face-first into the canal.

Kirwan couldn't tell how deep the water was. Hanson splashed once, went under. He floundered there, got his head above the surface for a moment, gulped air, then went under again.

Kirwan found a stone the size of a basketball beside the canal, lifted it high, then dropped it into the water where he'd last seen Hanson's head. Water spattered his pants.

He dusted off his hands, picked up the flashlight, and shone it down into the water. Hanson was a shadow just below the surface, not moving. A dark red cloud bloomed in the stagnant water, then dissipated.

He stood there for a while, watching to make sure there were no bubbles. Then he went back to where he'd dropped the wallet, took out the bills, and folded them into his shirt pocket. He kicked the wallet into the canal, then stepped out onto the flat rock, unzipped, and urinated into the water, a long stream that caught the light from the bridge, the pressure in his bladder finally easing.

When he was done, he zipped up, walked back to where the bike lay. It ticked as it cooled in the night air. Strewn on the grass were a pair of jeans, dark T-shirts, a sleeveless denim jacket. An insignia on the back read WHISKEY JOKERS DAYTONA BEACH above an embroidered patch of a diving eagle, claws out.

He reached into the open saddlebag, rooted deeper through more clothes. And there, at the bottom of the bag in a flat pancake holster, was the gun.

He drew it out, looked at it. At some point, maybe at the diner, Hanson must have holstered it in the saddlebag. But this gun was a revolver, and the one he'd seen had been an automatic. Or had it? Was this a second gun?

He went around to the other side of the bike, stepping over torn foliage. Using a pair of T-shirts to protect his hands, he took hold of the frame. It was still warm. He grunted, lifted, vines pulling at the ruined front end. The bike rose and then fell on its other side. The gasoline smell grew stronger.

He got the flashlight, opened the other saddlebag. More clothes, a full carton of cigarettes—Marlboro Reds—and a lidded cardboard box about half the size of a hardback book. No gun.

He opened the box, saw tissue paper. He peeled it back and in the middle was a cheap cloth doll—a cartoonish Mexican with a sombrero and poncho playing guitar, his floppy hands sewn to the cloth instrument.

Was this what he'd been checking in the saddlebag? A gift for a child? Then Kirwan squeezed the doll, felt the unyielding lump inside.

He turned it over, lifted the cloth flap of the poncho. Stitches ran up the back of the doll, thick ones, a darker color than the material. He tucked the flashlight under his arm again, pulled at the stitches until they were loose. The back of the doll came apart at the seam, revealing more tissue paper packed around a metal cigar tube. He unscrewed the top of the tube and pulled out a tightly rolled plastic bag. He poked a finger in, teased out part of the clear bag. Inside was a thick off-white powder, caked and compressed.

He pushed it back into the tube, screwed on the top. He put the tube in his pants pocket and tossed the doll out into the water.

He picked up the holstered gun, walked back up the slope to the Volvo, the road still empty in both directions. The yellow light blinked in the distance. The Volvo's hazards clicked, insects flittering in the headlights. A breeze came through, moved the sugarcane on the other side of the road.

He opened the Volvo's tailgate, pushed aside the sample boxes to get at the spare-tire compartment. He lifted the panel, pried up the spare, and put the tube and gun under it, then let the tire drop back into place. He closed the panel, shut the tailgate.

Back behind the wheel, he put away the flashlight, shut the glove box, gave a last look at the cell phone.

He reversed onto the road, swung a U-turn, headed back the way he'd come. He was calm inside, centered, for the first time that night. At the intersection, he turned the radio back on.

After a while he began to feel sleepy again, a pleasant drifting. He looked at his watch. If he kept going, he could push through to New Smyrna by three-thirty or so, find a motel, get five or six hours' sleep before the meeting. It would be enough. Maybe he'd ask Lois out to dinner that night, divorce or no.

He had two free days after that. He could stay down there, figure out what exactly was in that tube, what it might be worth. There didn't seem to be much of it, whatever it was. Maybe it was just a sample for some larger deal to be made later.

Rain began to spot the windshield, thick heavy drops. He turned on the wipers. They thumped slowly, and on their second arc, he saw that the chip in the windshield was gone. He touched a thumb to where it had been. Nothing there now, the glass unblemished. One less thing to take care of, at least.

He was humming along to the music by the time he reached the on-ramp for 95. What had happened had happened. There was no going back. Not now, not ever. The road and the night were his.

Contributors' Notes

Other Distinguished Mystery Stories of 2016

Contributors' Notes

The author of 11 novels and more than 120 short stories, **Doug Allyn** has been published internationally in English, German, French, and Japanese. More than two dozen of his tales have been optioned for development as feature films and television. Allyn studied creative writing and criminal psychology at the University of Michigan while moonlighting as a guitarist in the rock group Devil's Triangle and reviewing books for the *Flint Journal*. His background includes Chinese language studies at Indiana University and extended duty with USAF Intelligence in Southeast Asia during the Vietnam War. Career highlights? Sipping champagne with Mickey Spillane, waltzing with Mary Higgins Clark, and cowriting a novel with James Patterson.

• A few years ago, on a flight from New York, my seatmate was a former heavyweight contender from a famous Flint, Michigan, boxing family. For a lifelong fight fan, it was like sitting next to Elvis. We chatted the whole trip away. He'd suffered an injury similar to the one depicted in "Puncher's Chance" and continued to fight for several years afterward. Consider that a moment. This man stepped into the ring with skilled fighters, two hundred pounds and up, who were trying to knock him into next week, *knowing* that his chances to win, or even to defend himself effectively, were limited by his injury. Why would anyone do this? "I was trying to salvage my career," he said. "And hell, I always had a puncher's chance." And he was dead serious. Awed by his courage and commitment, I couldn't wait to get to my desk to start weaving it into a story. Sometimes writing is work. Not this time.

Jim Allyn is a graduate of Alpena Community College and the University of Michigan, where he earned a master's degree in journalism. While at Michigan he won a Hopwood Creative Writing Award, Major Novel Division, and also won the Detroit Press Club Foundation Student Grand Award for the best writing in a college newspaper or periodical. Upon graduation he pursued a career in health-care marketing and communications, working at major hospitals in three states. He recently retired as vice president of marketing and community relations at Elkhart General Healthcare System in Elkhart, Indiana. His first short story, "The Tree Hugger," appeared in *Ellery Queen Mystery Magazine* and was selected by Marvin Lachman as one of the Best Mystery Short Stories of 1993. Six other stories have been published by *EQMM* since then, including "Princess Anne," which was selected for inclusion in *The Best American Mystery Stories 2014.* Allyn is a U.S. Naval Air Force veteran, having served in a helicopter squadron aboard the aircraft carrier USS *Intrepid.*

• I found "The Master of Negwegon" very difficult to write. It began as a novel about five years ago and kept morphing and morphing so that I wound up with a couple of banker's boxes full of rough copy and nothing that resembled a coherent plot or story. I realize now that I made the classic mistake of "If you warm up too long, you miss the race." In an attempt to stay timely and relevant, I was continuously adding fodder about the war in Iraq, ecological problems such as the emerald ash borer, the utterly amazing lack of accountability among politicians, and developments in our understanding of TBI/PTSD. I got distracted and buried. So after walking away for a while, I decided to try it as a short story. Reduce it to bare essentials. That worked, but it was tough to extract and refine a short story from the morass that was to be a novel. The novel remains a target. Negwegon, at least, is stationary. Dynamic, but stationary. This beautiful wilderness park is located just a mile or so from my home in Black River and allows me to step back in time at will. When you emerge from the forest path to the broad, dune-swept horseshoe beach that fronts the bounding waters of Lake Huron, however far you've had to travel to get there will be worth it.

Dan Bevacqua's stories have appeared in *Electric Literature*'s "Recommended Reading," the *New Orleans Review Online, Tweed's Magazine of Literature & Art,* and *The Literary Review,* among others. A chapbook, "Security and Exchange," was published in 2015. Bevacqua is the fiction editor at *Jerry Magazine.* A visiting assistant professor in English and creative writing at Western New England University, he lives in Northampton, Massachusetts.

• For lots of reasons I won't get into, "The Human Variable" started in my mind with the image of a man driving through the night toward a marijuana farm. For weeks I didn't know why, until my friend and neighbor Krzysiek, a Polish engineer and climate scientist, told me about an app he was developing that would more accurately predict horrible weather events, like tornados and hurricanes. Somehow these two ideas, marijuana farming and climate change, got all mixed together, and then everything in the story started to click and work toward its violent end.

C. J. Box is the number-one *New York Times* best-selling author of twenty-one novels, including the Joe Pickett series. He won the Edgar Allan Poe Award for Best Novel (*Blue Heaven*, 2009) as well as the Anthony Award, Prix Calibre 38 (France), Macavity Award, Gumshoe Award, two Barry Awards, and the 2010 Mountains and Plains Independent Booksellers Association Award for fiction. He was recently awarded the 2016 Western Heritage Award for Western Novel by the National Cowboy & Western Heritage Museum. The novels have been translated into twenty-seven languages. *Open Season, Blue Heaven, Nowhere to Run,* and *The Highway* have been optioned for film and television. Millions of copies of his novels have been sold in the United States and around the world. In 2016, *Off the Grid* debuted at number one on the *New York Times* bestseller list in March. Box is a Wyoming native and has worked as a ranch hand, surveyor, fishing guide, and small-town newspaper reporter and editor, and he owned an international tourism marketing firm with his wife, Laurie. In 2008, Box was awarded the "BIG WYO" Award from the state tourism industry. An avid outdoorsman, he has hunted, fished, hiked, ridden, and skied throughout Wyoming and the mountain West. He served on the board of directors for the Cheyenne Frontier Days Rodeo and currently serves on the Wyoming Office of Tourism board. He and his wife have three daughters and one (so far) grandchild. They split their time between their home and their ranch in Wyoming.

• With each short story and novel I write I draw from the landscape and terrain around me, and "Power Wagon" was written while elk hunting in northwestern Wyoming near Big Piney, with the Wind River Mountains to the east and the Wyoming Range to the west.

There's a rhythm to each day while hunting that involves leaving well before dawn in subzero temperatures, returning to the camp for the middle of the day, and going back out into the mountains to hunt in the evening. Most days result in seeing no elk, but every foray is an adventure that may involve wading across ice-covered swamps and fording freezing rivers. There is also the opportunity to encounter local ranch families and to hear their stories and witness the history and culture of the area from the ground up.

I wrote the story in the hours between the morning hunt and the evening hunt, when everything I'd seen or encountered was still fresh in my mind.

Big Piney is in rough country. It's located in Sublette County, and family histories and feuds spread out along Lower Piney Creek, Middle Piney Creek, and Upper Piney Creek. There are four-generation homesteads scattered through the pine trees, and the memories of the locals are long. There are splits and divisions even among those with the same family name, and keeping track of who likes whom and who hates whom becomes a full-time job that was almost beyond my capacity.

The isolation of the area and the independence of the locals breed long memories and colorful stories. There's the one about the dead trapper found in a cabin in the middle of the winter, who was hauled by sleigh down to a ranch, where his body remained in the barn for three months until the ground thawed out. There's the one about a water-rights feud between two old-time ranchers on the same drainage that ended with a tractor battle and high explosives.

And there are stories about the tangled relationships of families who grew up and either stuck or dispersed.

That's where "Power Wagon" came from. It's about the four adult children of a malevolent Big Piney patriarch and how they deal with their father's death as well as a high-profile unsolved crime. Brandon, the youngest son, returns with his pregnant wife, Marissa, to sort out the financials of the inheritance. But it isn't just the surviving children of the old man who have come back to the ranch for a reckoning.

On a bitterly cold night, when Marissa sees a single headlight strobing through the willows on the way to the house, she senses that trouble is on the way. When four disturbing people climb out of the car and approach the front door, she's sure of it.

And so are we.

Soon Brandon will learn that the key to everything is the ancient 1948 Dodge Power Wagon that's been parked for years inside an outbuilding. It's described by one of the strangers as follows: "The greatest ranch vehicle ever made. Three-quarter-ton four-by-four perfected in WW Two. After the war, all the rural ex-GIs wanted one here like they'd used over there. That original ninety-four-horse, two-hundred-and-thirty-cubic-inch flathead six wouldn't win no races, but it could grind through the snow and mud, over logs, through the brush and willows. It was tough as a damn rock. Big tires, high clearance, a winch on the front. We could load a ton of cargo on that son of a bitch and still drive around other pickups stuck in a bog."

"Power Wagon" was written for an anthology called *The Highway Kind*, which was edited by Patrick Millikan. The subtitle describes it thus: "Tales of Fast Cars, Desperate Drivers, and Dark Roads"—even though the vehicle in question in this tale may not ever run again. But it does hold secrets.

The story was constructed over a week filled with blood, sweat, mud, ice, and some of the most awe-inspiring Rocky Mountain terrain in the country. I hope that atmosphere seeps through to the story itself.

Gerri Brightwell is originally from southwest Britain. She is the author of three novels: *Dead of Winter* (2016), *The Dark Lantern* (2008), and *Cold Country* (2002). Her short stories have appeared in such journals as *Alaska Quarterly Review, Southwest Review, Redivider,* and *Copper Nickel,* as well as on BBC Radio 4's *Opening Lines.* She lives in Fairbanks, Alaska, with her husband, fantasy writer Ian C. Esslemont, and their three sons.

• One year I went through a phase of being obsessed with westerns — something about their grittiness and bravado fascinated me. There are some wonderful western novels out there (Portis's *True Grit,* Williams's *Butcher's Crossing,* McCarthy's *All the Pretty Horses,* deWitt's *The Sisters Brothers*) and spectacular films (*The Revenant,* the Coen brothers' *True Grit*), but so many of the movies were disappointing: they relied on the same stock characters in the same stock situations. You could pretty much guess how the story was going to play out from the first few scenes.

One afternoon I found myself writing my own western (it just happened — I was working on something else when suddenly there was Matthis riding his horse down a slope, and the story took off), and though he looked every inch a hired gun out of one of those disappointing films, he had to be more than that. I wondered, What if he isn't such a good guy? What if the point of the story isn't a gunfight but something else? What if it's a slow unveiling of what's really going on?

I ended up with a story I wasn't sure anyone would want: Who publishes westerns nowadays, especially mysterious ones? Thank you, *Alaska Quarterly Review,* for starting "Williamsville" on its journey.

S. L. Coney obtained a master's degree in clinical psychology before abandoning academia to pursue a writing career. Currently residing in Tennessee, the author has ties to South Carolina and roots in St. Louis. Coney's work has appeared or is forthcoming in *St. Louis Noir, Noir at the Bar Volume 2,* and *Gamut Magazine.*

• When I quit my doctorate program and moved to St. Louis, I immediately fell in love with the city and its people. Scott Phillips mentored me and influenced a lot of my early work, so when he asked for a contribution to *St. Louis Noir* I jumped at the chance. I was living in the Clayton-Tamm neighborhood — also known as Dogtown — and I am enamored of this area, with its Irish charm and St. Louis spunk. But most of all, with the old Forest Park Hospital that sat on the eastern side of the neighborhood. This was a huge brick building with contrary angles and seemingly inexplicable corners. It was torn down the year I wrote "Abandoned Places," and so this story became my love letter to that particular bit of history.

Trina Corey is the pen name of Trina Warren, an elementary-school teacher who lives in California. Her five mystery stories have all been published in *Ellery Queen Mystery Magazine,* beginning with the Department of First Stories. They have received nominations for the Edgar, Macavity, Barry, and Derringer Awards.

• "Flight" began, as many mysteries do, with a *what if?* What if a serial killer who had always targeted elders ended up living with his target demographic? In the long process of answering that question, characters came and went, or stayed and changed. Jenny, the new nursing assistant, was originally going to be the main character. (She and her fiancé, Brian, are the wife and husband in "There Are Roads in the Water," a story I wrote set many years later.) Mina is a composite of several women I knew whose principal shared characteristic was kindness. But it was Rachel, the heroine, who most surprised me. She was originally slated to be one of the victims. Over the six years that it took to write this story, Rachel didn't so much change as I just got to know her better, and she changed the story. That a voiceless, seemingly helpless woman came to be the narrator and savior of others is a case of a character who would not be denied.

A former journalist, folksinger, and attorney, **Jeffery Deaver** is an international number-one best-selling author. His novels have appeared on bestseller lists around the world, including the *New York Times,* the London *Times,* Italy's *Corriere della Sera,* the *Sydney Morning Herald,* and the *Los Angeles Times.* His books are sold in 150 countries and have been translated into 25 languages. The author of thirty-nine novels, three collections of short stories, and a nonfiction law book as well as a lyricist of a country-western album, Deaver has received or been shortlisted for dozens of awards, including the Lifetime Achievement Award by the Bouchercon World Mystery Convention, the Raymond Chandler Lifetime Achievement Award in Italy, and *The Strand Magazine*'s Lifetime Achievement Award. Deaver has been nominated for seven Edgar Awards from the Mystery Writers of America.

• When Larry Block contacted me about the idea of writing a story inspired by the American artist Edward Hopper for an anthology entitled *In Sunlight or in Shadow,* I jumped at the chance. I was familiar with Hopper from my visits to Chicago's Art Institute when I was young and had long admired his subdued and yet mysterious work. As for the painting upon which to base a story, contributors could select anything but *Nighthawks* (the iconic late-night diner). I picked *Hotel by a Railroad,* 1952. I had several stories in mind based on the couple in the image, but, curiously, it was the date of the painting that sent me to my word processor. I thought —as one would—the Cold War! And I was off and running.

Brendan DuBois of New Hampshire is the award-winning author of 20 novels and more than 150 short stories. His latest Lewis Cole mystery, *Hard Aground,* will be published in early 2018. He's currently working on a series of projects with the *New York Times* best-selling novelist James Patterson. His short fiction has appeared in *Playboy, Analog, Asimov's Science Fiction*

Magazine, Ellery Queen Mystery Magazine, Alfred Hitchcock Mystery Magazine, The Magazine of Fantasy & Science Fiction, and numerous anthologies, including *The Best American Mystery Stories of the Century,* published in 2000, and the *The Best American Noir of the Century,* published in 2010. His short stories have also appeared in Gardner Dozois's *The Year's Best Science Fiction* anthologies. His stories have twice won him the Shamus Award from the Private Eye Writers of America and have earned him three Edgar Allan Poe Award nominations from the Mystery Writers of America. He is also a *Jeopardy!* game show champion as well as a cowinner on the trivia game show *The Chase.* Visit his website at www.BrendanDuBois.com.

• As a lifelong resident of the small state of New Hampshire, I've seen the tension and conflict between local townspeople and visitors from out of state, most often called people "from away." No matter how much you read about how the culture of the United States is the same from one coast to the other, the truth is that we are very different indeed. Sometimes these differences are something to be celebrated, as when a New Hampshire guy like me can travel and enjoy Kansas City barbecue, or go to New Orleans and try Cajun cooking. But at other times, as in my story, the differences can lead to tension, conflict, and—eventually—death.

In my story, an avoidable accident on a lake in New Hampshire that ends in a woman's death causes her husband to go on a long and exhaustive search for her killers and to find justice, ending up in the urban sprawl of Massachusetts. It's the classic tale of city dwellers vs. country.

But in writing this story, I also wanted to play with the cliché of the suffering husband seeking revenge for his loved one, and I did so by making the wife a very unlikable character, in the slow process of divorcing her small-town husband. But after she is killed, it's her small-town and apparently simple husband who makes things right. She was still his wife. It's his duty. And he intends to complete his duty.

When he's finally captured by the husband, the urban man responsible for the woman's death can't believe it. Why would this simple country man do so much and risk everything to get justice for an unlikable woman who's about to divorce him?

The answer shows the gulf between the two worlds, and the two ways of life, as the two "men from away" have their final, violent confrontation.

Loren D. Estleman, the author of more than 80 books and 200 short stories, has won 20 national writing awards and has been nominated for the Mystery Writers of America Edgar Award and the American Book Award. He served as president of the Western Writers of America, and in 2012 that organization presented him with the Owen Wister Award for Lifetime Achievement in the western field. The Private Eye Writers of America honored him with its lifetime achievement award in 2013. (How many lives can a writer have?) He lives in Michigan with his wife, author Deborah Morgan.

• I always had a hunch my ten-foot shelf of books on Jack the Ripper would pay off someday, but no one was more surprised than I when, once the opportunity came to write about him, I chose to leave behind 1888 London and move the action to World War II Detroit. Maybe it was inevitable, as I spent most of my youth listening to my parents sharing their experiences of the era and watching 1940s noir thrillers on early TV. Despite the time jump, "GI Jack" gave me the chance to use my late close friend Dale Walker's pet theory about the Ripper's identity, which makes as much sense as any.

Peter Ferry's stories have appeared in *McSweeney's, Fiction, OR Magazine, Chicago Quarterly Review, StoryQuarterly,* and *Fifth Wednesday Journal.* Ferry is the winner of an Illinois Arts Council Award for Short Fiction and a contributor to the travel pages of the *Chicago Tribune* and to *WorldHum.* He has written two novels, *Travel Writing,* which was published in 2008, and *Old Heart,* which was published in June 2015 and won the Chicago Writers Association Novel of the Year award. He lives in Evanston, Illinois, and Van Buren County, Michigan, with his wife, Carolyn.

• "Ike, Sharon, and Me" is a story that has been bumping around my head, my heart, and my portfolio in various shapes and forms for about thirty years. It is inspired by events and people in my life, not the least of whom is my old friend Patrick Snyder, who took a proprietary interest in "ISM" and would not let it die, even when I sometimes wished that it would. I wrote the last line just a year ago. That the story is finally amounting to something makes me proud and happy.

Charles John Harper is the pseudonym for Minneapolis attorney Charlie Rethwisch. His noir stories featuring 1940s PI Darrow Nash appeared in the February 2008, March/April 2008, and July 2009 issues of *Ellery Queen Mystery Magazine* under the name C. J. Harper. A fourth Darrow Nash tale, "Lovers and Thieves," was the cover story for *Alfred Hitchcock Mystery Magazine*'s April 2016 issue. Stand-alone stories have also appeared in those magazines. Harper has twice been shortlisted for the British Crime Writers' Association Debut Dagger Award. He lives in Minnesota with his wife, Dana, and their two itinerant kids, Ellen and Bobby.

• Heading to my day job one morning seven years ago. Slogging through traffic snarled by dreary Minnesota weather. Sick of the repetition of a mostly unfulfilling job. Frustrated at not having—or making—the time to do what I really loved to do. Feeling trapped. Seeing no end in sight. And worst of all, out of ideas for a new story.

Then Darrow Nash popped into my head. And all he did was simply give me a weather report of the world beyond my windshield: "It was a misty November rain." Hmmm. Sounds like an opening line. Immediately my mood brightened. The gray skies took on some color. Even my day job became bearable. I had found a story.

A story from a line that seemed to offer very little. No plot. No clever twist. No distinct setting. No unique characters (other than Darrow, of course). But in fact it had something very intriguing to me: it had a feeling. An atmosphere. And out of that atmosphere arose a story. A story that grew more complicated the more I wrote. Luring me to two dead people on a couch in an apartment, a strangled man and a woman with a gun in her hand and a bullet hole in her head. To the police it was a clear-cut case of murder-suicide. But to Darrow Nash, all was not as it seemed. It sounded perfect.

So perfect that it took me four years and two rejection letters to finally figure out what really happened inside that apartment. But those four years not only helped me find the solution to the puzzle, they helped me uncover the issues that became the true heart and soul of the story:

The treatment of gay men in postwar America.

The differing attitudes that veterans had toward their service in the war, from bragging tin soldiers to silent heroes, some silent for decades.

And, ultimately, the contradictions that live in all of us and the facades we create to disguise those contradictions. Our immutable predisposition to be, like the crime in the story, not as we seem. To be in our hearts both the lover and the thief.

Craig Johnson is the *New York Times* best-selling author of the Walt Longmire mystery novels, which are the basis for *Longmire,* the hit Netflix original drama, now in its sixth season. The books have won multiple awards: Le Prix du Polar Nouvel Observateur/Bibliobs, the Wyoming Historical Association's Book of the Year, Le Prix 813, the Western Writers of America's Spur Award, the Mountains and Plains Book of the Year, the SNCF Prix du Polar, *Publishers Weekly* Best Book of the Year, the Watson Award, *Library Journal's* Best Mystery of the Year, the Rocky Award, and the Will Rogers Medallion Award for Fiction. *Spirit of Steamboat* was selected by the Wyoming State Library as the inaugural One Book Wyoming. Johnson lives in Ucross, Wyoming, population twenty-five.

• As Jean Luc-Godard once said, "It's not where you take things from, but where you take them to." I have a weakness for quirky or forgotten writers from different geographic regions across the country, and one of them is Davis Grubb, the Appalachian author of such luminaries as *Fool's Parade, Cheyenne Social Club,* and the better-known *Night of the Hunter,* which was nominated for a National Book Award in 1955. Though his output was small, many of his best-selling novels were adapted as feature films with actors like Jimmy Stewart, Robert Mitchum, Shelley Winters, Kurt Russell, and George Kennedy.

There is a scene in *Fool's Parade,* one of Grubb's lesser-known works, where a paroled convict, Mattie Appleyard, intimidates a guard, and that scene stuck with me since I read it many years ago. My protagonist, Walt Longmire, is the sheriff of the least populated county in one of the least populated states in the country, and in *Serpent's Tooth,* the ninth novel in the series, the deputy, Double Tough, loses an eye and has a little trouble getting it replaced, in that he's colorblind in the remaining one.

Every year since the debut of my first novel, I've written and sent out a holiday story to all the readers on my website newsletter, *The Post-It,* and last year I couldn't help but do my take on Grubb's gruesome display— even going so far as to include his novel in my short story.

In the idyllic setting of a country church in Story, Wyoming, an evangelical heroin addict has taken the congregation hostage, and particularly a young woman from the choir. The Highway Patrol, an adjacent sheriff's department, and even a SWAT team have cordoned off the church, but there doesn't seem to be much hope of resolving the situation without deadly violence when Double Tough, having also read *Fool's Parade,* comes up with a unique response in "Land of the Blind."

William Kent Krueger (he goes by Kent) writes the *New York Times* bestselling Cork O'Connor mystery series, which is set in the great Northwoods of Minnesota. His protagonist, Cork O'Connor, is the former sheriff of the fictional Tamarack County and a man of mixed heritage—part Irish and part Ojibwe. Krueger's work has received a number of awards, including the Minnesota Book Award, Loft-McKnight Fiction Award, Anthony Award, Barry Award, Macavity Award, Dilys Award, and Friends of American Writers Prize. His stand-alone novel *Ordinary Grace* received the 2014 Edgar Award for Best Novel. He lives in St. Paul, where he does all his writing in a couple of wonderfully funky coffee shops.

• When I was invited to submit a story for *Echoes of Sherlock Holmes,* the anthology in which "The Painted Smile" was first included, I drafted two stories. My initial attempt was a straightforward take on Holmes and Watson, with a ghost in an English castle thrown in for good measure. The story felt too derivative, so I bagged it and tried another approach altogether. I'd been writing about adolescents for a while, an age in which innocence and worldly understanding tug ferociously at opposite ends of the psyche. The idea of a child, incredibly bright but terribly vulnerable, appealed to me enormously. During the writing, I kept trying to imagine what Holmes might have been like in his childhood. Of course, the story had to be set in St. Paul, a city I know well and dearly love. And instead of a ghost, I decided to throw in a clown. Those guys are really scary.

Karen McGee grew up in Berkeley, California, but has spent the past few decades in Tokyo, where she teaches at Nihon University College of Art. She is the co-organizer of the Tokyo Writers Workshop. Her stories have recently appeared in *Bête Noire, The Font, HiddenChapter, Twisted Vine,* and *9Crimes,* and she is currently working on a novel. She is an avid reader of mysteries and a big fan of Lucas Davenport and Virgil Flowers.

• I was inspired to write "Dot Rat" after watching *The Drop* and then tracking down and reading the source material for the film, Dennis Lehane's brilliant short story "Animal Rescue." I have never been to Dorchester, but I was attracted to the setting as a town with a tough reputation, a place that might be home to an old-school organized crime head. I was also interested in creating a character that appears vulnerable but is actually dangerous. As with much of my work, I subjected a draft of the story to my monthly workshop. At that time it was titled "Fence" (for lack of a better idea). The title inspired much confusion and several fascinating theories. As usual, the group was also a big help.

Joyce Carol Oates is the author most recently of the novel *A Book of American Martyrs* and the story collection *The Doll-Master and Other Tales of Terror.* Recently inducted into the American Philosophical Society, she teaches alternately at Princeton University, New York University, and UC Berkeley. A new poem of hers will appear in *The Best American Poetry 2017.*

• "The Woman in the Window" was first imagined as a dramatic monologue giving voice to Edward Hopper's mysterious woman in the window (*Eleven A.M.,* 1926). The young woman in the painting is sensuous, pale-skinned, lost in thought. My evocation of her was originally in the form of a poem of long slow meditated lines that replicate the thought-patterns of one contemplating her future (suggested by the window in front of her, through which the viewer can't easily see) as well as her past.

In transforming the poetic monologue into prose, I opened up the story considerably, providing the young woman with a revealing backstory and also with a lover, a married man who has paid for her apartment and is locked into an intense emotional relationship with her, which, we are allowed to see, will not come to a happy ending.

Steven Popkes's work is found largely in the science fiction and fantasy world. His first sale was in 1982 to *Asimov's Science Fiction Magazine.* Since then he has published three novels: *Caliban Landing, Slow Lightning,* and *Welcome to Witchlandia.* He is better known for his short fiction. Since 1982 he has published about forty stories. In 1988 his story "The Color Winter" was nominated for the Science Fiction and Fantasy Writers of America Nebula Award. Since then he's been collected in several year's best science fiction and year's best fantasy anthologies. His novellas, *Jackie's Boy* and

Sudden, Broken, and Unexpected, placed second in the 2011 and 2013 Asimov's Readers' Award Polls. He lives with his wife in a Boston suburb, where he raises turtles and bananas.

• There are a couple of sources for this story. One is very personal. I was born in Southern California and lived there until we moved to Alabama in 1964. My parents both loved horse racing. I have many memories as a child hanging out with them in the stands watching magnificent animals run their hearts out for us. I remember my parents shoving me forward to shake hands with someone they said was Willie Shoemaker. I was probably around seven.

Another is more writerly. A number of years ago I wrote a novella entitled *Mister Peck Goes Calling.* This involved Cthulhu and the Boston Irish gang wars before Whitey Bulger got involved. It provided the character that ended up in "The Sweet Warm Earth." I live in the Boston area now. After being here for over thirty years, it's not hard to imagine an Irish mobster falling in love with California.

William R. Soldan received his BA in English literature from Youngstown State University and studied creative writing in the Northeast Ohio MFA program, where his focus was fiction. He teaches Writing at YSU and is a board member of Lit Youngstown, a nonprofit organization focused on facilitating and nurturing the literary arts. His work has been nominated for a Pushcart Prize and has appeared or is forthcoming in a number of publications, such as *New World Writing, Thuglit, The Vignette Review, Kentucky Review, Jellyfish Review, Elm Leaves Journal,* and others. He currently lives in Youngstown, Ohio, with his wife and two children.

• Stories often first present themselves to me in the form of an image or an ending. Or an ending image. But in the case of "All Things Come Around" it began with a situation and grew from there. My wife and I had decided to stop at Popeyes for some food on our way home one night —the same Popeyes in the story. Our son was about a year old then, and he was teething and miserable in his car seat, screaming and crying something fierce. So this element of the story—a fast-food chicken joint and a shrieking child in pain—was drawn straight from real life. As for the rest of the story, let's just say it could have happened, or something close to it.

In my twenties I lived a reckless life and kept company with some rough individuals, some of whom did their dealings in the neighborhood my family and I found ourselves in that night. Some of whom still do, for all I know. As is the case anytime I find myself in a place where I used to run around during the darker days of my youth, I began to imagine what might happen if I crossed paths with someone from back then, back before kids and marriage and making other positive changes in my trajectory. That was when the idea began to take shape, while still sitting in the drive-through, waiting for my chicken. I must have had a faraway expression on my face, because my wife looked at me and said, "You're writing a story, aren't you?" She knows me well. Now, rarely does a story come into view fully formed, this one being no exception. However, the scenario and the players for this one came in a flash, and the rest was really a matter of organizing the content.

I originally started at the end, with Travis lying on the cold concrete with a bullet in his chest (I drew some inspiration for the scene from Tobias Wolff's story "Bullet in the Brain," in which he does some wonderful things with time and perspective). As Travis lay there, the events of the evening leading up to his being shot swirled through his mind, during which time the story slipped into flashback and came around full circle, ending where it began, more or less. I soon scrapped that idea, though, deciding it was better told in a linear fashion. Evidently my instinct was right, because Todd Robinson over at *Thuglit*, who had previously published another one of my stories, "The Long Drive Home," loved it and included it in his journal's farewell issue, *Thuglit: Last Writes*. I owe Todd a huge debt of gratitude for that. Now more than ever.

Peter Straub is the author of seventeen novels, which have been translated into more than twenty languages. They include *Ghost Story, Koko, Mr. X, In the Night Room,* and two collaborations with Stephen King, *The Talisman* and *Black House*. He has written two volumes of poetry and four collections of short fiction, and he edited the Library of America's edition of H. P. Lovecraft's *Tales* and its two-volume anthology *American Fantastic Tales*. He has won the British Fantasy Award, ten Bram Stoker Awards, two International Horror Guild Awards, and four World Fantasy Awards. In 2008 he was given the Barnes & Noble Writers for Writers Award by Poets & Writers. He has won several lifetime achievement awards. His most recent publication is *Interior Darkness* (2016), a collection of selected stories.

• "The Process Is a Process All Its Own" is the first real product of a long, long meander through the interior of a novel very much in progress. It was short of tumble-dried on its way toward the finish line, so I was obliged to start over. From the first page. I wanted to see what I could come up with and, because neuropathy had buggered my typing, also wanted to experiment with dictation. The act of dictating into my phone somehow suggested the synesthesia that begins the story. Most of the middle came from material already written. The ending is the development of a situation that had been considered but not yet written. And not long after I started, I bought a large-key keyboard, because typing was easier than talking.

Wallace Stroby is an award-winning journalist and the author of eight novels, four of which feature professional thief Crissa Stone, whom *Kirkus Reviews* called "crime fiction's best bad girl ever." He's also written for *Esquire Japan*, BBC Radio 4, *Reader's Digest, Salon, Slant, Writer's Digest, Inside Jersey,* and other publications. A lifelong resident of the Jersey shore, he was an editor for thirteen years at the *Newark* (NJ) *Star-Ledger,* Tony Soprano's hometown paper.

• When editor Patrick Millikin—a longtime bookseller at Arizona's Poisoned Pen Bookstore—invited me to contribute to his collection *The Highway Kind: Tales of Fast Cars, Desperate Drivers, and Dark Roads,* my thoughts immediately went to that greatest of all road-rage stories, Richard Matheson's classic "Duel." I was intrigued at first with the idea of telling a similar story from the antagonist's perspective—the hunter rather than the hunted. Once I began writing, though, the story veered off into unexpected directions, fueled by memories of my own long late-night commutes from a newsroom in North Jersey to my home at the shore. I began to riff on the idea of a cat-and-mouse game played out on a lonely stretch of highway in the middle of the night, with a driver so exhausted that his own senses are playing tricks on him, and where paranoia, fear, and danger are always waiting just up the road.

Other Distinguished Mystery Stories of 2016

ARTHUR, BRUCE
    Beks and the Second Notice. *Alfred Hitchcock Mystery Magazine*, December

BEARD, JO ANN
    The Tomb of Wrestling. *Tin House*, vol. 18, no. 2

COSBY, S. A.
    Slant Six. *Thuglit: Last Writes*

DAVIS, ARTHUR
    In Innocence and Guilt. *Mystery Weekly*, July

DAY, DENNIS
    The Fixer. *Midwest Review*, Spring

DOBOZY, TAMAS
    Steyr Mannlicher. *New England Review*, vol. 37, no. 3

DRISCOLL, JACK
    Land of the Lost and Found. *Prairie Schooner*, Winter

FAYE, LYNDSAY
    The Sparrow and the Lark. *The Big Book of Jack the Ripper*, ed. by Otto Penzler, Vintage

FLANAGAN, ERIN
    The Rule of Three. *Hayden's Ferry Review*, Spring/Summer

FLOYD, JOHN M.
    Jackpot Mode. *The Strand Magazine*, October-January

GRAY, LUCAS
    Eternity Met. *Alfred Hitchcock Mystery Magazine*, January/February

HANN, KEITH
    The Last Man. *Ellery Queen Mystery Magazine,* February
HART, ROB
    Last Request. *Thuglit,* no. 22

IDASZAK, JOSHUA
    The Last Laz of Krypton. *Boulevard,* Fall

JENSEN, WILLIAM
    A Quiet Place to Hide. *North Dakota Review,* Spring/Summer

KOZAK, CATHY
    Dirty Girls of Paradise. *The Fiddlehead,* Spring

LAWTON, R. T.
    May Day. *Alfred Hitchcock Mystery Magazine,* May
LIMON, MARTIN
    The King of K-Pop. *Alfred Hitchcock Mystery Magazine,* June
LISS, DAVID
    Me Untamed. *Crime Plus Music,* ed. by Jim Fusilli, Three Rooms Press

MARTIN, VALERIE
    Bromley Hall. *Conjunctions,* Fall
MCFADDEN, DENNIS
    Tillie Dinger. *Ellery Queen Mystery Magazine,* March/April
MERKEL, WARREN
    Giddy. *Mystericale,* December

OPPERMAN, MEG
    Murder Under the Baobab. *Ellery Queen Mystery Magazine,* November

RICHARDSON, TRAVIS
    Cop in a Well. *Spinetingler Magazine,* May
RUSCH, KRISTINE KATHRYN
    Overworked. *Alfred Hitchcock Mystery Magazine,* December
RUTTER, ERIC
    Proof. *Alfred Hitchcock Mystery Magazine,* November

VLAUTIN, WILLY
    The Kill Switch. *The Highway Kind,* ed. by Patrick Millikin, Mulholland

WILEY, MICHAEL
    The Hearse. *Ellery Queen Mystery Magazine,* April
WILLIAMS, TIM L.
    What We Barter, the Things We'll Trade. *Ellery Queen Mystery Magazine,* April

THE BEST AMERICAN SERIES®

FIRST, BEST, AND BEST-SELLING

The Best American Comics

The Best American Essays

The Best American Mystery Stories

The Best American Nonrequired Reading

The Best American Science and Nature Writing

The Best American Science Fiction and Fantasy

The Best American Short Stories

The Best American Sports Writing

The Best American Travel Writing

Available in print and e-book wherever books are sold.

Visit our website: *www.hmhco.com/bestamerican*